Magical Midlife
Awakening

Magical Midlife Awakening

By K.F. Breene

Contact info:
www.kfbreene.com
books@kfbreene.com

CHAPTER 1

Sebastian

"I'M IMPATIENT TO get into his files." Sebastian waited behind Nessa as she used her instruments to cut through a chain-link fence on the outskirts of Malachi's extensive property.

"It's a wonder how he got so high up in the Mages' Guild hierarchy, considering his sloppiness in the shadow markets." She finished the circle of fencing and carefully pulled it away to create an opening.

"He wanted people to know who he was." Sebastian took the wire from her and set it aside as she analyzed what lay beyond. "He must've. In the past we barely found a trace of him, remember? He wants people to know he's doing high-level work for Momar. That he's helping him with his endeavors."

"Not smart."

"Why? Who's going to oppose him? Who's going to go after him?"

She turned back with a quirked eyebrow, highlighted by the bright moon overhead. Sebastian felt a smile curl his lips.

"Who's afraid of the big bad wolf?" she asked with a glint in her eye.

"Elliot Graves is a has-been." He nearly laughed as she crawled through the hole. "A 'would-be' that never was. He reached his stride and then disappeared. There is no coming back from that. Not now that Momar and the Guild have essentially joined forces. Resistance is futile. Submit or be destroyed. Did I miss anything?"

"Yes, actually. Momar's silent partner, who has all the power." Nessa turned once she was through the hole and pointed at a couple of wires running along the fence. "One above." She moved her finger down to point near the bottom. "One below. Don't touch either or the whole world will light up. He went mundane with the perimeter security. Too lazy to do spells, maybe."

"Got it." He handed through his pack before crawling in after it. When he was halfway across, she hissed and grabbed his head, forcing it down a little. She was better at this stuff than he was.

Once he was on the other side, they gathered their packs and looked out through the trees at the massive house sprawling just over a berm in the distance.

"The Guild is nothing but Momar's puppet," Nessa

whispered, scanning the grounds. "They think they have joined forces with him, but in reality they have rolled over so he can do as he pleases. He has all the power. Those magical twins from the attack on Kingsley's territory and their legion of magical workers are working together in a way the Guild mages can't comprehend."

"Seems like Momar learned a thing or two from shifter unity and teamwork."

"He hates them, but he's not stupid. He recognizes their power now, and he's trying to create something to combat it. He would've won if not for gargoyles' selflessness."

"The one thing we have at our disposal that he never will. Mages might be working together right now, but that battle showed selflessness is definitely not in their wheelhouse."

She didn't comment, and he knew what she was thinking. Sebastian and Nessa would have to use—and abuse—Jessie and her crew's selflessness if they wanted to end this thing.

Nessa did not like acknowledging the reality of the situation. Sebastian didn't either, but he was pragmatic. His visions, as sporadic and distorted as they were, didn't lie. They needed to walk this path to the end. As terrible and heartbreaking as that might turn out to be, the alternative would probably be many levels of magnitude worse.

"Come on." Nessa started forward, directly across the grass.

Sebastian quickly used a spell to distort them from view on the camera footage.

"Pretty soon…we'll need to scramble," Nessa informed Sebastian. The melancholy he sensed in her tone wasn't like her. "Here we go," she said, starting to jog.

Two black phantoms raced through the evening, teeth bared but utterly silent. Dobermans, one from each side, locked in on their prey.

"I should be more scared," he said as he matched her pace and quickly flung spells. "I should be much more flustered in this situation. I usually am."

He headed one off before working a little harder to trap the other. The dog hit his magical barrier and snarled, breaking the silence to loudly bark and continuously lunge, trying to break through the four invisible walls that now surrounded it. The other dog found its way around the detour he'd thrown at it and sprinted after them.

Sebastian was ready, blasting the ground near it to put it off its stride and then locking it into a second magical cage. He'd release them after they got into the house, allowing them to roam and quiet down. The dogs tended to ignore anything that went on within the house. Sebastian had organized a few surprise deliveries to ascertain that fact.

Near the house, they slowed, hardly out of breath. In the weeks since the pivotal battle between Momar's people and the motley crew led by Jessie and her people, they'd worked hard to get in better shape. They'd gone off on their own, so they didn't have anyone to fly them around anymore.

"You aren't scared because shifters are much scarier than dogs," Nessa said, watching her feet as she made it onto the concrete pathway toward the side entrance they planned to break into. "You aren't flustered because you've had experience scrambling. Dogs are predictable and mostly straightforward. Gnomes are not."

"All good points," he said as the familiar pang hit his heart. It had been a little over a month since they'd had any direct contact with Jessie or her crew. Sebastian missed them terribly. He missed working in the bowels of Ivy House and laughing at the crew's antics. He even missed the tremors of fear he'd feel around Austin or Broken Sue or Tristan, that sort of primal terror that affected a person at their basic level.

He probably should've been afraid in his current

situation, too, but he wasn't. Not even slightly. He was back in his element as Elliot Graves, the feared and fearsome mage. This was a game he knew how to rig. He knew what he was up against and felt nothing but expectation and confidence. He had a score to settle, especially now, and he had the tools to do it.

He'd played nice for Jessie. He'd been Sebastian for her, hiding his worst self, but he wouldn't play nice as Elliot Graves. Never had, not since the Mages' Guild had taken him in for questioning and ended up extorting and torturing him.

"Here we go." Nessa stopped beside a closed door. A sensor light clicked on overhead, showering them with a harsh blue-white glow.

Sebastian checked out the magical shield glimmering over the door with a gossamer sheen. He worked his spells, digging a little here, poking a little there.

"Decent magic," he said, finding the current of the spell and the release that would pry it from the door.

"Stronger than yours?"

"No. He was working alone to create this. The weave of it is complex, though. Not as simple-minded as I'd expect from him. He must have learned from better spell casters."

"Stands to reason, since he's in the Guild, doesn't it?"

"No. They don't like to share. He must have gotten it from Momar's people. They don't keep such a tight leash on their creations anymore. They don't have to, right? No one in the Guild can compete with them. I'll just pop this off and…" His words died away as he encountered something along the edges of the spell, lining the doorframe. "Well now, hold on…"

Nessa stepped closer to the wall and turned, probably so she could better see his face.

"Looks like our mage has a spy." Sebastian delicately sussed out this secondary spell, feeling out both its connection to the other and how it would work. "Very clever. It fits within his alarm spell seamlessly. I'll bet Momar's lot shared—or let him snoop—for a reason. This spy has a lot more power. A *lot* more. This spell is deliciously complex." He sucked his bottom lip as he studied it.

"The goal?"

"To let the spy know when he is coming and going. Malachi has a sort of magical base along the edges of the doorframe. It makes it easy to erect spells. It's like a starter—"

"I know, I know. You won't use them because it is lazy spell work, which makes it dangerous."

"Case in point. They wove their spell into his base spell. It's always here, monitoring when he erects his protection spell and when he takes it down. They know when he comes and when he leaves. I'm sure there is one on every door."

Nessa checked her watch.

He nodded, reading the silent cue. They didn't have time for him to geek out over this little slice of spell work. The mage would come home soon, and they needed to be lying in wait when he did.

"Can you break it?" Nessa asked as Sebastian stepped away.

"Can I break it? Yes. Just. Can I do it in a way that the spy won't detect? No. It has too much power. Even if I had time to figure out a dainty way through, without Jessie's power to aid me, I'd have to bust parts and it would shatter. Shattering—"

"It'll set off alarms, I get it." She looked up at the second floor. "Think they have it on the second-story windows?"

"No. This mage doesn't fly. It wouldn't make sense for them to bother." He scanned the house. Time was ticking. "We have to do this backwards. We'll go in through the second floor and leave out this door."

Nessa hiked her backpack farther up her shoulders. "So the proverbial bells will go off after we leave. Think the spy will swing by to check it out?"

"I don't know. It won't matter if they do or don't.

Not with how we're going to leave the inside of the house. They'll come to the same conclusion regardless of whether they witness a fresh murder or a stale one."

She jerked her head in a nod and found the easiest way up to the second floor.

✧   ✧   ✧

NESSA

THE WINDOWS ON the second story were unlocked and unguarded. The mage hadn't bothered with the simplest of protections. They easily made their way inside. He wasn't worried about flyers. Shortsighted, and because of what she and Sabby were about to do, the Mages' Guild and Momar would soon realize it. The test was if they would announce it to the world of mages. She had her doubts, but they were only just testing the waters of the organizations still. They had a lot of work left to do before they had a handle on the changed landscape of the world of mages.

"Don't close that window," Sebastian said in a hush.

She froze with her hand on the top of it.

"Remember?" he whispered. "Open a few others. Punch out the screens."

She pulled her hand away slowly as the gentle breeze ruffled her hair. She swallowed and then nodded.

"I'm going to hit the records room." He moved toward the door. "You rig up your trap and I'll meet you down there. Watch the time."

He was in his Elliot Graves headspace, where only logic and plans existed. He felt very few emotions, and in these situations, those usually only revolved around Nessa's wellbeing. Everything else was magic and math and a means to an end. It was how he could get through this next phase of their plan.

She was not lucky enough to have an Elliot Graves headspace. Killing to survive was one thing, but it made her uneasy to sacrifice others for an end goal that was so far in the distance she couldn't yet see it.

If there were literally any other choice…

She stilled for a moment and collected herself. Time to get to work.

With quick economy, she stepped down the way to another large window and popped it open. She punched out the screen like a gargoyle might and watched it tumble onto the roof. That done, she shoved furniture out of the way and pushed a few items on tables to the floor, liking the violence of glass shattering against the ground. She needed to let out some aggression.

She tipped a globe over and then randomly pulled some books off the shelves. Gargoyles were vicious, messy beings, or so the mages would think. They were violent, uncouth, not house trained. They destroyed every home they entered.

That done, she flitted out of the room and down the hall, catching Sebastian in the records room, carefully using his magic to reveal any little traps or secret vaults. Once he'd found them all, since there were bound to be some, he'd go through the files, also with a careful hand. Only when he'd gotten all he needed would he then ransack the place, tossing papers everywhere, ripping out drawers.

"Pull some books off the shelves for funsies," she called, hitting the stairs. Might as well keep things consistent.

On the ground level, she made herself familiar with the layout. Viewing a map of the interior was not the same as being in the space. Here there were currents of energy and intent, of motivation. It revealed a hint of the owner's personality. She took all this in, understanding far more about what she'd always done intuitively because of a few books she'd gotten anonymously, delivered to a hideout no one should've known about.

Tristan was forever dogging her heels.

In this, though…she had to admit that she was glad for it. Excited, even. He'd seen something in her that no one else had bothered to, a sort of energy magic that she wasn't even aware existed. She still wasn't quite sure what she could do, or how to control it. All she knew was that he thought she had an incredible amount of strength and potential. He believed in her…and she'd end up having to betray him.

What a shitty fucking life.

She walked around the island in the kitchen, paused by the fridge, and then walked out again. When he came home, he would order something for dinner. He always did on Wednesdays after his Guild meeting. He wouldn't stay in the kitchen long.

At his wet bar, she looked things over and then headed out again. He'd make himself a drink to relax after his meeting. Normal people would hit the couch or head to the library to watch TV or read. Not this mage. No, first he'd go to his office. Every day, right after getting home, he went to that office.

She headed that way now, feeling the need to pick up her pace. It wasn't because of the time, but because the energy that seemed to pull at her, urging her faster.

Complying, never realizing this was actual magic and not just intuition, she passed the library and stopped at the door of the home office. The black-and-white checkered floor disappeared under sea-foam-colored cabinets that spanned one whole side of the large room. A white counter had been arranged on top of a break in the cabinets, creating a desk. Two large computer monitors sat atop it, along with a desk lamp and a frame showcasing two knotted ropes. They were probably sentimental, the mage having escaped out of them or trapped a victim with them or something. Sebastian would know.

A window waited to the right of the setup, and long, low storage cupboards spanned out beneath it.

Nessa stood behind the desk. That computer would require a password she didn't know. She'd need to spring the trap after he'd logged on.

After taking in the area for a little longer, she got to work. The ceiling would support the mage's weight and then some. The furniture was sturdy and heavy. It would easily act as anchors. Everything else was child's play. She could rig up one of these traps in her sleep. For a mage, anyway.

Her mind drifted, thinking about how she'd have to alter the setup for Tristan. He could've broken out of the trap she'd laid for him in Kingsley's territory, and she'd put a lot of effort into that one, using pulleys and her own body weight. She'd even punched nails into the floor! She wouldn't be able to capture him with the trap she was currently setting up. He'd yank the ceiling down on top of them or pull the furniture away from the walls. He'd capture her, his grip tight around her throat, her back against the wall. His lips would barely glance off the shell of her ear as he whispered a vicious threat.

She shivered as she finished what she was doing, wiping a little sweat from her brow that hadn't come from her efforts.

"How goes it?" Sebastian waited at the doorway.

She startled and let out a slow breath. "Good." She cleared her throat and looked over her setup, glancing at the moonlight streaming through the windows. "Unless he comes home early and notices the little visible strand of parachute cord there, we're good."

Sebastian glanced at the lighting setup. "The ceiling is mostly shadow. It's like this mage *wants* to be strung up and tortured."

"After the role he played in helping orchestrate the attack on Kingsley's territory, I have to conclude that's exactly what he wants. He'll appreciate us for this, I am positive."

"Yes, I think so. He'll beg to be tortured just a little more."

"Or…killed a little faster, but…" She shrugged. "Same thing."

"Exactly the same." He hugged her tightly. "I know this is hard—"

She held up a finger. "I'm in the right headspace for

it right now. Let's leave it at that."

He nodded and stepped away. "Right then, Captain. Because of your quick work, we have an hour to kill. What shall we do with ourselves? Raid his pantry or raid his valuables?"

"Valuables, obviously. I had some Goldfish before we came. Let's see if our mage has anything special we can take off his hands and show to our enemies as a threat…" She flashed Sebastian her teeth. "Damn it! I keep forgetting that we won't be able to take credit for any of this. How annoying."

"For everyone involved, yes. Jessie and her crew think they're going to have a nice little reprieve while Momar scrambles to understand his loss."

"Well…" She followed him toward the stairs. They always started with the master bedroom first. "They would if we didn't interfere."

"Right. Except we are, so…"

She didn't comment, trying desperately to stay focused as they strolled into the bedroom. They were in this one alone. She wouldn't have Edgar to stand in the corner and act…like Edgar. Or Niamh's cool-headed logic. Or the shifters to wither the bowels of their enemies. Or Tristan to handle the violence. It was just her and Sebastian again, getting their hands dirty in the least honorable ways possible.

"Are you sure you're okay?" Sebastian asked softly as he paused in rummaging through the mage's closet. Lord only knew what he was looking for.

"Yeah. No sweat." She headed toward the safe, getting out her tools and setting to work.

Sebastian curled his lip, pointing at a little statue in the corner. "It's all pricey but…gaudy. He shouldn't have decorated his own house."

"Nice collection of watches." Nessa stepped back after she'd opened the safe.

"Wow, Captain. That was quick. It must've been a record."

"The safe needs to be replaced. It's way too old. It was child's play to break into." She passed a few of the nicer pieces over.

"Meh." Sebastian paused on one. "Oops. This one has a magical tracker. Let's not take it."

"Would Jessie know which have trackers and which don't?"

Sebastian hesitated. She could hear his release of breath. It was enough to prove she'd been wrong about him—he wasn't impervious to all emotion when he was in his Elliot Graves mode. He was having some guilt issues about what they were doing, just like her.

"We'll take the three best," he said, "and leave the rest scattered on the floor. The one for tracking is ugly, thankfully."

"We should be making more of a mess."

He hesitated again. "Yeah, you're probably right."

They picked their way through the house, noting things of value and not making a mess in any of the rooms the mage might see before they sprang their trap. They had a van parked on the backside of the property, across the street, near where they'd cut through the fence. They would drive it around to the front of the house to gather their spoils once the mage was dealt with.

Down in the three-car garage, Sebastian pulled off a car cover and then whistled softly. "I think we've missed a new fad, Captain. Look at this baby!"

A sleek, old-fashioned automobile sat to the side of the garage, in the farthest position from the door leading into the house. Cherry red and in pristine condition. All Nessa knew was that it was some sort of Ferrari, it was a classic, and it was expensive.

"This thing is a beauty," Sebastian purred as he ran a hand over the fender. "Kingsley would kill for this. I mean…Austin would, too—anyone would, but Kingsley would understand it for the true gem it is."

"How many fancy cars have we found since we started this thing?" Nessa asked as she looked around the rest of the garage. The other cars in the mage's collection were new luxury models, nothing too excit-ing. They weren't worth the hassle of selling them to a chop shop.

"There are fancy cars and then there are collector's items. This is the latter. So are the other ones we've seen or procured. Watches are still a *thing*, obviously, and clearly used for tracking and communication, but it seems like the big players are moving on to cars. He sank a lot of money into this thing. Money I'm not sure he has. He'd have to stretch for this sort of price tag."

"Or else he killed for it."

Sebastian put up his finger. "Or else he killed for it. Is this the new way to get status, then? You take some-one important down and show up in his collector's-item car?"

"That certainly sounds like a fad Momar would like."

Sebastian looked at her for a long moment, and she could tell the wheels were turning. He nodded slowly before going back to look at the car.

"We're taking this," he said, grabbing the car cover and pulling it back over. "This is perfect on so many levels. We're on the right path, Captain. The way is shitty, but it is right, I can feel it. Let's get ready for our host."

They had all their tools ready by the time Malachi

walked in. He passed through the kitchen, went to his wet bar, fixed himself a drink, and headed to his office, following the same routine they'd logged over the past few days. He didn't notice the intruders in his space until after he'd logged on to his computer. They sprang the trap, and a cable looped around his neck, his hands, and then his upper body as Nessa hoisted him into the air. His eyes bugged until she lowered the blinds and then loosened his neck loop just enough so that he could breathe.

"Here's the thing," she said in a silky voice, having taken the time to do up her makeup and put on something that would identify her as the Captain. "Elliot Graves and I haven't done this solo in a while. We've been pampered. Now I'm missing my friends."

She pouted as Sebastian walked in. He'd changed into a suit and slicked back his hair. Now, he made a show of taking off the jacket and rolling up the sleeves on his dress shirt.

"By the time we're finished here"—he gave a cocky grin, stopping in front of the now-struggling mage— "my lovely white shirt is going to be sprayed red." He held up his hands. "And I'm not even sorry about that fact. Let's get into it, shall we, Malachi? I have so many questions."

"Please," the mage said with a wheeze, licking his

lips. "Please, they have a magical spell on my head. I can't talk. It'll kill me if I try."

Nessa laughed, picking up one of her more pain-inducing instruments. "We've run into that before. It was very frustrating. Luckily…" She hooked a thumb Sebastian's way.

"I'm smarter than the person who designed that spell," he said. "It hurts like hell to strip it away, but that'll be nothing compared to what's coming if you don't talk. Here we go…"

NESSA SLUMPED AGAINST the wall as she waited for Sebastian to bring the van around. Her nails were stained red even though she'd scrubbed them in scalding water, and the clothes she'd been wearing were ruined. She'd forgotten how hard it was to get information out of someone who'd been magically induced not to give it. Sebastian could do a lot, but nothing could help like the magic of Jessie and the pizzazz of the Ivy House crew. Nothing was so neat as however Tristan had gone about it on Kingsley's land.

Fuck, she missed all of them. So badly. They'd made her forget this life a little. They'd made her feel less wicked. Less monstrous. With them, she was doing things like this within the unity of the crew for a common goal. Now…they had that same goal, but she felt raw. Lonely.

She glanced back at the torn-up house. They'd even affected claw marks in the sofa and walls just to be very clear that it was the gargoyles behind this mess. That it was Jessie who had done this. She was being thrown into the big players club whether she liked it—or knew about it—or not.

A knock sounded at the door. That meant Sebastian had torn down the protection spell—and the spy's spell layered into it.

She flipped the latch and shoved it open.

Sebastian looked at the framing. "If there is a countdown, that's going to start it. Everything ready?"

"Ready. Let's—" She grabbed his shirt and yanked him around, rubbing at his face. "Wait, you have some blood…"

"Thanks," he muttered, glancing at her face as well. His expression crumpled. He wiped at her cheek. "Tears come off a little easier than blood, at least."

"Not when they come from a wounded soul."

"Look at you," he whispered with a sad smile. "So poetic." He put his hand on her shoulder. "We'll talk about it when we get home."

"There's nothing to talk about. I just need to get used to this kind of thing again. It's fine. I'll be fine."

"Yeah," he said noncommittally.

In silence, they started loading stolen items into the

van. He'd be taking the fancy car out of here. It would be covered in a spell that made it look like the van she'd be driving. When they were loaded up, they did a last sweep through the house.

"It's convincing. They'll believe Jessie's crew did this," he said, knocking over a small porcelain statue just for fun. It shattered across the ground.

"Either that, or they'll think shifters are behind it."

"Shifters can't pull down spells like this. That takes power. They know she has it." He nodded and took Nessa's arm, guiding her out. "It'll work. In Kingsley's battle, she was pushing her little cart to the top of the hill. This shove will send it careening down to Momar."

"Your metaphors need work."

She passed him by and headed to the van, soon relishing the silence as they drove to their current hideout. The streets were mostly deserted this late at night—early morning, actually. Country roads took them to the estate way outside of town, over an hour's drive. They tucked the automobiles into the empty garage and left them for the time being.

"Do you want a nightcap?" Sebastian asked when she stopped in the bare kitchen to grab a glass of water.

"No, it's okay. I'm going to head to bed. See you tomorrow."

"Okay," he murmured, his façade fading away and his tone dripping with sadness. "I'm sorry, Nessa.

Truly."

"It's not your fault. This is what needs to happen. I know that. I'll adjust. I just…need some time."

She closed the door to her bedroom with a sigh and leaned against it for a moment, closing her eyes. Her heart was beating too fast and her insides felt hollow.

"Stop feeling sorry for yourself," she berated herself quietly, pushing off the door. She'd always known she would end up in this situation. She needed to just get on with it.

An unexpected flash of color had her reaching for a knife. Adrenaline dumped into her body as she focused in on what it was.

Sitting on her desk in the corner, beside her laptop, was a crystal vase filled with deep purple tulips. The computer was opened and turned on, a green rectangle flashing in the upper corner of an otherwise black screen. A little card sat in front of the tulips, folded in half.

She approached it slowly as tears sprang to her eyes. With a shaking hand, she picked up the note.

Call me next time, little deathwatch angel. I told you—I don't mind getting my hands dirty so that you can keep yours clean. No exceptions.

– YM

YM. Your Monster.

Tristan.

How the hell had he found her this time? After he'd found her last time and sent those books, she'd been so careful.

And *how* had he possibly known what she did tonight?

She looked at the screen, her fingers itching to reach for the keys. To talk to him. He was on the other side of that blinking green rectangle, she knew. This wouldn't be the first time she'd told him to get lost by these means.

It was the first time she needed to talk to someone, though.

She leaned on her elbows, staring at the note.

No exceptions.

That sounded so good right now, but there were always exceptions if you were rotten enough.

She needed to close the laptop down. She needed to disconnect it from the network and change the IP. They'd have to move *yet again*. They'd planned to anyway, but they hadn't wanted to do it so hastily. Tristan had found her, though. He had a knack for doing so. He'd told her once that he could anticipate her. That he could discover her plans as quickly as she made them.

Damn him. If he didn't keep his distance, he would ruin everything.

She grabbed the top of the screen in a rush and tensed, ready to slam it down.

Another tear fell.

She glanced to the side, wiping it away. Her resolve cracked.

We have to stop meeting like this, she typed.

The cursor blinked. She stared at it, wondering if he was sleeping. If he'd gotten tired of waiting for her to return.

I'll meet any way you want. Next time maybe I'll stay for a while so I can see you in person. I need to collect on that promise.

She frowned at the screen, wiping away another tear. *What promise??*

Your kiss held a promise. I'm eager to collect.

He meant the kiss in Kingsley's territory after she'd taken him down on his porch.

She rolled her eyes. *I wasn't in my right mind.*

Not ready yet? No problem. I've got time.

She tapped her fingers against the desk, not sure what else to say, knowing she couldn't say much. She wanted to ask after the crew but was worried it would hurt too much. Nothing could be said about her life, because it was all work and no play right now. She barely even baked, working feverishly to close the gaps in knowledge that had formed between the time they'd stepped away from the mage world and now. There was so much happening, so many secret deals and improbable alliances.

Momar had a firm, solid hold on the majority of it, but there were cracks. There were fragile areas. It was those areas they had to burrow into and exploit while also driving holes anywhere else they could. They had a lot of work to do. Dirty work.

Hell, maybe they had a lot of cars to collect. They'd probably need to get a garage, and her new hobby would become learning about automobiles, where once it had been knowing the ins and outs of watches.

She'd just decided it would be safe to ask after a coffee recipe, something she knew Tristan liked creating for Mr. Tom, when green words flashed across the screen.

Those flowers are called Queen of the Night tulips. I didn't know that when I went to purchase them. They grabbed my eye because they reminded me of your haunting beauty. Of your ability to stand out. After learning the name, I figured they were perfect. Get some sleep, little monster. When you need to talk, I'm here. If you need help, I'll come. No exceptions.

Him and his "no exceptions." Clearly he didn't

know what she was up to.

He would soon enough. He'd learn what a real monster looked like.

She sighed, thought about typing goodnight, and then reached to close the computer down. Before she could, one more message came in.

By the way, your bed is too small. My wings don't fit. Get a larger one when you settle into your next residence. I'll bang you against the wall, no problem, but we do have to sleep sometime.

She narrowed her eyes at the computer before turning slowly to look at her bed, made crisply like usual. Nothing was out of place.

Slowly, knowing a smile was threatening, she pulled back the sheet and bent to sniff. His mouthwatering cologne hit her immediately, followed by his special and unique fragrance, wood and amber.

"That little…" She pulled it back more. His scent was everywhere. "Bastard," she whispered, laughing to herself.

She crossed back to the computer.

Have fun pining. You're never going to get a taste.

The green rectangle bleeped. Then: *Liar.*

Her smile stretched. She finally closed down the computer. He was insufferable, but if she'd stuck around, she probably *would* have succumbed to his charm. She did like them dangerous. And hot. And holy hell, he smelled good.

She stripped and slipped into bed. His smell reminded her of Ivy House. Of a really bright point in an otherwise shadowy life.

It smelled like…home. She wondered how long it would take to fade away, and if her memories would fade away with it.

Regardless, she needed to get her head in the game. They couldn't allow for distractions. Her focus had to be acute. They needed to be vigilant if they hoped to survive long enough to reach the end.

CHAPTER 2

JESSIE

"EDGAR, I GET what you're saying," I attempted to explain patiently, "but we cannot have violent attack flowers hidden within the wood. We have hikers that accidentally come through here."

"We wouldn't have hikers for very much longer."

I stared at him.

He stared back at me, blinking far less than I was.

My patience waned. "We can't randomly kill hikers, Edgar. We have to share this town with non-magical people. Murder is against the Dick laws, remember? And it's morally bankrupt. I know we've dabbled in a lot of gray areas when dealing with the mages—"

"I wouldn't call torturing and then killing the enemy for information morally gray so much as mostly heinous…" He put up a finger. "And that is okay, because they are the enemy. Much like trespassing hikers."

"No…"

I took a deep breath and counted to ten. There were some things I was not overly proud of having done in this new magical life, and most of them stemmed from the questionable practices of mages.

Nessa and Sebastian, experts in the dirty underground of the magical world, Niamh, and the newest installment of our antihero squad, Tristan, had all assured me these acts had been necessary. Expected, even. The mage world was ruled by despicable sorts, and our enemy, Momar, sat at the top of that pile. People like him and the Mages' Guild were squeezing out or outright killing anyone with an intact moral compass. That was something Austin and I wanted to fix, but until we could take the high road…we were reduced to arguing about killing hikers with violent magical attack flowers, apparently.

"Just…no, Edgar. If you must have the flowers, at least ensure they have no poisonous thorns. Scratching and scaring, sure. An angry flower behind a 'beware' sign, great. But a killing flower that looks like an innocent sunflower until it is literally gouging a lost hiker? No. *No!* You must see the logic there."

He heaved a sigh and bowed in defeat. "Okay, Jessie. I guess I'll pretend to see the logic, since you are making me feel guilty about not seeing it. But I'd like to go on recording history by saying that I think this is a mistake and these flowers could also work against the corrupt mages sneaking on the property to check you out…"

His brows lifted slowly. It kinda looked like they were attached to the corners of his mouth, because his hopeful smile was slowly spreading.

"No attack flowers!" I yelled at him, my usually calm and patient demeanor exploding into frustrated anger.

I tried to breathe. To calm down.

Instead, I yelled louder, "Solve the gnome problem! That's what we need. A gnome-killing flower—"

"But Jessie, as I explained—"

"*Solve the gnome problem!*" I hollered at him.

He spun and burst into his insect cloud, zipping away.

I stared after him, perspiration coating my forehead. Immediately I felt guilty, knowing he was just trying to help. We were all trying to find a new normal.

It had been months since the big battle at Kingsley's. Since my team had devastated Momar's, even with his impressive display of magic.

Since we'd lost Nathanial, and I'd almost followed him into the grave.

The loss had affected everyone differently, and to be honest, I was having a hard time consoling everyone through their grief. The guilt I felt had a constant hold on me, even in my nightmares. I'd try to change the outcome, try to dislodge Nathanial from my body as we hurtled toward the magical barrier that would kill him. But nothing made a difference.

Nothing could change the fact that he'd given up his life to save mine.

Without him, I wouldn't have made it. I wouldn't have taken out those mages and destroyed their spell. Without him, we would've all died.

Austin hadn't been sleeping well, either. He constantly woke up, clutching for me, dreaming I hadn't come back from the brink. That I was one of the people he'd helped bury.

I ran my hand down my face and turned, startling when I caught Niamh standing not far away. She wore black pants and shirt with a neutral expression, patiently waiting for me to notice her.

"How long have you been there?" I asked, checking to make sure I had clothes on.

That was another little trait I'd picked up—I just randomly worried I was naked. It was like I'd stopped remembering when I'd last bothered with clothes. We were going to my parents' for Christmas in a week, and I needed to keep things in check. I would not end up like my father, wandering around the house with his begonias hanging out.

"Long enough to wonder if we should have left that vampire behind at Kingsley's."

"Yeah, right." I huffed, starting toward the house and a meeting with Tristan I was probably late for. I did, in fact, have clothes on, so that was something. "He gave us a pass with the gnome situation even though they turned feral relatively quickly. There was no way he would consent to keeping Edgar."

"Especially now that Aurora has refused Kingsley's final ultimatum about going home."

I groaned, reaching the back door and pushing my way in.

Before taking off without another word, Nessa and Sebastian had arranged a little surprise for us. They'd helped Aurora, Kingsley's daughter, stow away with the basajaunak on the way back to O'Briens. She'd taken up residence at Sebastian and Nessa's abandoned house. Kingsley hadn't known any of this until he'd found her "goodbye, don't worry about me" letter, which had been before we even found out.

Commence his worrying.

"What was the latest ultimatum?" I asked, passing by Mimi at her desk and knocking on the nearest wall in hello. We didn't waste words when we didn't have to.

"He cut her off."

K . F .   B R E E N E

Mr. Tom wasn't in the kitchen, so I pulled open the fridge door and stared at the contents for a moment. Then shut it. The interior looked like a grocery store had thrown up in there. I wasn't hungry enough to bother figuring out lunch.

"Cut her off from communication?" I frowned at Niamh as I headed for the hallway again. "That seems a little harsh. What if she wants to go back?"

"He's desperate fer her to go back. No, he cut her off from the money teat."

"Gross. So she's broke?"

"Are ye jokin'?" Niamh gave me a side-eye. "She's got plenty to be gettin' on with around here. No rent to speak of, and she's gettin' a nice little income from the pack. She's moving up in the ranks faster than anyone can believe. She's got a lot of drive and a good head on her shoulders. No, she'll be just fine."

"Kingsley's going to appeal to Austin next," I said, knowing how these things went.

I approached the bottom of the stairs as Ulric was coming down. He hopped off the last step and then put out his arms for a hug. I complied, as I always did, closing my eyes when he held me tightly and rocked me a little. He'd been doing that often since we'd come back from Kingsley's, silently offering his support or needing some of mine.

When he stepped back, he pointed at me. "We're not inviting my mom to Christmas, right?"

"Oh…" I let out a breath. "Um…sorry, Ulric, I thought you knew. Austin and I will be going to my parents' house for Christmas. We'll be meeting my ex and his new woman and doing holiday parties and all that. You guys will all be staying here. But you can have her here, if you want? Mr. Tom was intending to make a big dinner and all that stuff."

He gave me a strange look. "No, then. Okay." He headed past me.

"I can't imagine she'll be overly pleased about that," I murmured, pausing to watch his wings swing as he walked away.

"She'll be grand."

"Did you need something?" I asked as I headed for the front sitting room. Niamh didn't give or need subtle support like Ulric and a few of the others. She usually just forced me onto a barstool and helped me make bad decisions.

"Not a thing. Just passin' the time, is all," she said, following me in.

Tristan sat on one of the couches with a book in hand and his ankle resting on his knee. An empty coffee mug sat on a coaster. A little froth and whipped cream clung to the sides of the mug. He liked to challenge Mr.

Tom's coffee-making prowess.

"Hey," I said, taking a seat facing him.

He held up a finger, continuing to read, before picking up a bookmark from beside him and fitting it into the pages. He set the book on the coffee table before standing.

"Oh." I stood with him. He'd wanted to see me about something. I now wondered if this would be a walk-about situation like with Edgar. I had high hopes that this meeting wouldn't be nearly as annoying.

He stopped in front of me and bent to wrap his arms around my shoulders, holding me tightly before letting me go again, only to hold on to my upper arms and look down into my eyes.

"How are you?" he asked, his gaze searching.

"She'd probably do better if people would stop pandering to her," Niamh grumbled, heading to one of the couches in the back.

Her surliness didn't stop a wave of emotion from filling me. My lower lip started to tremble.

Tristan nodded, pulling me in tightly again, hugging me for a long moment as I got myself back under control. They'd stopped telling me that it hadn't been my fault, or asking if there was anything they could do. It wasn't logic I needed, or some magical recipe to forget, especially since I didn't want to forget. I just wanted it to get a little easier.

When he finally released me, he regained his seat, watching me silently.

"I'm fine," I said, wiping my eyes and then grabbing a tissue to take care of my nose. "What do you need?"

"Two things. The first is that I'd like to work the basajaunak into the gargoyle flight training, but I need you connecting us all so we can be spatially cognizant of each other."

"My, my. Spatially cognizant, huh?" Niamh drawled. "They must've had schools in yer previous life."

Tristan's roots were still a mystery. Or maybe Niamh knew everything, and she was just poking fun—I didn't know. I'd asked to be left out of any discoveries about his past. Plausible deniability was just fine for my current mental situation. I didn't want to accidentally out the guy, and right now, I couldn't even remember if I had clothes on half the time.

"Timing is going to be a little tough," I said, reaching for my phone in my back pocket. It wasn't there. "Dang it," I muttered, wondering where I might've set it down. "I'm leaving in a week, remember, and I have a list of things I need to do before I go. I'm sure I can squeeze it in, though. I just need to find my phone and then pull up my schedule so I can figure it out."

"Of course. The second is that—"

A ringing phone growing in volume pulled my attention, because it was my ringtone. Jasper walked into the room a moment later, just as the ringing stopped. He held the phone out to me while nodding hello to Tristan.

"Found this in my bathroom," he said. "The caller tried twice."

"In *your* bathroom?" I asked.

"Yeah. What would I be doing in yours?"

"Well, what was I doing in—" The truth dawned on me, and I nodded. "Delivering towels, that's right. Mr. Tom has been absent on and off all day running errands."

"You don't need to deliver my towels, Jessie. I know where the laundry room is." He gave me a side-hug. "But I appreciate it."

My phone started ringing again, and I tilted it up, seeing my ex-husband's name.

"Tristan, do you mind if I—"

"Not at all." He leaned forward for his book.

I swiped my finger across the screen.

"Hello?" I asked, crossing over into the seldom-used sitting room across the way for a little privacy.

"Jacinta," came Matt's stuffy, arrogant voice. "Yes, hello."

"Hi, Matt, what's up?"

"Jacinta, I had thought we were on the same page about the holiday plans. I don't like hearing that they've been changed at a moment's notice. Now, Jim—"

"Whoa, whoa." I squeezed my eyes shut and waved my hand through the air, trying to make sense of him but having a hard time not being incredibly irritated by his tone. "What are you talking about? I haven't changed any plans."

He paused for a long moment. "I was hoping to have a reasonable discussion with you, not be interrupted and barked at."

My hand tightened on the phone, but I paced a little, counting to ten.

"I apologize," I said in an even tone. "But I don't know what you're talking about. I haven't changed any plans."

"Jimmy was supposed to fly into LAX in three days, whereupon Camila would've picked him up, and we would've all seen you for—"

"*Camila* would've picked him up?" I asked, standing in front of a little table by the window. "He was excited for you to do it."

His pause stretched again, and I didn't have enough numbers to count to calm the irritation.

"Matt, look, I'm in the middle of something. Could

you put in a new battery or something and get the words out a little faster?"

After another pause, I pulled the phone away from my face to make sure he hadn't hung up. That was a usual occurrence when he thought I was being "difficult." I was sure this was one of those occasions. He hated when I interrupted him for any reason, especially if it was to argue.

"Not that it is any of your business, but I have a meeting scheduled," Matt finally said, his tone highly disapproving. "I planned to see him right after work."

"Not any of my business? He's my son, Matt, and it breaks my heart when you hurt him. He was looking forward to your making the effort. You never used to when he was younger, and he thought it meant you—"

"Jacinta, I didn't call you to get into my work schedule," he said tersely. "Camila is no longer working and has the time to devote to this. I do not. I do not want to speak of this any longer."

I threw up my hand. "Great, fine, whatever. You do you, bro. But you called me about a supposed change in plans, and so far, you don't want to talk about the only change that I know of."

His words came slowly, as though he were talking to someone hard of thinking.

"Jimmy was supposed to come *here*, and you were

to meet *us* for dinner at my house, not the other way around."

"And that's what's still happening. I'll see you on the twentieth. Or twenty-first, or whatever it is."

"Christ," he said, pulling the phone away. That meant he was very frustrated with me.

"I have the date somewhere. Calm down," I said, rubbing my palm against my forehead. "It's in my phone, which is next to my head. It's fine. We'll be there. All is well. No change in plans…"

The Porsche that Gerard the gargoyle had given me pulled up to the curb. Mr. Tom almost never drove it because it went too fast when he stomped on the gas. He couldn't be talked into *not* stomping on the gas. I hadn't understood why he'd wanted to take it today, but the answer to that question stepped out of the passenger seat. He had a look of wonder on his face and his hair was badly in need of a wash. His clothes were a little too small, rumpled, and probably sporting stains. His face turned toward the house, and through the window I saw his beaming smile.

"Oh," I said, my heart lurching and excitement flaring through me. "Jimmy is coming here first instead of going there," I said in a rush. "He just got here. I see him through the window now."

"Yes, exactly. I would say that is a huge change in

plans—"

"Matt, honestly, I didn't know. Mr. Tom must've set this up to surprise me—"

"Do you actually expect me to believe that?"

"I don't give two shits what you believe. You screwed up by telling him work is more important than him, and this is clearly Jimmy telling you how that makes him feel. This is between you and him. If he wants to come here for a week instead of going there, he's an adult. That is his decision to make."

Mr. Tom came around the car and wrestled Jimmy's bags away from him.

No sound came from the phone, and a quick check verified that Matt had hung up on me this time.

It was just as well. The conversation would only have gone downhill from there.

"I thought you got along with your ex?" Jasper asked, waiting in the hall. He'd clearly been eavesdropping.

"I did. But I guess that was before I developed a spine. We haven't really seen eye to eye since I moved here."

"Fair play to ya," Niamh called, but I was already jogging for the door.

"Mom!" Jimmy's face had an attempt at a five o'clock shadow, his few whiskers a long way from a full face of hair. His eyes had dark circles under them, but otherwise he was practically thrumming with excitement. "Surprise! Are you happy?"

I tackle-hugged him, squeezing him tightly. The pain from the last couple of months threatened to break free as he stepped back. His eyes shadowed immediately, and he stepped in for another hug.

"Mr. Tom told me about you losing your friend. Sorry, Mom. That's why I thought you wouldn't mind if I came here instead of going to Dad's. And not to throw him under the bus or anything, but Mr. Tom said it would be okay."

"Of course I don't mind!" I stepped back and wiped my face, smiling. "You are always welcome, you know that. Maybe a little heads-up would've been nice, though, *Mr. Tom.*" I leaned around Jimmy to give Mr. Tom a hard look. "The Christmas party is going to be tense because Jimmy's dad is less than thrilled that I didn't clear this with him, but it'll be fine."

"The nature of a surprise means there is no heads-up," Mr. Tom intoned, not at all apologetic.

"Yeah." Jimmy headed toward the house. "I figured Dad would be pissed. That's why I didn't tell him. But he canceled all the stuff just he and I were going to do together. I'd have been stuck hanging out with Camila all the time, and…" He shrugged. "I figured he wouldn't really care, since he wasn't going to be there much anyway."

"We'll smooth it over. It'll be fine. Are you tired? Hungry?"

"Is Austin still—"

The words died on Jimmy's lips when he saw Tristan waiting just inside the doorway. He stopped dead and then started to back-pedal.

"What's wrong?" I put a hand on his back to stop him. "That's Tristan. He's with us now. He's a new hire, so to speak. Well…not *new* new, but new since you've been here."

"Don't mind him a'tall." Niamh shouldered the huge gargoyle-monster, something we'd taken to calling him because he wasn't full gargoyle, out of the way and held out her hands for Jimmy. "He's only incredibly dangerous to yer enemies. Come in, come in. How about a *cuppa*? Do ye want a sandwich? Ye do, o'course. Come in and I'll make something fer ya."

She turned for the kitchen.

"You do not get to offer your terrible sandwiches in this house," Mr. Tom called, dropping Jimmy's bags and hurrying in through the door. "Don't touch those, Master Jimmy." He hastily pointed at the bags as he moved through the foyer. "I'll be back for them promptly. I just need to get that horrible old woman out of my kitchen before she wrecks everything. Don't you touch my bread," he yelled, running down the hallway.

Mimi flattened herself against the wall down the way. Mr. Tom's wing fluttered by her, and then she pushed off again as if an old butler hadn't just sprinted past in a mad dash for kitchen dominance. She held herself as regally as usual, stopping in front of Jimmy and clasping her hands in front of her.

"Hello," she said. "I hear you are Jessie's boy. Well met. I am Naomi, Austin's Grandma Mimi. Since you are part of our family, you may call me Mimi as well. Given you are a Dick, I will inform you that I am not a hugger."

"What'd she just call me?" he murmured, hesitantly putting out his hand for a shake.

"Dick—like a non-magical person, remember?" I said.

Mimi looked at his outstretched hand before shaking her head. "No."

"Okay. Good times." I rubbed Jimmy's back. "And yes, this is Tristan." I motioned to Tristan, who had taken a large step away to give Jimmy some space. "He's one of us. A very large one of us, but still on the team."

Tristan put out his hand and stepped forward slowly, trying not to spook Jimmy.

My heart melted and tears came to my eyes. With

sudden fear, I quickly patted myself, affirming I was still dressed. My God, when would I stop being so horribly scattered?

I pointed at Tristan. "Do you mind hanging out for a moment while I get Jimmy settled, and then we can talk about the second thing you needed?"

He finished shaking Jimmy's hand and stepped back. "It's not urgent. Enjoy your time. I'll connect with you later in the week, how's that? And don't worry about training. We can do it after the holidays."

"We'll figure it out." I nodded at him, removing my hand from behind Jimmy and pointing down the hall. "Head to the kitchen, bud, okay? I'll grab your bags and meet you there. Tell Mr. Tom to make me whatever he's making you."

"Here we go." Jasper came in holding the bags before motioning upstairs. "His room is down the hall from mine, right? I can just go put these away."

"Yeah, please, if you wouldn't mind. Thanks, Jasper."

Jasper hefted the bags in response and headed up the stairs.

My phone rang again, the name this time coming up as "Camila (Matt)." I stared at it for a moment and then sighed in defeat. I'd been in her shoes. Matt would find a situation impossible to navigate, decide it wasn't worth his time, and hand it over to me. He had a secretary at work, and one at home.

Ultimately, this situation wasn't Camila's fault, and she didn't need my censure. But man, I wanted to lay into both of them.

I took a deep breath, had a seat, and prepared to rework the holiday plans for the guy who simply could not go with the flow unless the flow directly benefited him.

I had the distinct impression the holidays were going to be a lot tougher this year. At least it would only be Austin and me going home. I wouldn't have to explain away a bunch of capes.

CHAPTER 3

JESSIE

"WHAT DO YOU mean you told them they were going?" I demanded of Austin the next morning, standing at the edge of the bathroom as he exited the shower.

I didn't even care about the rivulets of water running down his glistening, cut body, or the light playing across his handsome features, or the part of him that was standing at attention after seeing me in my birthday suit. We were about to do battle, and those things would only distract me.

"Babe…" Austin grabbed a towel and started drying himself. "It's not safe for just you and me to go on trips, you know that."

"Except it is. The word on the street is there's another superpower mage in town, and she is working alongside shifters. The mage community has given me a wide berth. You've seen that yourself—there've been no attacks, no threats, no invitations to dinners, even. They are wary and they are giving me space for now. We should be fine."

I didn't mention—because Austin already knew— that we didn't know how long this break would last. We also didn't know what would happen when it was over.

Momar must want to wipe me off the face of the earth, and all the shifters with me. He'd retaliate at some point. The Mages' Guild... Well, we didn't know much about them. We might have some idea if Sebastian and Nessa had been in touch, but they hadn't, not in all this time. They had sent me an encrypted phone, which had arrived shortly after we returned to Ivy House, but all my texts and voicemails to them had been met with silence.

I still tried, though. I missed them. I often walked through the bowels of Ivy House, looking at Sebastian's abandoned equipment, changing out various ingredients as they went bad just in case he might show up. I went over to their house and helped Aurora garden, not talking much with her (she was like Mimi and not chatty) but enjoying some time and company in their space. They were part of my life here, and their absence had left a hole. I worried about them getting into trouble and not having my help. Or, God forbid, never seeing them again. It felt like too big of a disturbance after Nathanial's sacrifice, and even though Sebastian and Nessa had assured me it was necessary, I couldn't shake the feeling that it would lead to more danger for all of us.

"We're not bringing everyone," Austin said, wrapping the towel around his waist and doing nothing to hide the now tented fabric. The guy was insatiable. Normally great, right now distracting. "We'll only bring a few shifters and a few gargoyles to the parties—"

"Are you out of your mind?" I hollered, and then put up my hand, a signal that I realized my reaction had been out of proportion. I wasn't very good at handling grief, anxiety about my friends potentially being in danger, or the sense of impending doom that dogged me everywhere I went.

After a deep breath, I tried again, with Austin watching me patiently.

Softer this time, I asked, "Are you out of your mind?"

He started laughing.

"It's not funny," I said, unable to help the edges of my lips from twitching upward. "Austin, no. How am I going to explain the gargoyles' capes? Or the shifters' unbridled intensity? These are all Dicks and Janes, and none of them know I am magical."

"They probably all think you're in a cult." He took

out his toothbrush. "Don't your parents still think that from the time they were here?"

I put my hand over my face. "*Please* try to see this from my point of view. My ex is being really uppity, and his mom is just the worst, and I had hoped to dazzle them with my wealth and pretend social status and hot new boyfriend."

"Life partner."

"What?"

"I get that we can't say *mate*, but the term *boyfriend* implies temporary status. We'll use *life partner*."

The suggestion would be sweet in any other situation, but he didn't know what sort of world he was about to step into.

"We can't use that, because then they'll talk about you not having proposed," I said. "They'll question our whole situation. Do you not have enough money for a ring? Are you not ready for commitment? Maybe I'm your mistress, and you're trying to keep me around by promising me you'll leave your wife and marry me. Sound insane? I know, but these are seriously things I have heard them say. I don't want to be part of that rumor mill. The result is snide remarks and sly grins and things I really would prefer to avoid."

He finished brushing his teeth and walked up to me with swagger, a handsome smirk on his face. His hands settled low on my hips.

"They won't question my devotion to you, Jess." He leaned down slowly and kissed the side of my neck. "Boyfriend, live-in partner, love of my life…" He kissed the other side of my neck, and shivers coated my flesh. "Showing love is about actions more than titles. Touching. Possessive posturing. The women will know, without a shadow of a doubt"—he softly kissed my lips—"that you are my everything. You're the woman whom I've pledged my life to protect, to care for. The men will know"—he slid his hand up my stomach and cupped a breast—"that you belong to *me.*"

I fell into his kiss greedily before I remembered my point and backed off again.

"Stop that. You're intentionally trying to distract me."

He laughed again, sauntering out of the room. He was confident and eager to prove his claim in front of my family and the people from my past. I was eager for the same thing, as long as everything went well. Bringing any part of my crew would ensure *nothing* would go well.

"Please, Austin, I don't want to be the talk of the town this time. Negatively, I mean. I've always been the one who doesn't fit in. The one who doesn't belong. This time…I just want to shut them up."

"You will, baby. I promise."

I followed him into the bedroom. "Okay, but… You must see how showing up at a family gathering with a bodyguard detail is overboard. And if those bodyguards wear *capes*? Are you kidding me? First, they'll think I'm faking. Of course they will. I manage a house. Why would I need bodyguards?"

"Because of the cult? Or, like…a cult war?"

"It's not funny. Then they'll think I'm unhinged because I believe my bodyguards are actually superheroes." I shook my head, leaning against the wall. "Please, Austin, no. I'll be a laughingstock. I'll consent to having them at the house we're renting, but that's it. They have to stay inside at all times. Like prisoners."

Jeans on, he came up to me again, pulling me into his warm embrace.

"Jess, I'm just messing with you. I am taking this seriously, I promise. We *do* need to have a detail with us. That is not up for negotiation, but the gargoyles can blend into buildings. They'll stay out of sight in a way shifters can't. I checked out the topography of the area. There are enough trees and natural life that the basajaunak can also blend in. So we have them by parties and the shifters can guard the temporary residence. Okay? I'm assuming everything will go smoothly, because we are in a sort of magical bubble, but I want us covered."

I let my hands hang limply at my sides as he hugged me close.

"I hate you," I said with a pout.

"You hate losing arguments."

"That's what I said."

He chuckled as a knock sounded at the door. Cyra poked her head in with a plastered-on smile that meant terrible things.

"Hey, Jessie, how are you?" she asked. A doll tottered in behind her with a glass of water. That usually only happened after Cyra had recently died. It took her a while to learn how to control her fire again, and in those weeks and months, she tended to shed lava in the house. Sebastian had created a brooch to magically control that, though. I wondered what was going on.

"Fine. Good," I said. "Maybe borderline super angry, depending on why you're here."

She put out a finger. "Maybe. But hear me out. Edgar mentioned that you really wanted those gnomes gone, right? And I get it. Those little suckers somehow got a hold of a butcher knife and ambushed me the other day. It took three of them to wield the thing, and they hacked at my legs until I fell down."

"Could you not shift and fly away?"

"That's what those little bastards wanted. I wouldn't

give them the satisfaction. But unfortunately, they weren't trying to sever my neck. They were trying to get my magical brooch, which I was wearing at the time. And…well…they did. They yanked it off and ran."

"But…why were you wearing it? You haven't died in…months and months."

"I died during the battle at Kingsley's." She glanced at Austin. "Crap. I forgot I wasn't supposed to say that. Or was I not supposed to say Aunt Florence nearly died? I forget which one."

"*What?*" I asked, my heart lurching painfully again. Aunt Florence was Patty's sister, Ulric's aunt, one of the garhettes that helped in the battle.

"Both," Austin said in a deep voice. "You weren't supposed to tell her either of those things."

I rounded on him. "You're keeping things from me?"

"We all agreed to keep that from you because Cyra can come back from the dead and Aunt Florence didn't actually die. Indigo left you to heal her, nearly losing you because of it. One of the many times." His expression was stark, haunted. "It would've done no good to tell you, and I didn't want the reminder. We nearly lost many of our people. That we didn't lose them all is outstanding news. That you were nearly sacrificed time and again to save them is—"

"*Shh*," I said, stepping closer and wrapping him into a hug. "I'm okay. I made it."

His fingers dug into me for a moment, and the world stopped as he held me. He kept himself together almost all the time. That was part of alpha training, apparently. You learned not to lose control, including when people were killed in battle. You stayed strong for your pack. But it was different with a mate.

In these moments, I felt normal again. I felt like I wasn't alone in processing the terror of life's fragility, our loss, and how close I'd come to leaving my people and my family. But they always passed too quickly, putting me back on the unfocused, messy, emotional rollercoaster of grief. Still, I'd rather stay here than swing over to the opposite side and steep in cold, calculated vengeance. I felt it pulling at me. I felt the need to yank out Momar's heart with my bare hands. I felt the violent darkness within me like never before, devoid of humanity. Devoid of emotion. Devoid of anything familiar.

For that reason, I wouldn't hide from my grief. I wouldn't try to escape it. I didn't want to find out what I would become if I did.

When he'd regained his balance, Austin nodded and excused himself to the bathroom.

"I was a hero, by the way," Cyra continued. "In case

you didn't assume." She shrugged, and I couldn't help a half-hysterical chuckle.

"How many did you save?" I asked her, trying to keep from tears.

"Ten. Maybe twelve? Well…" She adjusted her fake glasses. "Maybe I didn't save them, per se. I took out half the mages who'd joined forces to send rapid-fire spells at our people. There were just four mages left after I got done with them, but Jessie…" She leveled me with a look, and I saw something spark in her eyes. Something that made me somewhat uncomfortable, although I couldn't discern why. "They were more intense than you and Sebastian together. And they weren't cowards."

I reached out to grab the post of the bed, my eyebrows pinched together. "They were working together like Sebastian and me?"

"No. They were working together like one entity. *Better* than Sebastian and you."

A flare of fire dripped from her and singed the rug. The doll threw water at it quickly, accidentally dropping the glass. It *thudded* against the floor, thankfully didn't break, and rolled away a little.

"I caught their combined blast," she continued. "It killed me almost instantly. That's not an easy feat. Hollace was above, moving into position. Niamh was there, too. Hollace let down his lightning, and then Niamh swooped in. She speared one of the twins—oh, yeah, I forgot to add that two of them were twins. The kind that look alike. Anyway, Hollace killed the two non-twins. But there was some sort of blast or explosion—I don't know, I was dead—and the twins got away. One of them had a hole in her side. Hopefully she bled out." She crossed her fingers. "But they were gone in a moment."

Two things pulled at the gargoyle part of me, lighting up my intuition.

"Twins," I said, leaning harder into the post as I considered the first thought that had grabbed at me. "Twins."

Who would work together better than twins? They'd be accustomed to sharing everything. A strong magical worker…doubled, the sum worth more than its parts. Then, using their affinity for working together, they could bring others into their fold. People without huge egos and a *me, me, me* attitude. I'd fall into that mold, no problem, because I liked the unity of working with others. Clearly there was strength in that.

It was a good strategy.

The bad news? They were working for Momar.

"I need to find some mage friends," I murmured to myself. If Momar could orchestrate a magical collective,

I could do it better. I knew I could. Probably.

I'd just need to scour the books in Ivy House for more information. If only Sebastian were here to help.

The next issue slithered into my brain.

…they were gone in a moment…

Like how they'd shown up in that territory out of nowhere, without any clear point of entry. We still didn't know how they'd gotten there. There had been no signs of helicopters. No sounds of automobiles. No strings of cars going through the surrounding towns. Their appearance was a mystery, even after the fact.

That hadn't sat well with Sebastian. I had a feeling that was why he'd left—to find out how the mages had done it. He and Nessa had dark ways of accruing information, and they wouldn't want to drag me down with them.

Niamh and Tristan were working on finding them. On tracking them. I had no idea how, but I knew they had a knack for that kind of work. All I could do was wait and hope our friends were okay. No news was definitely good news, because we'd hear in an instant if Elliot Graves and the Captain had been captured.

"Sorry…why are you here again?" I asked Cyra, my mind whirling.

"As I might've said—we've gotten off track and I can't remember—Edgar expressed an interest in getting rid of the gnomes. Given I'm now holding a grudge, I firebombed one of their larger nests. The basajaunak were not impressed. They're trying to put out the fire, but—"

"Wait." I held up my hand, realization dawning, and rushed toward the window.

Out in the back third of the wood, billows of smoke rose into the sky.

"I think it's spreading," Cyra said, joining me. "We—well you, I guess, since it's your territory or land or whatever—could use some elemental magic to stop it. Because, strangely, I don't know that fire kills those things. What even are they? They aren't plastic like the dolls. I can melt the faces and limbs off the dolls."

Two dolls, who'd been lingering in the doorway with glasses of water, suddenly backed slowly out of the door.

"You couldn't have started with this immediately?" I yelled, and this time I didn't hold up my hand for going overboard. In fact, I wanted to try again, louder.

I reached down to rip off my clothes, but I didn't have any on. I'd been naked this whole time.

"Do you need me?" Austin asked, emerging from the bathroom, still dressed in only his jeans.

"Not unless you know elemental magic." I sprinted out of the room, running full speed into Mr. Tom's back.

"Miss! Now, you don't want to end up like your father. Put on some clothes!"

"The wood is on fire," I said, shoving him out of the way.

"Well, then use the secret passageways!" he called after me. "You'll traumatize Master Jimmy."

I hadn't been thinking. Going through the passageways was the faster option anyway.

Reaching the nearest entrance, I quickly got inside and ran along until I hit the stairs. Up a little higher, and I emerged onto a type of shelf on the roof of the house. I heard sirens in the distance.

"It's under control," Ivy House said as I shifted into my gargoyle form.

"What are you talking about?"

"You think I'd survive this long without being able to control the elements on my land?"

I jumped off, flapping into the air. *"You're not doing much to stop the fire."*

"As I said, it's under control. I'm just allowing it to burn that nest the phoenix was talking about. The gnomes are getting a little out of hand. That vampire is too preoccupied with his flowers."

"What…"

I kept flying, suddenly feeling the flame. It was hot

in an unnatural way, sucking the life out of that area. I hadn't thought to set my inner alarms for fire or natural phenomena. I hadn't known it was possible until this moment, quite frankly.

"*Do you ever think that maybe your heirs die because you set them up for failure? Why didn't you give me this information sooner so that I could protect this place and myself rather than letting it burn? Physically and figuratively.*"

"*That thought recently crossed my mind.*"

"*It* just *crossed your mind?*"

"*Well? No one has ever called me out like you do. The other heirs were too busy living the good life and loving bad men.*"

They'd been too busy being young, was what she meant. They clearly hadn't been jaded enough going into all this.

The sound of wings caught my attention. I glanced back, seeing Tristan rushing toward me in his gargoyle form. He'd been incredibly protective since the battle at Kingsley's. He'd taken damage but hadn't allowed Indigo to heal him, wanting her sole attention on me. He'd saved my life. Which was another reason I couldn't care less about his secret origins. Whatever was discovered about him, it couldn't alter my opinion of his loyalty and good heart.

Nearing the smoke, I saw and felt the basajaunak below, running with water. Before I could use my magic to pull the heat from the flame, Ivy House did it for me. She sucked the fire from the land, pulling it back into the ground.

I flew around the smoke as it quickly shifted from a lighter gray to white, trying to see down through the lush branches and leaves.

Only a small portion of the area had been burned. It was probably the area Cyra had sent a jet of fire into. The damage was contained to the ground or the base of the trees.

"*How do you do that?*" I asked, mystified.

"*Magic,*" Ivy House responded.

"*Are you worried I'm going to learn how and then burn you down?*"

"*Now I am, yes.*"

I landed near the toasted area and shifted, shielding myself from the lingering heat. Dave the basajaun met me immediately.

"I do not want to throw anyone under the rat," he said, and I shook off the mixed analogy, "but *someone* lost her temper and caused this. She went to get help as we ran to get water."

"It's okay." I touched his arm.

"Oh yes, the needed hug. Here." He bent toward me

63

suddenly, more of a lunge, really, and it took everything in my power not to zap him with a nasty spell. He enveloped me in a hug, and his hair tickled my face and stuck into my partially opened mouth.

"Thank—*pfft*. Thank you—*pfft*. I'm good." I sneezed and rubbed my nose, trying to dislodge the hair. "Apparently Ivy House can suck the heat from flame. I found out about thirty seconds ago. So I guess we don't have to worry about fire on the property?"

"I did sense some very old growth," said *Her*, the young basandere working on the essence of the wood, trying to make it feel more inviting and homelike. "I do recommend a controlled burn through here to get rid of all the small things. But this magical wood is fantastic. I am glad we have made this connection with you."

More basajaunak materialized around us, probably over three dozen. I'd felt presences but hadn't counted everyone up. It was kind of a moot point with these creatures. If they weren't visible to you, they didn't want to talk. There was no better hint to *get lost* than that.

"Ivy House let it rage for a few minutes because it was trying to trim down the gnome nest," I informed them. I edged toward the charred area.

"Oops." *Her* put an arm out in front of me. "Here." She then side-hugged me, cracking something and popping something else.

"I really am okay," I wheezed. "But the gnomes stole Cyra's magical brooch, and she is dripping fire all over the floor. It's best for everyone if we find it."

"Oh…" another basandere said, leaning forward and putting a hand above her eyes to block the nonexistent sun. It was caught in the canopy above. "I saw a gnome fighting another for a shiny thing earlier. There's no telling where it might be. We can look."

"Wait until it's safe, obviously, but if you all wouldn't mind…" I let my words trail away, looking at all the shrubs and char and leaves and… They'd never find it. That brooch was small, and the smoke and fire would cover the shine.

After accepting another dozen or so hugs, remembering to close my mouth those times, I finally wandered away, readying to head back.

"Jessie, a word?" Tristan waited close by in his human form, leaning against a tree.

"Yeah, what's up?" I asked, trying to feel the land in this new way I was privy to.

His eyes barely glowed as he studied me. "I'd like to talk openly with you, and I want you to know that I'm here if you need to cry."

I sagged. "Well…at least you're not hairy, I guess. And have hopefully showered."

He shook his head in confusion.

"The hair—" I pointed back the way I'd come. "Never mind. It's fine. What's up?"

"Nathanial had a sixth sense where it concerned you. He could anticipate you better than anyone aside from Alpha Steele. Maybe even better than Alpha Steele when in the sky."

"Yeah," I said darkly. "And look where that got him."

"A hero's death."

I lifted my eyebrows, not having expected that answer. I definitely hadn't expected to hear the raw longing within it.

"Without him, we are weaker in battle," Tristan went on, stating fact as he knew it. "You are our most prized weapon. In order to best utilize you, we have to help you overcome or conceal your weaknesses. He could do that. No one else can. We're weaker without him."

"Maybe I do need a hug," I murmured. "But the thing is, I can't allow you to hug me right now. Not while being naked and…you know. Being *you*. I might need to go get Dave."

"Being me… Meaning being incredibly dangerous?" he asked with a crease in his brow.

"Yes," I said sarcastically, "in order to avoid your *incredible* danger, I'm going to go hug a completely safe

MAGICAL MIDLIFE AWAKENING

and not-at-all-deadly basajaun. Yikes, bud. How do you fit that ego through doorways?"

A crooked smile worked at his lips. "Ah." He spread his arms and looked down at his body. "I'm *incredibly* handsome, is that what you mean? Well built, glistening, nice dick—you're afraid you'll make your mate jealous?"

"Now you're just making it awkward."

He laughed. "You started it. And yes, I do somehow manage to fit this enormous ego through doorways. It just took practice. Listen, Jessie, no one could ever take Nathanial's place. We can all agree on that. He will be missed and remembered forever. I do think, however, that someone needs to try to assume his role. We can't have you passed around from person to person. You have to have a proper wingman. After speaking to the others, I would like to request the honor of that position." He put a hand on his heart. "I'm not asking for admittance into the Ivy House circle. I am simply asking for a job that cannot be left vacant. I'd like to shadow you and try to better understand your movements and motivations. I'd like to include you in more of our trainings so I can learn what it is like to lead a team while half carrying, half throwing someone around." He smiled briefly, but his eyes were sad. "I'd like to know your battle strategies well enough to anticipate when you plan to sacrifice yourself so that I can take your place."

I shook my head, turning away. "If you knew me better, you would've never uttered that last bit, because that's a hard no."

"If I had understood you better, I would've been the one flying you," Tristan said urgently, stepping forward. "I could've lasted longer. Protected you better. Not because of size and strength, but because of my ability to repel magic. I would've lived longer than Nathanial. Maybe I would've lived, full stop."

"And if not, we both would've died because no one would've been fast enough to get us to Indigo in time to save our lives. *You* did that."

He stared at me for a long beat and then deflated. He blinked a couple times, dulling his eyes even more.

It became suddenly clear to me how deeply this had affected him. He blamed himself for what happened, just as we all did. The *what ifs* were preying on us.

"Dave," I called, realizing I was crying. I had no idea for how long.

He came jogging through the trees immediately.

"I need a hug. Can you get someone to hug Tristan?" I asked. "We're too naked to hug each other."

"But I am almost naked," Dave said, stopping close to me.

MAGICAL MIDLIFE AWAKENING

I didn't know how to explain that his extreme hairiness and small loincloth negated the naked factor. I worried that I'd somehow cause offense, and we'd be in a weird situation where his culture dictated that he should kill me to make it right, but his place on my team meant he really shouldn't.

So I just said, "The loincloth is…enough."

The rest of the basajaunak were clearly eavesdropping, because *Her* burst out of the trees in an instant. I really needed to start paying attention to where my team was located. Although…that seemed like so much hassle.

Tristan tried to wave her away. "No, no, I'm—"

She wrapped him in a tight hug, her hairy bosom in his face, and his hands dropped limply to his sides. His expression—what I could see of it—was one of deadpan annoyance, and for some reason, that was utterly hilarious.

"You should let him have the position," Dave rumbled as he enveloped me in a hairy hug. "He is dedicated to our team. Whenever another creature spoke ill of our people in Kingsley's territory, he defended us aggressively. He even defended the vampire, and while I am also loyal to our team…I might have hesitated about the vampire."

For some reason, his last comment amped my

chuckles into guffaws that demanded release. It felt good to laugh, to push away that horrible, dark rage building up within me. I needed to focus on helping people out of Momar's umbrella of tyranny, not exacting vengeance. There was a difference, and I couldn't lose sight of that.

So for now, I laughed. I laughed and laughed and made everyone nervous.

Tomorrow I would grant Tristan his wish, I'd hang out with my son, and I'd get ready to meet my annoying ex and his stupid family. I'd enjoy this break I was taking from the magical world and try not to think of what might be around the corner.

Basically, ignorance was bliss.

CHAPTER 4

JESSIE

"CAN YOU CALL Mr. Tom and ask him to bring up my clothes?" Tristan asked after we landed on the platform on the second floor and shifted into our human forms. "Unless you're cool with my jogging through the house really quickly to grab them? I left them just inside the doorway."

I pulled open the door to the inner passageway of the house. "He's probably moved them by now, and Jimmy doesn't need to see naked people running around. I'll get Mr. Tom to meet us in my room."

I led the way to my bedroom.

"How'd you know where to find me earlier?" I asked, knowing all the twists and turns of the passageways by heart now. I no longer needed the house to help guide me, although it was debatable if I ever had. I'd always had a sixth sense about this place.

"I was in the front room talking to Niamh, and she

mentioned the fire. She agrees that we need someone to step up into the wingman role. She's not sure I can handle it, though."

"Why is that?" I entered my closet and waited for him to go through before shutting the door, making sure it latched. Sometimes it bounced off—it needed to be fixed—and while the dolls kinda just wandered around protecting the house, I still didn't like the idea of their creeping through the passageway into my room without any warning. I had enough nightmares without adding that to the list.

"She thinks I'm too self-centered. Nathanial was a giver, putting more value on you and this team than himself. She doesn't think I have the ability to do that."

"And what do you think?" I asked softly.

I took up my phone to text Mr. Tom, noticing one of Austin's T-shirts lying at the foot of the bed, slightly rumpled and ready for the laundry. Mr. Tom must've snagged it and left it for me, because Austin didn't like Mr. Tom cleaning up after him. He put his own clothes in the laundry.

"I think I have many abilities, most of which I don't put on display," he said as I picked up the shirt, giving it a quick sniff test.

Hardly used—my favorite. It still smelled deliciously like Austin but not like body odor. Perfect.

Feeling Austin heading out the front door—he still didn't know I used his dirty laundry as bathrobes—I pulled the shirt over my head before looking for the cup of coffee Mr. Tom would've usually brought up by now. It wasn't there, so I texted him and asked if he could bring one up when he came. He'd probably gotten sidetracked with my son, who was his first priority whenever he was in the house.

"And which of those abilities would apply to our present situation?" I took the encrypted phone off the charging stand.

"If you don't mind...I'd rather attempt to show you instead of telling you."

I sent off a message to Sebastian, asking for the spell to make another brooch. He hadn't answered any of my texts yet, but I'd never asked for something specific. Maybe he'd get around to it if I asked for something magic related.

"Man, I hope he responds this time," I murmured, "because I'd really rather not have to search for that spell myself. Tracking down spells or creating them out of thin air is not my strong suit."

I took a deep breath and set the phone back down, giving my attention to Tristan again.

"It's no big deal if you want to follow me around all the time. I'm pretty used to it with Mr. Tom. I do need someone to help me in the air, and there is literally no one stronger or more capable in the sky than you. But I will also say this: the strongest teams are the ones where everyone trusts each other. Not just with their lives, but with their true selves. If you fall, Tristan, we will catch you. If you fail, we'll help you try again. If you open up to us, we'll protect your secrets." I crossed the space to put a hand on his shoulder. "When you're ready, and if you need help, just let me know, okay? I'm always here."

He nodded silently as Mr. Tom bustled into the room with a cup of coffee and a pile of clothes.

"I apologize for the tardy coffee, miss. I realize you are unbearably grumpy until you have it." He handed off the cup to me, clearly not noticing my intense scowl. "Master Jimmy awoke, and I wanted to see his face when he opened all his Hanukkah gifts. I know you're only supposed to do one per day, but I rounded up to an even ten, since we've missed the entire holiday already."

"Hanukkah?" I asked in confusion, sitting at the little table by the window. "We're not Jewish."

"Yes, that's what he said. But judging by the severe disregard you have for any sort of faith-based activities, I figured we might as well support all the major holidays."

Tristan snorted and turned away, hiding a laugh.

"Is this your way of smothering him with presents?" I asked, shaking my head. "He doesn't need—"

"How dare you!" Mr. Tom's wings rustled, and he braced one of his fists on a hip, pausing in handing over Tristan's folded clothes. "I do not *smother* anyone. I merely look after their every need. Master Jimmy *needs* things. Like socks. I found one with a hole big enough to allow his toe through!" He finally handed over Tristan's things. "Now, Tristan, what am I making you this morning? How about a French press coffee? I realize that sounds horribly simple, but sometimes simpler is better, I think. Master Jimmy called it 'dope,' so it is clearly very popular with the younger generation. I could also do some sort of—"

"French press sounds great, thanks," Tristan replied, putting on his clothes.

"Fantastic. Miss, I'll have breakfast up shortly. I'm thinking an omelet sounds good, don't you? Master Jimmy raved about the one I made him. I'll just—"

He whizzed out of the room, muttering to himself the whole way.

"I'll give you some time in silence," Tristan said with a grin, heading for the door. "You don't have to worry about my being intrusive."

"No one could be more intrusive than Mr. Tom, no."

But he'd only been gone for a moment before I realized something…

I didn't much want silence.

I didn't want alone time.

I also didn't much want someone else stepping into Nathanial's position.

It was a dangerous place to be. I didn't want anyone else's blood on my hands. I needed someone, though. I couldn't deny that. I needed someone helping me in the air. Tristan would be the obvious choice, someone I literally trusted with my life.

"Your mate protector should be the one guarding you," Ivy House said.

"Except Austin can't fly, so it doesn't really matter if he does or doesn't take the magic."

"The mate protector will be able to magically communicate with your army. He can move the pieces into the best positions to protect you. He won't need to fly."

That I hadn't known. Not specifically.

"Or," she went on, *"make the alpha gargoyle your second mate. He'd be good in the sack, I bet you anything. You don't have that kind of swagger without something to back it up. That would be a nice man-sandwich."*

I stared at the door because she had no eyes. She'd said something along those lines before. If she had a body, she'd be chasing Tristan, I had no doubt.

"*Austin is my mate. Only him. He'll take the magic when he's ready. Leave it alone.*"

I hoped he would, at any rate. Because she was right—there was no one I wanted guarding my back more than him. There would be no one better at protecting me. If he could connect with everyone like I could, he'd find a way to make our unit stronger than ever.

He just had to take that magic.

With a sigh, I took another sip of coffee and stood, turning for the bathroom and the much-needed shower Cyra's visit had put off. It was only then I noticed the presence at my door. He'd come back to the house and walked onto the grounds completely unnoticed by me with everything else that was going on.

"Hey, baby," Austin said, raking his gaze down my body. "Comfy?"

"Oh. Uhm." I looked down at the dirty, rumpled shirt. "This isn't what it looks like."

"And what does it look like?" He prowled closer to me, a predator with his prey in his sights, his eyes on fire. "Other than my very sexy mate wearing my T-shirt in the morning." Reaching me, he slid his hands up the outsides of my thighs and then over the swell of my butt. He growled softly. "Without any underwear."

I set the mug down quickly, spilling a little out of the side, and gripped his shoulders.

"I just felt like wrapping myself in your smell," I said with a soft moan as he dipped his fingers between my thighs. "That's not weird."

"It's not at all weird, no. It's incredibly hot." He ran his scorching lips up the side of my neck. "The smell of basajaun on you is not as hot."

He scooped me up and carried me to the bathroom.

"I've wanted to catch you in my T-shirt for some time," he said, putting me down in front of the shower. "But whenever I try to sneak back in, you're always too quick taking it off."

"You knew?" I asked, suddenly embarrassed as he stripped off his own not-as-rumpled T-shirt and then pushed out of his jeans.

"Of course I knew. Who do you think left this one on the bed for you?" He grabbed the side of my neck and tipped me back so that he held most of my weight, kissing down my throat before consuming my lips. "Before we stayed together every night, I'd occasionally smell you on my dirty clothes. Never the ones that were *too* dirty, though. I figured it out pretty quickly. What I couldn't understand is why you were trying to hide it."

He slid his hand up my belly to cup a breast, the touch scorching, and his thumb traced across the hard peak. Pleasure shot through me as he sucked hard on the sensitive area of my neck.

"Mr. Tom was essentially rifling through your dirty clothes and stealing the best selections," I said in a husky voice, closing my eyes and magically shutting the doors to my room and the bathroom. Everyone else would feel me muffling the Ivy House link and know not to enter, but Jimmy didn't have that.

"I would've told you that all you need to do is ask if you want something of mine, and it will be yours," Austin said, his lips now hovering over mine as he trailed his fingers through my wetness, "but I liked the idea of your feeling like you were getting away with something naughty."

His lips touched down as his fingers plunged in roughly. His growling words and the rough treatment, mixed with his grip on my neck, sent a shock wave of carnal bliss racing through me.

"Tell me," he rasped, his thumb touching down right where I needed it, making a circle as his fingers worked, "do you get yourself off when you're wearing them?"

"Sometimes," I said, too hot to be embarrassed. On the verge already.

His lips skimmed my throat now. "Did you moan my name as you worked yourself hard?"

"Yes," I said in a breathy whisper.

"Lift up my shirt a bit," he commanded, pulling back slightly so I could comply. His fingers still worked me. His thumb rubbed, now excruciatingly slowly, keeping me right on the edge.

Once my breasts were bared, he leaned in and flicked a nipple with his tongue, making my eyes roll back in my head. His hot mouth closed down on it next, sucking hard. I rolled my hips into his hand, needing more, needing to crest.

His dark chuckle said I wouldn't be getting there quickly.

He backed off with his fingers, switching breasts, letting my nipple out again with a *pop*.

"Did you taste yourself?" he asked softly, now crouching and skimming his lips down my stomach. "Did you suck your taste off your fingers?"

I hadn't, of course, but that was obviously not what he wanted to hear.

"Yes," I groaned as he flung a thigh over his shoulder. "*Yes*," I said again as his tongue traced my sensitive flesh.

He sucked on me hard, working his fingers again, rough and fast and *oh my God,* he was so damn good at this. I gripped his hair and pushed myself harder into him, gyrating against his mouth. My groans increased in pitch, in fervor, and then I exploded, the climax crashing over me and sweeping me away.

As the waves of pleasure ran through me, he stood and flicked on the shower before rubbing between my thighs again, looking down at me, still in his T-shirt, like he couldn't get enough.

"If we were at our house in the woods with nothing to do all day," he said, "I'd never let you change."

He ripped off the shirt in a quick movement before grabbing me and pulling me into the shower. He backed me up against the tiles, pulling one of my knees to his hip. He pushed into me so hard and fast that I saw light dance behind my eyes. Water streamed down his gorgeous body as he reached low, working me as he repeatedly plunged in.

I groaned his name, holding on for dear life.

"That's right, baby," Austin murmured, slapping against me. "Tell me who you belong to."

I said his name again, over and over, as the pressure mounted. His hips swung hard, and I loved every second of it. His kiss captured my scream of release as he shook against me.

He was still shaking when he backed off, easing my leg down so I could stand on my own.

"I didn't realize the T-shirt would be such a turn-on for you," I said, still breathing hard as he grabbed the loofa and soap.

"It always would be, but now it is particularly so."

"Why is that?" I turned and leaned against him, my back to his front. He washed me, now slow and delicate.

"You've been embracing a lot of people these last few months, seeking and giving comfort. A primal part of me wants you to do that with only me. Obviously I am ignoring that part because I logically know you mean absolutely nothing by it, and also that you and your team need it, but sometimes I need to express my primal desire."

I reached back to cup his muscular thighs, letting the back of my head hit his shoulder and then roll so that my face was buried in his neck.

"I like when you express that side of yourself," I purred, nipping at his neck.

He paused in washing me, going languid against my body. He cursed softly before dropping the loofa. "I turned back because my niece said she was coming over to talk to you, Mimi, and me. We should probably hurry up and get down there, but…" His soapy hands glided up my body. "Maybe just one more."

IT ENDED UP being two, because he never felt like we got enough out of quickies and had trouble tearing himself away. I almost always gave in because I was just as insatiable when it came to him. I suspected I was now stuck in my sexual peak with a man I ardently loved. Our desire for each other would very likely not wane for quite some time. After years of having a subpar sex life, I was totally okay with that.

Hair and teeth brushed and clothes definitely on, Austin and I made it to the kitchen hand in hand. Jimmy sat at the island, his crimson face pointed down at his hands. Aurora sat beside him, a gorgeous twenty-four-year-old woman with long brown-blond hair, a steely demeanor, and absolutely no interest in my nineteen-year-old son.

"And there they are, right on time," Mr. Tom said as we entered.

"On time?" Aurora looked at Austin. "I said I'd be here twenty minutes ago."

"And so you were," Mr. Tom said, bustling for the door. "*They* get here when they have a notion, and whenever that happens, it is right on time. I'll just go get Naomi—Ah. Here she comes."

"This alpha pair isn't like most," Mimi said, entering the room with an electronic notepad. She handed it off to Austin. "I need those amounts approved," she told him before heading to the island. "Their love for each other is wild, and neither care to rein it in. It's necessary to allow leeway because it's good for the pack to see their leaders showing the strength of their bond."

A little crease formed between Aurora's brows as she glanced between Austin and me. Given she was very like other powerful shifters and didn't tend to show much of a reaction to things, I had no idea what that meant.

"What's this meeting regarding?" Mimi asked brusquely.

"Wouldn't you care to adjourn to one of the sitting rooms?" Mr. Tom held out his hand for the door. "That would be much more comfortable, I think. How about a coffee or something to eat? Miss, you must be hungry. You never did get your omelet. We don't want to see you *hangry*, right? So let's get some food in you. I know! How about I whip something up, and you can all have a seat at the table. What are we thinking, maybe some eggs Benedict? How about a sloppy Joe? We could go brunch or lunch at this point, dealer's choice."

"Hello, Jessie," Edgar said from his position in the far corner of the room. Aurora's shoulders tensed and Jimmy startled. "I have an update on the dreaded gnome situation, if you'd care to hear it."

"Don't loiter around like that, Edgar. You're creeping out the younger people," Mr. Tom admonished him.

"You mean the fire that Cyra created earlier?" I

asked Edgar. "Mr. Tom, did you know that Ivy House can control the elements? Like…she can stop fire."

"Well, of course I knew that. How do you think she brings in the fog or dims the light from the sun? Those involve controlling the elements."

He had a point. I really should've put two and two together.

"Yes, Jessie," Edgar said. "It seems the nest is gone, but many of the gnomes escaped, so—"

I held up my hand. "Don't. Do not ask me to retire you."

Mr. Tom scoffed. "Oh now, miss, he would never be so insensitive as to ask you to retire him so soon after losing one of our team members, *would you, Edgar?*"

"No, Miss Jessie," Edgar said, now stepping along the wall toward the doorway. "No, I sure wouldn't. That would be mighty insensitive of me, yes. No, no, I was just going to… Let's excuse this interruption. I was just—"

He burst into his insect form and hightailed it out of the kitchen.

"I think maybe we should stay at the other house tonight," I murmured to Austin. "I need a break from the madness."

"Maybe the sitting room would be a better place for us to talk," Mimi said, quickly leading the way.

"I should stay here, Mom, right?" Jimmy asked. "Not go to the sitting room with you?"

"Yeah, why don't you? Then we'll figure out what we want to do today."

Once seated in a seldom-used room—Ivy House had far too many sitting rooms that we hadn't converted to better use yet—Aurora started to speak.

"First, I want to apologize for putting you all in a tough position. When I came out here, I figured I could use it as a bargaining tool. Say, if my dad kept pushing for me to come home, I could ask him to make a compromise to give me something I wanted. Like a small pack not too far away from home to take over, or something like that. But now, after being here for a while… Honestly, Uncle Auzzie, I don't want to leave. I love it here. I love the pack's edginess and the high-pressure feel of everything. I love your wilder style of leadership and the camaraderie of the people who work under you, even the gargoyles and the basajaunak. The challenges are harder here and the ladder is so much higher, what with your beta being an alpha in his own right. I won't ever run out of runway in this pack like I mostly have with my dad's. I just… I don't want to leave."

She paused, and silence rang around us. It felt awkward to not immediately reassure her that she was lovely to have around, I enjoyed it when she came for dinner, and I hoped we could figure it out. But the situation wasn't mine to solve, so I held my breath.

Then I realized why no one else had spoken. It was because Aurora hadn't finished. Her body language was incredibly subtle.

"I already told you that Dad has now cut me off from the family fortune. And while that would hinder me if I were trying for a placement as alpha, it doesn't matter to me in my current position."

"You told him you wouldn't relent?" Mimi asked.

"Yes. I assume he'll appeal to you next, Uncle Auzzie. So I've come for two reasons. The first is to plead with you to treat me solely as pack in business matters, not as your niece. You won't interfere with my challenges, you won't pay me a penny more than what is due, and you won't force me out so that I have no choice but to go home. I'm asking you to tell my dad that you have no power or control over my personal life."

"Done," Austin said immediately. "This territory has always been a safe haven for people."

Her smile was slight but her eyes glittered. "I love that about this place. I love that everyone feels welcome regardless of who or what they are. Even the Dicks and Janes."

"And the second thing?" Austin asked.

"The second is personal. Even though it would be easier for you if I just went my own way…" She shrugged. "I love having you back in my life. I love your choice of mate"—she nodded to me—"and the feel of your home. I humbly request to still do family stuff, like meet for holidays and dinners and things."

"Of course we'll still include you in family things!" I said without thinking. Then I pressed on because I had every intention of being stubborn about this. "You're always welcome at our house, Aurora. And I don't know if Austin extended the invite, but you're welcome to come to Los Angeles with us for Christmas. You'll have to deal with my parents, who are…eccentric, and my ex's mom, who is the worst, but there'll be presents and clam dip and whatever else."

Her nose crinkled. "Clam dip?"

"It's actually not bad," Austin said with a chuckle. "I was going to say, Jess would never allow you to be excluded from the family, even if I would."

"She won't even exclude that vampire," Mimi grumbled.

"Uncle Auzzie did extend the invite, yes," Aurora said, smiling a little. "Thank you. I'd love to come. I've never been to L.A."

"I'm going too," Mimi told Aurora. "Though I can't

for the life of me understand why you would willingly attend a party with an ex."

"It's…" I leaned back. "It's complicated. We divorced a little over a year ago, and the idea was to provide a unified front for our son, Jimmy. The guy at the kitchen counter?"

"Mr. Tom introduced us," Aurora said with a nod.

"Our combined families usually got together the day after Christmas. This year he'd planned on having Jimmy stay with him and mentioned that it would be nice for our son if we could stick to that tradition. So I said fine. He also invited me over for dinner to meet his new fiancée."

I'd found out about the fiancée situation right before going to Kingsley's, having seen it on social media. It had led to a mild freak-out that had, in turn, motivated me to show off Austin on my social media. Matt had then called me, after what was probably a mild freak-out on his part, and said that I should go to their wedding because I owed them my support. The call had gone downhill from there.

"Ah." Mimi nodded. "He's trying to rub his new life in your face."

"Instead, Jess will be rubbing her new life in *his* face," Austin said, draping his arm around my shoulders. "I will personally see to it that he minds his manners when he speaks to you."

"Anyway." I shrugged. "This might end with us sev-ering our ties, but at least I can say I tried."

"It's not like Jimmy is a kid," Aurora said. "At this point, he doesn't really need his parents to get along."

"Like your father and uncle?" Mimi quirked an eye-brow. "Big words coming from someone in your position."

Aurora looked down at her knees, clearly her way of saying, "Touché."

"Is that all?" Mimi asked, leaning forward to get up.

"One more thing." Aurora glanced at Mimi. "This place is absolutely incredible. You've done a really great job, Mimi. Remind me never to listen to Mom's deco-rating advice over yours again."

Mimi finished getting up. "You couldn't afford an outfit like this. Not until you build yourself up a pack and replace all the money this move will cost you."

"It'll be worth it," Aurora mumbled.

"That's my girl," Mimi said as she walked out the door.

"About that, though," I said, stopping Aurora from getting up. "I know we're not supposed to give you any money or anything, but I need you to look the part if you're going with us to the ex's party. Non-negotiable. Mr. Tom will connect with you about what sorts of things to buy. We need to all look amazing."

Aurora's grin was smug and confident. "Not a problem."

CHAPTER 5

JESSIE

A WEEK LATER, Austin, Jimmy, and I pulled up to my parents' house for dinner. The stark sun shone in the pale blue sky on the outskirts of Los Angeles. Given no one else on my team was from the large, crowded, sprawling city, they were already complaining about the traffic and how long it took to get anywhere.

We'd checked into the Airbnb not long ago, but we'd been running late and left the details of sorting out who would sleep where to Mr. Tom. He'd assured us that everyone would fit, since each room was outfitted with multiple beds and people would be doubling up. Thankfully, there was a hotel not too far away in case that didn't turn out to be the case.

Neither Mimi nor Aurora would be coming to my parents' for dinner. After a nearly six-hour drive, I'd let them off the hook—easy to do, since my parents didn't know them. It would just be Jimmy, Austin, and me weathering my parents' weirdness.

I hoped to hell my dad had clothes on.

"I don't see why you can't just tell them you're magical now," Jimmy said as he climbed out of the back of the Mercedes, one of our "house" cars. Austin would save his fancy sports car for when we met my ex. I didn't need my parents asking if the cult they thought I belonged to was now in the crime circuit or money-laundering game.

"I told Grandma. She seemed to be okay with it, unless she's convinced herself that never happened. You just never know with her. But I can't tell Grandpa. He's not that open-minded. He'd think it sounds crazy and that I need psychiatric help," I said, shutting the door and moving to the trunk to grab the wine and beer. They'd told us not to bring anything else, and when given that option, I always complied.

"And a cult doesn't sound crazy?" Jimmy asked.

"Did your arms break when you went off to college? Come here and help me with these." I handed over the case of beer. "We're going to tell him I'm not in a cult anymore, all is well, and I have the means to keep the house because Austin is a rich investor and he's footing the bill for the renovation. I'll just mumble and talk quietly and hope they lose interest. You know that

Grandpa only needs the barest hint of rationality to make something irrational make sense. It's how he made it through Ivy House's teasing and then a magical battle. It'll be fine."

"But didn't you tell them Austin was a park ranger or something?"

"No, I didn't specify, I don't think. It's fine—whatever they remember, we'll say we told them that because he wants to keep his investing mostly a secret. They'll go with it, trust me. Especially with the mumbling. Worst case, I'll just talk about the rat problem at Ivy House. That'll throw them off the scent."

"Ew, it has rats?"

"See? Immediate reaction. And no, it doesn't. Though I'd choose rats over animated dolls and garden gnomes…but we didn't get that choice."

"I can't believe you left Edgar at home," Austin said as he took the two bottles of wine from me. "Or that Cyra and Hollace said they'd stay and watch him."

I shook my head about Edgar. There was no way in hell I was bringing him anywhere near my ex in-laws. Besides, it was on him to figure out that gnome situation.

"I think Cyra wants revenge on the gnomes, and Hollace is taking one for the team by making sure they don't cause too much havoc. He's the best at talking her out of terrible, destructive ideas."

"Oh, look, Mom." Jimmy pointed at one of the old trucks in the driveway. A rusty, worn-down trailer was parked beside it. "That old Wagoneer is gone. The one with the weeds growing up out of the floorboards."

I lifted my eyebrows, glancing around to see if it was poking out from around the house. Didn't appear to be, and it didn't run, so it couldn't have gone far.

"Did he finally get rid of it?" Jimmy asked, stepping up onto the creaky and cracked wood of the porch.

"I can't imagine he did." My dad never got rid of anything. He collected and collected and just piled the new things up.

Jimmy opened the faded brown door with the orange-brown paint covering decades-old scratches from a dog long gone. Duct tape covered a crack in the stained-glass window.

"Duct tape fixes everything," Austin murmured, looking at the patch.

"You know how Kingsley's house was immaculate?" I asked, edging around a lemon tree in a large pot that blocked part of the entryway. "This will be nothing like that."

My dad sat in the far corner of the living room with an iPad balanced on his large belly and his hands on the armrests. The TV blared from not far away, but Dad was wearing headphones and couldn't hear it as he watched the iPad screen. A couple of corners of his green blanket stuck out from under his legs, and even while we stood there, we heard why we christened it his fart blanket. He was at least clothed. Small miracles.

Austin looked at the deer heads mounted on the wall and then at the many pieces of furniture placed around the living room, three steps down. Most of the pieces were from a matching black leather set, but one orange couch circa 1970 sat in front of a sliding glass door that no longer opened. A large potted plant stood on the bricks in front of the fireplace, and the coffee table held two huge stacks of magazines.

"Dad," I called, stopping at the steps leading down into the living room. "*Dad!*" I waved my hand. Nothing. "Let's go find Grandma."

She was at the stove with her hair in curlers, wearing faded maroon sweats covered in holes and bleach stains. Our movement caught her eye because she glanced up. Her expression turned joyful as she set down her spoon.

"Jimmy!" She hugged him before clamping her hands on his cheeks and kissing his forehead. "I'm so glad you could come for dinner! I'd thought you were supposed to be at your dad's?"

"I'm going over there tomorrow," he said, looking

around for a place to put the beer.

"Oh here, let me take that. I'll put it in the cooler in the garage. Are you hungry? Do you need a snack? I didn't make any clam dip today because we'll have it on Christmas, but I do have a cheese ball if you want that."

"I'm okay," he said, opening the pantry. "I'll just have some chips."

It was my turn for a hello. She smiled at me and gave me a hug before beaming at Austin.

"And here is Austin!" She put out her arms for a hug, and it occurred to me that I'd better stop her from doing that when she met Mimi. "I'm so glad you could come." She patted his shoulders before stepping back. "Jessie talks so much about you. I hear you two have moved in together?"

"Yes." I hooked my arm around his, filled with joy and pride. Our relationship felt more real, somehow, now that I was bringing Austin into what I thought of as my past life. My non-magical existence.

"Well, that is just great news. I knew you were perfect for each other." She beamed at me. "Want a beer?"

Having a beer soon after walking through the door was basically a rite of passage in this house. It was just what one did.

"Sure," I said as Austin pulled his arm from mine and wrapped it around my waist.

"Austin? Beer?" She picked up the case from the counter, pausing to get his answer.

"Please," he replied.

"We can just take it from there." I pointed at the case she held, stepping forward to help.

"No, no." She twisted to the side, sticking out her elbow to keep me from grabbing it. "I have some cold ones in the cooler."

"I can do that." Now Austin reached for the case.

"No, that's okay. I'll just put these out there. It's no problem." She twisted the other way, trying to stick an elbow into Austin this time. She pushed past him, clearly intent on not accepting help from anyone.

"We're going to have lamb, hon. I know you love lamb!" she called as she jiggled the beer around, trying to open the garage door.

"Here, please, let me help." Austin met her at the door, opening it with one hand and reaching for the beer with the other.

I watched as he delicately pulled it from her hands with what I knew was a stupid grin on my face. Handsome, kind, and a gentleman. I'd chosen a winner.

Then my smile grew the second he stepped into the doorway of the garage and went completely rigid. He was seeing the garage for the first time, and there were no words. None at all.

I couldn't wait to hear his thoughts!

✧ ✧ ✧

Austin

Austin nearly dropped the beer when he saw what lay before him. Jess hadn't at all prepared him for their house. In fact, she'd said very little and mostly just snickered. Now he saw why.

The garage was indescribable. Big enough for two cars side by side, with another in the back. He could see a car carcass on the right, near the garage door, but the rest of it was full of…stuff. Wall-to-wall…*stuff*. Heaps of it, piled in the carcass, in front of it, beside it. On racks near the ceiling, on shelves at the back, heaped on what might've been another non-functional vehicle on the other side. He couldn't make sense of it.

"Just down there, next to the cooler. We'll load them in when there's more room."

He paused as he stepped down the makeshift stairs—a couple of blocks of wood precariously nailed together. A large blue cooler sat on a concrete floor in front of…an engine of some sort, with shoes and boots heaped to the side. Other car parts were haphazardly piled on top and an old Jeep at the back of the garage with an unattached, crooked hood and no glass in the windshield. More stuff, like a rug, maybe, some boxes, and other debris littered the inside.

A small clearing beside it served as a walkway, and on the other end there was a large white refrigerator with an office-sized fridge next to it, sitting on some sort of box.

"The cooler…or the fridge?" Austin said, answered in a moment when the cooler lid creased open and she reached inside for a cold Pabst Blue Ribbon.

"The what?" Jess's mom straightened up to see where he was looking, but his gaze had slipped back to the array of *things*, picking out deer antlers without heads from the tangled mess.

"Don't mind all that." Martha waved the stuff away. "Pete never gets rid of anything. He has more projects around this house than he knows what to do with. He keeps saying he's going to get to them, but he's retired now, and do you know what he does? Argues with people on YouTube. Here, just put that down here."

She got out of the way so he could set the beer on the ground.

"Do the refrigerators not work?" he asked, unable to help his curiosity.

"That's a freezer." She pointed at the larger one. "This one works." She shifted her point to the office-sized fridge. "But it's already full of beer. Jessie's brother, Chris, will be coming for Christmas, and he likes IPAs and other hard-to-drink stuff. We keep that in there."

"Gotcha." He put the beer down and grabbed out two cans from the cooler for him and Jess. Martha grabbed another, probably for Pete, and then headed back inside.

Austin gave a last look around, kind of in awe of the garage, really wanting a photo, before turning off the light and shutting the door behind him. Projects, indeed.

"Where was I?" Martha looked around the kitchen before popping her beer and taking a sip. Jimmy sat at a dining table beyond the island, eating the chips. Martha set the beer on the counter before moving to the other side of the kitchen, leaning over the island, and yelling, "Pete!" She shook her head. "I swear, he has the volume on everything turned up so high—Pete!"

Jess was watching Austin closely, a knowing grin on her face.

"Jessie, go say hi to your dad." Martha turned and messed with the stove. "I'm just going to take this off the heat. Did you hear what we're having?" She half turned to look at Jess behind her. "Lamb, your favorite."

"It's Chris's favorite, Mom," Jess responded as Austin went to stand beside her, noticing more piles of stuff on the edge of the counter next to the stove: a wallet held together with a rubber band, washers and electrical tape, various paper items… "I don't like lamb, remember?"

"Oh, no?" Martha paused in what she was doing. "I could've sworn you did."

"I like lamb," Jimmy called.

"Oh good. Well, there you go." Martha resumed what she was doing.

"I might as well be the red-headed stepchild of this family," Jess told Austin in a murmur. "She never remembers what I do and don't like. One year for my birthday dinner, she made stuffed shells." She paused and gave him a deadpan look. "I *hate* stuffed shells."

"Okay." Martha wiped her hands, took a sip of her beer, and smiled at them. "I'm going to head up and change." She pointed at Jess. "Say hi to your father. Go give him that beer there."

"The garage," Austin whispered as Jess led him into the other room.

She laughed. "Right? It's something."

"It sure is something, yes…like a fire hazard…"

"Dad," she yelled when they were standing about three feet from him.

Finally Pete looked up. He was an aging man with gray hair and wiry eyebrows that lifted immediately. He brought up a hand, one finger out, to stab at the iPad before removing his headphones.

"Jessie!" He set all of his things on the edge of the orangish seventies couch, which had no business in that room, and stood from the recliner that was crammed up against it. "Oh. Thank ya."

He took the beer and smiled at Austin. "Austin! Pleasure to see you again." His handshake was firm and eye contact direct. "I hear you're dating our girl."

"Living with her, yes, sir," Austin said. "I plan on being around forever, if she'll have me."

Jess's smile was radiant, her eyes sparkling. It made him feel like a million bucks.

"Well then, as the kids all say, put a ring on it." Pete laughed, his belly shaking, before turning to Jess. "Where's your mother?"

"She went to get dressed. I'm just going to show Austin my old room."

"Uh—" He pointed a finger at Jess. "No hanky-panky. Leave the door open."

Jess frowned at him and then took Austin by the hand, leading him across the living room, around the banister near the door, and up the stairs. The décor in this place was strange. The worn carpet was brown, the wall to his right was a different shade of brown, and the nice, rustic wood ceiling offered yet a third brown. Oh, and the polished banisters added one more brown to the collection. None of the rooms or areas had a unifying concept. The curtains were cream, the other walls were a different cream—

Mimi would lose her mind if she saw all this. He couldn't wait to see her face on Christmas. He'd definitely be showing her that garage.

A little landing at the top of the stairs had a painting sitting on the ground. He assumed it was eventually supposed to go on the wall. Or maybe it had fallen there and never been replaced. It was hard to tell.

"They're not really into the details, huh?" Austin asked, passing hall closets with no doors and trim that hadn't been nailed to the wall. "How long have they lived here?"

"Most of my life."

Around the corner and straight ahead was what he figured was her old room. It appeared to have been turned into a sort of library with no shelves or organization. Books were stacked on all available surfaces.

"I don't really get this place," he said, looking this new scene over and over.

She slid her arm around his waist, hugging him close. He dropped his arm around her as he took in the place where she'd spent her formative years as a Jane. Back then, she'd had no idea that someday she'd grow into a magical powerhouse capable of shifting into a gargoyle and leading an army.

"I'm not sure why I wanted to show you this." She looked around the space. "I don't really have anything in here left over from when I lived here. Except maybe those." She pointed at some glass canisters screwed into the wall with decorative rocks inside.

"What are they?"

"Candleholders. They should have water and floating candles in them, but the water kept evaporating and leaving lines on the sides, so I gave up."

"And left them there?"

"Yeah. I didn't want them. As you can tell, no one really cared."

He laughed, shaking his head. "This place is a trip."

She turned to him then, leaning in. "I like having you cross over into this life. I feel more excited about our relationship for some reason."

"You like showing me off?"

She tilted her head up for a kiss. "Yes. I found someone extraordinary, and I want everyone to know it. Even if you didn't have magic, or that face, or this incredible body, you're kind and supportive and my biggest fan. You treat me like a priceless treasure, and I want people to know how lucky I am."

He kissed her, his body tightening with need. It was

the way wrong time for that, unfortunately.

He backed off, rocking her gently, pressing his cheek against her forehead. "That's how I thought about things when I was introducing you to my family."

"Except your family is a lot nicer."

"Your ex is no longer your family, and while your parents are…one of a kind, they are plenty nice and a lot more expressive than my family."

"They are certainly more expressive, I'll give you that. I'm wondering how Matt's…people will react to Aurora. A pretty young woman who *never* smiles. Also who is intense and capable of staring down adult men."

"Not well?"

She laughed. "I don't know, but I can't wait to find out."

"I thought you didn't want to be the talk of the town?"

"*I* wouldn't be, and I know she won't care. She's much too strong-willed and confident for that."

"After the holidays, you will be, too, I guarantee it."

CHAPTER 6

AUSTIN

T HE NEXT MORNING they pulled up to a little coffee shop off a side street, not terribly far from their Airbnb, but it had taken half an hour to get there. Traffic, even in residential districts of L.A., was nothing to sneeze at. The huge and busy freeways were never far away. The bustle was enough to make a guy want to give up and go home. He saw now what an incredible change of pace O'Briens had been for Jess.

They'd come here to meet Jess's good friend, niece to the former legal owner of Ivy House. She had the family legacy but apparently not the right personality to be granted *heir* status. But she'd brought Jess to Ivy House, and for that he'd be eternally grateful to her.

"Did Mimi and Aurora decide to go check out Hollywood?" Jess asked as they circled the block for the second time, looking for parking.

"They'll go a little later. Ulric and Jasper are going

with them. Jasper will drive. He says the packed free-ways don't bother him. I give them a one-in-four chance of bringing the car back without a scrape."

"I can't believe no one in our crew has been to L.A. before. That's craz—There's one!" She flung out her hand, indicating a parking spot in a cramped corner of a nearby strip mall, a couple of blocks from their location. Given her urgency, they likely wouldn't do any better if they kept circling.

He eased into the parking space, a tight fit. Other luxury cars were all around, suggesting this place was in an upscale part of town. It was hard to believe. The strip mall looked a little dirty and run-down, with average shops, a few blinking signs that should be fixed up, and grimy pavement. The air smelled stale, as though it had been left in a sweaty locker for too long, and a brownish haze colored the sky.

No gargoyles had come with them this time. Jess had convinced him it was unnecessary—the outing would take hardly any time, and besides, if they brought even one gargoyle, Mr. Tom would definitely show up. She didn't want anyone in a bad disguise peeking in through the windows.

A valid point. Besides, they'd only just arrived in town. If they stuck to Dick establishments and kept a low profile, they should be safe enough. Especially since the mages still seemed to be keeping their distance.

She met him at the back of the car and slipped her hand into his, lacing their fingers.

"Have you talked to Kingsley since he demanded you send Aurora home?" Jess asked as she steered them to the sidewalk.

Kingsley was not pleased that his threats weren't resonating with his strong-willed and capable daughter. Austin had no idea why his brother would have expected otherwise. She was a determined young woman and knew the value in further training, which Austin's setup could provide.

"No. He cut off all conversation for the present."

"For the present?"

"He's too levelheaded and rational to cut her off forever. She's too young and hotheaded to realize that, but they'll come to an understanding eventually that'll benefit them both. I've been in her shoes before. I know how he works. And how she does, to some extent, though she's a lot smarter than I was at her age."

"You got lucky with a brother like Kingsley. He really is the salt of the earth."

"He is."

They entered the busy coffee shop and paused as Jess glanced across the filled tables. Roasted coffee beans flavored the air, and the whir of espresso machines interrupted the soft murmur of conversation.

"There!" She smiled and tugged him forward, weaving through the space to a table in the corner. A brunette with reddish glasses sat with her head bowed over her phone and a white mug in front of her.

The woman in question looked up. A wide smile crossed her face when she saw Jess, and she stood, vibrating with happiness. The two women hugged and squealed and bounced a little, like teenagers, before Jess stepped back and put her hand on Austin's arm.

"Diana, this is my boyfriend, Austin. Or life partner. Whatever. The guy I'm living with."

"Pleasure." Austin stepped forward with his hand out.

Diana's eyes lit up, but a moment later her face drained of enthusiasm. Her posture bowed and body mechanics turned mousy, as though she sensed a predator and was now a flight risk. Austin could immediately see why she hadn't been chosen by Ivy House.

"H-hi." She gently took his hand, her grip lax, and pulled away quickly. Tucking a strand of hair behind her ear, she averted her gaze.

"So what have you been up to?" Jess asked, pulling out a chair and then looking around. "Wait, we'll go grab some coffees. Do you need a refill?"

"I'll do that." Austin kissed Jess's temple. "What are you having?"

"Oh. Uh." She glanced at the counter. "A cappuccino. This place does great cappuccinos. I should get one to go for Mr. Tom."

He nodded, sighting in on Diana, who'd been looking up at him from under her lashes.

"Diana?" he asked, his touch on the small of Jess's back to establish his claim. It was probably overkill in a place like this, but it was ingrained behavior. Not to mention that he had an uncontrollable urge to always touch her after almost losing her. He had to be sure she was real and this wasn't some lucid fever dream while he endlessly waited by her side, pleading for her to return to him.

"Just, um…just a black coffee, please. It's my fourth cup."

"How long have you been here? I thought we said we'd meet at ten?" Jess asked.

"We did. I just needed to get out of the house. The kids are driving me nuts."

Austin nodded and slid his hand from Jess, letting the ladies talk.

People cleared out of his way as he walked through the place. He wasn't the only muscular guy in the coffee shop—nearly everyone seemed in great shape—but the other patrons still gave him a wide berth as he joined the back of the line.

The guy in front of him glanced back, physically fit and half his age. His eyes widened before his gaze snapped downward.

"Excuse me," the guy said, slinking out of the way, clutching his phone.

The woman in front of him, about the same age and dressed in a strange, colorful outfit that somehow worked, glanced back as Austin took the other guy's place in line. Her eyes widened and a small grin played around her lips. Her gaze dipped down his body.

"Hey," she said softly.

He didn't respond, hitting her with a no-nonsense, blank stare.

Her smile slipped a bit, but hunger grew in her eyes. She half turned, giving him more attention in a way that sent warning shivers racing through his body. If she did something stupid, like touch him or push in too close, it would set off Jess's beast. Jess had great control, better than any alpha shifter and certainly better than him, but it wouldn't do to use any kind of magic in the Dick world.

"I have a fiancée," he said in a low growl, increasing the menace in his gaze and posture. His magic pulsed out, hot and dangerous. People around him tensed, those in line ahead of him glancing back, their backs bowing.

The woman put her hands up in surrender, her smile dimming, but her eyes still sparkled with desire. She clearly liked dangerous men.

"Can I help you?" the woman at the counter called to him, looking through or over everyone ahead of him. She waved everyone else out of the way, clearing a path for him to step up next. The patrons in line complied immediately.

✧   ✧   ✧

JESSIE

"OKAY, REAL QUICK—HOLY cow, Jacinta!" Diana put her elbow on the table and cupped her hand over her widened eyes. "Talk about a complete one-eighty in men. You went from posh and proper Matt to Mr. Rugged Growly Guy."

I glanced back at the counter where Austin was strutting through the line and up to the counter like it was his birthright. Surprisingly, no one questioned him or griped. Everyone kinda just bowed out of his way and waited for him to be done.

You could take the alpha out of his territory, but you couldn't take the alpha out of the man.

I grinned like an idiot. "Yeah. But he's really sweet, actually. He's honestly a big softie."

Diana watched him place an order. She shook herself out of studying him, took a deep breath, and smiled at me.

"Tell me everything," she said. "It's been so long since I've seen your face! Talking on the phone is not enough. How is Great-Uncle Earl?"

"Is he really your great-uncle?" I asked, forgetting that she'd called Mr. Tom that before I met him.

She furrowed her brow. "He's related to Aunt Peggy in some way."

"And Aunt Peggy…is not magical?"

"What?" Diana asked, the sort of confused reaction you get when you've said something completely outlandish and the other person is hoping they've misheard.

"You've never heard of…you know…" I dragged my lip through my teeth. "You don't think magic exists, right? Like…the house isn't magical, and Aunt Peggy is normal…"

Her eyebrows started to rise. "Is this part of the cult thing your mom told me about? I thought she was exaggerating."

"Oh yeah. Totally." I waved it away. "No, I mean, I'm not in a cult. My parents are…"

MAGICAL MIDLIFE AWAKENING

I made a face—*no explanation available*—and she laughed, albeit a little nervously.

"It's just that Great-Uncle Earl—who still works there and has changed his name to Mr. Tom for reasons no one understands"—more nervous laughter—"is very...strange. And he wears a cape and claims he's a gargoyle. So I didn't know if your Aunt Peggy... I don't know. I'm trying to make sense of it."

"*Oh!*" She nodded like it suddenly made sense, and then leaned back as Austin approached the table with our coffees. He set them in front of us before heading back to grab his drink. "Right, all that. Well, I've never met him. But Aunt Peggy said he was really old and a little addled, and you're supposed to just go along with his fantasies until they all make sense."

...until they all make sense...

Aunt Peggy might not have gotten the house magic, but she knew both the house and Mr. Tom were magical. She'd been made privy because she'd been in line to become an heir and instead was nothing but the legal guardian of sorts.

How crazy to know magic existed in the world but not be able to experience it. I was pretty sure that would drive me crazy. I wished my life wasn't as dangerous, or lately as heartbreaking, but I wouldn't trade what I'd gained in O'Briens for the world. I loved having magic and learning about the magical community.

Austin pulled his chair a little closer to mine and put his hand on my thigh, getting comfortable.

"So how'd you guys meet?" Diana asked, not looking at Austin. I got the idea he made her nervous.

"No, no. No way!" I waved my finger at her. "Tell me about the kids and husband and how everything is going."

"How is that even remotely as interesting as a new life in a creepy old house with a new boyfriend?" Diana returned, mock-scandalized. "I saw your instas. Are you guys living a lavish lifestyle, or what?"

I launched into our fake investor story for Austin, sharing the parts of my life that she could understand. It felt frustrating and strange to leave out the magical aspect of our lives, but I doubted Diana would even want to know the truth. She had her life set up the way she'd always wanted it, even if the family was currently driving her crazy. Blasting her world perception to make my life easier would be a crappy thing to do.

"So what's next?" Now Diana did look between us, lingering on Austin a little longer. "Living together, life partners, maybe a little pitter-patter around the house?"

I scoffed. "I had one of those, remember? Much younger than you. That part of my life is over."

"But Austin, you don't have kids, right?" Diana

pushed.

"I don't, no," he answered, laying his hand over the back of my chair. "That wasn't part of my life's plan."

My heart squelched with the memory of why. He'd gotten a vasectomy a long time ago, after nearly killing his brother. He'd been trying to do humanity a favor, apparently, by not duplicating what he thought of as a danger to those around him. It was untrue, and while I was plenty fine not having another kid, I *knew* he would've made a great father. Maybe not back then, but certainly now. He'd been wild and young, that was all. I hated that he'd thought so poorly of himself that he'd decided to prevent himself from procreating.

I rubbed his leg in support. "We're middle-aged now, anyway," I said, making light of the whole thing. She didn't know that we were paused at this age forever. "That time has passed."

"Not even remotely." She shook her head adamantly. "My friend Clarice—you remember Clarice, the one with the long blond hair who always buys expensive sunglasses she can't afford?" She waited for my nod, though I barely remembered her. "Well, she just had an oops at forty-two. Talk about a surprise! They hadn't been able to get pregnant since the last one nine years ago. She thought she was going through early menopause. Nope. Surprise baby."

I grimaced. "Helluva surprise."

"Yeah. She had a mini breakdown, but they're happy now. It *is* possible."

I nudged Austin's arm. "Or maybe we'll just enjoy our lives with no kids in the house, able to leave and vacation whenever we want."

She looked at me whimsically. "Yeah," she said with a pout. "I'm already envious."

I laughed and used the opportunity to shift the conversation to her. Diana told me stories about her kids and husband, and we chatted as though no time had passed. Austin listened silently, getting another round of coffees when we needed them, with a couple of bakery items to go with them. He never showed boredom or impatience, though he didn't have much to add. After about an hour and a half I checked the time, knowing we should probably get going. We were supposed to have an early, getting-to-know-Camila supper with my ex when we dropped off Jimmy, and then I hoped to take a drive with Austin and show him a few of my favorite places in the area.

We didn't get the chance to wrap up the conversation, though, because the magical world came crashing into the Dick coffee shop.

CHAPTER 7

AUSTIN

AUSTIN GRIPPED JESS'S shoulder as the three shifters walked in the door, their gazes and bearing leaving no doubt as to why they were here.

"Stay here," he told Jess quietly, pushing back from the table and standing.

"Why, what's—" She caught on, and a pulse of magic pumped through the space. People looked around, their brows furrowed. A few clutched the edge of the tabletops and looked down at the ground, apparently wondering if there had been an earthquake. "I'll go with you."

"No." He partially stepped in front of her chair, blocking off her view of the newcomers. They stood just inside the door, staring at him. They didn't show any interest in her, and his current posture would alert them to her status as his mate. It would advertise how ruthless he would become if she were jeopardized in any

119

way. "You stay here and finish your coffee. I'll be right back."

"But—"

He put his hand on her shoulder again. "They aren't here for trouble, Jess. And they aren't here for you. Let me handle it, okay? You'll feel it through our bond if something goes wrong. Then, by all means, raise hell."

"Are you in some kind of trouble?" Diana asked Jess with alarm.

He waited for Jess to hesitantly nod her acceptance at him before he wove through the patrons of the café, many of them sending furtive glances at the wall of lethal muscle by the door.

"No, no, don't mind this," Jess said, clearly trying to hide her nervousness. "Sorry, I should've told you. He's a huge nerd. We play this killer tag thing where—"

He shut out her voice and focused on the situation.

Unlike a lot of the Dicks in this coffee shop, these shifters hadn't cultivated their muscle in a gym. Nor did it look like they led a mostly sedentary lifestyle, like Kingsley's shifters, with a little padding layered over their hard-earned strength. No, these guys, in their late twenties or early thirties, seemed hungry to prove themselves. At a guess, they were in the process of defining a territory, enforcing new rules.

All three of them put together wouldn't be able to

take him.

He stopped in front of them before making a show of glancing around.

"Shall we step outside?" he asked.

The guy on the end, a blond with tousled curls and sun-kissed skin, about Austin's height but slimmer through the chest, took a small step back and half turned. *After you.*

The others watched him warily.

Austin inclined his head, an exercise in trust. *Don't give me a reason to turn this violent.*

Outside and down the street a ways, Austin stepped into a break between buildings and turned, putting his hands in his pockets. *I'm not looking for trouble.*

The three fanned out just a little and stood in front of him, blocking off the street and exits. He'd already put his back to the little alcove for garbage cans. *If this kicks off, we've got you outnumbered.*

Austin inclined his head again, with a tiny twitch of the corner of his lip. *Sure you do.*

Their nervousness showed in their shoulders. These guys weren't used to dealing with alphas of Austin's caliber. Not outside of their own pack, at least. That suggested they were part of a new pack, one that wasn't listed in the detailed directory Kingsley had shared with him of prominent, known packs and territories. That directory was currently a Google document shared between some of the larger packs across the nation. It really should've been open to all and updated formally. If they ever hoped to unify, they'd need to know where other packs and leaders resided. Until now, he'd thought this area was devoid of organized packs.

"What can I do for you?" Austin asked, his bearing relaxed, confident in his dominance.

"We represent the Agoura Pack," the blond guy said, "and you are currently in our territory. As I'm sure you know, it's customary for a visiting alpha to announce himself to the residing pack alpha and state his intentions, typically within twenty-four hours of entry. Are you rogue?"

The term *rogue* was generally applied to an alpha, or an otherwise powerful shifter, who didn't have a pack. They were the shifters no one wanted around. The fear was that the rogues would make trouble or rip a pack out from under a weaker alpha.

Austin had been a rogue for years, starting the moment he left Kingsley's pack and ending when he officially created a pack in O'Briens. Brochan, too, would've been considered a rogue during his travels. In fact, all of the shifters Austin had brought with them on this trip would likely make these guys nervous.

"No," he said, not offering any more information. "I

wasn't aware there was an established pack in this area."

"You're new in town?"

"I'm visiting my mate's family for the holidays. They are not affiliated with magic."

Creases formed between their brows. They didn't know what to make of that.

"The Agoura Pack is newly established with firm territory markers in place," Blondie said, adjusting his stance to be more authoritative. "You'll need to request passage at your earliest convenience." He pulled a card out of his back pocket. "This is the information. Your call will be expected within twenty-four hours, but because of your stature, it would be better for all parties if you didn't wait so long."

Despite the tension at the onset of the meeting, Austin had to own that these territory enforcers were keeping things professional. Regardless of how new their pack was, they were adhering to the accepted code of conduct. He'd do them the favor of backing down on his dominant posturing.

He took the card and slipped it into his back pocket, softly blowing out a breath. *I've got a conflict of interest.*

"I'll see what I can do," Austin said, releasing his other hand from his pocket but hooking his thumb in his belt loop. "My mate has a dinner scheduled tonight with her ex-husband. It's the first time she's seeing him since the divorce and the first time I'm meeting him. I can't miss that dinner. I'm sure you understand. I'll call after we leave the coffee shop and explain."

Blondie nodded, stepping back a little. "Very good. I fully understand the need to enforce your claim. I've done likewise a time or two, and my girlfriend at the time was always glad for the backup."

"Fact," one of the other shifters said.

Austin turned to leave but hesitated. "Are there any other packs in the Los Angeles area I need to be concerned about? I'd thought the whole area was devoid of organized packs."

Their shoulders tightened, one and all.

Blondie said, "At present, no other packs are established." He paused for a moment, like he was wrestling with something. Then, "Watch yourself, though, alpha. We have mages in the greater Los Angeles area, and they don't like shifters on their doorstep."

It felt like a bolt of lightning had lit Austin up from within. He understood the message—any packs that tried to form were being steamrolled by mages. He should've expected it. Sebastian had told him before that mages infiltrated Dick establishments and businesses, going where the money was. Mages didn't like to share, and Momar didn't like shifters in particular. It made sense that the mages were running powerful shifters out of town.

Austin nodded just as Jess walked around the corner, her eyes ablaze and her hands out, ready for war. She'd felt Austin's thrill of adrenaline and thought the worst was happening.

"Whoa, we're good." He quickly stepped out in front of the shifters and put his arms out. "We're fine. It wasn't them I was responding to."

She continued walking, looking over his shoulder before slowing down. "What's going on?"

"Nothing. I'll explain in the car. What's the status with Diana? Are you two still having coffee?"

She veered a little into the street so that she could see the shifters, now behind him, her bearing hostile. "No, I said goodbye shortly after you left."

He reached for her when she was in proximity, reeling her in, and thankfully, she let him. "We're good," he said again, feeling her very slowly start to relax. "They're friendlies."

"What is she?" one of the shifters murmured as Austin firmly turned her so they could head back the way they'd come. Maybe her control wasn't as solid as it had been before Kingsley's battle.

"She's something the mages definitely won't like on their doorsteps," he replied, escorting her away.

She didn't utter a word during the walk back, and

he didn't want to insult her by making small talk. Nor did he want to repeat the conversation in the streets. He'd be able to feel presences of anyone invisible, but there was no telling what sort of listening devices or surveillance existed in a city like this. Call him paranoid, but he'd seen what organized mages could do en force. When dealing with mages, paranoia was a survival tactic.

Thankfully, the shifters had found them first, but they'd need to alter their plans to ensure they *only* met shifters.

"What's the situation?" Jess asked as soon as the car doors were closed.

As he began driving, he quickly walked her through what had been said and how.

"Mr. Tom can take Jimmy to Matt's this afternoon," she said once he'd finished. "I'll tell Matt something came up. We need that pack to grant us passage, and anyway, it's a good excuse to make contact. I know you've held off on trying to organize against Momar, but we need to strike while the iron is hot. If we let too much time pass, people will get complacent. That can't happen. Momar's already planning his next horror, so we need to be strengthening our position."

He put his hand on her thigh, not mentioning that he'd been waiting for *her* to emotionally heal. As much as the battle had hurt everyone involved, it had hurt her in a special way. It had been her first experience with personal losses, and unlike other alphas, she hadn't been raised to expect it. She hadn't had the resources to emotionally deal with it. She'd needed the break.

Or so he'd thought, anyway. Now, it seemed like she needed action.

"It also wouldn't hurt to ask them what they know about the mages in this town," she continued, clearly on a roll. "If only to help us avoid them for now. Tristan and Niamh are great about some things, but they don't have the network Nessa and Sebastian did. We could be missing a whole lot that goes on in this town."

"Agreed. No more leaving the house without back-up, either. We'll need to arm people with potions, just in case, and keep an eye out. I'd rather overreact than get another surprise."

She looked out the window. "How'd they even know we were there? Do they own it?"

"They might. Or a shifter stopping in for coffee, or…" He paused. "Or it might've been the woman at the counter who waved me to the front of the line. If she was a low-powered shifter, I wouldn't have noticed unless I was looking for it. In that busy spot…I definitely wasn't looking for it. I'm not acclimated to the population of this place."

"I can see that after spending so much time in O'Briens and your hometown."

"Or it could've been someone else. I had to posture in a couple of instances, and it's noticeable to someone who knows what they're looking for."

She slid her hand up his arm and to his shoulder before dusting her fingertips along the skin of his neck. "I like how noticeable you are," she purred.

Tingles worked at the base of his spine and his groin tightened. He pulled a hand from the wheel and rubbed it along her upper thigh, squeezing.

"Why were you posturing, though?" Her light touch traced along his stubble. "Is it because you worried about what I would do to defend my claim?"

He swallowed, painfully hard now. "Something like that."

"I felt your annoyance through the bond, followed by your release of power, and turned to see what was going on." She pulled her hand away and then reached lower, yanking at the top button on his fly. Not one to pass up a good time, he slid his butt down a little to give her better access. "Diana commented that you seem to like public displays of affection, and that was good because I clearly like them, too. She was right. I *do* like them."

He took over the buttons, and she reached in to

wrap her fingers around his length.

"I really like them." She pulled him out and stroked, slowly at first, then speeding up. "Turn left here."

He complied, though going straight would take them in the direction of the house.

"When you postured with that woman, whatever expression I wore made Diana blush," she breathed, rubbing him up and down. "I'll give you a hint—I was thinking sexy thoughts. Take a right here."

The roads reduced to three lanes, still wide but not as crowded at this time of day.

"Ten and two," she said, pulling her seatbelt away from her chest and getting her other arm out.

He adjusted his grip on the steering wheel, starting to breathe heavily now.

"At the light, get in the left turning lane. After you turn, just go straight."

She bent down into his lap, and he groaned as her hot, wet tongue moved over him. It circled before she sucked him in as far as she could go, the angle not giving her the usual range, although he was not at all complaining. He focused on driving straight as her hand followed her mouth up and down. Her tongue swirled, and it was a struggle to keep his eyes from rolling back in his head. The lane came up, and he took it, stopping at a red light, gripping her hair.

She hummed softly, and the vibration went straight down to his balls. He dropped his head back for a second, closing his eyes, groaning in pure bliss.

A horn sounded, and he came to, belatedly noticing a truck to his right. The driver, a younger guy, glanced over as the person behind honked. He did a double take, his eyes widening as Austin took his foot off the brake. Then he flipped Austin a thumbs-up.

The voyeur situation, and how cool his mate was, accelerated his lust.

"Faster, Jess," he said, hand still in her hair.

She moaned, tearing at her own button and sliding her hand down the front of her pants. Both hands worked now, one on him, one on herself. Her hot, wet mouth repeatedly sucked him in and out. The pleasure mounted. It was hard to concentrate.

"I'm getting close, baby," he said, looking for a spot to pull over. "Come with me."

She groaned again and worked herself faster. Sped herself up until she was bobbing her head furiously.

He jerked the car to a stop on the side of the road, leaned back as the pleasure crested, and then groaned long and low. She shuddered even as she drank him down, her hair in his hand.

He closed his eyes in the aftermath. The glove box opened, Jess getting something to clean herself up with, and then he felt a wet wipe on him.

"I can do it," he grinned, opening his eyes now and taking over.

Once everything was squared away and they were back on the road, she rubbed his shoulder and then put her hand at the nape of his neck, clearly wanting to be closer than they could be with him driving.

"Diana said she's never seen me look happier," Jess mused, pointing to get him to turn back toward their Airbnb. "That she's never seen me look more in love."

He felt her glow to match her words, her thumb stroking his skin.

"I think she's also afraid of you a bit." She laughed. "You make her nervous."

"I got that impression. I see why she didn't make it as an Ivy House heir."

"She wouldn't have taken the magic." Jess leaned her head back on her seat and looked out the window. "She wouldn't have wanted the responsibility. Money wouldn't have swayed her. I definitely didn't take anything away from her."

"Is that what you've been thinking?"

"No. It just randomly occurred to me while we were chatting." She sighed. "It was nice to see her. I've missed having friends who are more my speed. Or what my speed used to be. But things are...complicated. My whole world has changed. In the years to come, I won't be able to explain to her or anyone else why I'm not aging. Today, my explanation of why you were leaving the coffee shop was absolutely terrible. She probably thinks you're in the Mafia or something. I don't know. This is all so much harder than I was thinking it would be, and we both know I'm potentially in danger all the time…" She shook her head. "It won't be safe to be around her. I won't even entertain the idea of her kids coming around. I could have her at Ivy House, I guess, but she hates that house. I doubt she'll want to visit."

"What are you saying?"

She sighed again. "I just don't know how our friendship can stay consistent, you know? I'm worried about our future as friends."

He placed his hand on her thigh. "You have some time before the aging thing becomes a problem. If we can get Momar out of the way, things will slow down. Let's not write her off just yet."

She turned her face toward him, her smile soft. "Matt always tried to push my friends away. Here you are, trying to help me hang on to them."

"I'm not threatened by your friends or insecure in your love and affection for me."

"I know," she whispered, gazing at him for a long moment. "But speaking of that clown, I'd better give him the bad news."

"Why do you sound so giddy?"

"Because it'll ruin his day. Why do you sound so glum?"

Austin grinned. "Because I was looking forward to meeting him."

CHAPTER 8
MR. TOM

T HIS MADE TWICE today that Mr. Tom had not been allowed to escort the miss on an errand. Or to storm the castle, as the case may be. First coffee—she'd forgotten to grab him a cappuccino—and now to see the shifters. No matter. He would be guarding the most important thing in the miss's life: her son.

It was Mr. Tom's job to make sure the young boy had everything he needed and then some. To spoil him, as the case may be. He could do a much better job than any grandmother, that was for sure.

"Do you have everything?" he asked as they pulled up to the curb of an unoriginal establishment in a cultivated bore of an area.

"Yeah," Master Jimmy replied.

Mr. Tom put the ridiculous Porsche in park. The ride was terrible. The seat made his butt hurt. Master Jimmy loved it, though, and that was all Mr. Tom cared about.

"New game console for the lulls when your dad is gone?" Mr. Tom pressed.

"Yes," Master Jimmy said, staring straight ahead, not reaching for the door handle.

"New VR gear for when he is there and you would rather escape to your room?"

"Yes, but you guys got me one last time. You didn't need to get me another one."

"The second installment of your favorite game is only available on this new one. Plus, it's lighter and better for your head."

Master Jimmy twisted his mouth to the side. Who could argue with logic?

"I packed you cavity-causing snacks as well as plenty of caffeine-enhanced drinks. I heard that your father detests both, so there will be none in the house."

Master Jimmy gave him a funny look, a mixture of bewilderment, nearly laughing, and gratitude.

"Most importantly…" Mr. Tom held up a finger, leaning in a little. "In the inner pocket of your suitcase, the one with the clothes, is a throw-away phone, compliments of the Irishwoman and the very strange person posing as a gargoyle. It's not traceable to you. They seemed to think that was important for some reason. I've also put in cash and a credit card with a very large ceiling. If you need to leave, or you need help, or you simply need to talk, there are options. Ask for help immediately. I am always available. The miss would want you to be my top priority." He tilted his finger a little more. "Do you understand?"

Master Jimmy blinked at him for a moment and then said, "This sounds incredibly stupid, but are you a guardian angel?"

"That does sound incredibly stupid. Angels don't exist. Have some sense, boy."

Mr. Tom exited the car and retrieved as much as he could from the tiny trunk before fetching the rest from the itty-bitty backseat. What a nuisance of a car.

"Here—"

"Don't you dare!" Mr. Tom yelled at the young master. "The heir's son does not carry his own luggage!"

"I mean…" Master Jimmy shrugged and got out of the way. "Okay."

When it counted, the boy was as lovely and pliant as his mother.

"Here we go, let's step lively now—your father was in all sorts of a bad mood with your mother earlier." Mr. Tom followed Master Jimmy up the walk. "If he gives you any grief, you call me and I'll come pick you up directly. I never sleep."

"You don't?"

"Don't question me." He put the bags down on the grass just below the three steps leading up to the blue door. "Now, let's look at you. I hear your dad is an anal sort of character."

Mr. Tom ran his arms down the boy's sleeves, obviously freshly pressed but having endured a car ride. He adjusted the collar and straightened out the boy's hair. When all was settled, he nodded.

"What sort of welcome will this be, do you think?" Mr. Tom rang the doorbell.

"I don't think it'll be great. Dad doesn't like when Mom changes plans." Master Jimmy paused. "Or does her own thing." He hesitated again. "Or kinda has a life of her own. He likes to be in charge."

"What an interesting bit of information." Mr. Tom ruffled his wings in distaste as footsteps sounded beyond the door. It swung open to reveal a nice-looking woman with lovely, moisturized, tanned skin, a pleasing sort of aura, and a fine cut to her shiny black hair. Her clothes were bland but made with expensive material, her shoes were also expensive but appeared comfortable, and her engagement ring was probably one and a half carats and of decent quality. She seemed intent not to make any kind of personal statement with her *look*.

Her smile was wide and her eyes sparkled with genuine excitement about seeing Master Jimmy, though, and so any flaws were immediately forgotten.

"Hello, Jimmy!" she said, holding her arms wide for a hug.

Mr. Tom stepped out of the way so Master Jimmy could get the warm welcome. The boy didn't receive it as eagerly as it was given, though, delivering a weak pat on her back and a lackluster expression.

"And…hello." She greeted Mr. Tom with confusion. Her gaze flickered to his wings before returning to his face. "You're Jacinta's…friend, correct?"

"I am her butler, madam," Mr. Tom responded. "She has been called away on important business."

"Her…butler?"

The woman didn't seem to understand the word.

"Yes, well." He touched Master Jimmy's shoulder. "You have all you need? Besides your bags, of course. I'll bring them in momentarily."

"Yeah, I'm okay." Master Jimmy hesitated before entering the house. "You guys are coming tomorrow, right? Or the next day?"

"We're not sure yet, young master. It'll depend on how today goes. You'll be safe here." Realizing what he'd just said in front of a Jane, Mr. Tom cleared his throat. "Looked after, I mean."

The woman picked up the baton immediately. "Of course!" She touched Jimmy's shoulder while still beaming at Mr. Tom. "We'll take great care of him!"

She really did mean well. You couldn't fault the woman for that.

"Fantastic. Well. If you'll show me to his room?" Mr. Tom turned to pick up the bags.

"Oh…" The woman looked at him in confusion again. "Um… I can get those." She stuck out her hand. "I'm Camila."

"Yes." Mr. Tom hefted the bags, ignored her hand, and waited for her to grant him entry.

"Oh…uh…" She backed away, clearly out of sorts.

"Master Jimmy can lead me to his room, madam. Be at ease." He pushed his way into the residence, barely passing a glance at the store-bought art and uninspired furniture. Mimi would have something to say about this décor. Then again, when didn't she?

"I assume your bedroom is upstairs?" he said to Master Jimmy.

He followed the boy upstairs to a bare room with zero personality. Sure, Mr. Tom had gotten it all wrong the first time he tried to dress up the boy's room in Ivy House, but at least he'd tried. Through many phone calls and texted pictures, he'd managed to perfect the look, and it had been in perfect shape by the time Master Jimmy returned. This was…worse than a hotel.

"No, no." Mr. Tom put the bags on the bed. "This

won't do. Don't worry, I will fix this. Let me just bring in the other bags, put everything away, and then I will go shopping to make this room nicer for you to inhabit."

"No, Mr. Tom, really…" Jimmy's eyes were doing that thing the miss's always did when she was overcome with emotion, appreciative of someone looking after her. It was a look Mr. Tom strived for. It was his benchmark. If he hit that look, he knew he'd achieved success.

"Don't be ridiculous, boy!" he admonished Master Jimmy, knowing that the miss accepted his help easier if he yelled at her. Such strange creatures, these Dicks and Janes. "Find a place to hide the…" He gave a *look* that indicated he was referring to the cash and credit card and left the room.

The soon-to-be stepmom was quarreling with the father in the living room, easily seen from the stairwell, since it clung to the wall and descended into that space. They didn't look up until he was halfway down the stairs, slow to register his presence.

She smiled in a disarming way. The man's look was reproachful, full of disdain and arrogance, and with an air of dominance.

Why he'd attempt to claim dominance, Mr. Tom couldn't say. His suit was made well, a somewhat expensive purchase, but the tailoring was off. It was as though his body had changed since it had been fashioned. The coloring, a light blue, was currently out of fashion and much too bright. He had a small pot belly, a fragile sort of frame, and narrow shoulders. He'd lose a fight with an old Jane woman over a stolen handbag.

His chin was tilted up, though, like he fancied himself some kind of king or emperor.

"Hello," the man said, walking forward to meet Mr. Tom at the base of the stairs. He put out his hand. "You're Jacinta's…butler, I hear?"

Mr. Tom shook the hand, a little put off by the waxy skin. "Yes."

The man stared at him. But while his gaze was direct and expectant, there was no power behind it—not the kind that required a response.

"Right," Mr. Tom said, turning. "I have one more bag to bring in, and then I must go shopping for Master Jimmy's room. It is devoid of décor that interests him."

The man didn't stop him from leaving or prevent him from taking the last bag upstairs. Upon delivering it, though, Mr. Tom could tell Master Jimmy was uncomfortable.

"Listen," he said to the boy gently, "you currently seem to be a pawn in the schemes of…some of your parents, but you are not a child. At any time, you can stand up and be your own man. You needn't allow

yourself to be passed between your parents like luggage.
Let me put you up in your own room at the hotel near
the house. Naomi and Aurora are staying there, as well
as a couple of the shifters and gargoyles. Or you can
take your emergency money, leave whenever you wish,
and do whatever you like." He pointed a finger at the
boy. "As long as you let your mom know you're safe.
We don't want her leveling the city because of you."

Master Jimmy smiled at that—a good sign.

"Don't spend the holidays unhappy," Mr. Tom finished.

Jimmy reached out to hug him, the first time he'd
ever done so. "Thank you," he said, backing away
quickly. "I'll stay for a day or so. Don't bother outfitting
the room. But can you ask Mom to either come for
dinner tomorrow, or maybe the day after so I can go
back with her? I mean, it'll be fine here, but…" He
shrugged. "I prefer staying with you guys. I don't really
have much in common with my dad."

The earnestness with which the master spoke broke
Mr. Tom's heart. He didn't want to leave the child. The
woman here certainly seemed loving, but she was
mostly a stranger. The man…

Well, Mr. Tom didn't quite understand the particu-
lars, as the miss said very little about her ex other than
that he worked a lot, but the reception here was certainly stale. Austin Steele was gentler on a shifter's first day

in the pack, and that was a work affair.

The situation was altogether strange, and Mr. Tom did not like strange things.

He lifted his chin. "Remember that phone. I am a spectacular wit when one is bored."

There was that grateful smile again. "Okay."

"Good." Mr. Tom nodded. "Sweet dreams. Bedbugs biting and all that. Monsters under the bed. Don't let limbs hang over the edges. Etcetera."

"Riiight…" Master Jimmy drew out with a goofy smile.

The father was waiting on the couch in the living room, a magazine open on his lap, but he was clearly too tense to be reading it.

Mr. Tom didn't bother to engage him as he reached the bottom of the stairs, something that clearly flustered the man. No comment came, though, as Mr. Tom headed for the door, feeling anticipation through many of the Ivy House bonds. The team must be getting ready to head to the shifter compound.

Mr. Tom wouldn't be joining them, of course, even though he could arrive in time. He wouldn't even be leaving the area and would merely hide the car and then return to sit on the ground below the boy's window. The miss had convocation business to attend to. Mr. Tom would guard her child.

CHAPTER 9

JESSIE

NERVOUS TREMORS MADE me shiver as we headed to the meetup with the resident pack. Terrible fears plagued me. The battle at Kingsley's was still so fresh. Our losses weighed too heavily on my mind for me to relax.

Austin drove the souped-up sports car I had gotten him before we headed to Kingsley's. It was a flashy, fast thing that we'd gotten to impress my ex-in-laws. It would serve us much better in this situation. With a car like that, there would be no question that Austin had means and our convocation was successful. We just wouldn't mention that the funds had come with my house.

Our team followed behind us, heading to what satellite imagery had revealed was a sort of office complex with a sprawling parking lot all around it. We'd gotten directions to assemble near one of the buildings, and while it hadn't been specifically requested, Austin had told them how many people they should expect. He wanted to be open about the power we had at our disposal so they wouldn't feel threatened in any way.

Based on the confrontation he'd had with the shifters earlier, Austin assumed this was all just a formality. That we might even be making a useful connection.

I was mentally preparing for war.

I couldn't help myself—my mind automatically jumped to the worst-case scenario.

We slowed as we rolled down a dimly lit road on what was probably the very outskirts of the pack's territory. Los Angeles had a bunch of little suburban neighborhoods scattered all around and often melting into each other. It was hard to tell where one ended and the next began.

Austin pulled into the parking lot of the meetup, an office complex, this building exactly the same as its neighbors except for the sign posted out front. No business names were posted next to the four suite letters. High bushes ran between the buildings, stopping at the edge of the parking lot. A few vehicles were parked away right and left, Dicks and Janes not all having left their place of work for the day, but there was not one car in front of the building in question.

We'd been told to take the parking spaces farthest

from the building and walk toward Suite A. While the rest of the crew did use those spaces, Austin parked at an angle right in the middle.

He took his time adjusting his gold, gleaming cuff links with the diamond studs, another thing he'd brought to show off for my ex-in-laws. His tailored suit screamed *rich* while the cut and style softly purred *posh*. His watch was a gift from me, which I'd given him at the same time as the car on the perfect date I'd tried and mostly succeeded in taking him on. He looked every inch the part of a successful alpha, or so he said.

I wore a suit as well, something we'd had to go out to buy earlier. I'd brought clothes for a dinner party, not for a big boss meeting. My suit didn't fit as well as a tailored suit would've, but the alterations Mr. Tom had made with a ten-dollar sewing kit would have to do.

"This is the part of shifter life you haven't experienced yet," Austin said, releasing his car door and waiting for it to swing upward at an angle. They were kind of annoying to get in and out of, but they looked *very* cool. "Glitz and glamour and swagger while subtly threatening to kill the other party if things go south."

We'd had mage dinners like that, and the gargoyle dinners weren't too different, but none of them had the subtlety shifters used with their body language. I'd be out of my league where communication was concerned.

He got out of the car and came around to my door. I waited patiently, knowing he wanted to make a show with his swagger.

I took his hand when my door reached its zenith and tried not to look like I needed to be hoisted out. Our people drifted in around us, gargoyles on one side and shifters on the other, their lines headed by Tristan and Brochan and fanning out in a V. Dave led the basajaunak, filing into the empty space behind me. Indigo and Niamh pushed in front of them.

Austin and I walked toward the suite in question and stopped just before the curb leading up to the sidewalk. The others gave us space, stepping back a ways.

The moment we stopped moving, the door to the suite opened and their team of shifters walked out. Their suits were black on black, with black pocket squares, black ties, black dress shirts, and shiny black shoes or pumps. Their hair was greased back if it was short or tied in a bun if it was long. Very fashionably organized—very Los Angeles.

Every other person went right or left as they emerged, and they filed in around us, curling until they'd locked us in with a small opening in front, waiting for their alpha.

My alarm bells clanged. Who the hell trapped

someone in if they were friendly? Did they *want* us to fight our way out?

Because I'd do so dramatically.

Austin's hand, still holding mine, tightened. He clearly felt my turmoil and wanted me to chill out a little.

Sure, fine. For now.

After a pause, another man walked through the door. He had dark skin, short-cropped hair, a fantastic suit with *chic* flair, and an athletic build. His walk held swagger but was confident and refined, suggesting he was owning his space rather than showing off.

He stopped on the walkway in front of us, and it felt like everyone held their breath.

"Austin Steele," he finally said, his voice deep and rich and, thank God, not obviously hostile. "Your reputation precedes you."

Austin didn't move but for his thumb, gently shifting it back and forth over mine. "I don't believe I've had the pleasure."

"Terence Fortua, original alpha of the Agoura pack."

"Well met, alpha," Austin replied, and inclined his head, giving him his due as leader and alpha.

"And this is the infamous Ironheart," Terence continued, looking at me now. "A female gargoyle, did I hear that correctly?"

"Yes," I said, still simmering on *don't mess with us* setting.

"Correct me if I have this wrong, but you attempted to sacrifice yourself to break the spell during the Gossamer Falls battle. You saved your people from total annihilation, Alpha Steele and Alpha Barazza among them?"

Now it was me squeezing Austin's hand, emotion welling up, wanting to just walk away. "I only lived because of my pack, Alpha Steele among them."

"The reports of your being humble are correct, I see. You declined a mention of honor in the Gossamer Falls pack, a prestigious accolade. Honestly, I didn't believe it."

A slip of my magic made everyone bristle. "Forgive me, alpha, but this is still fresh. I'd prefer if we didn't discuss it."

He didn't show any emotion, not that I should've expected it. He didn't even nod, just moved on, for which I was grateful.

"Alphas," he said, giving us a vast amount of respect within his territory. He was claiming us as equals, something Kingsley had even been slow to do. "You have a large force here. A lot of power. Usually, this would set off warning sirens for us. Not just bells, but actual sirens. You also didn't declare yourself upon arrival—more warning sirens. However, I've heard how the encounter went outside of the coffee shop. I believe that you didn't realize we were established. I also appreciate you giving us numbers upfront, though…"

His voice trailed off as he looked over the people we had assembled. Broken Sue got an awful lot of notice, Niamh was another sticking point, and I could even tell he was wary about Tristan.

"Numbers have nothing to do with what you brought here tonight," he finally finished.

"Power is hard to quantify," Austin answered.

"Indeed. Why did you bring so much protection to a family event, or did my people get that wrong?"

"You've clearly heard about our battle with the mages," Austin said, and Terence nodded. "We were helping my brother. My mate has her own problems with mages, since she can do magic like they can. We've had multiple attacks and dealings with them, all hostile. She's the only one amongst us who can do magic. If she or we are attacked, she has to neutralize the threat while we take it out. When dealing with mages, we need strength. Living in their backyard, I would assume you'd know that."

Terence was quiet for a long time, no expression, no body movement. Finally he said, "I do understand that, yes. Alphas Steele and Ironheart, would you do me the favor of stepping into my office? There are matters I'd like to discuss."

Austin looked at me, waiting for an answer.

"Why is it up to me?" I whispered, trying not to move my lips. "I don't know what's going on. Is this dangerous? I'm not in a balanced headspace for danger. If he attacks, I might level the building, who's to say? I have a few new crazy spells that haven't seen the right type of practice but are itching to be used. It would be a mistake to let me get cornered."

I hadn't had a chance to practice some of the most dangerous spells because I didn't have Sebastian. He'd always ensured I stopped myself from causing the kind of destruction that couldn't be walked back.

My emotions wobbled. I missed him and Nessa, missed Nathanial. My beast sensed an opportunity and tried to feed my rage and need for vengeance.

I took a deep breath, willing patience, as Austin watched me silently. Why were his eyes glittering like this was funny? It was making us look bad.

"Seriously," I whispered through my teeth. "*Dangerous* isn't a strong enough word for me right now. You know this. This shouldn't be my call to make."

His lips stretched into a smile, totally unlike him when dealing with other strong shifters.

"Let's go," Austin said, sliding his arm around me.

"Okay, but…" I looked back at our people, suddenly worried they were trying to lure away the magical person and make good on the threat they'd issued when they surrounded us.

"It'll take a force much larger than this to take us down, Jessie," Tristan told me. "We're good."

Austin and I followed Terence and two of his shifters through the door. A lobby area was simply furnished and the door at the back led into a few rooms, all of them outfitted like offices. We took the one on the left, the office decently sized, with two chairs in front of an oak desk and a bookshelf lining the back wall.

Terence took the leather chair behind the desk, and two of his shifters filed in and stood near the door.

Butterflies fluttered in my belly as I took one of the chairs facing the desk, waiting for Austin to take the other.

"I can assure you, Miss Ironheart," Terence said as he made himself comfortable, "the last thing I would want to do is challenge shifter celebrities."

"My brother has been spreading word of what happened in his territory, I see," Austin said, leaning back and crossing an ankle over his knee. He stretched his big arm across the arms of our chairs and rested his hand on my thigh. It didn't seem completely professional, but nor did his slouching in the seat like a playboy. I had to assume he knew what he was doing.

"Very much so, yes. I'm surprised he didn't tell you. He's giving the heads-up that you two plan to organize the shifters under the umbrella of a convocation, is that correct? Encompassing not just shifters but other magical creatures like gargoyles? And the…basajaunak, another thing I didn't believe until tonight. That seemed like the tallest tale of them all."

"Correct," Austin replied. "We were letting the dust settle on the battle before we took our next steps."

"I see." Terence leaned forward, bracing his elbows on the desk. "Let me tell you how things work in this territory. We exist because we keep our heads down. Any shifter pack that tried to organize in the Los Angeles area in the past was pushed out, whether by political means, business, or just plain force."

"By mages?" I asked.

"Correct, by mages. In order to play their game, you need to have some serious connections and savvy, and most shifter packs do not. Not like they do." He spread his hand across his chest. "We do not. Instead of encroaching on their monetary territory, I purposely chose a small suburb and have contented myself with smaller businesses, like that coffee shop. I do not reach for more territory, I do not try to make political friends, and I stay under the radar. By doing that, I've mostly avoided notice."

"Mostly?" Austin asked, the word laced with a growl.

"I've received threats now and again, usually telling me to back off on the acquisition of one business or other. And I have. I gave them an *olé* as I did so. I let Dick police handle their laws, and my people coexist with zero flashiness. No pulling alpha in coffee shops, that sort of thing."

"I was about to be hit on," Austin replied. "I was trying to defuse the situation before Jess got involved."

"Ah." Terence surveyed me for a moment. "I see. Be that as it may"—he leaned back like he was suddenly tired—"I respect what you're trying to do with this convocation. I know quite a few people who are excited about it, and not just because they want an organized way to push back against the mages."

"You sound thoroughly connected in the shifter community."

"Yes. My brother and sister each head up a pack, one down south, the other on the East Coast. I moved out here for the potential before realizing the gridlock the mages have on the town."

"Why'd you stay?"

He was quiet for a beat. "Because I love a challenge.

Look, eventually I want to join this convocation. I want backup to push harder into this town. But for now, with things the way they currently are, I'm going to respectfully request that you keep a low profile in this area. Not because you're afraid of retribution from the mages, but as a favor to me. Mages can't or don't care to distinguish between shifter packs. A shifter is a shifter. If you're around town making noise, they'll assume you're with my pack and try to push us out. I'd rather not have that happen."

"And in return?" Austin asked, still mostly lounging, like this meeting meant absolutely nothing to him.

"In return," Terence said without hesitation, "I'll relay to my network what I saw here today. Your power, the truth of the rumors, my desire to join your convocation as soon as I'm not against a wall with mages… Ask around about my family. I'm sure you'll see the value in this trade."

Austin looked at me again, as if I might have any notion of playing hardball. Of *course* we were going to keep our heads down as much as possible. We didn't want attention from mages any more than Terence did. They might force him out, but they'd try to kill or kidnap me. I was in a much worse situation.

Or was he looking for more from Terence? I certainly wouldn't know what to ask for. What he'd offered sounded great. It would save us a lot of time and effort.

Austin's demeanor was patient, his emotions buoyant. I had a feeling I was missing something, and for some inexplicable reason, it made me irate.

"Austin, I have no idea," I blurted, and a pulse of magic flooded the room. The shifters by the door flinched, and their clothes rustled. Terence's eyes tightened.

Austin didn't react at all.

I held up my hand and closed my eyes, taking a breath.

"I apologize," I said softly, willing myself to calm down. I met Terence's gaze. "Really. I'm new to magic and the insanity that comes with being part beast." I swallowed. "Also to losing people in battle and the guilt associated with that. I wasn't lying when I said I wasn't balanced right now."

"Actually, you said *dangerous* wasn't a strong enough word and that you were a holy terror," Terence said, steepling his fingers. "And yes, I could tell you weren't lying. I think you make Alpha Steele's job quite a bit easier."

I lifted my eyebrows at him, wanting to ask, *How so?* but also not really caring. The idea of the mages in this area taking notice of us had struck a nerve. Without Sebastian and Nessa, we were flying blind.

"Staying under the radar will benefit us as much as

you," Austin said, pulling his arm away and standing. He reached down to help me up. "But I would be grateful if you'd pass on our information. I think we'll start taking steps toward a unified front sooner rather than later."

"It's honorable, what you're trying to do." Terence stood with us. "It's badly needed. Respect." He put a fist to his heart. "If I can help in any way, I will. You have my word."

"Honestly, it was my brother who started along this path. He didn't have the power behind him, though, or the urgency."

"You definitely have both." Terence came from around the desk, looking down on me. "It won't ever feel better, the loss. The guilt might always plague you. But remember this, Jessie Ironheart—you aren't forcing anyone to fight with you. To follow you. They are doing it because they believe in your cause. Honor their sacrifice, but don't let that sacrifice be in vain. Don't let it eat away at you from the inside out. It's not what they would have wanted."

Tears making my vision swim, I nodded. Austin hugged me close, giving me comfort.

"Until next time, alpha," Austin said, walking me out.

"Stay safe," Terence called. "And when you're walking the city streets, grow eyes in the back of your head."

CHAPTER 10

JESSIE

A STRANGE PRESENCE slowly pulled me out of sleep. Heat coated my bare skin—Austin's body curled around me protectively. His breathing was slow and even, washing against my shoulder.

The confusion of having just woken up cleared slowly as I clued in. We had people watching the yard in shifts. If they'd spied someone, or felt someone, their alarm would filter through their connection to me. Not to mention I had magical alert spells set up along the perimeter, enhanced last night, ready to warn me if anyone wandered close.

Only silence existed around us, though, interrupted by Austin's steady breathing.

Those footsteps niggled at me, wandering closer, at the side of the yard and heading for the house.

Then a flash of understanding hit me. It wasn't this house they were approaching.

Ivy House.

Slowly they moved, two people, clumsy and seemingly heavy of step. They weren't shifters. Not decent shifters, at any rate. Maybe hikers, but why would they enter at the side of the yard and aim directly for the house? Hikers were usually lost in the back wood somewhere, ambling and taking in the surroundings.

Could be tourists, wanting to see the large, shadowy house.

I clued into the grounds at large, kind of a trip from so far away. The basajaunak wandered through the wood, some of them starting to move quickly toward the disturbance. Shadow leaked into the sky, Ivy House readying for action.

"Let's not jump to conclusions," I told her, monitoring the situation. *"They could be just checking out the house."*

"Don't you think I know what's a threat and what's benign?" she responded. *"I've been doing this for a lot longer than you've been alive."*

She had a point.

The intruders started to zigzag now. The area they were walking through was mostly clear of trees, but they darted from one area of cover to the next, not wanting to be seen.

"There are different levels of threats, though," I ar-

gued. *"We don't need to bury them in the yard if they are just trying to steal a TV or something."*

"Why not?"

I huffed as the basajaunak neared the area with incredible speed, clearly hidden from view because the people didn't slow or freeze. They continued on to the area where the grass should start, no more cover unless they tried to work their way around. Which was exactly what they did. Within view of the house, they circled in, moving about ten feet away from the first basajaun, then past the next, having no idea how close to certain death they were.

They finally stalled near the back of the house, basajaunak all around them.

"Did the basajaunak just reveal themselves?" I asked Ivy House as I tried to push up to sitting.

Austin's arms tightened around me and he nuzzled his face into the crook of my neck. I ran a palm up his arm before sliding free, and he quickly came awake as I did so.

"What is it?" he asked, rubbing an eye.

I grabbed my phone from the nightstand by the bed, only then realizing Cyra, Hollace, and Edgar were no longer on Ivy House grounds. This was the first time I'd mentally checked in. They were together, traveling fast, quite a distance from O'Briens. Given the direction they were headed, I had the distinct impression they were coming to us for the holidays after all.

"Someone's sneaking onto Ivy House soil," I answered Austin, trying to figure out what to do. "The basajaunak are all around, but none of them have phones. We need to remedy that. Cyra and the others are…coming here, it seems like? Or they're on a car trip, at any rate."

"The intruders are readying a spell of some sort," Ivy House said, and I could feel her magic building.

"Crap," I said, then relayed this to Austin.

"Tell her to take them out," he said immediately, reaching for his phone. He would send people in to check it out. "If they were friendly, they'd have knocked on the door like anyone else."

Of course, he was right.

I didn't get the opportunity to give her the go-ahead.

The basajaunak rushed in, five of them at a time. The feet of the intruders left the ground. My phone rang a moment later, Cyra's number.

"Hello?" I answered.

"Jessie, this is *Her.*" It sounded like the basandere who'd moved into my wood before the rest had followed. I felt her right next to what remained of the intruders.

"Hi. What's going on?"

"Cyra gave me her phone in case something like this happened."

"Where'd she go? Did she expect intruders? She hasn't contacted me."

"She did not tell us either of those things, just that we should let you know if anything seemed suspicious. Two men were just about to shoot a spell at Ivy House. We felt the alarm roll through Ivy House's wood and figured we should stop them."

"Are they still alive?"

"Yes, in case you wanted us to ask them questions. If not, we can kill them easily."

"How much longer will you be?" Ivy House said, and I knew she was asking if this meant I'd cut my trip short.

I bent forward and cradled my forehead in my hand. *"At least until the day after Christmas. I can leave early in the morning and skip the holiday party with my ex's family. I'm sure my parents will thank me. Can we tie the mages up and keep them in the bowels of the house? Their magic won't be an issue for you. The dolls can monitor them. The basajaunak can leave food."*

"They might be mad by the time you get back…"

It was clear she didn't mean mad the emotion.

Austin barked orders into his phone as I told the

basandere to tie them up, making sure their hands were separated and at their sides. If they were powerful enough to do spells without hand and body movements, this would still cut out the most dangerous magic available to them.

"The gargoyles will fly them to the Box," Austin told me, hanging up the phone. "We'll keep them there until we can get back and sort this out."

The Box was a special holding area for mages he'd built in his storage facility. Sebastian had put up safeguards to deaden magic within the walls, keeping everyone on the outside safe. Food could be slid in through a slot in the door, like in a prison.

My magical alarms vibrated through me as I relayed that information to the basandere. A stranger was crossing into the yard. *This* yard, in the house we were currently inhabiting.

I sprang out of bed. I'd learned the hard way not to trust coincidences.

"We've got company," I told Austin, throwing on a muumuu.

He followed me out of the room, not bothering with clothing. On the landing, I saw Tristan cross to the door beneath us, glancing back and up as he did so.

"A man with a hazy face," Tristan said. "He's obscuring his appearance with magic."

"Or trying to look younger," I said. "They do that."

"I've got two gargoyles blending into the house, ready to step out and block his retreat. Not that I'll give him the opportunity to run. Brochan is guarding the rear, leading the shifters, who are getting into position around the sides and back in case this isn't an isolated visit."

Tristan waited just behind the front door. When I descended the stairs behind Austin, he put out a hand to ensure I didn't take point. A knock sounded. Tristan grabbed the door handle and paused for a moment before swinging it open and filling the space with his body.

My view of the man beyond was obscured by fluttering wings and massive shoulders, but I could just barely make out someone that appeared to be in his mid-thirties. He gasped at the appearance of the huge gargoyle-monster. The mage's rounded eyes meant he had the ability to form facial expressions. He wasn't trying to disguise himself with a completely different face like Sebastian did, just smoothing out the wrinkles and lines.

"Yes?" Tristan asked in a dark, whiskey voice that promised horrible things.

"Here!" The man thrust out some sort of envelope. It almost looked like one you'd use to send documents via FedEx but for the blue holiday decorations lined with silver foil. "This is for Jacinta Evans. Please, I don't mean anyone harm. I'm just the messenger!"

…Jacinta Evans…

They had my legal name. That didn't mean much, really, but people from the magical world tended to call me Ironheart. It felt like the mages wanted me to know they'd looked me up and had dirt on me. Or maybe there were a thousand layered meanings that Nessa and Sebastian could have deciphered for me.

"I got this," I told Tristan, putting a hand on his arm to move him out of the way.

Instead of moving aside, though, he crossed the threshold and stepped beyond the man, coming to a stop just to the side and behind him. The man flinched and then visibly cowered within the proximity. He lifted his shaking hands.

"Please," he said. "I'm just delivering the message. They aren't—*we* aren't hostile. We don't mean anyone any harm. We try to stay out of all of that." He looked over his hunched shoulder at Tristan. "Please don't hurt me."

If mages weren't so dangerous, I would've laughed at this display.

Austin leaned against the wall beside the door, just out of sight of the mage, letting me handle it.

"He's not going to hurt you if you mind your manners," I told him, taking Tristan's place in the doorway.

The man flinched again before shifting his gaze to me. Gratitude eased the anxiety in his expression. I was reminded of the first time Sebastian had met shifters.

"I will!" he said urgently. "I promise I will."

"You asked for me?" I said as my magic curled around me, ready to be released at a moment's notice.

"Y-yes." He looked over his shoulder at Tristan again and then startled, probably because he'd just noticed there were two more gargoyles beyond Tristan, standing to either side of the walkway. His tongue darted out to lick his lips. "Yes." He cleared his throat, clutching the very fancy-looking envelope to his chest. "I apologize. I'm just the messenger, like I said. This is all Arthur's doing. He's the one organizing."

"Organizing what?"

He thrust it out, and his whole body shook like leaves in a gale. "You've been noticed. Your allegiance h-has been noticed." He must be talking about our stance against Momar. "Given your visit to the area, Arthur would like to invite you to dinner with a small collection of like-minded mages. They have an interest in speaking with you. Just a small dinner. T-tomorrow night. He knows you are new to the magical world, so he's included guidelines for dinner." He coughed into his fist, waving the envelope a little. "He wants to help so you know how to behave."

I lifted my eyebrows, and Tristan stepped a bit closer, bristling in reaction to the slight.

The mage flung out his other hand. "N-no, not like that. He isn't trying to offend you. Honest! He just wants to h-help. To make things clear so you don't run into any problems with the others. The number of people you're allowed to b-bring, the acceptable and non-acceptable use of magic and potions, dress code, stuff like th-that. It's all…in here."

He pushed the envelope out a little farther.

Tristan's nightmare magic swirled for a moment as he stepped closer, staring down at the mage. Slowly, deliberately, he took the envelope. The mage cowered a bit lower. He'd probably never want to be a messenger again.

"Tomorrow night?" I asked as Tristan held out the envelope for me, not backing off from the mage.

The poor creature looked up at the big gargoyle-monster, hunched in a stance that reminded me of Edgar, and if not for the turmoil mages in general had caused me, I probably would have called Tristan off. As it was, I looked forward to the messenger trying to relay his terror and his master probably not believing him. It would make for an eventful dinner.

"Tomorrow night is Christmas Eve," I mused, running my finger over the foil symbol. The image within was some kind of coat of arms, though I couldn't make out the significance. I'd need to save it in case that was a big mage thing Sebastian hadn't mentioned. I certainly didn't have one.

"Arthur assumed you'd want to…alter your plans," the mage said, scooting a little farther away from Tristan.

They were trying to seem important, he meant. More important than any prior engagements. Then again, maybe this situation was similar to the one with the shifters—they wanted to know who was invading their territory within a certain time period so they could determine if the person was hostile or benign. I'd have to mull all this over.

Which I was about to say when Austin stepped into sight, his arm coming around me, every cut, tense muscle on full display. Power pumped off him in heady waves, raw and intense, full-scale alpha.

The mage let out a strangled sound, clutching his throat.

"You tell Arthur that if I get one whiff of foul play"—Austin growled, and Tristan's magic also intensified—"or if my mate is in danger in *any* way, I will rip your spleen out before I ruin his whole world. I have the money, connections, and aggression to shut him out of this town. He'd best ensure this dinner is in good faith."

The mage's eyes widened until he looked like a caricature. His magic failed him, showing his age, and his face drained of color.

He didn't even get a chance to speak before shifters walked up from the sides of the house, moving onto the lawn. Naked, one and all. Strong men and women, tits and balls out, muscles shown off. They made a line beside the walkway, past the gargoyles already standing there. More gargoyles stepped forward from beside the house, suddenly visible. Basajaunak showed themselves around the bushes and trees in the perimeter.

The mage screamed, tried to get around Tristan, and hit the step wrong. He fell, twisting an ankle and crying out again. Once on the walkway, he hobbled toward the curb, limping as fast as he could go. His car was a little down the street, a Jaguar, and the tires screeched as he peeled away.

"That was almost too easy," Tristan said, watching the scene.

"That's because of his status and magical level." Austin gently pulled me back from the door. "You know firsthand how dangerous mages can get."

"Dangerous from a distance." Tristan followed us

in, and Broken Sue came in after him. "They clearly don't deal well with unbridled hostility in close proximity."

Austin caught a pair of sweats that Broken Sue lobbed at him and then stepped into them. "At the moment, no." He shook his head slowly, lowering into one of the overstuffed couches in the large living room that attached to the kitchen. "I wonder, though. Momar was incredibly prepared at Kingsley's. He left virtually nothing to chance. If he hadn't underestimated our magical power and the lengths our people would go in order to save our own, he would've destroyed my brother's pack. I think we should expect these mages—the high-level ones—to learn quickly and seek to cut out our advantage as fast as possible. This is just a gut feeling, but I think we need to lean on our robust viciousness and primal power right now, and when they adjust, so do we. We disarm them by shifting to a more polished look. A housebroken look."

"And that's when we show them we've been playing their game all along," Tristan said, nodding as he stared off into space. "Niamh and I need to make some trips after the holidays. There are some people I need to reconnect with, and she thinks she has a line on a few of her old cohorts, whatever that means. We'll both work some new connections we've made in our research. We have the ability to establish a much more robust network than the shadowy world of mages is capable of. They might as well be sleeping with a nightlight compared to a few of the players we can bring to the table."

"But can you control those players?" Austin asked as I sat down beside him.

"Can *I*? Yes. Can Niamh? I don't know. I get the feeling she's dabbling in things not even I have dared to mess with."

"I'll talk to her," Austin said.

"There's another matter we need to discuss as well." Tristan rubbed his chin in thought, still looking out the window. "A certain well-connected mage has gone missing. The connected parties have been incredibly tight-lipped, but...I have...thoughts."

"Is it urgent?" Austin asked.

"No." Tristan glanced at me. "Didn't the ex change the dinner to tonight, since you couldn't make last night?"

Butterflies swarmed my belly. As I'd expected, Matt hadn't been pleased about the change in plans. "Yeah. It's a late afternoon supper."

Tristan nodded. "It can wait, alpha, until you get a chance to talk to Niamh. I don't have anything concrete, just some connecting of the dots and a hunch."

I pulled up Hollace's number on my phone then

handed off the envelope for Austin to open.

"Yup," Hollace said when he picked up. "Jessie?"

"Yeah, hi. What's the situation?"

Cyra's voice drifted in. "What's she saying?"

"Hang on, Jessie, let me put the call on speaker." Hollace's phone was muffled, and then he spoke again. "Did you notice we were gone, or did something happen?"

"Two mages snuck into the yard and attempted magic," I told him as Austin broke the foil sticker sealing the package. "*Her* called me. The original basandere."

"We're calling her June behind her back," Cyra said. "Otherwise it gets too confusing."

"June, then. They're taking the mages to the Box. Why did you leave?"

"Not to sound cloak and dagger, but you'll see when we get there," Hollace said. "There's a box for you. Or a package or whatever. We should be there in about…" The phone muffled again. "How long, Edgar?"

"You're letting Edgar drive?" I asked in sudden alarm.

"Oh heavens no," Hollace replied. "Only one of us can come back from the dead. No, Patty is driving. She insisted."

"Hello, Jessie," Patty, Ulric's mom, called from

somewhere in the car. "I didn't mind at all, don't you worry. We have only one pit stop to make along the way—a friend lives near there. She gave up the garhette life and moved in with a lovely Jane woman. I'm just going to say hello really quick—"

"No way," Cyra said. "No—Edgar, tell her. We can't stop along the way for *any* reason. It's in the note. We have to go straight there. You promised."

"Yes, but—"

"I have an early supper with the ex tonight anyway," I interrupted, not needing the argument. "You—"

"What's a supper?" Cyra asked.

"An afternoon delight," Patty helped.

"No—oh my God, no. Not an afternoon delight. You need to look that term up. It's basically an early dinner. Matt has always been very concerned about his evening routine and his bedtime. When it comes to gatherings like this, he prefers to start and end early."

"Why not just call it Early Bird Special, like the diner in town?" Cyra asked.

"Because *early supper* sounds better. He thinks it's posh."

"Weird," Hollace said.

"Anyway, doesn't matter." I waved the thought away. "You don't have to hurry, basically."

"Who is Matt again?" Patty asked.

K . F . B R E E N E

"Her ex-husband," Cyra responded. "Even though there is a holiday party with both families, he's insisting on Jessie meeting with him and his new squeeze alone. He's obviously trying to flaunt his status."

"Well, we probably won't do the holiday party because—" I started.

"Oh my—well, Austin Steele will put a stop to that," Patty interrupted. "I need to get an invite to the holiday party, though. I don't know anyone who can talk up Jessie better than I can. I've practically made a science out of it. Why—"

"No, no." I squeezed my eyes shut. "No. We're not even—it's fine. It's all going to be fine. Just get here. Bring the box, or whatever you have. And there better not be a severed head in it."

There was a pause.

"This just got super dark," Hollace murmured.

"Oh, she's not at all as wholesome as she seems," Edgar said in the background. "Sometimes she comes out with things that make you worry you may not wake up the next morning. You know, for those of you who sleep."

"No—I mean, because of the movie *Se7en*?" I said. "With Morgan Freeman and the—Never mind. Just get here."

I tapped the end button and noticed Tristan's grin.

"What?" I asked.

He chuckled. "You and your crew provide endless entertainment."

"I'm glad you're amused." He laughed harder, and I pushed up off the couch. "I'm going for a shower, and then we'll go through what's in that envelope. We need to figure out if we're going to go to that dinner."

"We're definitely going to the dinner," Austin said. "What we need to figure out is how dangerous it's going to be before we enter their world."

I paused and pointed at Austin. "Could you really force them out of L.A.?"

"At present? No. It was a bluff. But if they pushed me?" He thumbed through the documents. "I'd come up with a way."

"You won't have to," Broken Sue growled. "If they threaten Jessie or us, no one will be leaving that party."

CHAPTER 11

JESSIE

MY DEEP CRIMSON, plunge-necked dress hung to just past mid-thigh. A little black sweater hugged my shoulders, and I had on a simple strand of pearls that didn't at all go with the outfit but would be expected by Matt and likely worn by his fiancée. I didn't intend to stand out at this dinner beyond the "loud" color I was wearing. I didn't want Camila to feel like she was underdressed or her jewelry was outclassed. I remembered what it was like when I was in her shoes. If I dressed up, Matt would reproach her for being underwhelming in otherwise sparkly company.

Not that he'd ever let me buy expensive jewelry. It was only now that I realized he'd essentially set me up to fail and then blamed me for it. Hopefully he was a lot more lenient in his expectations with her.

My hair was in a loose curl, not the French twist I'd often worn to these things with him, and my nails weren't polished. He'd notice that.

Shrugging it off, I did a final check in the mirror, wishing Nessa or Mr. Tom were here to offer a final yay or nay. I knew Austin would be fine with whatever, but Matt had exacting standards. I'd never been able to get it right when I was married to him and wanted to knock it out of the park now that I had been cut loose.

Why was this whole situation wreaking hell on my nerves? It was nuts. I should've been over all of this and worried about the very real dangers converging on us, but something about being back here, in this city and his circle again, had shoved me back in time. It was becoming hard to again crawl my way out of the expectations that had hemmed me in for half my life.

A knock sounded at the door. Tristan stepped in a moment later, sweeping the room with his gaze before finding me at the mirror.

"You look lovely, Jessie," he said, and I knew it was entirely for the purpose of support. He'd always been upfront that female fashion mystified him. He'd had to learn men's fashion, but that was as far as he planned to go.

It made the sentiment mean that much more. Like when Edgar inquired after the food Austin made me. My team was exceptional in their kindness to me and each other. I was truly fortunate.

"You okay?" Tristan asked, walking over. "Need a hug? We're dressed."

"No, no." I blotted the corner of my eye. "Thank you for saying that. I'm just grateful, that's all. We have an awesome team."

"We do." He leaned against the wall next to the mirror. "It's rock solid, both in power and in unity. You and Alpha Steele have created something amazing here. You two lead how you'd want to be led, with genuine hope and heart, and people can feel it. The fact that you're trying to bring other packs and cairns under your umbrella setup rather than conquering them is…heroic."

"How is that heroic?"

"You're making yourself a target. If the mages kill you two, they kill the organization. They kill the power."

I let that sink in for a moment, looking at the reflection of my blank expression. Memories popped up like champagne bubbles.

"I was always going to be a target," I said, smoothing my dress out of habit. "All of the heirs have been. Might as well do something better with my privilege and growing prestige than get presents from kings and eventually be killed by my mate, right?"

Tristan put a large hand on my shoulder. "I can't

take Austin Steele by myself, but if he turns on you, I'd lead a host to take him down. He won't, not ever, but we've got your back if that should happen. And if the magic drowns you and you lose your head and decide it would be fun to try to take him out, then we'd stand in your way. We've got your back there, too. Everyone else?" He smirked. "They'll rue the day they came up against the Dusky Ridge convocation. We'll make sure of it."

I put my hands out like a child, gladly accepting his hug now.

"But first?" I said after I'd stepped back. "I have to get through a dinner with my ex."

"If you don't mind my asking…" He followed me to the door. "Why did you agree to it?"

I shrugged, walking down the hall. "We got along just fine after the divorce. It's only lately that we've started to clash again. It'll be good to show Jimmy that we all get along."

"*If* you get along."

"I'd be lying if I said that wasn't now a chief concern of mine, especially after all the changing of plans. Matt always gets flustered when plans change. It makes him unreasonable." I paused. "No, unreasonable is too soft of a word. He turns into a passive-aggressive Satan. He learned it from his mom. It is not…pleasant. Hopefully he's not that bad today."

I heard a commotion as I reached the stairs, finding Cyra and Hollace standing next to a large powder-blue box that had been set on the coffee table in the front room. Aurora and Mimi sat on the couch across from them, listening to Cyra animatedly tell a story.

"It was the craziest thing, wasn't it, Hollace?" she was saying.

"Oh yeah, and I was supposed to tell you that they finally arrived," Tristan told me.

"I really don't know how it happened," Hollace said, nodding. Edgar stood in the corner with his hands behind his back, surveying everyone. "We all agreed to skip the detour to Patty's friend's house and come straight here. And then we were somehow having tea with Patty's friend."

"It was like an out-of-body experience, I'm telling you," Cyra said. "None of us could remember when we'd changed the agreement. We just ended up stopping by for a nice bit of tea while they gossiped."

"The detour was happening and no one so much as asked why," Hollace said.

"No, Jessie."

It took me a moment to realize Mimi had spoken to me.

"What?" I asked as I reached the bottom of the

MAGICAL MIDLIFE AWAKENING

stairs.

All eyes turned to me.

"No." Mimi shook her head. "The necklace is wrong and not at all you. The sweater is unsuccessfully trying to make the dress more conservative. Don't dull yourself to please other people."

Tristan stopped beside me, glanced down at my outfit, and continued forward again without comment. He didn't plan on getting involved.

"I get that, but Matt makes these snide comments about the dress code. It's a mood killer. I'd rather avoid it."

Tristan stopped and turned back, his eyes glowing brightly.

"Since when are you the type of woman to alter your taste because of a man's snide comments?" Mimi pushed.

"Honestly, it'll just be easier if I tone things down a bit."

"Easier for whom?" Mimi lifted her eyebrows.

I froze on the word *me*.

Awareness seeped in slowly. I remembered all the times I'd come downstairs and he'd say something like "Is that what you're planning to wear?"—his voice dripping with disdain. Then he'd go on with something like "Well, we don't have time for you to change. Just try not to embarrass me."

Nothing I'd ever worn was right, even if he'd been the one to suggest the outfit. One time I wore *exactly* what he'd said would be best for a corporate function, but when we got there, I was overdressed. He'd turned around and blamed me for getting it wrong, saying, "No, you obviously misheard me." When I recounted the conversation, he'd continued, "For someone who thinks she's so smart, you certainly have a bad memory. I told you *not* to wear something like this. I distinctly warned you that the event would be business casual."

He'd been so adamant, so confident, that I'd almost believed him. If he hadn't also been overdressed, I would've thought I was crazy, remembering something completely different than what had happened.

He'd always made me question myself. It was why I was now so relieved when Mr. Tom picked out crucial outfits or Nessa helped me accessorize. Clearly, I was still worried I'd get it wrong. I'd done exactly as Mimi had said and dulled myself to ensure his approval. That, to me, was knocking it out of the park.

Unsettled and a little confused, I blinked stupidly for a moment. It was like looking in a mirror and not recognizing the reflection in the glass.

"Wear what *you* want," Mimi said softly, as though I needed to be handled with care. "Be confident in yourself. You'll never please others if you can't first please yourself."

"That sounds like good sexual advice, too," Cyra said, nodding.

"Here." Aurora pushed up from the couch and glided over to me, taking the predatory grace of a shifter to new heights. "I'll help. I have an eye for rubbing it in exes' faces."

Up in my room again, I picked through my necklaces while Aurora brought over different options for a cover, one a silk wrap and the other a cashmere shawl.

"Uncle Auzzie always says that you're really easygoing...until you're not." She held up one, and then the other, before lifting the cashmere. I nodded to approve it. "Being easygoing has the potential to attract controlling partners. My first boyfriend was a gaslighting jerk. He had my brain so twisted, I was essentially reduced into a shell. And you ask yourself...*how*, you know? How could I end up in a situation like that? I'm better than that. I don't let others push me around."

She helped me take off my sweater before moving around me to look at the necklaces.

"But they are so charming at first," she went on, picking up a sparkly diamond necklace Austin had bought me a few months ago for no other reason than he thought I might like it. She draped it around my neck and fixed the clasp. "They compliment you endlessly, fawn all over you, tell you you're pretty... The manipulation is gradual. First they blame you for something innocuous. Then they start telling you to calm down when you call them on something they did, or they ignore you when they think you're behaving badly. They pick at you for the very things they once praised you for, right? 'Why are you wearing so much makeup? Are you trying to entice other men?' I got that one a lot. Or 'Why are you so dressed up? You look like a slut.' He got his hooks into me, bro. In the thick of it, he made me start to question reality. He gaslit the fuck out of me. Excuse my language."

I stared at her within the mirror in utter bewilderment. It was the most I'd ever heard her say in one go, and she'd just perfectly described the beginning of our courtship and marriage. Totally spot-on. I felt like I'd been slapped.

"I...feel like my confidence is slowly draining away," I said honestly, suddenly unsure about this dinner. I hadn't expected to feel like this. I hadn't, in a million years, expected to start sliding back into my previous headspace as his wife.

"Hey." She put a hand on my shoulder, connecting with my gaze in the mirror. "I get it. You were with him for twenty years. I was with my ex for less than two. It was hard for me to find my strength after, and my whole world, my *entire* future is predicated upon being strong. It's essential in an alpha. He could've jeopardized everything. That's why my dad is so protective of me now. He saw what I'd been reduced to. But listen, you're not under his thumb anymore. You've found your strength, even after all that time. Now you just have to find a way to assert that you're out from under his control forever." Her fingers squeezed. "You can do it—you just have to keep your head above the bullshit."

My bewilderment was back. "You sound way too mature for your age."

Her smile was dazzling, and I was happy she was relaxed enough around me to show it.

"Honestly, my generation is talking about this stuff a lot more. It sounds like your ex was trying to reduce you to make himself feel more powerful. He tried to control you so he felt in control. Right? Or I am missing the mark?"

"You're...exactly right." I took one final glance at the mirror and left the room, Aurora following me, and started downstairs again.

She nodded beside me, her lips pulling to the side. "Yeah. So many men do it, it's insane. Fragile egos. Women, too. Uncle Auzzie's ex twisted him all up and made him incredibly dangerous. Different scenario, but same manipulation and abuse. People can be the worst."

Back in the front room, Ulric, Jasper, and Patty had joined the others in the gathering around the box.

"I don't think it'll hurt to open it just a little," Patty was saying. "She won't even notice."

"Mom…what?" Ulric demanded. "How would she not notice—and what would even be the point of opening it *a little*?"

"Ah. Here she is." Patty clasped her hands together as I reached the bottom of the stairs. "Oh, Jessie, you look *beautiful*!"

"Yes," Mimi said with a nod of approval. "You do. You're more yourself now."

"Where is Mr. Tom, by the way?" Cyra asked. "I could use a coffee, and I know that he falls all over himself to get those."

"He insisted on guarding Jimmy." I stopped next to the coffee table and looked down at the box. "And considering what's going on with the mages, it probably isn't a bad idea. What is this?"

"It's the delivery," Hollace said. "A courier dropped it off last night with a note from Sebastian saying that Cyra, Edgar, and I should deliver it to you personally."

"From Sebastian?" I asked, feeling my heart rate increasing as I bent to the box. "Why didn't he text me on the encrypted line? Or call me? I've been contacting them for weeks and getting zero in return, and now this?" I paused. "We should probably grab Austin."

"No, no, he's probably busy—let's see what it is," Patty urged, bending over the box with me.

I lifted the lid, pulling the top away.

"It would've been just that easy," Patty murmured. "It could've accidentally happened in the car, even."

Ulric rolled his eyes.

A rectangular envelope lay atop a plastic garment bag. I pulled out a handwritten note.

Jessie –

You need to go to that dinner tomorrow. Wear this dress. Mind the pocket watch. That's now your thing. Play with it as much or as little as you want. Tell Austin to wear the watch you gave him.

Bring Cyra to test the food, though it shouldn't be needed. Bring Dave but use his alternate name. Edgar and Tristan should be there for magical detection and overall scariness.

Try to make friends. These are the good sort of mages you'll be helping. They might be a little arrogant, but most mages are.

Broken Sue should guard the outside door, no watch, along with Mr. Tom in his disguise. You shouldn't bring any more than that or they'll balk.

Most importantly, if <u>anyone</u> attacks you with magic, <u>return fire</u>. It doesn't matter who it is, <u>attack back</u>.

Miss you.

Sebastian

Then, below, in a different pen and clearly as an afterthought, he'd written:

I also put in another brooch for Cyra and the associated spell. You really ought to do something about those gnomes. And don't thank me for the watch. I took it from Ivy House for just such an occasion.

"So he *is* getting my messages," I said, handing the note to Patty because I was sure she was bursting with curiosity. "Yet he hasn't ever replied."

I pulled out the garment bag, handing it off to Tristan to hold, and unzipped it. The dress inside was a silky powder blue with a full skirt. On one side, a pocket had been sewn in with a little loop at the top. A metal chain descended from the loop into the pocket and attached to a very cool gold pocket watch with an intricate, flowerlike pattern. I hadn't even known this was in Ivy House.

"Oh, Jessie, that is just gorgeous," Patty exclaimed, looking at the dress.

"How'd he know about the dinner?" I asked, pulling a pair of white silk gloves from the bottom of the box. "Cyra and Hollace were already on the road when I got the invitation."

"They're clearly doing a great job of strengthening their network." Tristan turned the dress so he could re-zip the garment bag. "Can I see the note?"

Patty handed it over before taking the dress from him. "I'll go hang this in your room, Jessie. We don't want it to get wrinkled."

"He didn't choose a very strong group to go with you," Mimi said with a sniff. "No offense to Edgar, but it might be better for Broken Sue to be on the inside, not guarding the door."

"Mages fear the weird," I told her, checking the time. We needed to get going. "He suggested bringing the people who will make the mages the most nervous. It'll in turn make them think I'm more powerful. I'm not quite sure about the logic, but he'd know. If he's telling me to go, he's not worried about the danger they pose."

"Except he told you to return fire if anyone attacks,"

Ulric said.

"That's just common sense." I replaced the lid on the box for unknown reasons before heading into the kitchen to see how Austin was doing. He'd wanted to make a dessert to bring.

He was sitting at the round kitchen table, his black dress shirt crisp, his shoulders looking fine and muscular, with the harsh afternoon light glowing through his tousled hair.

"Hey," I said, noticing a serving platter with chocolate-covered strawberries wrapped with cling film.

He stood, checking his watch for the time. The face glittered with diamonds. "Hey, baby." He looked me up and down and smiled, his swagger prominent as he crossed the distance to wrap his arms around my waist. "You look beautiful. Are we really supposed to be so dressed up just for a dinner at their house?"

"Yeah, it's his thing. He'll have Camila pull out all the stops. I thought you were going to make a Bundt cake."

"I was, but I like this option better. It'll remind me of our fondue forays when you wrap those lips around the fruit."

I ran my palms up his chest as fire flashed through my body. "And now I will think of that, too."

"That was my hope." He kissed me lightly and waited for me to wipe the lipstick away. "Ready?"

"Yup." A wave of butterflies filled my middle. I sure hoped this didn't go badly.

CHAPTER 12

JESSIE

AUSTIN ROLLED UP outside of the house in his fancy car, still sporting all of that swagger. He didn't get out of the car right away, though, even though we were ten minutes late. He stalled, capturing my hand.

"Why are you nervous?" he asked, lacing his fingers through mine.

I took a deep breath, not really wanting to be honest. I knew he was giddy about staking his claim in front of my ex, and the magical part of me was eager for him to do it. The Jane, though, still had a lot of misgivings. Those feelings Aurora had picked up on weren't so easy to shake.

"Matt hates any sort of confrontation," I admitted, looking out the window because I didn't want to look at Austin.

I felt weak, like I wasn't in control. Like I'd fail at any moment, which was insane, because it was just a semi-casual dinner and I wasn't hosting. Unlike with my last couple of formal dinners, this one posed zero risk. So we didn't get along—so what? My son was grown, and his dad and I didn't need to be best pals. We could be civil when we had to see each other, and that was that.

But my stomach was churning and a cold sweat had beaded on my skin. This was exactly how I felt when I'd gone to gatherings with Matt in the past. If things didn't go perfectly, I'd get the fallout. His words could be so cutting, so terrible, that I'd be reduced to tears and a lack of self-worth. The memories were suddenly so fresh that I was choking on them.

"He can make a night utterly miserable," I said, struggling to get my bearings.

Keep your head above the bullshit, Aurora had told me before we walked out the door. I was suddenly so glad she'd come to Los Angeles with us.

"I'm here." Austin reached over to put his fingers on my chin and pull my face his way. His eyes were so gorgeous and blue, so open and raw. "I'm here for you. Always. Don't forget that. The past is a hard terrain to walk through, but we'll do it together. I guarantee he will not make your night miserable. I will not let that happen, okay? Trust me."

I let my head fall against the headrest and gave him

a thankful smile. Because I was with this man, not the one lurking inside, and my life was so much more beautiful than I'd thought possible. "Okay."

"Okay." He let go of my hand and opened his door. I did the same, waiting for him to come grab the chocolate-covered strawberries from my lap and help haul me out. He laced my fingers with his again as we walked toward the front stoop. "I thought you said he had a new, big, fancy house."

I took in the surroundings, the stale neighborhood with no real personality, the yard with not one leaf out of place, and the moderately sized dwelling that looked like a toy compared to Ivy House. The land was mostly barren of natural trees; instead the streets had planted saplings affixed to posts with rubber ties to ensure they grew straight and uniform. The bushes were all…too perfect for my tastes. It was as though the builders had come through, purposely stripped away all that was natural and wild, and replaced it with uninspired architecture and unoriginal plant life, aiming for an all-American vibe and landing instead on "good enough."

I glanced up on impulse. I knew gargoyles were in the sky, circling until the coast was clear and they could come down and blend in.

"This is his version of a big, fancy house. Once it might've been mine," I said as I pushed the doorbell.

"Things have certainly changed. I wouldn't go back to living in a neighborhood like this for all the peace in the world."

"That's good to know," Austin murmured as heels clicked against hardwood behind the door.

"He would never answer doors," I mumbled. "I always had to do it. Not Jimmy, even. Me, as the woman of the house. If I wasn't home and he was, the door didn't get answered. Looks like Camila is running with that baton."

"I mean no offense, but that didn't strike you as odd?"

"It really should have, right?" I huffed as the lock clicked over. "He'd said it was how things were done in an affluent household. At the time, I wanted to please him and also…fit the image of a wealthy woman. You saw my parents' house. It felt like a big step up in life."

"And now look, you're beyond wealthy on your own terms. You can open doors without even getting up, but if you do, you'll get chewed out by your old-as-dirt, somewhat senile, very grumpy gargoyle butler."

I spat out a laugh as the door swung open to the woman I'd seen on social media with her new, gleaming engagement ring. Her pretty face was fresh, and her eyes sparkled with genuine happiness. She wore a gray dress, dusting just above her knees, with three-quarter-length sleeves and a cinched-in belt at her waist. It would've been plain if not for the interesting neckline, cut a little off center and connecting with a shiny black button on the right. The buttons continued down past her waist, adding a little flair. As I'd expected, a row of pearls adorned her neck.

"Jacinta, it's so nice to meet you," she said, her smile stretching wide. She reached out a hand. "I'm Camila."

"Call me Jessie, please. Hello, nice to meet you." I shook her hand before turning a bit. "Allow me to introduce my boyfriend—partner, I mean. Austin." Flustered, I finished, "We live together. Because it's permanent."

Abort! Abort!

"Hello." Austin balanced the dessert platter on one hand and reached the other forward for a handshake.

"Hi," Camila said, dazed for a moment as she took him in. She cleared her throat, stepping back. "Hello! Welcome."

"These are for you." Austin pushed the platter forward.

"Oh." The smile was back in full force. "Thank you so much! You didn't have to do that."

"Crap," I said, glancing back at the car. "I meant to bring a bottle of wine as well." I grimaced at her. "I'm so sorry. I totally forgot."

"Don't worry about it!" She leaned in a little. "We have plenty."

"Camila," came Matt's disapproving voice from the interior of the house. "How long do you intend to strand our guests on the porch?"

Her smile dwindled rapidly, and a cagey look lit her eyes. "Oh my—I'm so sorry. Please, come in."

She stepped to the side of the door, her shoulders tensed. I knew exactly how she was feeling—my heart also quickened upon hearing that familiar tone.

"It's fine, really." I waved away her sudden concern as Austin ran his hand along my shoulders, from one side to the other, before lightly trailing it down my back, offering quiet support. I leaned into his touch for a moment, stilling myself, taking a breath. Matt did not own my world anymore. This dinner was at his house, but that did not give him sole control of the proceedings. We could leave whenever we wished.

The front room was just as stale as the neighborhood, with light gray walls, a dark gray wraparound couch, and a plain beige rug beneath it. A glass coffee table held a vase filled with a bouquet of white roses, a necessity for Matt every time we'd entertained. A painting one might find in a hotel hung on the wall behind the couch.

Matt stood from his seat at the end of the couch,

laying a Pottery Barn catalog down on the coffee table. He wore a light blue button-up shirt with black slacks and black shoes he'd probably had Camila polish. Jimmy, on the opposite side of the couch, stood as well, his smile bright and his clothes equally formal, if a little rumpled.

I could feel Mr. Tom moving around the perimeter of the house, checking things out or maybe just stretching his legs. He hadn't been moving much while he was here, and I guessed that was because Jimmy had stayed in his room a lot. I wasn't sure how the eating and bathroom situation was working for him and was honestly a little afraid to ask. I wasn't sure what lengths Mr. Tom would go to watch over Jimmy (though my heart squished every time I thought about his devotion to my son).

"Hey, bud." I gave him a tight hug. "Did you guys have fun the last couple days? Have you settled in?"

"Jacinta, please," Matt said, his tone disapproving. "You're suffocating the young man. It has only been a couple of days. He's well able to live his life without his mother hanging over him at every turn."

"I already don't like him," Ivy House whispered in my mind. *"Set him on fire, lock him in a closet to burn up, and be done with it."*

It really spoke to my anger and frustration at Matt's

comment that I half contemplated her suggestion. He was definitely in one of his moods.

Trying to keep the peace and hopefully lighten things up, I widened my eyes at my son, who was accustomed to his father's outbursts, and dropped my hands. I faced my ex. He looked older than I remembered. His eyes were tight and his jaw clenched, etching the opposite of laugh lines into his skin from years of disapproval. His hair was slicked with a severe part to the side, and while before it had somehow seemed refined and cultured, now it seemed uptight and too greasy. His posture was still great, but his affluent air seemed strangely lacking. His power and dominance definitely were. Time had altered my perception of him.

"Your wrap is gorgeous," Camila said, still holding the dessert. "Just let me know if you get too hot and would like me to take it."

"Oh, here." I unslung it from my shoulders and crossed to the coatrack by the door. "I've got it."

"I see not much has changed." Matt gave Austin a commiserating smile. "She never did know how to dress for the occasion. One would think we were headed to a disco."

I barely stopped my shoulders from tensing. *Here we go.*

When I made it back to him, Austin slipped an arm

around my waist. His anger burned through the bonds, but his tone was easy and nonchalant.

"Disco… When's the last time you heard that term?" He chuckled as he looked down at me intimately, creating a private joke at Matt's expense. "I'd like every day to be a disco if it means you're going to dress this fancy and look so gorgeous."

I smiled at him gratefully and snuggled in a little closer. A soft smile soaked into Camila's expression as she watched us.

Matt's eyes narrowed slightly. "And what is it you do…" His smile was condescending. "Forgive me for not knowing your name. Jacinta has forgotten to introduce us."

"Austin," he said as he stepped forward with his hand out. "I'm an investor, but I also deal in manpower and textiles, selling services and some wholesale products. It's a family business, handed down, though my brother is heading up his leg of the organization from Wyoming."

"I see," Matt said, his gaze shrewd as he shook Austin's hand. It was a look I'd seen a million times. He was sizing up Austin's possible net worth. "Lucky our Jessie found someone like you so quickly. I worried she wouldn't be able to make it on her own."

Power surged from Austin. His gaze turned vicious.

"All due respect." His hand visibly tightened, and he yanked Matt a little closer. "She isn't *our* Jessie," he growled, and Matt's eyes rounded. "She is *my* Jessie. Take care when you address her."

"S-sure. Yes, fine," Matt stammered, pain flaring in his eyes from the punishing grip.

Austin let go and leaned away, hugging me closer. As though none of that had just happened, he continued in a neutral tone, "I couldn't have done it without her. She's been integral in building our investor list." His anger still burned bright through the bonds, but he'd smoothed it from his face. "She's the co-leader of our organization."

He looked down on me with a soft smile, his devotion to me evident. I knew it wasn't just for show. I could feel the sentiment through our bonds. He was just making sure Matt saw it, too.

"Should you not put that in the kitchen?" Matt asked Camila in a sharp tone. "We'd hate for Jacinta's hard work to melt."

"Oh, actually, Austin made those." I put a hand on his chest and smiled in pride. "He is excellent in the kitchen."

Camila smiled tightly at Austin, apologized, and hurried away.

I watched her, memories of those hurried strides

rising to the surface.

"I apologize, Austin," Matt said, inching away but with squared shoulders. He wanted distance but was trying to save face. "We didn't want to put you out. Jessie always made the desserts and things around here. She never did have an affinity for it, I guess. You weren't too fond of it, were you, hon? That sort of thing shows in the finished product."

"Then it's a wonder why she didn't have help." Austin's gaze was intense. "Don't call her *hon*. I will not tell you again."

His unbridled intensity pulsed through the room, coating my body in goosebumps. The threat was plain, and it was equally plain that he could carry out said threat with zero effort. He would play "easygoing" for many things, but someone being too familiar with his mate was a line he wouldn't allow to be crossed.

CHAPTER 13

JESSIE

HEAT COURSED THROUGH me, my gargoyle responding. I ran my hand up Austin's chest, not hearing Matt's response. I only registered that he quickly crossed the room to exit toward what must've been the kitchen. I pulled Austin's face down and captured his lips for a moment, sinking into his kiss.

"I love you," I murmured before wrapping my arms around his neck for a hug.

"And I love you," he replied as I finally pulled away.

It was only then I noticed Jimmy still standing by the couch.

"Sorry," I said immediately, crinkling my nose at him. "Too much mushy stuff, I know."

He shrugged. "It's fine. It's nice to see you happy. But…" He stepped closer, shooting a glance toward the kitchen. "He's been livid since Mr. Tom dropped me off. He's in one of those *moods*. It probably just got worse. Watch out."

"What does that mean, one of his *moods*?" Austin asked.

"Jimmy, why don't you…go see what they're doing. We'll be there in a minute," I said, not wanting to have this conversation in front of my son.

He nodded and left before I tried to explain to Austin.

"Matt gets…like…intensely passive-aggressive. There's no pleasing him. If you try to make it better, he belittles you. If you try to push back, he minimizes you until you feel like you're in the wrong."

"Is there physical violence?" Austin asked in a low, rough voice.

"No, nothing like that," I said quickly. "It's just… It's a head-wreck. It's what I was worried about in the car. It makes you feel like garbage, basically. It happened every so often when we were married. I tried to shield Jimmy from it as much as possible, but…he knows the signs."

Austin's eyes sparked fire. His hand found the small of my back, guiding me forward. Under his breath, I barely heard him whisper, "We'll see about this *mood*."

"Just kill him," Ivy House said. *"You could snap his neck like a twig. End him."*

But even if I'd be fine with killing my son's father,

this wasn't that kind of battle. It wasn't a fistfight, or a magical attack to be thwarted.

No, this was a mental battle—the kind of fight I'd never learned how to protect myself from. At the time, I hadn't even thought it necessary. Other moms in my circle had seemed happy in similar situations. They'd seemed well adjusted.

Or maybe they were just better actors…

I took a deep breath.

"It's fine," I said for no reason as we walked through a formal dining room with the place settings perfectly laid out, the napkins matching the table runner in the middle. Two tapered candles waited to be lit on either side of a basket of fresh flowers.

I'd laid out a very similar table, picking the pieces out of a catalog so I was sure they'd go together. I remembered agonizing over the flowers, knowing Matt would point out my lack of etiquette if I got it wrong. He'd never helped me learn, though, if there was even a guide.

I hadn't thought about that since the divorce. The supposed need for "proper" flowers and place settings had never once crossed my mind since our parting. If I hadn't come to this space and seen the same thing play out with a different actor, I never would've remembered.

My grip was tight on Austin's hand where it rested on my hip as we entered the kitchen. Matt was just around the edge of the island, leaning down into Camila's space, murmuring to her.

Her face was drawn, her knuckles white from grasping her hands in front of her. I knew the sort of "pep talk" she was getting. He was taking out his frustrations over how it was going with Austin and me on her. He was blaming her for any number of things that were not her fault, but that she would feel responsible for.

My stomach knotted at the sight. At the memory of what it had felt like. During those moments, I'd wanted so desperately to cry and give up, but doing so would only have ended with his taunting me over my "hysterics." He would cite how emotional women were, ineffective at even the simplest of tasks. He'd tell me to stop sniveling or, worse, ask why I couldn't be more like Charlie's wife, with her perfect taste and beauty, or John's wife, with her amicable chatter and exceptional cooking prowess. He'd then flirt with those women, usually in front of me, shedding his charm on them while I struggled to fix the many things that had somehow been my fault.

"I would've gotten that account if the dinner party had gone more smoothly. Why did you have to tell that joke? Why didn't you get along with his wife a little

better? I swear, you weigh this family down. If it weren't for me, I don't know how you'd ever survive, Jacinta."

Once again, I felt steeped in memories of the past. Why had I agreed to come at all?

Keep your head above the bullshit.

I shrugged off the memories, feeling my anger kindle as Matt straightened up and stepped away from Camila. His smile was charming.

"We were just finalizing our dinner plans," he said, walking away from the island a little.

"Where's Jimmy?" I asked. "I saw him come in here."

"I sent him up to his room for the time being," Matt replied. "I figured it would give the adults a chance to talk. He'll meet us back down here for dinner."

"You sent…" I swallowed my irritation and tried to steady my anger. He would stonewall me if I seemed cross. "Forget for a moment that he's an adult now, not a child you can send to his room. He's only home from college for a short time. The whole point of having this dinner was to present a united front as a family. Sending him away doesn't do much to promote that ideal. Don't you want to visit with him?"

"Jacinta, please." Matt's smile tightened. "You don't need to make this into an argument. Let's just *try* to have a good time for once, can't we?" He shifted his focus to Austin without skipping a beat. "Austin, would you care for a glass of scotch?" He put one hand on his stomach and lifted the other, motioning in the direction we'd just come from. "I'd love to hear more about your business while the girls finish up in the kitchen."

"A glass of wine would be fine, thanks," Austin said, pulling his arm from around me and unbuttoning his shirt sleeves. "Camila, I can give you a hand. What do you need?"

She paused in grabbing the wine bottle, a confused smile on her face. "Oh no, that's okay. I have it all organized."

"Yes, don't trouble—"

"In my family," Austin interrupted Matt, rolling up first one sleeve and then the other, showing off his muscular forearms, "food is a love language. I love to cook, especially for my m—partner. I'd be honored to cook for her extended family. How can I help?"

"Be that as it may, I think we can give the girls time to get to know each other," Matt said, raising his voice to reclaim the group's focus. His nerves were starting to fray, I could tell. "It's much more fitting if we head out for a scotch. Leave them to gossip. I'm sure they would thank you for it."

Staying calm was not easy with Ivy House drum-ming power through me, muttering about flames and rope and closets. Why she wanted him thrust into a small space while lit up, I couldn't say, but she wouldn't let it go.

"I'm fine where I am," Austin said. His demeanor, the strength of his stare, and his rush of intensity made it clear he would not be backing down.

Matt flinched, bowing his usually straight posture just a little. In a moment, though, he lifted his chin in indignation. Frustrated anger made his shoulders tense. This man could bounce back on a dime. Likely it meant he'd zeroed in on someone to kick around until he felt in control again.

"Here, I'll just get that scotch." Camila hurried to a cabinet at the side of the kitchen. "I can get it right here."

"Jacinta, might I have a word?" Matt's tone was ice.

My stomach rolled.

I knew how he could hurt me. It was worse than a knife wound, worse than injuries sustained in battle, because this was personal. He would hold up the most vulnerable aspects of me—the parts only a loved one would know about—and use them to cut me to the quick.

"Yeah, sure." I caught Austin's wary look as I followed Matt out into the front room.

Keep your head above the bullshit.

He stopped in the center of the space with his hands on his hips like he was surveying a pothole that might damage his Lexus.

"You've sure got him fooled, huh?" he said.

"What do you mean?" I asked guardedly.

"How else would you find someone so forgiving? Then again, you haven't been together long. If he really knew you, like I know you, he'd know how erratic you are. How incapable of living on your own. You can't provide for yourself. You didn't even to go college."

He'd gone for the throat right out of the gate.

I balled my fists, because he wasn't entirely wrong. Not finishing college was one of my biggest regrets, and yes, I'd had no idea what I was going to do with myself after the divorce. If it weren't for Ivy House, I had no idea what sort of career I could've put together. How I would've paid the mortgage on a house after using the divorce settlement for a down payment. Austin had given me half of his estate, but I had nothing solidly my own, not without Ivy House.

Struggling with self-doubt, I pushed back. "*You* were the reason I didn't finish college, and you know it," I gritted out. "Remember? You convinced me to drop out after two years, saying it was time for marriage and a family. That I could go back later. But then *later*, when I could've gone back, you said we didn't have the money and I was needed at home. I sacrificed for this family, for what *you* wanted. Holding it against me is—"

"Yes, because I was supporting you. You wanted to go to school when you should've wanted to get a job and help with the bills. But no, you were more than happy to spend my money, and now you're blaming me for your life's choices."

"What are you even talking about? First of all, it was *our* money. Second, you wouldn't let me get a job! Not to mention being at home *was* a job. A very demanding job."

"Being a wife and mother was somehow more demanding than being a husband and father who worked sixty hours a week? You got to stay home all day while I put a roof over your head and food on the table."

"All you did was work. That's it! I took care of literally everything else in your life. Food was bought and made for you, your social engagements planned, your errands run, your child—"

"Jacinta, I have given you the courtesy of listening to your wild opinions. Now you will listen to what I have to say. I find it incredibly disrespectful that you would change my plans with Jimmy on a whim. Even more disrespectful that you would allow someone *else* to drop him off. Someone clearly unhinged. Do you know that person was wearing a cape and talking about being a butler? You allow this character to hang around our son?"

"First, it was Jimmy who originally changed plans, and that was because *you* arranged for someone else to pick him up after saying you were going to do it. Second—"

"That is utterly incorrect. This is what I mean. You twist words and now events to try to suit your needs. *I* was going to pick Jimmy up. We discussed that."

"Except you changed the plan and were going to have Camila do it."

"I did no such thing. I was always going to pick him up, and he knew that. He said you missed him and wanted him at your house, so he went to make you feel better. Jacinta, is this what you need to do to be the center of attention? Lie?"

"What are you talking about?" I said, desperately trying to think back through the muddle of my thoughts to when Jimmy had arrived. My frustration and anger were making things slippery. "No—"

"We had the whole week planned, and then your selfishness made him feel guilty. That isn't fair to the boy. To make matters worse, you specifically told me that you would personally drop him off, and then you send him with some strange character in a superhero outfit. He just waltzed into this house like he owned the place. Is this your version of a joke, jeopardizing our child?"

"I'm not jeopardizing anything! Mr. Tom looks after Jimmy like he's his own child. More so, actually, and I didn't say I'd be dropping him off. I knew that I couldn't, so—"

"His own child? Just how many people are you dating?"

The whiplash of that comment pulled me up short for a moment as I tried to process what he was accusing me of this time.

"Besides," he went on, not allowing me to have a moment to form any semblance of an educated rebuttal, "I distinctly remember your telling me you were going to drop him off."

"I couldn't have said that, Matt," I replied, now trying to remember specifics from our previous conversation so I could prove him wrong verbatim. My voice rose, because I knew he was trying to twist me up. "I had something come up, and I knew I wouldn't be able to. I remember that specifically. Besides, what does it actually matter if—"

"You need to calm down. There is no need to shout." He blew out an exasperated breath. "I don't know why I bother trying to speak to you. You always blow everything out of proportion."

My mouth dropped open. "*I* blow everything out of proportion?" I said incredulously, my volume still high and my anger rising. "You're the one—"

"No." He put his hand in front of my face. "I will not tolerate yelling. You are clearly too emotional to discuss this in a rational manner. When you've calmed down, maybe we can have an intelligent conversation. I swear, Jacinta, when your new man-friend realizes how you change facts and bend the truth, he won't be around much longer."

He shook his head in disdain as he about-faced and strode from the room.

"Kill him," Ivy House said as I watched him go. *"He's the sort of man the last heirs would've gone for. He'll end up trying to kill you, trust me. Kill him before he gets the chance."*

CHAPTER 14

NIAMH

"THE TRICK IS, girl, you have to establish yerself in a place before ye go plying people for information."

Niamh sat slightly hunched over the bar, at the end, a couple stools from the wall, where she could see most of the comings and goings. The size of the place made it easy. A fairly tiny affair, it had a few booths, a few high tables, and a row of ten barstools before the corner and three after. A door at the front allowed in all the traffic, and one at the back led to the *jacks*—two toilets, one urinal, and a couple of twisted holes where the signs used to be. It was a free-for-all back there, pee everywhere. At least the locks worked, not that Niamh cared. When she used the loo, not many guys were thrilled to witness it. She had no idea why. Maybe it was the large silver bush or the inviting wave she gave any looky-loos. Semi-innocent Peeping Toms were an uneasy sort.

"Ye don't just waltz in, ask a bunch of questions, slurp down yer beer, and sashay back out again. That's a surefire way ta get noticed."

Niamh rattled her ice in her glass and settled it at the end of the bar. The barman, a portly fellow with no real interest in the patrons, making drinks, or moving, took a little encouragement. It was why Niamh had two drinks going at the same time. One to drink while the barman loaded up the other, then switch.

"Ye especially don't go all dolled up to a place like Bruster's or the Dirty Puck, are ye jokin'? Ye're much too pretty to go doin' something like that."

Aurora leaned heavily against the bar top, a shot of whiskey in a double glass sitting in front of her with soda in a glass behind it. She'd asked for a whiskey sour, and this drink was the barman's response.

"How'd you even know I was out?" the girl asked, clearly bewildered.

"Do ye think I'm an *eejit*, do ya?"

Aurora gave her a blank stare.

"A drop-dead gorgeous young woman walks into a bar…" Niamh started.

"I think I've heard this one," the barman said as he moseyed his way closer and reached for the empty glass. "Oh wait, no. I haven't. Because hot chicks do not walk into bars like this unless they are selling something.

Usually themselves."

Niamh stared at him with a dispassionate expression. "Well, God almighty, he can speak. What a real fecking treat."

He shrugged. "You're the one telling the joke."

"I'm not tellin' a joke, I'm lookin' at one. And yes ye have heard of it, or didn't ye just mention the hot chicks sellin' themselves? Get on wit' ya and get me that drink. Ye're as *slow*… If I had a horse as slow as ye, I'd sell it to the glue factory."

"You should drink faster. It might improve your personality."

"The logic train doesn't stop at yer station, does it?" She tsked at him as he walked away, staring holes in his back. She raised her voice. "If ye'd move faster, I would drink faster!"

Aurora watched the scene with her father's straight face, giving absolutely nothing away.

"Do ye play poker?" Niamh asked her. "If not, ye should. Find some Dicks, start a game, and clean up. Anyway—"

"Why doesn't the bartender kick you out?"

There it was, hidden in her tone. She was incredulous and bewildered. Figured. She was a novice at the pubs, only having been in the ones around her pack. The people there probably treated her as the alpha's daughter. Royalty, or near enough.

Not here. Here, she fit in with all the pretty, rich Los Angelenos, a face for the big screen and a body from (they would assume) the gym. She wore nice clothing, hair and makeup like she should be hitting a posh club…but she was on her own in seedy bars without the least bit of nervousness. None of it added up, and guys in bars talked. A lot. They were the biggest gossips in the history of the world. Not even Patty could compete with the likes of them.

"He doesn't kick me out because he likes being razzed. Ye gotta know yer crowd and how to talk to them."

"And why do I need to know that?"

"Because if ye are gonna go out, ye should at least help the team. And I knew it was ye because of yer description, including the failure to smile or show any sort of emotion. That description and the distance from the bar hotel were dead giveaways, like. Far enough away to take too long for a human, but just close enough that a big tiger, who made a couple homeless men question their sanity and/or proximity to the zoo, could make it there handy enough. If Naomi goes out lookin' for ya, she probably won't find ya. I assume that's why ye chose a dive bar. Or should I say dive bar*zzz*, since this is the third one ye've hit up tonight."

Aurora sighed. "Yes, which is why I was obviously surprised when you *did* find me."

"Different league, kid. Take a lesson. Literally. I'm handing 'em out free; write them down."

Aurora stared at Niamh for a long moment. "You have cased all the bars in the area, got gossip on me, *and* made friends with homeless guys?"

"Aye."

"All in three days?"

"Three days and one evening. It's real easy in this town. Dicks and Janes aren't suspicious creatures when it comes to old women, mages aren't suspicious of Dicks and Janes, which is what I look like, and I stay out of the shifter territory where they could smell me. Ah, here comes Broken Sue. He probably followed the breadcrumbs as well. He's not real pretty, but he's got a little something between his ears."

"You don't think he's handsome?" Aurora looked at Niamh. "Are you blind?"

"You might use a *little* expression, girl, or people are goin'ta think ye're stuffed full o' Botox. No, he's too troubled to be pretty. Too much baggage makes Dick a very dull boy."

"I feel like you're just talking nonsense."

It was a fair assessment.

Broken Sue stalked down the bar like he'd just won

a bar fight and intended to start another. The handful of patrons gave him a wary look, the rougher among them staring hard. That was, until he stared back. Then they dropped their gazes down to their hands and slumped over their beers. It seemed no one in this bar was drunk or stupid, and certainly not both.

The barman put Niamh's filled cider on the bar, and she drained the current one and pushed it forward. He wrapped his chubby hands around it but didn't move, watching as Broken Sue stopped at the corner and stared down at Aurora.

"You shouldn't be out by yourself," he growled. "And you *definitely* shouldn't have left without telling anyone where you'd gone."

"I'm not out by myself." Aurora hooked a thumb Niamh's way.

"Are you calling me stupid?" His intensity increased, his power swirling around them.

She looked up at him as her own power started to pump out, two alphas not liking the other throwing their weight around. The difference was, one of them held seniority in the pack and a lot more experience, and the other had better lower her gaze or there would be hell to pay.

As if hearing Niamh, Aurora dropped her eyes before taking a sip of her whiskey. She crinkled her nose.

"What'd they call you?" the barman asked Broken Sue.

"Sue." He sat on the stool kitty-corner from Aurora. He reached for her glass, stopping with his big hand around it, but splayed his fingers out a bit, asking permission to take it.

Aurora's movement was so subtle, Niamh would have missed it if she hadn't been watching. She only knew what it meant because Broken Sue's question had been so clear.

His fingers touched down, and he pulled the glass to him, running it under his nose before pressing it to his lips. Aurora watched his mouth, then her gaze dipped to his bobbing Adam's apple.

Broken Sue lowered the glass to the top of the bar and then pushed it. "Pour that down the sink. It's garbage."

"What are ye on about?" Niamh scoffed. "Here, send it over here. Don't waste whiskey, are ye mad?"

"It's cheap," Broken Sue replied.

"So are ye, but we don't throw ye out, now do we? Aurora, give that here." Niamh waved it on.

Aurora did as she was told, now watching Niamh as she upended the glass and drank down the contents.

"How do you do?" the barman asked Broken Sue.

"Ah, fer feck's sake," Niamh murmured, pushing

the glass forward. "C'mere, get the ugly man an expensive whiskey, would ya? Get the girl a girly drink—"

"Two shots of Woodford Reserve, one neat, one with a couple cubes of ice and a twist. Make sure the twist is clean."

"Ah…" The barman scratched his stomach as he looked toward the containers down the bar. "Yeah, I can do a twist."

"It's scrapin' off a part of the lemon rind," Niamh said as the barman moved away. "Don't put yerself out, like."

"Never do," he called over his shoulder.

Aurora half glanced at Broken Sue, and apparently that meant something, because he replied, "I didn't want bad whiskey to put you off the drink. They don't have any good whiskey, so I ordered you a bourbon. If you don't like it, at least you gave it a fair shot."

Niamh didn't notice any movement from her, but his slight incline of the head was usually his way of saying, *You're welcome.*

"Crap on a crust of bread, yis are a coupla mimes. I'm regretting ye tracking us down," she told Broken Sue.

He stared at her. Aurora stared at her. Neither had any expression whatsoever.

"Forget thinking ye have Botox—people are goin'ta

think yis are a coupla mannequins. It's disconcerting. Try a smile or a frown or a fart, I don't care. Do *something*, like."

"How'd you find me?" Aurora asked Broken Sue.

"Your scent. It's distinctive. And it lingers."

"Why aren't ye with Jessie and them, though?" Niamh asked.

"Naomi said Aurora was missing. She hadn't checked in or told anyone she was leaving."

"In my old pack, when we were off duty," Aurora said, "we were *off* duty. We didn't have babysitters."

The two stared at each other for a long moment before Aurora slowly pulled her gaze away, a beat shy of a challenge.

Broken Sue continued to look at her. "You are not in your old pack. You are also not in the home territory of your new pack. You are traveling in hostile conditions. In this situation, we *check in*. You report to the alphas or to me. If all of us are indisposed, you report to the most senior of the pack. I was told you'd had extensive training and think you're ready for your own pack. I shouldn't have to explain the basics to you."

She snapped her head back to him, her body minutely tensing.

"You are also here for family reasons, invited personally by the alphas," he went on, his powerful stare beating into hers. She held it, refusing to back down.

Niamh watched with a small smirk. Maybe she was glad he'd tracked them down after all. This was bloody good entertainment.

"And?" Aurora pushed, clearly out to get his goat, because any fool would know what he meant.

"Given we are in a potentially hostile situation, or at the least an unknown situation, you need to communicate where you're going to your uncle or Naomi or Jessie, because she will worry the most and scour the world looking for you." He paused for a moment. "You know this, I see, so why didn't you check in?"

Again she held his stare. Niamh rested her chin on her hand and her elbow on the bar, watching them. Power coiled between them as if they were two rams gearing up to butt heads. This time, after Aurora finally turned away, Broken Sue softened his tone.

"I understand wanting independence," he told her, "but the timing isn't right for solitude. If you want to see the world away from your family, pick a partner on the team to go with you."

"Like who?" she asked. "Who's going to allow me to let my hair down without running to my uncle and telling him what I'm doing and who I'm doing it with?"

Niamh's grin spread as Broken Sue's eyes darkened. That had thrown him for a wee loop.

He didn't speak, and Aurora nodded slightly.

"Exactly," she said.

"Bollocks," Niamh said as the barman returned with the Woodford, lifting the straight-up shot until Broken Sue pointed at the bar in front of him. The barman delivered Aurora's before turning to get Niamh's next cider, always instructed to fill the empty glass. Two other people down the bar were waiting for their turn to order. It didn't hurry the barman in the slightest. "If ye'd take the lessons I'm tryin' ta feed ya, ye could hop around the bars with me. Tristan would keep yer secrets, no problem. And if it's a little fun ye're interested in, ye don't even need to leave yer room. The gargoyles would come to you. Line 'em up and take as many as ye want. They don't mind. They're happy to share. It's only this great lummox who's a spoilsport. Steer clear of him. Bad news. This is what I meant about baggage. Too much of it, if ye ask me. Way too much. And his stare is much too loud. It deafens me."

"Okay." The barman was back, setting down the bottle of cider. "Oh, right. Ice."

Broken Sue lifted his glass slowly, staring into Niamh's face. He was so easy to rile up now that she knew his buttons. At least the pressure was off Aurora.

CHAPTER 15

AUSTIN

"**D**O YOU HAVE an apron?" Austin asked Camila.

He didn't like the frame of mind Jess was in. Being here, she was clearly reliving old horrors. He knew what that was like, having done his fair share of it recently.

This situation was a little different, though. Jess had clearly been conditioned to act and react in a certain way in that relationship, living with a monster dressed in a businessman's clothing. She'd been stuffed into a box of expectation when she was young and manipulated and emotionally abused into staying there. Austin could see the signs.

Camila was walking down the same path: younger, impressionable, and now financially dependent as a stay-at-home wife. Austin would bet Matt would knock her up soon to trap her in. This guy had a system. A system that clearly worked.

It was hard to stay back and let that man talk to her so disrespectfully, but this was something Jess needed. She was struggling to throw off the chains of her Jane conditioning. She would, though. She'd snap and assert herself. When she did, the explosion would be epic. *That* was when Austin would lean in and seal this dude's coffin. Not before. He wouldn't deny Jess her glory.

For now, he would show Camila what a real man was like.

"An…apron?" Camila randomly walked to the oven, flustered.

He opened his arms and looked down at his dress shirt. "Food splatter is hard to get off."

She breathed out a small, nervous smile. "True. Good point. Um…" She opened the pantry door and lifted one of the aprons hanging on the back. "It's…kind of feminine."

"My masculinity isn't so fragile as to be threatened by an apron."

He waited patiently while she pulled out a white apron with black stencils of high-tea tables and candelabra and English-style cottages. The bottom was a little ruffled, like a skirt, the design incorporating black lines in what looked like an homage to a French maid mini-apron. It also had a large black bow accentuating the right hip. It was really cute, actually, and if Jess were wearing it without any clothes underneath, it would be incredibly sexy. Given she wanted to learn how to cook (in a fun and loving environment), he had a feeling this would be a perfect gift.

"I had to…" Camila, face tinged crimson, undid a knot she'd tied at the top to make it hang properly.

Raised voices drifted from the front room and raw emotion rolled through the bonds—anger and surprise and frustration and misery.

He took a deep breath as he pulled the apron on and tied it around his waist. "The contour is a little lost on me. I think this was made for people with hips."

Camila laughed, her face redder now. "Yes, I think so. I just… If I'd known you would be cooking, I would've gotten—"

"No, no." He held up a hand and began looking through the cabinets for a glass. "Don't apologize for having the right features to show this apron off. I'm jealous."

He gave her a disarming smile as he found a glass and poured himself some wine. Jess's anger was amplifying.

"Do you want a glass?" He pulled out one for Jess and hesitated before taking out a third.

"Oh…uh…" Camila was still standing in front of

the open pantry. "Yeah, sure. I'll just…" She hesitantly pulled out another apron, this one pink with darker pink flowers, lime-green straps, a matching belt around the middle, and pockets.

"Oh, I see, you gave me the one without pockets." He shook his head and tsked. "Selfish."

She laughed a little more freely, pulling it on. "Yes. You've caught me. Us ladies pine for pockets."

Shouting rang through the house, and Camila tensed.

"Wine?" Austin asked, monitoring Jess through the bonds. Intense anger and confusion. Bewilderment. Austin would bet he was spinning her head around. Matt seemed to have a knack for manipulation. It made Austin want to punch him, which wasn't something Janes could usually get away with. Dicks either. This guy was probably litigious.

"Sure. Sorry about—"

"No need to apologize." Austin poured her a glass and set it to the side for her. Usually a shifter wouldn't offer another female food or drink, but this woman didn't know those rules. She'd think it was a slight if he set down the bottle and expected her to help herself. He knew Jess would understand. Still, he was glad her gargoyle wasn't here to see it. "We are the support system. Whatever happens is between them."

"True," she said softly.

"So." He clapped his hands together and looked around the immaculate kitchen. "What are we having? How can I help? I'm all dressed up with nothing to do."

She laughed again as Matt entered the kitchen, flustered and obviously angry, though trying to keep his cool. He froze when he saw Austin in the apron, and a scowl creased his brow.

"Camila, putting our guest in that is entirely inappropriate. Don't you have anything more fitting?"

"N-no. I just have the two aprons. I didn't know—"

"Austin, this is embarrassing," Matt said, shaking his head. "Allow me to apologize for my fiancée. She clearly missed the mark. I'm sure no one would fault you for going back on your desire to help her."

Austin let his stare beat into the other man. "I think the ruffles really accentuate my hips, don't you?" he growled, his power promising pain. *Let it go.*

Matt froze. His tongue darted out to wet his lips, and primal fear made his body rigid. "Well then, if you'll excuse me, I have a few matters to attend to. I'll leave you to the kitchen with the women."

After delivering what he clearly thought was a dig that a shifter would deem a challenge, he hurried from the room and Austin's dominating presence. Fleeing, in other words, so he wouldn't be forced to face the fallout of his words.

The rush of anger that followed was a palpable thing, coursing through Austin's body and lighting him up with adrenaline. He was not the kind of guy to let a challenge go unmet, and he absolutely detested allowing that guy to issue it while running. What sort of coward was he? What sort of fool?

"I'm sorry—"

"Definitely do not apologize for that," Austin said, doing his best to quash the throbbing rage. "Unless he is a robot and you hold the remote control, you are not responsible for a grown man's actions."

He wrestled up a smile that was clearly startling, because Camila took a step back, her eyes widening. He needed Jess in here to defuse the situation. To help calm him down.

He felt her hurrying his way, clearly in response to his distress.

"What are we making?" he ground out, rolling his head. His neck cracked.

"Uuuhh…" Camila drew out.

Jess sauntered in a moment later, her face flushed with anger but her eyes hyper-focused. She moved slowly, like molasses, but graceful and outwardly calm. Concern flowed through the bonds, and her gaze raked over his body before settling on his eyes.

"Hey, handsome," she said with a beautiful smile, reaching him and running a hand up his arm and around his neck. Austin barely registered Jimmy following her into the kitchen. "Looking hot in that apron."

She laughed as she looped her other arm around his neck and then pulled him down for a kiss and a tight hug.

Her lips brushed off his ear and she whispered, "Not even you had the power to steer this dinner away from Shitsville."

He huffed out a laugh, holding her firmly. "I was blindsided, I will admit," he said in a whisper that would be undetectable to human ears. "He is…" He didn't have the words. "At least we're in it together. We've been through worse. Maybe later you can accidentally on purpose toss him through the window."

She laughed as he let her go. He could tell she felt worlds better—and so did he. It was true, they'd had worse. Much worse. A thousand times worse. In the grand scheme of things, this was less than nothing. She just had to realize it and then act on it, thereby allowing him to scare that guy so badly he wet himself.

He just hoped she made her stand soon. He wasn't going to be able to take much more of this torture.

CHAPTER 16

JESSIE

"U H…I HAVE…" CAMILA glanced at Austin as she opened the fridge and took out a rustic wood platter covered with cuts of prosciutto, slices of cheese, what looked like sun-dried tomatoes, and olives—a charcuterie board with the works.

"My favorite," I said as she placed it on the island in front of Jimmy and me.

She pulled a cutting board out from somewhere beneath the counter and grabbed a loaf of bread from near the wall.

"Usually the ladies chat in here, like we're fixing dinner," Camila said, "and the guys have an appetizer or two in the front room."

"Who is this for?" I asked, snagging an olive.

"This was for us because Jimmy mentioned that you like charcuterie boards. Matt—as I'm sure you know— thinks they are too frou-frou."

I honestly hadn't known that. Huh.

"Do you need me to cut that up?" Austin asked, holding out his hand for the bread.

"Sure." She put it onto the cutting board and slid it his way, her face red. "In thin—Oh. You know. Yeah, like that. Then we'll toast them."

"And for the men?" Austin asked, cutting the bread in fast, practiced movements.

Camila went back to the fridge, pulling out an oval plate covered with shrimp and sprinkled with green specks. She grabbed out a lemon and another cutting board. After slicing the lemon into quarters, she spritzed the juice from one piece over the shrimp before laying the others on the edge of the plate.

"This is cold marinated shrimp with some herbs and onion." She slid it gently next to the charcuterie plater. "Matt loves shrimp."

"You would've taken this out while I nibbled," I said, "expecting the guys to have settled in by now."

A soft line creased between her brows when she glanced up at me, her gaze wary.

I held up a hand quickly. "I didn't invent the schedule. His mother did. It took me a while to get the cadence of it, but I never mastered it. I wasn't an expert hostess like you clearly are."

She released a breath. "You're being modest. He's

mentioned a time or two how great your timing was."

I blurted out a laugh. "Only when he was preoccupied and forgot to notice me being late or early. I was compared to his mother, who designed the setup."

"There is no such thing as perfect timing," Austin said, finishing with the bread and placing it on a broiler pan to be toasted. "Every party or group of people is different, and unless you are in the room and can see the signals, it's all a guessing game. It's up to the waiting party to be patient, which I'm sure all your guests know. None of them are ever as frustrated or stressed as the hosts, trust me."

He bit into one of the shrimp, squinting and looking upward. Without asking for permission, he started opening cabinets.

"Do you...ah... What do you need?" Camila asked, watching him uncertainly.

He'd already found the spice rack, though, helping himself and turning toward the shrimp.

"A little dry mustard and some thyme will nudge this one to the finish line," he said.

"Well, that's his favorite recipe..." Her voice drifted away as Austin worked.

"Don't worry, Austin's a genius in the kitchen," I told her. "Worst case, if Matt doesn't like it, just blame it on Austin. Say he did it without asking."

"Which is exactly why I didn't ask," Austin replied, finishing up.

"You might get a plate and take him some, though," I mentioned, snagging one of the shrimp for myself. "Not that I want to get involved, but as someone who's been there, I know he typically hates missing out on the food more than he hates missing out on the company."

"Yeah, that's true." Jimmy nodded as he grabbed a piece of bread and piled on prosciutto and salami. He clearly didn't care about it not being toasted.

"Hey." I blocked his reach. "Save some for everyone else."

"Good…" Camila nodded, suddenly flustered again. "Good point, thank you. I hadn't thought of that."

She bent in front of the oven and pulled out another platter, this one covered with little crescent roll circles filled with what I knew was sausage and cheddar. It was one of Matt's favorite appetizers. I'd made it a zillion times.

I hated being faced with all these memories. It was probably why I'd been so amicable in the divorce—I'd been relieved to move on.

She placed the platter on the stovetop, then took a bite of the shrimp before pulling out a plate for Matt.

"Hmm." She furrowed her brow at Austin in that way people did when they were serious about the flavors in their mouth. "Wow. That does boost the flavor. Yum. If you'll excuse me, I'll be back shortly."

"I'll just get these toasted," Austin said, adjusting the oven settings to broil and slipping in the bread.

"I think you're making her nervous," I told him as Jimmy hopped off the stool.

"It's not his fault," Jimmy said, his cheeks puffed out with food.

"Don't talk with your mouth full," I admonished him automatically.

"Sorry," he mumbled before chewing and swallowing. "It's just Dad and his protocols. You know. He doesn't like when things don't go according to plan. He gets all riled up. She's pretty jumpy about it. More so than you used to be."

He pulled a plate from the cupboard and started filling it quickly.

"What are you doing?" I asked, sticking my hand in front of the charcuterie board.

He pushed my hand away. "Making Mr. Tom a plate. I think he'd starve out there if I didn't feed him."

"No, he'd just turn to stone until you needed him. For some reason I don't quite understand, gargoyles don't need to eat, drink, or use the toilet when they're in stone form. They can exist that way for years, I was told."

Jimmy paused in what he was doing and then looked down at the plate. "Oh. Should I not take him food anymore?"

"I'm sure he's tickled that you think of him. He loves that sort of thing."

Jimmy revved into action again, and I let him have more of the charcuterie board. He hurried across the kitchen and to the back sliding door, pushing it open and closing it behind him.

"You raised a good kid," Austin told me, leaning against the counter. "He's thoughtful and kind."

I smiled at him. "Thank you. It was just the two of us a lot of the time, even when Matt was home. I'm sad that he doesn't have a better relationship with his father, but I'm starting to think my being here is hurting rather than helping."

He didn't say anything, just crossed around behind me and massaged my shoulders before pulling me back against him.

"I don't love the stress and anxiety you feel here," he mused quietly, "but I'm glad I'm getting a fuller picture of where you came from."

"I felt the same when I was at Kingsley's." I leaned my head against his chest. "But while I want to go to Kingsley's a lot more often than we'll be able to, I'm good with not coming back here for dinner."

He laughed softly and leaned down to kiss my head. "I'm good with whatever you want to do. Except take a tour of your parents' garage. There has to be a portal to another world in there somewhere, and your dad is guarding it with heaps and heaps of junk. That can be the only explanation for all that stuff. Have a look around and then—whoops, you're in another dimension."

I laughed as Jimmy jogged back in. He barely had time to sit down before Camila re-entered, her face ashen and her eyes tight. She looked on the verge of tears.

"Here." I leaned forward, put two fingers on the base of her wine glass, and slid it forward a little. "This will help. Sorry about all this. I've had a few surprises from work and it's affecting my schedule. I know how that throws him off. It's my fault."

"No, it's fine," she said distractedly, going to the fridge and taking out various containers. "I'll just get dinner going now. Supper, I mean."

"Here, let me—"

"No." She held up her hand for Austin, her smile forced. "Thank you. I appreciate it, but it's best if I just do it. If you guys wouldn't mind, I'll go ahead and seat you in the living room while I finish up, okay? Matt will meet you both there."

She grabbed the wine bottle and the platter of shrimp and headed out in front of us. When my chest tightened this time, it wasn't because of Matt. It was because of what Camila was obviously going through. It was because I knew firsthand what it felt like. Austin and I had ensured this dinner party was the worst Matt had hosted in a very long time, on par with the time he'd accidentally insulted his boss's wife, made an ignorant joke to compensate, and prompted his guest of honor to leave early. None of that had been my fault, but it had been a helluva fallout to bear. Camila wouldn't have a great night.

"Should I go back into the kitchen with you?" I asked her once she'd deposited the platter of shrimp and wine bottle. "Austin can stay out here, it's fine."

Her look was grateful, but she shook her head. "This will be better. Dinner will be ready really quickly. I just have to put it all together and warm it up." She squeezed her eyes shut and put up her hand. "Supper, I mean."

"What should I do, Mom?" Jimmy asked me, having followed us out.

"Go to the kitchen or go hang out with Mr. Tom for a bit. Or go to your room. Let's just keep it civil to help your dad's mood, okay? You know the drill."

He nodded, heading for the stairs and his room.

Doing as one was told was the fastest way to bring Matt out of his funk. Or, in this case, the fastest way to get dinner over with.

No Matt currently in sight, I took a seat next to Austin, feeling his arm stretch around my shoulders. If poor Camila married my ex, she would get steamrolled. She was a docile sort of person. A people pleaser. She'd try her best, but she'd always fail.

"I always failed," I said softly.

Aurora's conversation came to the forefront of my mind, followed by a memory of how Matt had spun me around earlier. He'd built on his lie until I wasn't sure if I was remembering correctly and then jumped to an accusation before I could get my bearings. The minimizing. The interrupting. Calling me hysterical. Emotional. Unreasonable. A liar.

"I *always* failed," I said. "I never got the timing of these things right, even if it seemed like I had. But he told her the opposite, the same way he was always telling me that his mom was so accomplished. They're head games. His way of making us feel crappy about ourselves so that we try and try. We try to please, as is our nature, but our confidence stays low because we always fail. Sometimes in big ways, sometimes in small ways, but we always fail."

I took a shuddering breath, wanting to go back to

my youth and take that girl by the shoulders and tell her to raise hell. To fight back. To run.

"Let's go." I pushed to standing, then hesitated. "Wait, is that rude to Camila?"

I sat back down. I didn't want to leave Camila to my fate if at all possible. I wanted to help her, but I had precious little time to convince her to see what she could have: a guy like Austin. Like Ulric or Jasper. Like Tristan, even with all his secrets. Broken Sue wasn't ready, but even with all his pain he'd still treat a woman with respect. There were better men out there, ones who didn't need coddling. Ones who didn't twist up their partner's mind so they could always stay in control. Ones who didn't abuse.

"I'm not sure what's happening," Austin said.

Neither was I. The two of us were still by ourselves, sitting on our own in someone else's house. My son was sequestered to his room like a child. A woman was unhappily cooking for us in the kitchen. And the orchestrator of it all was twiddling his thumbs and stewing in the misery he'd created.

"We should leave, but I don't want to do that to Camila," I said, chewing my lip. "This isn't her fault. I half don't want to leave him alone with her, to be honest."

"Then let's stay and make this as easy as we can for

her. We've endured worse, remember? The wine's not bad, at least."

I turned so that I could kiss him. "You're a good man."

"That's why you put up with me."

I laughed as footsteps sounded on the stairs.

"The circus felt empty," I murmured. "But here comes the clown."

Matt descended slowly. Ice tinkled within his glass, swimming in his scotch.

"He's regrouped," I whispered, turning to Austin so that Matt wouldn't see my lips moving. "This will be his last stand. He'll be at his absolute worst right now, trying to regain control. Just play nice. Hopefully we can turn his mood, and Camila's night might just be a little bit better."

"I see your cooking forays are over," he said, crossing to take a seat. He quirked an eyebrow at Austin. "And you've lost your frilly apron."

I dropped my hand to Austin's knee. "How are you, Matt? I didn't get a chance to ask."

"Yes. Too busy arguing," he said with a condescending smile. Like a dog on a bone, this guy.

I didn't take the bait, just waited for him to either tell me or try to stonewall me. It was a favorite tactic of his, I remembered.

"I'm doing well," he finally said, crossing an ankle over a knee like he was once again the master of this dinner party. "Very well, actually. The company is five percent above last year, our investors are appreciative of the job my team is doing, I have this beautiful new home and a beautiful, *young*, soon-to-be wife. I couldn't ask for more. My life is finally perfect." He looked at me with a gleam in his eyes. "And how about you, Jacinta? You've lost weight, I see. Did one of your crash diets finally work longer than a couple of weeks?"

Ah yes, the ol' "you really should slim down, hon, everyone at the club is talking" or "if you stopped eating so much you might actually get rid of that baby weight."

"No, I had a little work done"—magic counted—"and I exercise with Austin a lot." Battles and training certainly counted as exercise.

He swung his gaze Austin's way and froze up for a moment before jerking it back to me. I had a suspicion Austin was giving him an alpha's stare.

"You two haven't been together long," he said, his tone even.

"Not as long as you and Camila, no," I replied, my tone just as even, waiting for the other shoe to drop.

"And you two are...serious?" He quirked an eyebrow again, flicking his eyes toward Austin.

"Very," Austin said, matching the tone.

"You must be a patient man." Matt laughed like that was a grand joke.

His voice from the past drifted in. *"You're lucky I'm patient, Jacinta. Most men wouldn't tolerate a wife like you."*

He'd said that or something like it all the time, as though no one else would want me. As though, if not for him, I'd be destitute and alone, not fit for marriage, and it was only his kindness that kept him from tossing me out.

I laughed to myself. It wasn't my insecurity that started to rise this time, but my banked anger. He was systematically hitting all the things he knew affected me, one by one, trying to break me.

He was trying to *break* me.

Power rushed through me from my gargoyle.

Many of the things Matt had said tonight were challenges, to me and also Austin. He was getting away with it because Dicks and Janes didn't punish mental or emotional abuse, just physical. If he were magical, though, he'd have been dead ten times over.

"I'm not very patient, no," Austin replied easily as I let out a long, slow breath, trying to calm myself. Ivy House started muttering about rope, fire, and closets again. "Thankfully, I don't have to be. Jess is patient enough for the two of us. She has shown she's able to deal with some truly unforgivable personalities. I once thought I was a nightmare, but I'm now convinced she's an angel for some of the garbage she's had to deal with."

Matt tilted his head just slightly, like a dog hearing a dog whistle. "Well, give it time. You'll see what I mean. She can try the patience of a saint, can't you, *Jess*?"

The way he repeated Austin's nickname for me, giving it emphasis, rankled in a way I wasn't prepared for.

Rage blotted out my senses. Power throbbed to the surface, ready to destroy.

"Here we go," Ivy House said. *"Now we're talking."*

"She used to ask for an increase on her allowance for the most far-fetched things," Matt went on as I struggled with the urge to destroy his whole world. I couldn't react in a Dick environment like a magical person. I couldn't react like I might at the mage dinner tomorrow. Matt had to be dominated a different way, and not just because I didn't need Dick police putting me on a most wanted list. Being destroyed emotionally would register with him more poignantly. It would create a lasting impression that cut much more deeply.

But my God was I struggling just now.

"The amount of books she purchased was bad enough," Matt said with a disbelieving smile, "but imagine trying to extend the allotted amount to include a computer, a TV, *and* expensive jewelry, all in the same month! She was always extravagant. You'll see. Though I don't see a ring, so maybe you won't get that far."

His smile was grating. His tone made me want to both shrivel up in remembered horror and go forth with firebombing this place.

"Imagine," Austin said lightly, though I could feel the rage running through him, "wanting to buy common material possessions with your half of the family estate."

"The computer was for Jimmy because we only had one and Matt wouldn't allow him to use it," I said in just as light a tone. "I was told to replace the TV by Matt because the other one was old—it looked bad when people came over, he'd said. His image was apparently more important than his son's education or desire to share. The necklace was a request for my birthday. The women at the social club whispered behind my back— loudly enough that I could hear—about my wearing pearls too often. I wanted to fit in better, as Matt said I should. Isn't that right, Matt? Or am I somehow remembering that incorrectly? Do you have a better account? Maybe you'd like to talk me through my experiences with childbirth, as well. I'm sure you know what happened much better than I do."

His smile was placating. He ignored the digs, focusing instead on his agenda. "You could've saved up for a nice necklace. Instead, you chose to spend it on other things."

"Yes. Like food for the family, bills, Jimmy's school supplies... Frivolous things like that. I took care of the house and child, with very little to nothing left over for myself, and you always got whatever you wanted. Looking back, that definitely seems fair."

Matt's eyes had a violent gleam. His smile turned brittle. "Just like usual, you're remembering the computer situation completely wrong. But that's fine." He shrugged. "I don't intend to argue. You can believe what you'd like." He looked at Austin. "This is what I mean about patience. She is prone to arguing and wild fabrications. Ask her about the necessity of always getting her hair and nails done." He nodded like he had me there. "Every other month. She certainly never shirked getting pampered."

"I did my own nails," I said, digging my fingers into Austin's thigh.

"*Kill him!*" Ivy House yelled. "*Kill him now!*"

I had a point to make.

"Like a *peasant*, as I recall your saying. I couldn't forgo the hair, or you'd ridicule me in front of your friends for becoming *homely*. I decided I'd rather be called a peasant than homely, so I chose to maintain my hair despite it costing more."

"Despite it costing more, yes. Amazing how you rationalize monthly haircuts." His laugh was incredulous. "Homely meaning your dieting was not going well, Jacinta, as you must remember. I stood by you through one diet after the other, paying for your ever-changing food needs, buying shakes you didn't drink... Do you remember that, or do you just remember the things you want to? And with all the time you had," he said slowly, his eyebrows arched high as he looked at me, "you didn't put any of it into exercise." He shrugged again, and I wasn't sure whom he was trying to fool. "Water under the bridge. You have her now, Austin. Or have I scared you off?"

Austin's fingers were now digging into me. "Scared me off? Hardly," he said, his tone still light. "I love her dearly and want to be with her for the rest of my life. Did you make me want to rip your spleen out of your mouth, hang your skin on it, and put you in the coat closet? Yeah, maybe."

"*See? He gets it,*" Ivy House said. "*Bad things get worse when shoved in a closet.*"

CHAPTER 17

AUSTIN

TEAR HIS THROAT out, or stick with the plan?

Tear his throat out, or stick with the plan?

Tear his throat out……

Austin took a deep, steadying breath, trying not to move much because he wasn't sure if that movement would turn fluid and end with Jess's ex bleeding all over the cheap, bland rug.

"But," he said to the frozen solid and incredibly rigid Dick, "that does seem like a very challenging situation. For her, obviously. You sound like a real piece of shit. Luckily, it isn't her situation now. This necklace"—he ran his fingers down her throat slowly, feeling her shiver, before running them along the diamonds— "was a gift from me. She was going to wear those simple pearls you apparently like so much, just to keep the peace, but thankfully she reconsidered. I like to see my baby sparkle."

Jess turned to show Austin her smile before kissing his jaw and relaxing against him.

Matt watched every movement with darkening eyes, probably not daring to move because of his obvious fear of Austin. He'd likely seem incredibly composed to most Dicks, but Austin could read this guy like an open book with large print. He'd been doing it all afternoon. Matt hated Austin's supreme confidence, his flashiness, his open intimacy with Jess. He hated someone with undefined social status sauntering around his house, no groveling, no deference to a reasonably wealthy businessman. Hated that his ex-wife was happy without him and no longer felt beholden to his schedules and his demands. The saddest thing? He didn't seem to particularly enjoy his son. It seemed like he'd just invited him to stay because he wanted to take him away from his mother. Jimmy was a way to control Jess even when she was technically out of his reach.

This whole "afternoon supper" was Matt's effort to bring Jess to heel, and it was turning out like a car driving across black ice.

"I did happen to notice your...eccentric vehicle parked out front," Matt said, not giving up. Now he was trying to weasel through Austin's confidence, it seemed. It was almost surreal. "You do like to throw your money around."

"I'm more apt to throw my money at businesses, actually," Austin said easily, running his fingertips along Jess's bare arm. "I own several and add more all the time. I do like fast cars, though. Which is why Jess bought that one for me."

A gleam lit Matt's eyes, and his gaze was calculating as it swung to Jess. "So I guess *I* bought that car, since you didn't have a dime before the divorce."

"*My* money from the divorce, you mean," Jess said. "Paid *to me* for services rendered to this family, a payment much lower than what I'm worth. That money is sitting in a high-yield savings account, largely untouched. The money and property owned by my employer are mine to control and spend as I would like until I die. I purchased that car with those funds, and it was a drop from the well of what I have within my disposal. But please, try to monetarily swing your dick around a little more, Matt. I so greatly enjoy playing the 'whose is bigger' game, mostly because I like winning."

The slight tic in his eye was the only facial expression that gave away his utter shock and disbelief. Soon his whole body screamed mistrust and disdain, though, and a condescending smile pulled at his thin, pale lips.

"Funny," he said, leaning forward to place his now-empty glass on the coffee table before snagging a piece of shrimp. "A woman with no budgeting skills or prior experience is suddenly in charge of an employer's fortune for the term of her life? This sounds like one of your fantasy books."

"It does, that's right," Jess said, still relaxed, though his tone and mode of questioning were similar to what they'd been before. This was about her magical life. A life this insignificant prick hadn't spent twenty years picking away at. She'd started fresh, as a woman who no longer gave any fucks, and it showed. "Just so we're all clear, I have amazing budgeting skills. You can't give a woman just enough to cover life expenses, demand she make it work despite fluctuating rates, reap the benefits of her frugal living, and tell her she has no budgeting skills. I did that for twenty years. I know plenty about budgeting."

He ate a piece of shrimp and then grabbed another. "I've had about enough of your dramatics. I'm going to go see where dinner is. Camila cannot seem to figure out how to be a good host."

Jess watched him go, irate and frustrated.

"You did that for twenty years," Austin said, not able to help laughing in utter bewilderment. "*Twenty years!* How?"

"Right?" She sat forward and turned a bit to look at him, her face a little pale. He was relieved to see the haunted expression from earlier was gone. "In fairness, he wasn't like this all the time. This is one of the worst moods I've seen him in. If it weren't for you, I doubt he would've tried so hard. I think he was trying to put you off our relationship."

"He definitely was, yes. He doesn't want you to be happy without him, and he certainly doesn't like another man making him feel small in his home. I think we've addled that poor bastard's brain."

"Poor bastard, my ass," she breathed, snuggling back into Austin. "But yeah, he's terrible. Isn't he terrible? His opinions are somehow fact because that's the reality he wants to believe. No one else matters. It's…infuriating. And exhausting. I just hate it and want to go home. I hate being in his company."

"Yet you had an amicable divorce, right?"

"Yeah." She shrugged. "It was fine." Her eyes went distant. "I agreed to the parameters. It sounded reasonable. Half the house, half the liquid funds, a portion of his retirement. He agreed to pay for Jimmy's college."

A portion of his retirement…

Probably a small portion if Matt was paying for college, which he'd undoubtedly hinged on a book full of stipulations. She'd also said *liquid* funds, and Matt clearly hadn't let Jess have access to the books. There was no telling how large this man's stock portfolio was, how much money she'd left on the table.

Anger welled up in Austin again, but this time it was easier to let it go. She'd walked away amicably out of survival instinct. She'd made sure Jimmy was looked after, she'd felt like she'd gotten enough, and she'd gotten out. No more stress, no more *moods*. None of the stuff she was going through this evening. She was safe now. The past didn't matter.

"Well. Maybe someday you two can get along amicably again," he said, rubbing her back.

"I'd be fine to never see him again. We'll get along when Jimmy wants us to, and that'll be the end of it. I hold a grudge."

"Now you do, at any rate."

She laughed and stood. "Exactly." She glanced at the front door just in time for it to open and for Ulric's head to pop in.

"Hey," he said softly. "The Dick is in the kitchen yelling at the Jane. Well…talking sternly, at any rate, but she's crying. We're all spying, and Cyra is wondering if it's okay for her to make him cry?"

Jess wilted, her lower lip hanging a little. She really felt for Camila. "No. We can't treat this like a magical situation."

"She thought you'd say that, so she followed up by asking if we could go get Niamh, who doesn't need physical violence to make people cry?"

Jess stared at Ulric for a long, quiet beat. "No. But there's been a change of plans. Send word to the shifters at home. We'll be staying for that extended family party after all, and I'll be inviting some of you. Niamh can have her crack at messing with his mind then. How's that? Let's see how good he is at gaslighting her."

A wide grin came across Ulric's lips. "Perfect. Can I go to watch?"

"No, your hair is too loud. Your mom can, though. In fact, let's send her into some of his familiar haunts so she can get some reconnaissance on him. I feel like fighting dirty."

"Sounds good. Last bit of—" He jerked his head, looking back toward the kitchen. In a moment, he had reduced his volume and started talking faster. "Last bit of news. Mr. Tom flew up to Jimmy's room when he realized there was trouble in the house. Jimmy was…" He poked his head a little farther into the room, angling to see the stairs. "He was up at the top of the stairs listening, I guess. Whatever he heard upset him, and he asked Mr. Tom to help him clean out his room so he could leave after dinner. He doesn't intend to listen to you or your ex if you tell him to stay, which… He's nineteen. Why is he being pushed around by his parents?"

"That's his dad, not me."

"He explained about his dad. Your ex is trying to force him to stay by dangling some sort of allowance over his head or something?"

"*What?*" Jess asked. "He's using his *court-mandated* school allowance to *make* Jimmy visit?"

And there was the missing piece.

It always came back to control with this man. He used money or manipulation to maintain control of those around him. He must be a holy nightmare to work for. Or maybe that was the only place where he was okay, because the company title said he mattered. What he said went there, backed by his ability to fire people. It was only life that was messy. Family.

Jess ran her hand over her forehead. "I'd thought Jimmy was fine hanging out with his dad." She closed her eyes, swaying a little.

Austin jumped up to brace a hand on her shoulder, but she shrugged him off.

"Matt set a lot of that up, telling me Jimmy had agreed with the plan. Jimmy never mentioned…" Two hands went to her face. "But then, why would he? What would I do to help? I enable his dad. I tell Jimmy to go to his room to help calm Matt down. Instead of fighting for my son, I make him play along. I've been forcing him to stay in the same cage I'm trapped in. No…*was* trapped in. I got free and left him behind, still trapped."

She wiped a tear away from her eye. "What sort of mother am I?"

"Alpha Steele, I'll leave the consoling to you," Ulric said, "but Jessie, you should know that Mr. Tom thought that was ridiculous and will now put Jimmy on an Ivy House allowance. You'll probably want to make sure it's not too extravagant. Long story short, Jimmy is leaving with us after dinner—"

"No." Jessie straightened, tears dripping down her face, and tensed her shoulders resolutely.

Austin watched the theoretical straw rotate through the air, in slow motion, aiming for the camel's back.

"He's leaving *now*," she said firmly, and not even a hardened alpha would be comfortable looking into those wild, fiery eyes. "Get him out. I'll take care of his father."

She didn't bother to wipe at the trail of tears that lightly streaked down her cheeks before walking across the front room and toward the kitchen. Matt was just emerging, a fresh scotch in hand. No doubt he'd made Camila prepare it for him, and the composure and confidence he now exuded suggested he'd also used her to regain his footing. This guy did not know when he'd been beaten.

"Good God, Jacinta, look at the mess of your face…" His brow pinched. He was suddenly wary. The

MAGICAL MIDLIFE AWAKENING

hand that held his drink dropped a little, and it was clear he was looking into the eyes of a female gargoyle for the very first time.

A female gargoyle who was ready to protect her young.

"If you interrupt the payments for Jimmy's schooling for even one *day*, I will legally drown you, do you understand me? Controlling him with money ends *now*. If you think you can legally browbeat me, think again. I'll bleed you dry without even blinking. Try me and find out if I'm bluffing. In addition, I'll be sending an auditor by to look over everything that has transpired thus far. You'd better make sure your books are squeaky clean. There will be damages for any negligence."

His stance turned awkward, riddled with anxiety and unease that he was trying not to show. The sneer was obviously autopilot.

"Anything else?" he asked, his condescension wavering a bit.

"Yeah. This is the worst dinner party I've ever been to, and I've been to twenty years of them with you. Hell, I was at one where I threw a guy out of a window. This is still worse. My dad could walk around at Christmas with his balls out, and it would be better than this. You know, you're only as good as the women you corner into serving you. Camila is lovely. I hope she robs you blind and then leaves you. I won't be going to her funeral, by the way—your wedding—so don't bother sending an invite. From now on, I won't be organizing any interactions between you and Jimmy, either. He'll see you when he wants to. If he doesn't want to, that's on you. If you try to force him, you'll meet me, and trust me when I say"—she leaned in, and it was clear he couldn't help himself from leaning backward—"you don't want me as your enemy. Now *move*."

There was so much power in her voice, delivered in the tone of a commander talking to her league of gargoyles, that Matt wouldn't have been able to ignore it if he'd tried. He stepped to the side, dropping his glass. It shattered on the hardwood, washing scotch under Jessie's shoe as she stepped forward.

"Austin, remove him to the front room for a moment while I speak to Camila, if you don't mind," she said, and then she was through the kitchen door.

Now, Austin did posture. He let his power pump through him. The threat he'd felt all evening burned in his eyes. He didn't need to say a word. He stepped forward, and Matt scattered meekly before him.

"Now, it's my turn to talk," Austin said in a rough tone, following the man closely, full alpha. In the living room he grabbed the man's arm and whipped him around, leaning aggressively down into his space. "She is *mine*. That means she is under my protection, and so is her son. If you cause them any more discomfort, even *one* tear, I will end you, do you understand me? I will ruin your career, take your house, and ensure someone charms and steals your hopefully-never-to-be wife. You'll be penniless and destitute and then"—he grabbed the quivering man by his lapels—"I will beat you bloody. You don't know the meaning of pain, but I will gladly show you."

He let his feral gaze beat down into Matt, who issued a sound that was half wheeze, half whimper, and then the air was perfumed with the smell of urine.

Austin held the stare for one moment longer, showing this man what dominance really was, before flinging him away.

"Go get yourself cleaned up. We're taking your son with us. After tonight, you haven't earned a goodbye. He'll call you if he wants to. You will leave it at that."

✧　✧　✧

JESSIE

I ENTERED THE kitchen with my power pumping. It had taken me too long to realize it, to really accept it, but I was better than all this. Better than that idiot Matt, stronger than his *moods*. He'd dominated a different version of me. A younger version. I was older now, wiser.

I was the queen of my domain, and that fool was not my king.

Camila waited behind the island, her spine bent and her eyes puffy. The dinner lay finished behind her. Paella.

"That looks delicious," I said, softening my voice, walking around to pull her into a hug.

She resisted for a moment and then fell into it, crying softly against my shoulder.

"Listen to me," I said, rocking her gently. "First, this is not the worst it can get with him. He'll do exactly this in front of your respected peers and closest friends, in front of your kid, and it will feel like your whole world is crashing down around you. And when that happens, he won't let anyone comfort you. He'll ensure there is distance between you and any support system you used to have. So if you think this is just a one-time thing, you're wrong. Tomorrow he won't even say he's sorry. He'll blame you for it and go about his day. You need to know that before it's too late. Second…"

I pulled away so I could look into her eyes, which were filled with fresh tears.

"I am going to leave you my number. If this evening is unbearable, you call me, okay? Any time, day or night, you call—"

The sliding door opened, and Mr. Tom walked through it in a very rumpled butler's uniform, his chin held high.

"If I may…" He peered at Camila. "You remember me from the other day, I trust?"

She stared.

He clearly took that as a yes and continued. "I had left this to Master Jimmy, but given he is now coming with us and has no need of it, I will pass it on to you." He put a credit card on the island, followed by a wad of cash. "If you should find yourself in an emergency, this is a credit card with a very high ceiling and a lot of cash. Get yourself out however you can, and then call the miss—"

"I'm the miss," I said, dropping my hands from her shoulders. My heart expanded to fill my whole chest at this confirmation of what he'd done for Jimmy.

"Someone will be there to collect you promptly. This applies no matter where you are in the world. If you wake up in a coffin in Mexico with no recollection of how you got there, call us. An underground prison in Rome, call us. An—"

"She gets it, she gets it," I told him. "She's not in that kind of situation."

"You have no idea what kind of situation you might

find yourself in until you're in the thick of it." His wings fluttered, and I had to concede the point, though I couldn't imagine she'd find herself in such a situation and still have a phone. "And, might I just say, you are much too nice for someone who is unable to protect you in any helpful way. He is not your mate—"

"Your match, he means."

"I most certainly do not. If I meant match, I would have said match. There are a great many matches in the world, and candles that will steal their flame. But there is only one mate, and he is not it. Find your mate, as the miss has done. Find your mate so you may find your happiness in love. Until then, find happiness in yourself. He is not worth a ring and a"—he looked around the kitchen—"moderately sized and incredibly uninspired home. Now…" He looked at me. "We must be going. Master Jimmy is famished. He wants something called Texas Roadmap or some such thing. Apparently, there is one on the way back."

I looked through the drawers to find a piece of paper.

"I have it," she said in a small voice. "I have your number. Matt gave it to me a while back."

"Oh right, okay. Good. I didn't feel comfortable rifling through your things. Use it."

I veered to the chocolate-covered strawberries,

grabbed the tray—I deserved a treat after all that—and headed for the front door.

"Mr. Tom, where is Niamh? The night is young. Let's go see what she's been up to."

CHAPTER 18
NIAMH

"THAT'S NOT…REALLY WHAT I meant," Aurora said, her face turning red at the suggestion that she'd come out here so she could ride random guys. "I guess I wanted to go to a place no one knew me, somewhere I could swear and act out. Dance or dress sexy without someone running to tell my dad. Or my uncle."

Niamh's phone vibrated. A text from Ulric saying they were leaving the ex's house, dropping Jimmy off into the safety of the wards, and then going out for drinks. He wanted to know what bar they should head to.

Not this one. She didn't want any of them around here. They'd cause all sorts of ruckus and people would look at Niamh differently. Then they wouldn't talk so freely, and she had made some very interesting connections over the last few days.

She typed back, telling him to have Jessie pick one. Or he could. He'd circled some of the posher areas over the last couple of nights. According to him, the clientele got a kick out of his "vibe." She assumed they meant his cape.

"If that's all ye're lookin' for, ye could do that with anyone, like." Niamh waved Aurora's suggestion away. "Go out with Ulric and Jasper. Hell, go out with Jessie. She lets her hair down and does those things. We're not a bunch of nuns around here. And if ye need to sneak off into a quiet corner and get a little feather tickle, just ask Jasper which corner is the most discreet and mum's the word. He somehow finds willing partners to knock boots with just about anywhere. Ulric calls it a gift. I call it a sticky mess for some poor sod to have to clean up after closing. Anyway, the rest of them are going out for drinks here soon, so ye'd best finish up so we can get a move on…"

Her words dwindled away as a familiar smell wafted past her. It rode the currents of the air, leaking into the bar and all around her. The creature generating the scent wasn't moving past the place but lingering, ready to come in.

It had found her. She'd figured it might.

"Aurora, move to the chair on the other side of Broken Sue," she said urgently, applying the seldom-used power of command to her voice to get the young woman moving. "If ye feel fear for any reason, excuse yerself to the *jacks*."

"The what?" Aurora asked.

"The bathroom!" Niamh said. "Do *not* leave the bar, understand? Broken Sue, ye will go with her and protect her. Unless ye also feel fear, and then the two of ye lock yerselves in the *bathroom* together. They won't force a lock here. Not in a Dick establishment with me in the way."

"What is it—"

She held up her hand to cut off Broken Sue as the shape darkened the doorstep. Wisps like steam rose from the rotting flesh covering its body. Tattered gray-black robes covered most of it, ruffled by the wind of the closing day behind it. Its hands ended in glistening black claws, once broken nails from its having dug its way out of its own grave, that had become hardened and talon-like from age. The image of a scythe vaguely hovered behind it, as though fastened to its back, and its lips had pulled back from its shining, white, perfect teeth.

Odd.

It glided more than walked into the bar, the holes where its eyes had once been sensing more than seeing, similar to a bat's sonar.

Bar patrons tensed as they felt the presence passing them, looking back at it in sudden, anxious wariness. Non-magical people wouldn't see its true image. Nor could magical people without...darker origins. To everyone else, it would look like a businessman in a suave suit with a scheming smile, a vicious glint in his eyes, and slicked-back hair that wouldn't ever be affected by the wind or rain. His skin would appear sallow but human, and the sound of his soles on the run-down hardwood would faintly squeak in their perception.

Neither Aurora nor Broken Sue tensed or flinched in any way as the creature passed behind them and around the corner, stopping behind the seat Aurora had just evacuated. Broken Sue wrapped his fingers around Aurora's drink, pulling it a little closer to her. He then touched her upper arm briefly, a sign of comfort or support, showing he was there, before returning to his own drink. He took a calm, collected sip. The message was clear: he didn't see the being's true form, but he was ready to battle if necessary.

That was good. One needed to keep one's head around such creatures. This being was only a stepping-stone to the dark underbelly of the magical world, but if it took a notion, it could still rip out one's heart in short order.

"Puca," the creature rasped, a sound like insects scurrying over dried bones.

"Ezra, how goes it? Or are ye operating under a different name these days?"

He took the vacated seat, and his sigh sounded more like a hiss of satisfaction. "This seat is still warm. Full of conflicted emotion."

"I'm sure she's thrilled ye told everyone."

He touched the soda Aurora had left behind before swinging his gaze toward her slowly. His tattered clothes rustled like skeletons dancing, bone sliding on bone. The effect wouldn't translate into the image she could see, but she would nonetheless feel the being's presence, crawling in through the pores of her skin and tainting her blood like a disease.

She lifted her eyes from her drink and swung them Ezra's way, the movement both slow and deliberate. Her expression remained entirely passive, her body language loose. In a moment, however, she rose from her seat, bourbon in hand, and walked off toward the bathroom.

Broken Sue's eyes held pure carnage as he rose behind her, locking eyes with the creature for a solid beat before following her.

"The female is bursting with vivaciousness and vigor," said the revenant, a creature who'd crawled out of his grave over two hundred years ago, seeking vengeance on his wife, whom he'd thought poisoned him in a fit of jealousy over his many mistresses.

By rights, as soon as he'd gotten that vengeance, he should've returned to his final resting place, his undead purpose resolved and his presence no longer sanctioned in the world of the living.

But in life, the man had been shrewd and cunning. He'd inherited wealth and prestige from his father and poured it into the burgeoning industrial industry. He'd stolen and cheated his way to success, becoming a respected and feared businessman and compounding his wealth and his social status. His marriage had been calculated—he'd wed a plain woman of fortune who would join two competing businesses to monopolize their trade. He'd stashed her away in their mansion and then ignored her for more interesting pleasures, like pretty maids, friends' wives, and young *ingenue*.

A man like that didn't succumb to something so trivial as eternal rest.

Before claiming his vengeance, he'd managed to acquire an essential piece of ancient magic that had allowed him to avoid the fate of other revenants—he was able to avoid the compulsion to return to his grave and be sealed up in it.

Niamh's cousin had worked that deal and then taken off with just a fraction of the estate. Podrick had always been miserable at bargaining. It was a wonder he'd survived as long as he had.

Evading the grave was all well and good, but then the revenant had the issue of his flesh rotting on the bone and the inability to exist in modern society without some sort of magical cover to hide the funk of death and decay.

That was where Niamh had stepped in. For a sizable transaction fee, of course. A body didn't do something for nothing. There was a reason she'd outlived most of her kind. It took more than brawn and balls to slip through the rapidly changing centuries.

"I am jealous of the male you sit with," he mused, swinging his notice from Broken Sue's empty place to the bartender at the other end of the bar, currently glancing back at him. It was anyone's guess whether that bartender planned to budge from his location. Walking toward a nightmare wasn't usually particularly motivating.

"And why is that?" Niamh asked.

"He seems to be crawling out of the grave as we speak…but he got to keep his skin. What I wouldn't give for my former glory."

"It was only his soul that died. Ye never had one of those. Besides, he won't live forever. Ye certainly seem on that path, though. What are ye doin' roaming around a city? Shouldn't ye be off looking for a war or battle or some other sort of large, bloody skirmish? I assume ye still feed on the suffering and anguish of humans…"

"I do, of course. Not even magic can change the way a revenant gains sustenance. I've tried."

Risk, meet reward.

The second she recognized his scent, she'd wondered what lengths he'd gone to over the years to function within modern society. He'd know, at the very least, how things worked in the magical world. His personality, carried over from life, would still contain that original drive—that need to be a power player and reside at the top of a business empire.

Based on what he'd just said, he'd been in communication with mages. That, or he'd had someone reach out for him. It meant he had at least one connection, hopefully more.

Given he was still wandering the streets, visiting dive bars full of wayward individuals, that meant he had not reclaimed *any* of his former glory. He was hungry.

He had a use, and she knew his motivation. She was suddenly very glad she'd made her presence known in this place.

"And yet ye feed from scraps within the rank city streets, existing within the crusty folds of a Dick society?" she asked before finishing her cider in a couple of needed gulps, holding up the glass, and then clanking the ice around inside for another. "I figured ye'd be after inhaling the great misery that came with wars. The Dicks always have one or more of those happening at any given time. A little traveling and *voila*, eat like a king."

"If only that were the case. Now, they explode enemies from afar with fire and machines. It's not at all the same as the good ol' days. But luckily, there is plenty of sorrow and misery lining the curbs. I just need to wander by, and I soak up all that delicious sustenance."

"Sounds like a treat. And why have ye come to see me?"

"It isn't every day I smell an old friend in my neighborhood."

"Ye don't have any friends, Ezra."

"Neither do you, so we might as well pretend. And it's Volkan now."

"Volkan?" She gave him a side-eye while she rattled her ice in her glass again. "Did ye get that from *Star Trek* or what?"

"What?"

"Exactly. It's a stupid name. Pick another."

✧   ✧   ✧

MAGICAL MIDLIFE AWAKENING

AURORA

A BARE BULB shone down yellowish light from a dirty fixture in the ceiling. The toilet was eternally running and toilet paper was littered all over the floor. A small, empty baggy, which had probably held cocaine, sat on the edge of the sink, and the space smelled strongly of stale urine.

If this wasn't a fitting punishment for her cowardice a moment ago, she didn't know what was.

What had she even been scared of? That thing was gross, sure, and its magic felt like a sticky film along her skin, but its actual power hadn't somersaulted her like Auntie Jessie's or Uncle Auzzie's could have. And when Auntie Jessie let her magic surge, it was so powerful it threatened to drag Aurora down into the depths of subconscious.

But this thing?

She shivered.

It wasn't its power that had scared her. And, honestly, at any other time, she wouldn't have admitted to her fear. She'd been trained to keep all emotion behind a façade so that enemies couldn't see her weaknesses. Except her dad had never told her about creatures that seemed to *feel* weakness. Or maybe smell it.

There were clearly worse things than challenges in

the world, and some of them just turned up, willy-nilly, in dive bars.

Oh God, had that been one of Niamh's concerns? Was this why she'd followed Aurora? Why Sue had warned her against going out on her own? She'd assumed they were trying to rein her in for the same reasons her father, or her mother, or the last beta had: *Don't go out on your own, Aurora. You don't know who's watching. Don't relax too much. The pack has expectations.*

She'd wanted to finally…unwind. Laugh, if she wanted to. Smile. Show some sort of emotion, like the gargoyles did so freely. To not worry about anyone's expectations, or how much thigh she was showing, or how her actions might reflect on the alpha. Maybe flirt without worrying about the boy's status. Go home with someone without it being a huge event.

Suddenly the warnings made a lot more sense. She felt like a fool for making them chase her. For sneaking out and hiding.

She took another sip of the drink she'd carried in with her, the taste sharp but flavors coming through—cinnamon, cocoa, and citrus. The ice chilled it enough that it wasn't a punch in the face, and the rind helped bring forward the natural citrus in the bourbon. Sue had known exactly what would work. The man was perceptive.

Speaking of...

She pulled open the door a crack, leaning forward to speak.

He half turned, his gaze pointed toward the bar and his movements always so fluid. Reaching back, he grabbed the door handle without distinctly looking and pulled it shut again.

She sighed. Took another sip.

He always treated her like a treasured object, watching over her so Uncle Auzzie didn't have to, but this was a little much. She wasn't a Jane. She wasn't still learning the ropes, like Auntie Jessie.

She wasn't a child.

Taking a breath, she twisted the handle and pulled—

The door barely moved an inch before it was yanked shut again.

She had no idea why that made her look to the heavens with a little smile. Mr. Scary Alpha with all his scars. All the growls, the stern looks, the aloofness... Inside, he was a warm puddle of goo, hoping someone would make him a daisy chain and ask to be friends. He did a terrible job of hiding it.

"I'm good," she said brusquely through the door. "I'm good to return. I was just a little...taken aback, is all. I've never seen something like that before."

"Neither have I," he replied. "But it didn't have the same sort of interest in me as it did in you. Neither of us are wanted, anyway. This is Niamh's territory. We need to let her handle the situation without distractions."

"Heard." She paused for a moment. "Can I come out now, though? It stinks in here."

Nothing happened. She popped out a hip, happy no one was here to see her tantrum.

"Sue, I followed instructions. I did as she asked. I shouldn't be punished for that." Another pause. "It's making my bourbon taste bad."

The door bumped against the frame, Broken Sue releasing the catch, and then it swung her way. She caught it and opened it slowly, relishing in the clean— or, at least, not as rank as the bathroom—fragrance from beyond.

She stepped out with composure and allowed him to step to her right, positioning himself in the path of danger, should it come this way.

"What's happened?" she whispered, because his gaze was still pointed toward the bar.

"They're just talking."

"Body language?"

He barely moved, just a flare of certain muscles along his arm and through his broad shoulders. She understood every syllable in the way her father had taught her, a master at subtle body movement.

Touch and go. Tension.

One day she hoped to get Sue's history—to find out who'd trained him and how. She could learn a lot from him. When his pain wasn't so sharp, of course. When he wasn't guarding his heart with the claws of a hurt and desperate man.

She understood that pain, though it wasn't nearly the same as hers. She'd finally gotten her uncle back. Her broken family had reunited and become whole again. His never would.

"Niamh?" she whispered.

"Leading the conversation, though not relaxed. Not like she'd talk to me or you. Not like she'd talk to Tristan, even. She's wary of this creature, though it isn't a total stranger. That means it is highly dangerous. *Highly* dangerous. I hope she's doing damage control and not inviting it into the fold."

Aurora took a step forward to see.

Sue stepped in unison even though his gaze was turned away.

"Do you dance?" she asked, touching his arm lightly. He flexed, not planning on taking the silent request and stepping out of the way. "Those with a detailed understanding of body language usually make great

279

dancers."

He didn't comment, but the tightening of his body was answer enough. *Not since...*

"It isn't going to hurt if you just let me see," she murmured, persistent in her touch, showing her stubbornness.

He tilted his head just a bit. *You're annoying me.*

He did take a step back, though, just enough to let her peer around his big arm.

The angle of Niamh's body was off, not at all like when she'd been sitting at the bar earlier. She was leaning away a little, for one, as though she thought it possible the creature might lunge for her. Two, she was clearly ready to combat it, forearms on the bar and ready for use. And three, there was a strange sort of aura around her. Magic, definitely. Not shadows and darkness like Aurora might have expected from Niamh's personality, but a sort of shimmer, like a sparkle.

"Niamh is the last person I would've expected to sparkle," she whispered, edging out a little more to get a better look at the creature.

Sue grunted, his version of a laugh. *Agree.*

The suit was all wrong on that creature, but she couldn't pinpoint why. The jacket fit well enough, though it was a little too big in some places and small in others. From what she could see of the pants, they were the same. Black on black, matching. But there was a stretch in one shoulder and not the other. The hem seemed high on one side and not on the other. Or was that a trick of the eyes?

His feet hung strangely, too, one a little off kilter and neither resting on the footrest of the stool. His hands hung limp, as though he didn't have use of them, but she'd seen them move. The greased hair—

The list was long. All the little details didn't add up to the whole.

CHAPTER 19

NIAMH

THE DARK WISPS rising from his person intensified, heightening the smell. For anyone else, a shock of terror would've filled them with dread; their hearts would become hunted rabbits. She was immune, however—something about the origins of her magic reducing her susceptibility to creatures of the shadow and death march realms.

"You will not—"

"Can you fellas procreate?" she asked suddenly, noticing the similarity between his nightmarish magic and Tristan's powers.

"What?" he asked, thrown off his outrage a lot easier these days. His minimalistic diet was showing. "No." He looked into his lap. "My genitals didn't survive the rotting period." He shook his head at her as the barman very slowly worked his way down the bar. Most of the other patrons had left. "I see nothing has changed with you. Always poking right where it hurts the most."

"That wasn't intentional—"

"And for your information, Volkan means disaster, like a volcano. It's a fitting name."

"Is it, now? What disaster have you caused?"

"What is it the Dicks say? Dress for the job you desire."

"Aha. Well, the Dicks are gonna make fun o'ya if ye don't change your name."

The barman made it closer, licking his lips nervously. "Something for y-your friend?"

"A cheap whiskey will do him rightly," she said without missing a beat, sending him quickly away. "Cider first, though!"

"You run with shifters now?" the revenant asked, lacing his spindly fingers on the bar and staring out at the few remaining patrons. "Those two little mice who scurried away were shifters, correct? There aren't many in this city, but I come across their scents every now and again."

Oh yes, he'd been around. He was casing the city, it seemed like. Maybe had been for a while. Immortals didn't tend to move as quickly when they got older. Niamh had surely slowed down, content on her porch, happy in pseudo-retirement. She'd gotten a nudge, though, and was slowly but surely waking up. Stretching back into her old life. The process took some time, but as she got the wheels a bit more greased up and got rolling, things had started moving faster and faster.

This creature would be no different. He just needed to be properly fed. She'd have to speak to Tristan to see if he had any ideas about that.

"I run with some of them," she said. "Gargoyles, too, remember those?"

"Ah yes, gargoyles. Useless. Too stubborn to admit their fear, and because of that, dead too quickly to really suffer. I never had much to do with them. Bad feeding. I have not seen them in an age."

"They're mostly isolated these days. Anyway, Ivy House has found a new heir. Know anything about that?"

"Ivy House." His tatters rustled, the movement almost like gargoyle wings. "Yes. I met one of the heirs, visiting a king in…" He tilted his head upward in thought.

The barman hurried over with the whiskey and placed it on the very edge of the bar before backing away.

Niamh sighed. He clearly didn't plan on getting her the cider.

"Are you going to drink that?" She pointed at the whiskey.

Volkan slid it her way. "I would certainly rather not, but I would've if you'd insisted."

"That's why I got ye a cheap shot. Joke's on me."

He went back to thinking. "No. It was a queen I was visiting. Victoria, I believe. The heir was headstrong and powerful, I remember, but very fond of opium and the like. She was sent away shortly after arriving. Or was she assassinated shortly afterward? I can't remember the timeline. She *was* assassinated, I know, I'm just not sure when. I remember trying to get in contact with her for a trade she'd alluded to, but then I heard the news."

"Assassinated by her lover?"

"No, she had many of those, and they were all gargoyles. Loyal to the letter. Made it damn hard to get in a room alone with her. Always naked, too, flaunting their perfectly sculpted, intact bodies. Distasteful."

"The point?"

"Yes." His tatters rustled again. "Speaking to you is like trying to shake off the dust and wipe away the cobwebs in order to see out a window."

"Poetic," she said drolly before throwing back the shot. She needed a vat of the stuff to be comfortable in this thing's presence.

"She was assassinated over a deal gone bad, I think. She probably initiated it when she was out of her mind, didn't follow through or forgot about it entirely, and was held accountable. I have a feeling it would've gone similarly between the two of us if someone hadn't already gotten to her."

"That's the only dealing ye've had with Ivy House? I never interacted with any until I found myself in O'Briens, contemplating retirement. I don't know many details about its history."

His frame tightened a little. "Are you trying to get free information out of me, Niamh?"

She was getting nothing but, actually. That layer of dust was mighty thick. He had a lot of catching up to do.

Niamh wondered if she should point him in the direction of Momar so he could work his way up through the ranks. He'd be on the outskirts at the start, but there would be plenty of pain and suffering for him to consume, and he might eventually work deep into the organization. That or the Mages' Guild. There were options for him to exploit there.

Then again, he'd want to take over running it, and then they'd have a new, more sinister enemy to confront.

She needed a brainstorming session, not a hasty decision in a bar. Certainly not in *this* bar, at any rate. The stool wasn't comfortable enough for long-term seating.

"Just curious, is all," she said absently, checking the

time. "I've got to be running."

"The heir this time around…" He tapped his bony fingers against the bar. "Is she just as powerful? Does she show interest in…politics?"

"Ye don't know the first thing about magical politics right now, wandering around the streets like a zombie. But if ye did… Ye know how ye had a hard time getting the other heir alone because of all the gargoyles?" She paused before pushing off her stool. "Well, this time I handle the deals with dickless creatures. If ye have a query, ye go through me."

His hiss said she had the upper hand. It also said she had something he wanted.

He'd assume this heir could give him whatever the last heir hadn't. A willy, perhaps. Who knew? In life, the man had been vain. He'd always sought to improve his appearance. His image. He'd always wanted the prettiest women or men in his bed. The prettiest things around him.

And now he was a peeling flesh Popsicle. Fate could be a cruel mistress.

He talked of information? She knew more about him than he could dream to know about her. In truth, it was her cousin who'd poisoned the man. She had no idea why, nor did she know why the man had presumed it was his wife who'd done it. Nor had she cared. When she saw an *in*, she took it.

Just like now.

If Niamh judged the situation correctly, he'd get in contact again. He'd seek to make a deal. It would open a door for Niamh. She just had to figure out how a revenant, a dangerous creature to allow too close, could work into her plans.

What were the odds of coming across a creature like that, a master of disguises and the sort of fear only death could inspire, on holiday? She didn't yet know if it was a gift…or a curse.

✧   ✧   ✧

AURORA

"HE'S AN ILLUSION, isn't he?" she asked quietly, realizing she was now bodily leaning against Sue, clutching his arm. She couldn't seem to pull herself away. Despite her pep talk in the bathroom, she had to own that, yeah, that thing freaked her out. She didn't know exactly why, but something about the creature was a *nope*. For the first time in her life, she was happy to let someone else handle it.

"I don't know," he murmured in a rough voice. "It's not what it seems, that much I know. I'd like Alpha Steele's take on it. He's better at reading strange creatures."

"Or maybe Tristan's," she said, trying to will herself to push away from Sue but unable to do so. He didn't shrug her off, either, a rarity for a man who seemed to shrug everyone away. That thing out there had him rattled.

"Maybe Tristan's," he agreed as Niamh pushed off the barstool to standing.

Sue twisted a little and bent his arm around Aurora, pressing her into his broad back. She clung on like a spider monkey, leaning to peek around his bicep.

"I feel like a coward," she admitted, shaking a little.

"You and me both," he growled, and his body said he was laughing at himself to admit it. "I don't fear death, but I'm glad you walked away first. That means I get the job of hiding back here under the guise of protecting you. I have a reputation to uphold, after all. Pissing myself because of a creature in a slick suit doesn't fit my image."

If they were gargoyles, she'd have buried her face into his back to muffle her laughter. Instead, she had to settle for leaning harder into him, swaying, showing with her body how hilarious she found his joke. How welcome. Because no, he'd never have walked away first. He'd mastered his fear; she knew that. All the same, it was really nice of him to let her off the hook. It made the things he'd said earlier, when he hadn't, much more poignant.

"Right so." Niamh peeled some money off a wad that had been in her pocket and laid it on the bar. She paused then, staring at the creature. "Do ye want an invitation or what? Get on wit'ya. Ye're makin' everyone nervous, not to mention ya *schtink*. Clean yerself up, like."

"You have to hand it to her—she plays a really good game," Aurora whispered. She and Sue were still locked together, watching the scene from a distance. "Please don't ever tell anyone I needed an emotional support beta through all of this. I'm supposed to be the tough, fearless, budding alpha."

"I won't tell anyone you hid behind me if you don't tell anyone I made absolutely no move to back Niamh up. I'm pretty sure this is a breach of my duties, but I don't really care. That creature is getting worse by the minute, and I don't know why, and it is starting to really creep me out."

She *couldn't* help it. The situation was so surreal, so scary, so weird, that she buried her face into the crease of his back muscles and laughed.

"What have I gotten myself into?" she asked, pushing her forehead into his muscles and feeling them tighten. "I wanted a challenge and room to grow, but this… Mages, okay. Basajaunak, glad they are on our side. But *this*?"

"Working *with* a basajaun instead of veering away from one was a surprise to me," Sue said, stepping a little more toward the wall. She followed his progress easily, not needing to pull her face away from his back. This was highly unprofessional and un-shifter-like, but she didn't at all care, and thankfully he wasn't insisting on following protocol. "The mages were not pleasant for me to work with, given…"

He didn't finish, knowing he didn't have to. Everyone in the pack knew about his history with mages.

"The puca would drive a man to insanity." His arm tightened around her again. "The gargoyles were also an adjustment. Hell, Jessie's whole team requires constant adjustment. At this point I'd thought I'd seen it all. After getting familiar with her team and figuring out how not to kill the puca, I really thought I'd seen it all."

"At least you were eased in."

"True. But…" His shoulder bumped the wall. *Defeat.* "*Why* is that thing so scary?"

She laughed into his back again, shaking her head. "If I weren't so good at reading body language, I'd think you were trying to humor me."

"Which is why I'm being candid. You're one of the few shifters I can't hide things from. Your father is an incredible alpha. The best I've ever seen, Alpha Steele included. He has a temperament that lends well to leadership. A temperament Alpha Steele had to find in Jessie."

She flattened her hands against his slabs of muscle, soaking in their warmth. Thank God they were in the trenches and this didn't count as impropriety, because she was stepping over the line. He was a kind soul for letting her, for being her driftwood out at sea.

"Thank you for saying that," she said softly.

"Do you miss your family?"

"Yes and no. We're a very close group, but I crave a little freedom."

His arm came away, leaving her grasping at him for a brief moment before she regained her composure. He half turned to her, his dark eyes serious.

"You don't have to go out alone to find freedom when you're with this group. Your father is an incredible alpha for a pack of shifters, but Jessie and her gargoyles, her team, have inspired something no pack has cultivated. Alpha Steele is rolling with it in a way no other alpha shifter would. Niamh wasn't lying—you can go out with almost anyone and find the freedom you seek. Dress how you want, act how you want—within reason—and dance all night. We work hard and we play hard. We take care of each other, we're a team, and we don't sweat the details. And if you get challenged for letting loose?"

His eyes sparkled with the answer to his question. *Dominate.*

Hands at her sides now, composure finally sinking in, she inclined her head. *Heard/thank you.*

CHAPTER 20

AURORA

"**W**HAT ARE YIS at?" Niamh stopped beside them, her hands on her hips. "Ye better have change, because that barman took off, and all I have are twenties." She huffed, looking out toward the bar. "That clown of a revenant has made it impossible for me to come back to this bar again. There are many things I can bear, but being eighty-sixed from a bar when it wasn't my fault is not one of those things."

"It *was* your fault." Sue pushed forward, and Aurora realized she didn't have her glass in her hand anymore. It lay a foot away where she'd clearly dropped it, something she didn't recall doing. She wondered if Sue had even realized it.

"Me *bollocks*. I can't be held responsible for that thing tracking me to this bar," Niamh said, following him.

Aurora hurried to catch up.

"I'm certain, somehow, that it was," he replied.

"What was that thing, a rev…what?" Aurora asked as they left the now totally empty bar. Not even the bartender had stuck around. "Where'd everyone go?"

"That clown pulled down his businessman image, and everyone saw what he really looked like," Niamh said as they turned right, toward a busier street. "They shot out of the bar like the walls had come alive and tried to grab 'em."

"Let's grab a rideshare," Sue said.

"I can't be arsed." Niamh trudged on. "Nothing but chatty wankers, those. No, let's get a cab. Just up here. There's a whole bunch. They mind their business."

"Probably because they'd prefer to plead ignorance if there's a murder in the dirty back seat."

"Probably."

"What was the outcome of that meeting?" Sue asked, back to closed down and surly. He never seemed to let his personality out for long, a relic of his former job. It felt strange for such a powerful man—such an alpha in mind and in power—to be a beta.

Aurora took his transformation as a cue, though, to button up her personality as well. Back to business.

Niamh sighed, lifting her hand when they got to the curb. "Long story short, that creature could be incredibly helpful or a real nightmare."

"And you have no idea which?"

"Not one shred, no. But if he's helpful, he'll be *really* helpful."

"And if he's not?"

A cab pulled up as Niamh scowled at Sue. "Did ye trip back at that bar, knock yer head against the wall, and bust free all yer sense? Then he'll be a *real* nightmare, obviously. The risks are big, yes, we're all keepin' up with the conversation. Janie Mack, ye'd try the patience of a saint."

"How would you know?" he replied, humor in the lines of his body again.

"Because I am one. Saint McFeck-off." She turned for the waiting cab. "Now get into this cab. Don't embarrass me."

Stifling a laugh, because Niamh's surliness was a riot and somehow endearing, Aurora squeezed into the back seat, taking the middle, and Niamh gave the name of their destination.

"How many of those exist in the world?" Sue asked as they got underway.

"Oh…" Niamh let out a breath, looking out the window. "Probably only a handful now. It's not easy to thwart the grave, and once you exist the way he does, it's not easy to get along in modern society. As you saw."

"How do you kill them?"

"Same as most undead—tear out the heart, cut off the head. Things like that."

"How easy is that to manage?"

"Depends on how long they've been unalive and how many people have tried it before."

"And with that one?" Sue pushed.

"It would not be easy. He's never been well liked, in life or in death. Many have tried to take him down. He has a sixth sense for evading the grave, I think."

"His powers?"

"Speed, strength, hardiness, magic that makes you unnaturally terrified. He also looks a mess. Trust me, it's not nice to see." She thought for a bit as they slowed near a busy area filled with pretty people walking along the sidewalk, the men in tight clothes and the women skimpily dressed. "The magic is similar to Tristan's, don't you think?"

Sue shook his head slowly. "Both can make someone unnaturally terrified, but the feeling is much different."

"Except Tristan has never used his magic on you directly."

"He has. I asked him to. I wanted to know the effects...just in case."

Niamh bent forward to look across Aurora at Sue, a

grin pulling at her lips. "Just in case he turned out to be an enemy? Or double-crossed us? Or maybe you think that if we find out all his secrets, he'll seek to bring us down so we can't tell anyone?"

"It never hurts to be cautious," Sue replied, not looking at her.

"I bet ye aren't so cautious with shifters," she goaded him.

"I am exactly as cautious with shifters. I know what happens when a pack is too trusting."

Niamh frowned at him and leaned back again. "Why do ye always insist on clubbing people over the head with all that baggage? Ye take all the fun out of razzing ya, so ye do."

Sue's reaction was almost imperceptible, just a tiny relaxing of muscle. Basically, a smirk. He'd formed a camaraderie with Niamh, no matter how messed up. She might drive him nuts, but he took comfort in her flippancy regarding his past. Good to know.

"Well, anyway," Niamh went on, "a revenant couldn't be partially responsible for Tristan because their willies rot off. The mystery continues."

"Is that thing going to follow you here?" Sue asked as the cab stopped in front of a busy, upscale club in a hopping neighborhood. Lights flashed, people laughed, perfume wafted into the slightly open window. Bodies crowded the sidewalk, more than Aurora had ever seen in one place, never having traveled to a big city like this. The nightclub scene here was clearly very popular.

Sue paused with a foot out of the car, doing a double take back at her. He put out his hand, large and scarred, waiting for her to fill it with her own.

But they weren't in the trenches anymore. This was just normal life. Loud, chaotic, busy, but normal. It was outside of her comfort zone, sure, but that was no reason for the pack beta to give her special treatment.

"Nah, he'll get himself together before he makes contact again," Niamh said, leaning against Aurora to see the meter. "He won't want to risk being told to bugger off because he's not up to standard. *Jaysus*, I'd expect a happy ending for a price tag that steep. What kinda petrol am I payin' for, rocket fuel?" She handed two twenties forward. "Guess I don't need the change. Girl, take that lummox's hand so he can drag ya out. Hurry up now, let's get cracking. I'm dyin' of the thirst."

"I'm fine—" Aurora cut off as Niamh gave her a shove.

She sighed, taking Sue's warm hand and letting him help her out of the cab. On the sidewalk, he stayed close, posturing in such a way that the passing guys, their gazes appraising, found somewhere else to look.

"This way," Niamh said, peering down at her

phone. "Broken Sue, stay at that girl's back, would ya? We don't need one of these Dicks grabbing her butt and getting a deserved *baytin'*. They won't let us in if she does that."

Sue did as she said, his hand on Aurora's shoulder possessively, his body close behind. A wide berth opened up around them on the busy Los Angeles sidewalk. They threaded through a cluster of people to a bouncer at the front of a long line. Niamh yelled something at him, showed him the screen of her phone, and waited while he turned away to talk into his headset. In a moment they were through, Sue as big or bigger than their security, broader and more muscular. Tougher, too. Meaner. More vicious.

They sized him up as he passed, used to being in charge in this place, but quickly realizing they were outgunned. They dropped their gazes one by one, giving him the respect due to an alpha.

"Is it hard for you?" Aurora yelled over the sudden cacophony of music and laughter as they walked through a short hallway and were guided past a ticket booth and into utter chaos. Colored lights streaked through the air, white lights flashed, people shouted, bodies gyrated.

She stopped and then tried to back-pedal. Her senses were being *assaulted*. The noise alone felt like a suffocating bag that had been pulled down over her head.

"I've got you," Sue said, leaning down so his lips were next to her ear, his body pressed against hers. "Just follow Niamh. I'm right here."

He guided her on, pressing through the throng of bodies that Niamh somehow didn't seem to notice. They could've been walking into a half-deserted dive bar for all she paid attention to the mayhem.

"Is what hard for me?" he asked as they slowed when a people jam blocked the way.

"Is it hard for you being an alpha with a beta title?" she shouted, barely able to hear herself over all this noise. Someone belched. Another shrieked with laughter. And then they were moving again, Aurora grabbing Sue's wrist to keep hold of something. "With beta duties, I mean. You're an alpha, but you don't get the respect of one."

"If it had been Tristan's old situation, where the leader wasn't as good, or as dominant, or as respectable, I wouldn't be here. But this pack—even when it was just a pack—is different. Alpha Steele is more dominant than me, no question. More intense. More vicious. A better leader. Better for the team he and Jessie are putting together. Anytime I think I might be catching up, he bumps the ceiling a little higher. He gives me ample respect, and when we're in the company of other alphas, he treats me as though I am their equal. He doesn't make a show of my beta title when it's clear I have equal power to another. He only seeks to maintain our hierarchy, which I respect and the shifters need."

She turned a little to look up at him, gauging his honesty. He held her gaze, clearly knowing why she was looking. His intense, dark eyes were open, entirely serious. He was not just saying any of this for her benefit or to kiss the butt of the alpha's niece.

"You really respect him, huh?" she said as his hand shot out, catching a man who was just about to back into her. He gave the man a shove away.

"Absolutely."

"And being beta to Jessie?"

His exhale dusted her face as they slowed again, trying to work through a crowded bar area. He watched the path ahead, catching someone else before they could bump into her and then directing the woman away. The woman turned with a scowl, but her eyes widened at the sight of him. Red infused her cheeks, and it was clear she didn't know whether to be anxious or desirous.

"I'm not a beta to Jessie," he said as Niamh shouldered people out of the way and yanked Aurora after her. Sue kept pace. "Jessie doesn't work like that. I'm family. I would follow her into hell, but she would do everything in her power to keep me from trying. She's the glue that keeps the pack together, and I will help Alpha Steele protect her at all costs."

"Hey!" Jasper came out of nowhere, a girl on each arm and lipstick on his jaw. He smiled when he saw them and pulled his arms away from the women, pointing at Aurora. "They found you! Great. Come on, we're this way." He spoke to each of the women in turn. "Sorry, but I need to take them in. I'll talk to you in a while, okay? See ya."

He worked them through the crowd faster than Niamh had, probably because of his size, before leading them up a set of stairs and into an area with a lot of red ropes. Their crew had taken over the back corner, sitting or standing and looking over the balcony with drinks in hand, many of them swaying to the music.

Just inside the rope, Aurora saw that they had their own small but private bar, with a bartender who was currently serving Tristan and a couple other gargoyles. Sue headed that way, and Aurora followed as though caught in his undertow. She wasn't quite ready to be cut loose just yet. Her past desire to dance seemed a little too daunting in the insanity in this place.

Tristan turned as they got close, his pretty, glowing gaze taking in Sue and then darting down to her. His half-smile dwindled.

"What is it?" Tristan asked.

"You need to speak to Niamh about a revenant she met at the bar we just came from," Sue replied.

A hard edge lit those glowing amber eyes. Tristan's gaze almost seemed to flash, and power leaked from his person. "A revenant? You're sure?"

"That's what she said. She knew him. He walked into the bar and sat beside her. We gave her space."

Aurora couldn't hide the smirk at "we gave her space." It wasn't a lie…

Her subtle tell was too subtle for Tristan to pick up on, thankfully. He was learning fast, but he had a ways to go. He wouldn't know they'd been cowering in the back.

Sue looked down at her, though, catching it. His eyes glittered for a brief moment before he went back to business.

"You should probably talk to her before you two take this to the alphas," Sue said, and it was clear that he was passing off an ultimatum. *You'd* better *take it to the alphas, or I will.*

"Are those things bad news?" Aurora asked Tristan, and Sue adjusted his body to give her a bit of space.

"If you've wronged them, yes," he replied, looking at nothing. "I assume this one beat the grave? It captured its vengeance already?"

"Long past, I'm given to understand," Sue replied. "Niamh didn't seem comfortable around it. Said it would be hard to kill."

Tristan took a deep breath and held it for a moment. Oh yeah, this was bad news. Or good news, if it could be brought around to their benefit. "They're wily, above all," Tristan said. "It isn't their power that is the problem, or their magic. It's how they prey on their targets. They have a supernatural ability to seek out their enemy, blend in, and then kill when least expected. If you were to engage one with any kind of aggression, you'd better kill it then and there, because if you didn't, your chances of survival would be dismal. Eyes in the back of your head wouldn't be enough."

"You sound like you're talking from experience," Aurora said.

His posture screamed, *Danger: tread lightly.*

"I was a mark once," he replied slowly, beating his gaze into her. "I killed it in its life, and then I killed it in its afterlife. Not many people are that lucky."

"Let's hope we don't have to be," Sue said, angling a bit closer to Aurora. He was still playing protector, probably because of her affiliation to her auntie and uncle. She needed to cut him loose. Babysitting wasn't part of his job.

"Okay, well…" She took a step away. "I'll leave you

two to it."

With that, she turned and started walking, immediately bumping into Jasper, followed closely by Ulric.

"Hey," Jasper said, bending down to smile in her face. "Just the lovely lady I was looking for. Niamh said you needed help finding a dark corner." He spread his palm across his chest. "Is that to bang me specifically, or are you looking for help finding someone else? Either way, I'm in. It'll be easy, too. This place is full of corners and willing partners."

"It is *very* easy to find a willing partner," Ulric chimed in. "I mean, besides us, because we're always willing. But any Dick here would follow a woman blindly, it seems like—"

"Very sexually frustrated," Jasper said, nodding exaggeratedly.

"Well, yeah," Ulric replied. "They go about it all wrong. They're sleazy and pushy and act like they're trying to steal something."

"Did you hear that one guy? He called the girl a slut when she wouldn't give him any, which is the very definition of *not* being a slut."

"That just means he thought she was a slut going in, figured she would be an easy lay because of it, got pissed when she saw through him, and then tried to shame her for his crushed ego. Small dick energy."

"Well, right," Jasper put in, "but how are you going to look down on women for banging, and at the same time expect to be banged? There is zero logic there. Zero. Celebrate the fuck, that's what you gotta do. Celebrate the ladies who will give you the fuck. These guys are making their lives infinitely harder. It's very confusing."

"But helpful for us." Ulric grinned at him comically.

"This is true. Janes are even easier to please than shifters. Anyway, Aurora, all of that aside, you can have any Dick you want on account of your being super hot. Or us, obviously. We'll get you that big O, no problem. You're not as tightly wound as you usually seem." He used two fingers to point at her eyes. "I see that glitter, baby."

"We just need a direction so we know how best to fulfill your needs," Ulric finished.

She stared at them incredulously, which they wouldn't know because they were not nearly as good at reading body language as Tristan.

"I kinda just want to have fun without it getting back to my dad," she finally said. "Like…dancing. Slow dancing."

Ulric pointed at her, his eyebrows raised. "Grinding? Is that what you're really saying? I can't tell."

"Come on." Jasper took her hand, heading toward

the rope. "We'll figure it out."

"Okay, but being down there stresses me out," she said.

"We got you, baby girl." Ulric put his hands on her shoulders. "We'll be your bumpers. It'll be okay, you'll see."

Aurora glanced back at Sue as she let Jasper pull her along. He stood at the bar by himself, drink in hand, watching her go.

If their positions in the pack were different, she'd drag him with her, or stall the guys for a bit and go hang out with him until he found another group to join. But he was the beta, and she was a nobody right now. Pack protocol said that she needed to give him distance, regardless of how he'd helped her not one hour ago.

With a sigh, she followed Jasper and let herself laugh as she did so. Niamh had been right—these guys seemed like the cruise directors for people who wanted to let their hair down. She'd found exactly what she'd been hoping for.

CHAPTER 21
JESSIE

THE NEXT EVENING, after a really fun time hanging out and dancing in the club, I stood in front of a mirror with a grim expression. The fun and games were over. It was time for business. Tonight was the mage dinner.

"This can't be what they are going for," I said in my bedroom, looking at my reflection. This time, it wasn't my clothing choice that I was waffling about—it was Sebastian and Nessa's.

"Why, what's wrong with it?" Tristan stood from the bed, having come in a moment before to discuss the placement of the gargoyles tonight. We needed to keep them far enough away that none of the mages would know they were on hand, but close enough to get to us in a hurry if things went south. We had a strict limit on numbers for tonight, and I didn't want the mages to know, until it was too late, that I was breaking it.

"I mean…" I pulled my arms away from my body, looking down at the baby-blue ballroom-type dress. Lace dappled with little blue roses crossed the top of my chest and connected with the fitted bodice, perfectly contoured to my body. Sebastian and Nessa had gotten my size correct with impressive precision. The skirt puffed out over the hoop, reaching all the way down to the floor and dragging a little in the back. White gloves adorned my hands, up to my elbows, and a glittering diamond bracelet circled my wrist, jewelry I'd brought along. "Give me a black choker and a pair of glass slippers and I'd be Cinderella."

He squinted one eye as he took me in again, and then a grimace pulled at his lips.

"Ah," he said, and the grimace turned into a smile. "Well…she did look really good heading into that ball. What shoes do you have?"

I lifted the hem to reveal the white satin ballerina shoes, flexible but durable, with thick rubber soles.

"They aren't very glamorous." I dropped the dress again. "They'll be good if I need to run or shift, though, I guess. And like…" I ran my gloved hand over the pocket watch hanging from the sewn-on loop, running down a brief length before it nestled into the sewn-in pocket. I didn't have a pocket on the other side. The whole setup was specifically for the pocket watch they'd randomly found in Ivy House, a story the house told me after the dress had turned up here.

"Can I see the watch?"

I daintily pulled it out because I knew it must be valuable, if not a freaking relic. No one had said. I probably shouldn't be wearing it, or maybe even touching it. There was no telling what part of history it had originated from, like most of the other stuff in the house. It was too detailed, old-looking, and expensive-looking to be something mundane.

Tristan handled it gently, bending over to get a closer glance. He whistled softly. "This thing is pretty cool." He opened it as though handling something priceless before softly clicking it shut again. "You shouldn't keep something like that contained within a pocket."

"I know, but why would I take it out?"

"Appearances, I'd imagine." He backed off a bit until he was leaning against the wall like last time. "They must have had a reason for these choices." He shrugged. "Although it could very well be a joke. I don't want to spoil the surprise, but Sebastian and Nessa sent outfits or instructions for everyone. They put Edgar in that suit from when we headed to Kingsley's. Remember? The one that matched Niamh's but was too small in the…dick area."

I blurted out a laugh. "Nice phrasing. Very subtle." I

took a step back, giving him a hard look. "You think they're setting us up as a joke?"

"I think...they are operating in ways...they think they have to."

"What does that mean? Is that something you guys talked about in the brief meeting earlier?"

Tristan, Niamh, and Austin had gotten together to discuss some of the networking items Tristan and Niamh were up to. I'd sat in with them to hear about the revenant, but then left them to the more complex details of their efforts. Austin, knowing more about the magical world and political maneuvering, was better at strategy. I could never bring anything to the table until it was time to put plans into action.

"If this is a joke," Tristan said, "I truly believe they are doing it to benefit you, Jessie. They need you—our convocation—as an ally to reach their goals. They wouldn't want to ridicule you and kill any chance you have at making connections. Connections they need us to make."

I slipped the watch back into my pocket. He did have a point.

"Think of it like this—power is like money in the Dick world, right?" Tristan said. "If you have a ton of it, people shrug off idiosyncrasies as eccentric. The more you have, the more leeway your idiosyncrasies get.

You're basically rolling in there saying you are the most powerful person they are liable to see for a while, maybe ever, and you don't care that they know it."

I shook my head, looking at myself in the mirror again. "All my adult life I've been ridiculed for not dressing the part. Now, when I have the money and help to fit in, I'm intentionally coming off as an outsider."

His eyes softened. "Well, there you go—you're at least prepared for this sort of thing. Just think, if you'd always fit in and suddenly you weren't supposed to? You wouldn't know what to do with yourself. You'd have no confidence in being weird."

I chuckled and put out my hands for a hug. My heart was ragged after yesterday. I still felt guilty and raw after discovering what Matt had been up to with my son, bribing him for his court-ordered allowance. Jimmy hadn't said much on the topic, but I could tell he wasn't pleased with how his dad had acted to Austin and me. Heading into a situation where I'd really like to finally impress someone, but would instead look like Cinderella after being dressed by a drunk fairy godmother, wasn't great for the ol' confidence. All this over the holidays where I'd hoped to relax, rejuvenate, look successful to the people of my past, and generally kick ass. Nothing was going according to plan.

"Well, for good or bad, this is what I'm wearing." I pulled away. "I've put my trust in Sebastian and Nessa. This is apparently what it gets me." I went to the jewelry box to grab some earrings. I felt Austin downstairs, heading toward the front of the house. It must be about time to go.

"What's the status for tomorrow?" Tristan asked as I grabbed some lip gloss. "Christmas, right?"

"Yes. We're missing dinner at my parents' house tonight, but they'll come over here for Christmas Day. Tomorrow morning, Austin wants to see my favorite place to think, and then we'll come back and cook and open presents and do all that stuff. It'll just be immediate family and our people." I looked over his wings. "I wish there was a way to disguise those so we didn't have to come up with reasons why you all have superhero complexes."

I grabbed my small sequined clutch, utterly laughable, and put in the lip gloss while surveying him.

"I wonder if I can do...something..." I reached out to touch one of them, wondering if a salve would work, or some sort of magical oil, maybe.

He snatched my wrist out of the air.

"No," he said. "My wings are a lot more sensitive than a normal gargoyle's." He paused. "In ways you wouldn't want to stimulate."

I grimaced at him, taking my hand back. "Yikes. I didn't realize." Flustered and not sure why, I grabbed the encrypted phone from the shelf in the closet.

"What are you doing?" he asked.

"Asking the mages if they have any ideas. They haven't responded to a single message, but they did send that brooch for Cyra, so they must be getting them." I made sure there was no sadness in my voice when I added, "Maybe they're just…really busy."

"Can't you find that information about hiding our wings on your own?" he asked.

I scoffed. "Given how quickly Sebastian always found solutions, you'd think it was easy, wouldn't you? It's not. Like…at all. I have a crapload of books in Ivy House about magic, but the spells are very broad. This is for killing. This is for defending. There are nuances, sure, but Sebastian does truly out-of-the-box thinking. He has a talent for creation, for taking eight spells and making one spell from their roots. In Jane terms, he's a brilliant engineer. I'm just a powerful user. I have no idea what he was doing with me."

"Whoa, whoa." He pulled me into another hug. "I sense lots of emotions bubbling up in there, waiting to come out of your eyes and ruin your makeup. Now is not the time. Niamh isn't here, and Mr. Tom is getting Jimmy something to eat before we go. They aren't available to fix you up, and I am not good at that stuff."

"I could fix myself—Wait, where is Niamh?" I pushed away from him, not actually about to cry. I wasn't feeling sorry for myself. Not really. I just legit didn't know what a genius was doing working with someone who was basically a Jane. Didn't mean I wanted him to stay away, though. I was lost without him.

I felt Niamh's distance, only cluing in now because I'd expected everyone to be downstairs.

"She went to a posh wine bar where she's heard rumors of mages hanging out," Tristan said as I started for the door. "She wants to see if anyone shows, and if so, if they know anything about the dinner."

"That woman really gets around." We left the room and walked toward the stairs.

"Yes. Speaking of geniuses, I always wonder why she bothers trying to teach me how to hang around the pubs and extract information. She's as good as Patty when she's in her element. I don't have the knack to get on her level."

"She really is good at reading people."

"What's the story for the day after Christmas? Are you still going to the in-laws'?"

"Ex-in-laws, and yes. The mages in O'Briens can wait in their cells just a little longer. I want to show up at that party like a rockstar. Given Matt hasn't called to tell me not to come, even though I added a couple of people to the guest list, he probably thinks his mother can cut me down a peg. She is a real piece of work." I lifted my dress to take the stairs. "I will definitely wear something different than a Cinderella ball gown."

"Good for you. Give 'em hell."

The dress barely fit between the banister and the wall of the stairs. I nearly stumbled and fell...twice. Once at the bottom, I had a look around and just kinda...sighed in defeat.

"Really?" I said to Austin, who waited by the door in his expensive suit, looking for all the world like the rich investor we'd said he was. "You get to look good, and I have to look like Cinderella?"

His handsome smirk made me grumpier.

I took in Edgar's tightfitting suit with the bumble-bee brooch, a crotch not made for someone with a package, and the sleeves obviously too short and purposely sewn that way.

Dave lounged on the couch with a few leaves stuck in his hair, braids in strange places, wearing Phil's kilt and construction vest.

When he saw me looking, he used his thumbs and pointer fingers to pinch the edges of the vest and hold the edges out a little like it was the caliber of Austin's expensive and tailored suit.

"Edgar said that I should blend in, and I didn't know what else might do it."

"Not that," I said, shaking my head. "What's with the braids?"

He pulled out his leg, showcasing an impressive French braid that ran down his outer thigh. "I had too much grog last night, and a lady friend thought this might be nice."

"Grog? Were you sailing?"

His brow furrowed. "No, why?"

I let it go. What was the point?

Broken Sue looked great in his suit, and Mr. Tom held his typical suitcase of disguises.

"Fine," I said, noticing Cyra sitting on a beanbag chair in the back corner in a fitted orange suit with a red lacy shirt underneath, probably no underwear, and flip-flops. The outfit almost looked good. Nearly there. "Great."

The rest of the team members attending the dinner wore muumuus, even Indigo, who didn't shift. Those staying behind, which were a few pack shifters, Patty, Mimi, and Aurora would watch Jimmy. Aurora had wanted to come, but she apparently didn't have the seniority. She'd help guard with the others.

"Okay," I said, taking a deep breath. "I feel ridiculous, most of us look ridiculous, and it's time to go. Oh, I better bring a bottle of wine."

"I made more strawberries," Austin said, making no move to go and get them. "I didn't get to see you eat any of the last ones. The gargoyles ate the ones we took into the club last night."

"So good, bro," Jasper said from near the door with Ulric. "So, *so* good."

"They were," Tristan agreed.

"It's probably wrong to bring anything to a party like this," Mimi said. "But given…everything, it would likely be on theme."

"Fantastic," I said dryly. "Let's just go. We can bring the strawberries to the ex thing. Or just eat them here later."

"Hey, Mom…" Jimmy paused on the stairs, looking down at me. "Oh. Are you going to a costume party?"

"Super." I headed for the door. "What is it, bud?"

"Oh, just…" His face flushed when he saw Aurora on the couch. "Nothing. I was just going to ask if we could order something sweet, but if there are going to be chocolate-covered strawberries lying around…"

"We'll order in a few things," Mimi told him. "We wanted to see your mother off in her pumpkin."

"Why isn't Austin dressed up?" Jimmy asked.

"I'm a modern-day Prince Charming," Austin replied without skipping a beat. "The kind of guy who has evolved in his fashion sense."

"Yes, hilarious." I pointed at Jimmy. "No leaving tonight, remember." I swung the finger toward Aurora. "You, either. We don't know what's out there, okay?"

"We *do* know what's out there, actually, and that is why we will definitely not leave," Aurora murmured.

"Stay safe," Mimi told us as we headed for the door. "If anything seems odd, fire magic and run."

"It's going to be us," I said under my breath. "We're the ones that are going to seem odd."

It was not easy fitting the dress into the fancy car. I now had more than a few regrets about purchasing said car. When Austin parked twenty minutes later, I found it even harder to get out. He downright laughed when the hoop got stuck.

"This is seriously not funny," I said as he closed the door and we waited for the rest of our crew, who had much less trouble with their chosen forms of transportation.

"If it were a shifter situation, no, I would not see the humor." Austin held out his bent arm for me to take. "If it were a gargoyle situation, I would think you were on drugs."

"But since it is a mage function?"

"I'm just here to make sure you are safe. Everything

else is not my problem."

I had no idea why he was in such good spirits. We were heading into a potential trap, and I had no easy way out of this dress. The trust I was putting in Sebastian and Nessa was extreme.

The house was large, with tended landscaping in an interesting design and a little bridge that went over a koi pond. A double door was tucked under a large overhang with little benches off to the sides. Sconces hung to either side filled with what looked like fresh flowers.

"Knock or doorbell?" I asked as a metallic clang preempted the door swinging open to reveal a stuffy-looking man. He wore a black suit with a starched white dress shirt beneath. A white silk pocket square stuck out of his breast pocket, and one of his white-gloved hands was bent in front of his chest.

"Good evening," the man said, his voice a little scratchy and wrinkles lining his face. "Thank you for coming. I was told to mention that this door holds a ward. As you pass through, any magic or potions currently applied to you will be stripped away. Also, that the staff here is armed with various weapons that are studded with or shoot silver. Should there be a problem, they will use them."

Indigo, who was staying back with the part of our crew that would remain hidden, could fix Austin up if I couldn't. She'd had experience at the last battle. As for the magic...

"That ward is only good if it has more power than I do, correct?" I asked as the man who had to be the butler—one who lacked fluttering wings and was probably well trained at his job—stepped back and out of the way.

"Yes, madam," he answered.

"She would like to be called miss, actually," Mr. Tom interjected from the back of our party, waiting on the walkway to approach. "I tried 'madam' in the beginning as well. No go. You'll learn."

I was suddenly so glad he'd be guarding the door and not inside with the rest of us.

"Okay, let's do this." I went to step forward, but Austin put out his hand, his humor utterly draining away, his gaze on the butler.

"I'll go first, Jess." He pulled his arm from me and stepped. Almost in unison, Tristan stepped up to take his place at my side. Broken Sue pushed in close behind me, the three of them protecting me from all angles as if I weren't the one with magic in this outfit. Fine. It meant it would be easier for me to drape us all in a defensive spell. Thanks to Ivy House's collection of magical books, I now had a whole lot of those.

"How many staff did you say you had?" Austin

asked, putting out his hand for me once he'd crossed the threshold. I took it, letting him softly tug me in after him.

"I do not have the exact number, sir," the butler replied as I crossed the spell, feeling the magic slide softly over my skin.

"This wouldn't have stripped me of a spell," I mused, turning back to look at the doorframe. "It needs more punch. It's not grabby enough. Even with less power I could have devised something to slip past this."

"I think you do," Austin told the butler.

"Thirty-two, in total." A straight-backed man entered from a doorway on the left of what looked like a marble mausoleum, with marble pillars, floor, stairs—the works. His belly stuck out and a little black mustache lined his upper lip, curled at the corners. His gray hair was parted down the middle and a diamond sparkled from one ear. He wore a plain brown suit of excellent quality but no embellishments, which I found odd, given his choice of facial hair. Maybe that was his *thing*. His eccentric flair. The other was the cane he carried instead of used, and if it didn't have a sword you could pull out of the base, it was a waste of a party prop.

"They are all magical," he said, stopping about twenty feet from us and popping the cane tip off the floor. "Twenty-six of them, however, including Roberts there, don't have much power."

"He doesn't care about the magic—he cares about how many people will be wielding silver-tipped weapons," I said. "But it's fine. If they try to attack him, our people will kill you all. What's the story with this door ward, though? I don't get the point. Can't people just do magic once they get inside?"

A silent beat passed as he surveyed me, and I felt very self-conscious about the stupid dress.

"The point of the ward is to expose anyone trying to hide something," he finally said. "Like people with an invisibility potion."

"Ah." I nodded. "And have you applied it on all the doors and windows in the house, or just this front door?"

Again the silent beat. "Front, back, and side doors. Did you plan on sneaking people in?"

"If I did, they could just come through the front door, because that ward is pretty ineffective. If you want to be thorough, you should really do all the doors and windows."

"They are all locked."

"Locks don't matter for people who have sound-proofing spells and can break a window without being noticed. One of the heirs through the ages must've been a thief. I have a lot of magical spells for breaking and entering now. Anyway, no biggie. I was just getting the lay of the land."

His staring was starting to get annoying.

"You think you could get through that ward with magic?" he finally asked.

"Of course, but I didn't bring any potions or anything to prove it. I don't know how to do the ageless stuff, either. As you know, I'm new to magic. I've only focused on learning the useful stuff. Attack and defense. Breaking and entering. Well...and some horrible spells to get people to talk. Nothing that's good for dinner parties, basically. I could just fire a spell through it, if you'd like?"

My God, this guy had slow response times.

"No, that's okay. I'll take your word for it. Please, let's see the people you've brought."

Austin and I stepped to the side, waiting for the next in our team to come through. It should've been Tristan, but instead Edgar popped his head in, looked around, and sidled through like some sort of vaudeville demon.

"Well, hello," he said, his teeth elongated and almost neon white. "Thank you so much for inviting me to your show. I will greatly love watching the people who dine here."

Now, I was the one staring. This vampire could be

so incredibly creepy.

"Make room," I told him, gesturing him away.

"Yes, of course. I wouldn't want to intrude." He took two large sidesteps to the right with a strange smile, as though he were plotting something.

I really hoped he hadn't brought any gnomes.

Cyra stepped through next, giving everyone a wide, open-mouthed smile as she looked around. "Oh my," she said, pushing her glasses a little farther up her nose. Then she reached through one of the lenses and rubbed her eye. "This place is worse than the old Ivy House. Badly in need of a makeover."

"Come on, come on, out of the way." I waved her toward Edgar.

Finally Tristan entered, suave and huge and menacing, shadows curling through the air around him and the sheen in the doorway visibly melting away as he walked through.

I pointed. "Did you just…defuse that ward? With your body?"

He glanced back at it. "Melted it, I guess. It didn't have much power. It couldn't stand up to my magic, it seems."

His darker type of magic, he meant. I wondered what would happen if Niamh had walked through, whether the effect would have been the same or his mysterious blend of power was the culprit.

"Right." I turned back to the host. "These are the four for inside. I have two on the grounds outside. Would you like to see them?"

"Yes, please," the man said, his eyes locked on Tristan. It occurred to me that no one had exchanged names yet. He hadn't introduced himself, and it had made me forget my manners. Given he hadn't actually asked, maybe the crew didn't matter. Or maybe intros came later. I'd just roll with it.

"Broken Sue, if you please," I called.

He stepped inside a moment later, his body language that of a soldier going to war. His sway was exaggerated, like his gorilla form, and his menace doubled down on Tristan's, making the butler tense before stepping back.

"Excuse me…" The man coughed. "Did you just call this man…*Broken* Sue?"

"Yes. Mr. Tom, come in, please." And then, out of impulse, I said, "Don't embarrass me," as though that ship hadn't already sailed.

He appeared in the doorway, his disguise half on. A neck brace complemented Band-Aids on his face, and a strange gray wig stuck out from beneath a fedora. His arm was looped around a bundle of clothes.

"What is it?" he asked tersely. "I'm preparing for

guard duty, since you have relegated me to the wilds while that excuse for a butler parades around in those stupid gloves and unsigned shoes."

He'd probably meant to say "un-shined" shoes, but I didn't correct him. If Sebastian had been hoping for absurd, I was delivering it.

"Never mind. You're fine to secure the house."

He gave me a *harrumph* before disappearing again.

Tristan softly cleared his throat. "You're missing one," he murmured.

I stared at him blankly.

"Missus Smith," he prompted, reminding me that we would be using Dave's stage name, the one reserved for mages. "Alpha Steele doesn't count as one of your four."

Duh. How in the world had I forgotten the biggest and hairiest of our crew?

"Right. Mrs. Smith, if you please," I called, and a moment later, Dave stuck his head through the door with a gleaming smile, his teeth large, his smile insincere and threatening, and his hair puffed up. I wanted to take a step back myself, and he was on my side.

"Mrs. Smith," I said, holding out a hand for him. "Four, *not* including Austin."

The host had frozen solid somewhere between Tristan and Dave, his eyes wide, his head tilted up slightly.

"Did we break him already?" Edgar asked quietly. "Because usually it takes a little chatter to get to that point."

"*Shh*," I responded with a furrowed brow, wishing I could just be normal for once. But honestly, Edgar was right. We *did* tend to break people…in so many ways.

CHAPTER 22

JESSIE

"F O-FORGIVE ME," THE man stammered before clearing his throat. A light sheen of sweat covered his now-pale face. "Quite the team. I've had word that you also have a host gathering not far away."

Dang it. We'd done a bad job of hiding the extras. We'd need to work on that.

I figured it would be better to be open about it.

"Yes. Should this turn ugly, they'll be here in a moment. I'm sure you can understand my concern, given it's only been a few months since we dealt with a large-scale mage attack. We didn't kill them all. You're a stranger, and I have to think about protection. Rule of thumb, however—don't attack us, and we won't attack you."

His gaze was stuck on Dave, and his fingers were white from gripping the cane.

"I think we can abide by those rules. I'll explain

more in the presence of the others." He offered a stiff bow. "I am Arthur, your host for this evening. And you are Jessie...Ironheart, is that correct? That is your magical name?"

"Yes, given to me by our pack turned convocation."

He nodded as though he knew all about that, turning just a little to offer Austin a bow as well. "And this is Austin Steele? The local shifter pack seems all aflutter with the news of your arrival."

Now it was Austin's turn to stare, and I wondered if we would ever get out of this entryway.

The man shriveled a little where he stood, not able to withstand an alpha shifter's notice.

"That is my name, yes," Austin growled. "I wasn't aware you had any dealings with the local shifter pack."

"We don't," and the guy looked relieved to admit it. "They have been gracious in how they do business, and they stick to their defined area. We've seen no reason to...influence any of their business strategies. We are not enemies of the shifters, Mr. Steele. We are merely cutthroat business people. We'd seek to compete with any magical species in our area. We go head to head with Dicks constantly. It's the nature of a free market. I'm sure you understand, being a successful businessman yourself."

"I do. As I'm sure *you* understand, should the local

pack be physically threatened, my people will join their forces and terminate the threat."

I nearly tapped my foot in response to the lengthy stare-off this time. *Yes, it was a threat. There'll probably be plenty more. Let's move this along.*

"Then we understand each other. Please, follow—" The man gestured toward the doorway from which he'd just come, but Austin interrupted him.

"Forgive me for my ignorance, but is it customary for hosts to use magic to conceal their people when the guests are not afforded the same privilege?"

The man's eyebrows lifted. "Not typically, no. But this is not a typical situation. You are dangerous and, as Jessie has stipulated, have had some problems with mages in the past. You also gave my man a big scare yesterday, from which he has not yet recovered. I thought it wise to boost my safety."

Stupid! I hadn't sent out a feeler spell, taking what I saw for granted and trusting him to be a proper host. That was a good way to get myself and my people killed.

I did so now, easily finding the four people standing at the edges of the room. My ability to detect them meant the potion they used had been created by some-one on a lower power level. Austin had clearly felt their presence, and a glance back earned me a nod from Tristan. He could see them.

"They've got weapons trained on Alpha Steele, Broken Sue, Missus Smith, and me," Tristan said. "Crossbows with arrows that won't do anything to me or Missus Smith and wouldn't do much to slow Broken Sue or the alpha down. That is, *if* those mages managed to hit us, which is highly unlikely, given the amount of shaking two of the four are doing."

"They don't think I'm as dangerous as you guys?" Cyra asked, outraged. "Why, because I'm short? That's heightism!"

"It seems you could've proven the ward doesn't work on you all along," Arthur said, lowering his arm. "It also means you disobeyed the rules."

"You're misinformed," I told him, peeling off my gloves because they were really annoying and I wasn't sure how doing magic would work with them. If this kicked off, I wanted to be ready. "While, yes, my revealing potion would have been plenty powerful enough to get through that ward, none of us took it. Good shifters can feel presences. That's what Austin did. Tristan, however, doesn't need a potion to see through magic. He is immune to even the most powerful invisibility potions, mine included. The fact that you tried to hide your magic and gain the upper hand puts me off, to put it mildly."

He watched me pull out the pocket watch and then

stuff the gloves into the dress pocket. The pocket wasn't big enough to hold them both, though. Nor could I put the watch back into the stuffed pocket.

"Dang it," I muttered.

Austin held out his hand, his gaze never leaving Arthur.

"Thanks," I murmured, handing off the gloves. "So, Arthur, what happens now? Should we peacefully leave, or would you like to see what happens when mages shoot silver-tipped arrows at my team?"

Arthur licked his lips nervously. "I can see your point about my people. Given your accomplishments against Momar's organization, I should've realized the rumors were true and your power would far exceed my own. Forgive me. I was simply trying to instill confidence in my other guests by having a ready defense against a potentially dangerous adversary. Many of them were too scared to attend this dinner unless I took measures to ensure their safety."

"*Secrets, secrets are no fun,*" Edgar sang softly. "*Secrets, secrets, hurt someone.*"

"Thoughts?" I asked Austin.

"Up to you. Given what I've seen, I'm not at all worried for our safety."

I nodded. "I can see where you're coming from," I told Arthur. "I'll let this one slide. Do better."

"Yes, of course." He lifted his arm again, not at all sure. "I'll have my mages take off the revealing spell immediately."

"Don't bother." I waved it away as I started forward. Broken Sue took that as a cue to rejoin Mr. Tom outside, guarding the door. "It's neither here nor there if I can see them or not. My people will let me know if something's not right."

The marble continued down the hall. A large, gilded picture frame down the way held the mage's painted likeness. Big white flowers shot up from colorful vases on a thin glass table beneath it. It was pretty hideous.

The dark room on the right was decorated with muted colors and old-fashioned furniture. Half pillars holding vases of flowers dotted the sides, and more gilded frames hung on the wall. Given none of it seemed ragged and worn, the décor was a choice, and his taste was questionable.

Five men and women sat around the room with champagne flutes in hand, all held with the arm wearing a watch. Those watches sparkled and glittered, statement pieces, like Sebastian and Nessa had always said, and probably pricy. I, of course, didn't know anything about them. The men wore nice suits, not quite as fine as those worn by the host, Austin, or Tristan, and the ladies wore elegant, fashionable dresses.

I looked absurd, and so did half my team.

Everyone stopped talking as we entered. And then they gasped as my people walked in around us and spread along the sides of the room.

"Is that…a big—"

"Don't say it." I held my hand up for the woman wearing five strands of pearls, all different lengths. "He's a basajaun. He doesn't like being called the other thing."

Her mouth clicked shut, her eyes still wide.

"Excuse me." Cyra bowed at thin air. A bit of magic told me they had another invisible person there. She walked around but didn't go far, standing right beside the person.

"Yes, ah, some of the other mages employed invisibility potions for their people," Arthur told me. "For the reasons previously mentioned. Listen up, everyone."

"Did she get magic through the ward?" a man asked, his suit jacket open to showcase his rounded belly.

"I'll get to that." Arthur put up a finger for Belly Man. "Please, allow me to introduce Jessie Ironheart and her…mate, Austin Steele. Jessie and Austin, let me introduce the mages I have gathered here tonight." He indicated Belly Man first as a waitress with the same uniform as the butler stopped beside us and held out a silver tray with two flutes of champagne.

"Oops. That's my job." Cyra hurried back and took

one of the flutes from the tray. She took a large sip and grimaced. "I never much liked this stuff. The fizz makes me—" She sneezed, spraying the glass with spittle. Champagne sloshed out and dripped onto the deep brown rug. "Here, Jessie."

I took it with a grimace and then set it back onto the tray.

After taking the other, I said, "I'll take my chances with this one. I can probably heal myself if I'm poisoned anyway. Or we can rush Indigo in."

"Are you sure?" She pointed at it. "Do you want to just wait a minute to see if I die first?"

"A whiskey on the rocks," Austin murmured to the waitress.

Arthur's eyebrows were in his hairline.

I pointed at Cyra. "She's a phoenix. They come back to life after they die. She's the poison tester."

"And you have healing magic, did you say?" he asked.

"Yes. It's part of being a female gargoyle. We can heal as well as hurt."

"Well, that's just wonderful," said an older woman with bright pink lipstick and graying hair pulled up into a loose sort of bun with curls along the side of her face.

"Rest assured, Jessie, we don't mean to poison you tonight." Arthur smiled. The others chuckled as though that was some sort of joke. Politeness dictated that I should smile even though I didn't get it. "As I was saying, this is Farris Levine, specializing in mixed potions and practical application."

Farris smiled and patted his belly. His watch caught my eye—its face was crimson.

"Hello," I said, and left it at that because I didn't really know what mixed potions and practical application meant.

"Over here is Ester Bardot." He gestured toward the older woman with the pink lipstick before rattling off some other things that made no sense to me.

"Hi," I said.

The woman with the pearls, Tauna, did something called septic magic, which sounded gross, and I didn't recognize the words at all for the other two, Emma and Bert. They were all mages, though, and none had brought a significant other. In fact, there weren't any rings or anything, and it occurred to me that I didn't know if mages married or had mates or just partners.

Arthur then explained about our ability to feel presences or see past the potions, making Farris give me a placating smile.

"And you believed her, Arthur?" He tilted his head. "You must've been born yesterday."

"We can certainly prove it," I told him. "Just have

one of your people try to sneak up on someone from my team. Do it slowly, though. You wouldn't want them to react impulsively. That usually leads to violence."

That shut Farris up. He watched our people with a long face.

"Please, have a seat." Arthur indicated an empty couch.

Tristan drifted closer to the couch, staring down at some empty space until the person standing there must've moved. I didn't bother with magic, not getting any dangerous vibes from these people. They were clearly well below my power scale and didn't seem to intend any harm. They were trying to relax around my crew, even. At least, that was what it seemed like. I noticed them taking deep breaths after looking at Dave, or smiling nervously in clear determination not to seem wary of Edgar. They were doing their best to trust me.

"Jessie, if you wouldn't mind, would you walk us through how you came by your magic?" Arthur asked politely. "We've never encountered a...female gargoyle. They are quite rare, is that correct?"

Tristan tensed, turning his upper body quickly and looking at the wall behind him.

"You okay?" I asked before answering Arthur.

He didn't answer right away, his body flaring with muscle. "Yeah. We're good." He didn't turn back very quickly, though, and when he did, his eyes were glowing a little harder.

"There're no more surprises here, are there?" I asked Arthur seriously.

"N-no." He jerked his head from side to side rapidly. "No, not at all. Why? Is something happening?"

Tristan shook his head. "We should be good. If our outside people saw something, we would've gotten an alert by now."

He seemed a little on edge, though—something Austin must've noticed, because he was also studying the monster-gargoyle. Frowning for a moment, I checked in on my connections. Nothing abnormal came back—everyone was watchful but unworried.

"I actually feel safer with them here," said Emma, a woman in her mid-fifties with braided salt-and-pepper hair. "If any of the Guild try to break in, for example, they'd probably get an unwelcome surprise."

That brought me up short. "Is that a possibility? The Guild breaking in?"

Arthur gave me the kind of smile a grandfather might give a naïve *ingenue.* "Those of us with more power are constantly under threat from others of our kind, especially if magic is done on the premises. There are many things in this house they might try to steal, recipes for various potions being the most common.

I've had break-ins in the past, but no one has ever gotten past my wards and defenses."

"Wards like the one that was on the front door?" I pointed in that general direction.

"Similar, and some much more volatile spells."

"What I mean is, with that power level?"

"Yes. I've made all my own spells and potions." His smile was vain. It really shouldn't have been.

"That power is nothing compared to what Momar threw at us," I said seriously, wariness starting to creep in. "It's nothing compared to what I can do. Do you have enemies? Could Momar and his people know I came here?"

A crease formed between Arthur's brows, his pride in his magic stripped away.

It was Bert, an older man with a trim frame and bald head, who answered. "Mages usually set dinner dates such as this, a meeting of powerful people, with very little notice. It's specifically so enemies will not have enough time to properly prepare an attack."

"We don't have many enemies, though," Ester assured me with a comforting smile. "We mostly stay on the perimeter of the larger magical factions."

"The mage factions, she means," Bert said.

"We don't step on any toes—"

"When it can be helped, and it usually can," Bert

interrupted Ester.

She nodded. "We try to stay out of people's way. For mages like us, the most dangerous thing is getting caught in the crossfire. Or the Guild deciding we should pay more dues. If we don't fall into line, then yes, they might pay a visit."

"Yes," Arthur said. "That's how mages work in this day and age. If you get in the way of someone like Momar, for example, or even someone not nearly so powerful as him, you should fear for your life. It happened to me once in my youth, and I then took steps to ensure it didn't happen again. I stick to safer business and magical acquisitions and pursuits to relieve myself of intense scrutiny from the powerful players. When the Guild comes around, which is very rare at this point because I stay consistent, I pay what is owed and live a *mostly* peaceful existence. I don't stand in the way."

I stared at him incredulously. "And you invited someone like me into your home? Are you out of your mind? I am the very epitome of someone standing in the way."

There was that placating smile again. It was starting to really annoy me.

"All will be discussed in due time. For now, if you'd be so kind as to catch us up on…" Arthur gestured at nothing with the tip of his cane. "Well, how you came to be, I suppose. Then we could all have a little more insight into who you are."

I did as he said, paying attention to Tristan, who hadn't totally relaxed. I kept a firm eye on my connections.

Part of me wondered if I was being too honest and upfront with these people. Mages were sneaky, and what this guy had said did not line up with my dinner invite. The other part of me figured there was nothing to lose. I didn't tell him anything that could be used against me in any way but socially, and if someone wanted to sneak into Ivy House to steal my potions or spells, they were welcome to try. Already had, in fact, or at least onto the grounds, something I didn't mention.

A question-and-answer segment came next. Most questions I answered, and some I shied away from, like queries about my continuing education and whether I'd worked with any mages thus far. They didn't press, just moved the conversation along, which made me relax more in their presence.

When it was time for dinner, I sensed the conversation was about to get more serious. Which wouldn't have alarmed me if not for Tristan's continued apprehension. Though slight, it being present at all was unlike him.

"You okay?" I asked him as the party moved from the sitting room to the dining room.

He scanned the walls and even looked back in the direction we'd come. "Yes. Mostly. Something feels off. I can't put my finger on what, though." He glanced across me at Austin. "Anything on your radar?"

Austin shook his head. "Nothing."

"Do you want me to slink around the house a little?" Edgar asked quietly, following us.

"Yes," Tristan told him. "Don't get caught."

"Oh, I never do." Edgar drifted away, falling in too close to Ester, whose face lost its smile. She hurried to catch up to Bert in front of her.

I left him to it. He'd probably step on an invisible person and absolutely get caught, but I was confident we could explain it away. We were weird, and we did weird things. End of story.

"Maybe I'm just jumpy after hearing about the revenant," Tristan murmured, always scanning. "I really don't want to deal with one of those again, and that one seems worse than most."

"Niamh seemed confident that it wouldn't trouble us until it was ready to barter, and she seemed to think it would be a while before that."

"She's almost certainly right," Tristan said, shaking his head. "Something just seems…off, though. Here. In this house."

CHAPTER 23
TRISTAN

H<small>E COULDN'T SHAKE</small> his unsettled feeling. Like something was in this house besides them. Something was lurking with violent intentions, having slipped past the defenses. It wasn't his territory, though, which would make it easier for this theoretical predator to evade his senses. His magic was the strongest on his home turf, wherever he'd established himself for the time being.

He watched Edgar dog the heels of one of the mages, making the mage hurry up out of nervousness, before falling back and finally slipping into the shadows and through a doorway, unseen. That vampire wasn't good at detecting presences, but he had an amazing sixth sense for sussing out dangers to his clan. Hopefully he'd find whatever stalked these halls or plagued the large, spacious rooms.

Or maybe Tristan was just jumpy, like he'd said.

Maybe it was the effect of the nightmares from last night, dredging up terrifying memories of his being hunted. Of nearly succumbing to the clawed hands wrapped around his throat. Of staring into the murderous eyes of a dead man. His father.

The mages and the alphas sat down to a large table in the grand dining room. For all they were playing it safe with their business ventures, they were clearly very good at making money. It made Tristan wonder just what kind of holdings the more powerful mages and their larger organizations were sitting on.

"Jessie," Arthur began as the wine was poured. Cyra hovered behind Jessie and Austin, ready to taste. "You had asked why mages like us, who try to stay out of the way and lead mostly peaceful lives, would invite you here. It's simple, really. We live a caged life. There is always the fear that we'll accidentally get in the way. Or the Guild will want more than we can provide. Or that the mages' world will continue to devolve until we're faced with a situation in which we're forced to choose sides."

Waiters came out carrying two bowls of soup each, placing them in front of the guests. Cyra pushed between Jessie and Austin to taste, even though it was very unlikely there would be any poison at this dinner.

"*With* them means you will likely be forced to become involved in unsavory, despicable things," Emma said. "Things only a person with no morals would do."

"And against them means you are an enemy." Arthur pressed his lips together. "I'm sure you know what happens to their enemies."

"You made a statement to mages everywhere when you willingly stood in Momar's way and then beat him," Ester said. "It said that you not only oppose him, but you have the power to do so. That the shifters, working with you, are strong enough to take on the best, biggest, and most organized mages and win."

"But you are also so incredibly new," Bert said, steepling his fingers, not bothering with the soup. "And you also had a vested interest in the situation, right? Austin's brother?"

Austin inclined his head in the affirmative.

"So we then got to wondering, was it a statement, or merely an instance of your people defending your own?" Arthur said. "Allowances can be made for the latter. Which then leaves you open for alliances with the very people you fought against. People who, now knowing your power and seeing your potential, will probably offer you the moon."

"Such as what?" Jessie asked.

"Prestige in our society. Vast wealth. Power over others. You'd be like royalty. *They* are like royalty, and we are the lowly peasants."

"You are making a very compelling case...for them," Austin said, his confusion evident. Tristan agreed. This was the worst offer of friendship he'd ever seen. It was clear why these people didn't play politics and tried to stay out of the way.

"There is no sense trying to hide it," Arthur said. "Those are the types of things they offer the powerful members of our society. They reel allies in with promises of high social standing and riches, and then they use them. We wanted to talk with you before they got to you. Explain how things really work in magical society. How the Guild holds mages for ransom, basically—"

"They are more like a Dick mafia than a mage organization," Ester said angrily. "They extort, lie, kill—you name it. They run on greed. And after they reel you in with all their promises, they set you up as a mob boss, stealing and killing for them."

"Let me save you all a lot of time." Jessie set down her spoon. "While I don't know exact details, I have a very good understanding of how Momar functions. He has sent people after me in the recent past, and he's sent them after my family. I hold grudges. As far as the Guild, they did nothing to stop it, so they are clearly useless and need restructuring. I have chosen a side, and no amount of money or empty promises is going to change that. I've willingly put myself in the way, as you say, and now I'm readying myself for when someone tries to remove me."

Jessie's magic pulsed through the room, offering the people sitting there a battle. Offering them glory. A fight to the death. The message was from her gargoyle, whose magic was different from the mage's—it was showing them that while she could be considered part of their club, she wasn't one of them. Her differences made her stronger.

"That is…" Arthur smiled a little, dipping his spoon into his soup. "That is very good to hear."

"Those of us on the edges," Bert said, "have established a sort of network, trying to look out for each other. We in no way have the power and holdings to push back against Momar or the Guild, or even some of their higher-powered minions, but we are not useless. We could be your allies…"

Tristan lost the thread of the conversation as Edgar drifted back in, a little smile on his face. He showed zero alarm, but Tristan's warning systems were all still firing. The strange feeling persisted, almost calling for him to check it out. Tugging at him.

"See anything?" Tristan asked for the sake of being thorough.

"Only my shadow," Edgar said, standing a little too

close.

Tristan shook his head. The vampire was weird.

And then he nearly cracked his neck with how fast he looked back. "What did you say? Your shadow?"

"Yeah, she was—"

"Well, hello, everybody."

None other than Sebastian walked through the door the servers had been using, dressed in a suit, with his hair in the messy playboy style and his watch gleaming in the low light. His swagger said he was playing Elliot Graves, and his half-smile said he had something wicked planned.

Tristan's gut churned.

There had better be a logical explanation for why Sebastian was giving Tristan warning tremors.

✧　✧　✧

JESSIE

I STARED STUPIDLY, not believing my eyes.

"What are we doing here, boys and girls?" asked Sebastian—no, he wasn't Sebastian right now, not with that look. Not with how he was standing and the expression on his face. Elliot Graves had just walked into the room, uninvited.

"Arthur…" Elliot tilted his head and gave Arthur a

mock-disapproving frown. "Are you trying to set up an alliance with my new favorite mage?"

Arthur didn't get up. Actually, no one did. They all stuck to their seats like they'd been nailed down, their hands palms down on the table, looking at Elliot like they were staring a burglar in the face.

"I-I was ju-just warning her about the G-Guild, that's all. I sw-swear—"

"What the hell is going on?" I demanded, pushing my chair back so I could stand.

Elliot swung his hands out, firing magic at me blindingly fast. I barely got up a defensive spell, one that absorbed the hit but didn't negate the power of the blast.

It was a doozy. That bastard knew what spells I favored for my first line of defense.

I flew backward, tipping the chair onto two legs and then over. Austin tried to grab me but missed. I went crashing to the ground, my skirt pluming over me as I rolled. Austin was there, crouching next to me, helping.

"What do we do?" he asked urgently. "Do we attack?"

None of my people made a move as Elliot started talking again. I understood why. He was supposed to be on our side—they didn't want to hurt the guy that fought and bled with us.

I shoved Austin away, angry, hurt that Sebastian had never answered any of my messages. Fighting my dress and getting to my feet, I stood there with my hands fisted and at my sides.

"What are you doing here?" I demanded.

"I've missed you," he said with that cocky little smile, leaning against the doorframe. The other mages still hadn't moved, not even trying to fight back. "I thought we had a nice little rapport in my caves. Before you destroyed them, obviously. When you didn't allow Momar to question you about me, I figured you might want to reconnect, maybe form an alliance. But here you are with this weak lot of goodie two-shoes?" He put his hand on his heart. "You wound me."

"Are you high?" It was all I could think to say. I had zero idea what was going on. I knew there was a point to this, I just didn't know what it was or what part I was supposed to play.

"Nice dress. Did you come here in a pumpkin?" He laughed.

I grew increasingly angry. That bastard *had* set me up to be a punch line.

"Why are you here?" I asked tersely. "What do you want?"

"Simple—I want what's owed to me."

I put out my hands. "And what is that?"

"Why…*you*, silly. We're good together, you and me. We belong together." He gestured with his watch hand, circling the air toward me with his pointer finger. In a singsong voice, he said, "You're really powerful…and I'm really powerful…and together we can reclaim my throne and rule as king and queen of the mages." His grin was a little manic. "You'd have to get rid of the shifters, though. Mangy creatures. Now that you've used them to reduce Momar's battle prowess and knock him down a peg, you don't need them. You just need me. I can teach you the ropes much better than these idiots, trust me. I can teach you magic like no one else could." He winked at me. "What do you say?"

"You're batshit crazy, that's what I say. What's *owed* to you? That doesn't make sense, idiot. Now get out of here. You weren't invited."

"Aha, but you didn't ask how I got in. You know as well as I do that this fool has zero power. His spells are a joke, his booby traps laughable, and the potions and spell notes? Nothing to steal. I didn't even bother. You're the only valuable thing in this house, and you'd be the only valuable thing in an alliance. I, on the other hand—"

"Oh, shut up. I don't care. I gave you my answer: no. Now go away."

His smile was genuine this time. I could see Sebastian peeking through his pale blue eyes.

"Jessie, Jessie, so naïve. You really don't know how this works, do you? The things I could teach you. But alas, I see that you are stubborn. Must be that gargoyle, huh? Here, let me show you what happens when someone turns me down."

He pushed off the wall and fired another spell. My deflection spell this time was a new one I'd found. His spell hit it and bounced back. It fractured before hitting his defensive spell in a few spots and popping with corrosive magic. His eyes widened a little and then started sparkling. It meant he was intrigued by the spell and proud of me for doing it well.

He fired another, and another, throwing them at my people so that I would have to spread my power around.

"Should I just firebomb him?" Cyra shouted over the melee. The other mages yelled and screamed as they dove to the floor.

"No, you'll ruin Arthur's house," I said, remembering the note Sebastian had sent with the dress.

Most importantly, if <u>anyone</u> attacks you with magic, <u>return fire</u>. It doesn't matter who it is, <u>attack back</u>.

He'd clearly meant himself all along.

I didn't hesitate, deflecting his spells and firing spells back, faster than the last time he'd seen me. I'd been practicing. My spells were more complex, too, a few downright nasty and done to perfection. I didn't have a life anymore, not outside of our convocation and magic, so there'd been plenty of time to practice.

"My goodness," he said, standing in the middle of the doorway now, his hands moving faster. Faster than mine. He was still way more experienced. "You might be more powerful than me, my dear Jessie, but you have a lot to learn."

His spells started to eat at my defensive layers now. These were spells I hadn't seen before. Spells he'd probably created for just such an occasion. He got one and a half off to my one, still trying to hit my people as well as me.

I took the onslaught, pushing to go faster. Slamming spells home, hitting him with all my power.

"I *am* more powerful, yes," I gritted out, "and I have a bigger team."

I shot off what I called a time finder. It didn't do much but blast him with light. He squinted and flinched, giving Austin time to rush him. Dave was right behind Austin, snarling, his hair puffed out.

Sebastian swore, entirely genuine. The ground at his feet flashed, and then he was gone. Vanished.

Austin ran through the area, and Dave ran just beyond it, their arms out, searching.

"How did he do that?" Austin asked, out of breath. "Is he just invisible? I can't feel his presence."

"Tristan, can you see him?" I looked around, but Tristan was gone.

CHAPTER 24
TRISTAN

THAT FEELING HAD to be her. The tug. The pull he'd felt for the last hour. It didn't *feel* like her, though. He'd know her essence anywhere. He didn't feel it now.

He walked quickly along the hall upstairs, near the wall, blending in so thoroughly he'd be invisible to anyone but a gargoyle. His footfalls were silent on the plush carpet. His gut still churned.

They'd helped Jessie. They'd wanted her to come. This had to be part of their plan, somehow.

So why was his gut churning? He had an amazing internal warning system. It almost never failed him.

Had she…changed? Had something caused her to lose herself?

Had he failed her by not being there when she needed him?

The feeling was just up the way, in a room with a closed door. He snuck closer, standing outside of it. He could feel a presence in the middle of the room. Then it moved toward the outside, probably a window.

He burst in through the door, moving as fast as he could go. She turned around with a terrified expression that squeezed his heart. He hated seeing her scared and hated it most when he was the one who'd caused it. Her knife was up in a flash, though, her reaction speed amazing, and she slashed at him.

He batted it away with the same hand that reached for her throat, their version of a hello. He gripped then tightened, cutting off her air and carrying her onward. At the last moment, near the window, he veered and slammed her against the wall.

Her hands fell against his chest lightly and her eyes closed, as a little smile played at her lips. The energy around her, dulled a moment ago and now sparkling, danced and twirled between them—a relief the likes of which he'd never felt. Her eyes opened slowly and her pupils dilated with desire, her body relaxing as he pushed up against her.

Her scowl said her body was betraying her mind. She didn't want to like someone like Tristan: bad news, morally gray, unapologetic about either. She didn't want to like someone who had so many traits similar to her because she hated those parts of herself. She was in constant turmoil about them. About her past, one she'd never spoken about. He wished she'd trust him with the burden. That she'd trust him at all.

"Hello, little monster," he growled, loosening his fingers enough to let her breathe. He leaned down to run his lips along the shell of her ear. "What are you doing here?"

She shivered and dug her fingers into his pecs, pushing a little.

"How'd you feel me?" she whispered angrily.

"Your essence is altered. Why?"

"I got those books you sent me. On energy. It was you, wasn't it? You keep haunting my steps."

He'd been trying, but she was damn good at hiding in the shadows. She had a better network, more connections, and more knowledge about using the magical dark web. He'd been able to keep up at first, but she'd clearly taken it as a challenge and upped her game. She kept slipping away. He was starting to worry it was to her detriment.

"Why is your essence altered?" he pushed.

The little smile was back. "I knew it was you. How'd you know I could work energy? I didn't even know. Not the magical component of it, I mean. I still don't know how most of it works."

"I can see the effects of it in certain creatures. I can see how turned on you are right now, for example. How much you want me to tease you until you beg me to climax."

The sparkles between them sped up until they were swirling at a fever pitch.

"Lies," she whispered, her voice thick with need.

"I will not ask you again—why was your essence altered? Are you trying to hide from me?"

"Obviously. I'm supposed to be nulling my aura, what I assume you refer to as my essence. Looks like I'll have to try something else."

He hadn't known it was her—or been sure it was anyone, actually—so she'd probably succeeded. His internal warnings had only been triggered because of proximity. Not that he'd tell her that. He hoped she dropped the nulling effect, thinking it didn't work, and allow him to feel her. To better track her.

One thing that hadn't changed, though, was that tug he'd felt. The pull of her, of his need to see her again. To feel her lips and continue this dance of theirs. He liked the pace, each grudging step she took toward his bed.

"Why aren't you invisible?" he asked. "And why are you here? Why is Sebastian here?"

"I'm not invisible because I didn't think there was a point. Usually in a dinner situation like this, no one is allowed to wander away. Mages never totally trust who they're with. I didn't expect Edgar to be milling around."

"And the reason you're here?" He ran his lips along her jaw, liking when she shivered.

"Helping Jessie show off her magic, making it clear she is not connected to Elliot Graves, and proving she has more power than he does. It'll help her position."

"You guys play the bad guys so she can be the good guy?" He breathed against her neck before sucking in her heated flesh.

"That was always the plan," she whispered breathily.

He kissed her throat, creating a hot trail with his tongue.

"I have to go," she said, barely heard. Her fingers still clutched him.

"When are you coming back to O'Briens?" He kissed her chin lightly, then the corners of her lips. "I have a set of handcuffs and a blindfold I want to try on you."

She squeezed her eyes shut and murmured, "Oh my God."

"When you beg me to climax, I'll only let you if you call me Daddy."

He smiled wickedly when her fingers spasmed into fists, clutching his jacket and yanking him closer. She definitely liked the dominance games; probably praise, too. She'd likely never found someone she was really compatible with because she always presented the strong, independent sunshine girl, leading the way to the finish line. No one had probably read her desire to let someone else call the shots. To take her to the brink, to the very edge where she had no control, and keep her there until she screamed with pleasure.

It was a game he liked to play but hadn't found a woman who had given herself to it fully. Natasha had already done it, though, multiple times. Right now, as a matter of fact. Happily at his mercy, relinquishing control, her life or death in his hands. It was when she let down her guard and opened herself up that he got to see the real woman. The damage. The pain. The glimmer of hope.

"Jessie misses you," he said, kissing the corner of her lips again. "It hurts her that you don't respond to messages."

"If I did, you'd use it to track me. I know you know how."

He did, that was true. An encrypted phone was still a cell phone, and when it was on, it could be tracked if you knew the right information. They'd kept it off so that he couldn't, clearly charging it up at unpredictable times to get any messages that had come through before shutting it down again.

"You need to stop locking me out," he said, rocking

his hardness against her. "I know you want the help. I want to provide it for you." He captured her still lips. "Kiss me back," he commanded.

She whimpered in desire, doing as he said. Their kiss was scorching, unraveling his control. He thrust his tongue into her mouth, chasing hers before he backed off, sucking on her bottom lip. When he pulled back a little more, she followed, trying to keep contact. Her eyes fluttered, showing she was clearly lost to their chemistry. To his touch.

"I want to pleasure you, little angel," he murmured, sliding his free hand over her breast. "How much time do we have?"

She didn't comment, but her hands loosened and then slid up and around his neck. She pulled and stood on her tiptoes, trying to get higher. He lifted her, wrapping her legs around his hips, trapping her between him and the wall.

"I need to be going," she said softly, gyrating her hips against him. "I should've been out of here by now."

He captured her lips again. This woman had the ability to unravel him, shred all his control. His tongue picked up the same rhythm as his rocking. She groaned into his mouth. Their friction drove his need higher. Her mews of pleasure frazzled his ability to think. He gently caressed her breast while he roughly rammed against her.

"Yes," she said, and he backed off to watch her beautiful rapture. She rolled her head from side to side, her eyes still fluttering. "Oh God, right there."

He grabbed her hips with both hands. Something about this was so incredibly hot, more so than if they'd stripped off the fabric in their way and done it for real. He *wanted* to take it slow with her, to chip away at her distrust of him gradually, only going as far as she was comfortable. Never pushing. Never rushing.

He kissed her again, falling into it, letting it consume him. He felt her energy burning between them, soaking through his skin. Felt the movement of her, reaching for the finish line, about to crest—

He stepped back, letting her slide down to her feet. Her knees nearly gave out, dropping her to the ground. He caught her but didn't let her cling on. Removed her hand from groping him.

Her beautiful eyes sought his, wild, desperate. Her cheeks were flushed, her hair mussed. Great heavens, she was the most beautiful thing he'd ever seen.

"You didn't call me Daddy, little monster," he said darkly, so damn hard it hurt to walk. This would kill him just as much as her. But this was the game. They both liked to play. "Next time, I expect you to get it right."

He about-faced and headed for the door.

"*You*—" She cut off the insult he knew she was thinking.

But then, when he was near the door, he heard, "Tristan?"

He glanced back, and then staggered into the frame.

She had a hand down the front of her jeans, moving rapidly as she thrust against her digits. In a moment, she moaned long and low, jerking with completion. Her eyes drifted open, and he was in *agony*, huddled against the door, his dick pounding, his body uncomfortably wound up.

She slowly pulled her hand free and then lifted it before wrapping her lips around two fingers.

It felt like lightning had struck his body, the shock of desire so fierce he could barely focus. He rocked against the doorframe, of all things, rutting like an animal in heat, his knees too weak to stumble toward her, his brain too foggy to regain any sort of dignity.

She smiled sinfully. "Two can play this game, *Daddy*."

She winked, smirked, and strolled to the window. In a moment, she was gone, the pane whacking shut behind her.

"Well," he said to himself, slipping into the room and pulling himself out of his pants. "That backfired."

After he'd finished himself off, the release like a dam bursting, he found Brochan in the foyer downstairs.

"What happened to you?" Brochan asked.

It was clear he wasn't asking where Tristan had gone but why the hell he looked like a tormented man. And in that moment, knowing Brochan could have Natasha whenever he wanted, that she'd welcome it because the connection would be shallow, safe, he wanted to deck the guy out of frustration. Not because he was afraid of her being intimate with another—she'd never find in anyone else what she'd relish in Tristan—but because he knew he'd never read as safe, not until she gave herself to him. Not until she allowed herself to trust him, and to her, that was the biggest risk of them all. A greater concern than losing one's life, because this...this was talking about her soul.

He sighed and ran his fingers through his hair. "Nothing. What happened to—"

"Elliot Graves?" Brochan growled.

Right. He was only Sebastian behind closed doors. Tristan nodded.

"Apparently, he vanished. As in he teleported out of here or something. None of the mages have any idea how he did it, but I guess Graves made a whole truck disappear once, so who knows? The mages are talking about him like he's some sort of magical god. They are scared shitless of him. They're in awe of Jessie for holding her own against him and running him out of here."

"Which was the point. Show her power while showing that the two of them don't have a connection."

"You ran into Nessa."

"Don't think I can make that deduction on my own, huh?"

"Not with any certainty, no."

Tristan took a deep breath. "Edgar told me he'd seen his shadow. I went up to investigate, since I figured Elliot wouldn't be playing for keeps. She escaped—not that I tried to stop her."

Brochan looked at Tristan for a long moment. "She deserves better than you."

"There is no one better than me. Not for her."

He huffed. "Have to love that ironclad self-confidence. You're wrong, though. She deserves better. Than you, than me…"

"She just wants to bang you. You should let her."

Brochan shook his head and turned a little so that he was looking into the guts of the house, where the others were probably still talking to the mages. Or calming them down.

"She'd cease to exist for me if I did that. I'd cut off

all my feelings for her."

"Do you have feelings for her?" Tristan asked.

"She's beautiful. She's fun. She's a light in a dark place."

"She's a buoy you're trying to cling to in a storm, you mean."

"Yes," Brochan admitted. "It isn't fair to her." He paused for a moment. "Truth be told, it's hard for me, her being a mage. It's harder knowing what she does for a living. I don't respect it. I can't think too hard about it because...then I worry I might not respect her."

"Speak along those lines again, and I will make good on the impulse I've been fighting and beat the living piss out of you. She does what she does to survive. She's light and bubbly to hide her pain because, unlike you and Sebastian, she doesn't have a buoy to cling to. She's everyone else's buoy. She hates what she does, what she *is*, because people like you look down on her for it. But make no mistake, she and Sebastian are a huge component in why Jessie and Austin and Kingsley and his whole pack are still alive. Have a little respect for the sacrifice she's making to ensure the people she loves stay in the world of the living."

"I didn't know. I apologize." Brochan rocked from foot to foot for a moment. "You want to claim her, but you'd advise another male to bed her?"

Tristan chuckled. "It'll get you out of her system, and then she can focus on me. Gargoyle culture isn't like shifter culture. We experience sexual pleasure for what it is—a damn good time. If she wants to see a sword fight, or be sandwiched between two men, I'll oblige. If she wants to double-team me with a female friend of hers, no problem. A few friends? I've proven adept at multitasking. Until she allows me to officially claim her, I'm fine to help her experience the pleasures of the flesh she has yet to try."

"Until you officially claim her?"

"Yes. Because while I am part gargoyle, I am also a possessive motherfucker. Once she fully submits to me, she will be mine and mine alone. I'm sure you can understand that."

Brochan grunted, and Tristan knew that was a yes.

"What's the status with this dinner party?" he asked.

"Jessie can't seem to catch a break. Another dinner party cut short. She and Alpha Steele are talking the mages down from hysteria, and then we're going to head out. We'll either pick up dinner on the way home or make it when we get there."

"I'm ready for this trip to be over."

"Same. One more battle to go, though."

"The ex-in-laws," Tristan said.

"Yeah. And I get the feeling it'll be the worst of all."

CHAPTER 25

JESSIE

W E STROLLED ALONG a tree-covered pathway early the next morning. Austin had wanted to see my favorite spot from when I lived here, and I'd wanted to show him. Given today was Christmas Day and we'd have festivities from early afternoon until late, and tomorrow was the ex-in-laws' holiday party, we'd had to rise with the roosters to knock this out.

I inhaled deeply as we made our way to the beach, the winter bringing a chill but the fresh sea air clearing my senses.

"I haven't been up this early in a long time," I said. "I used to love it. I'd get up at five or so, before Matt went to work so someone was home with a sleeping Jimmy, and go out for a walk. I couldn't come here at that time because it was too far away, not until Jimmy was older, but the early mornings were always so peaceful. No crying kid. No demanding husband or huge list of chores. Just me, the fresh air, and a little time to think."

"When were you able to make it out here?"

The path turned a little, emptying onto a little-known beach in Malibu. The waves crashed down, the white foam crawling up the wet sand. A couple of seagulls flew by, looking for food.

"Usually never this early, but I'd bring Jimmy and he'd play in the sand, or we'd look for sea creatures among the rocks. Not a lot of tourists find this beach, and the parking is harder and you have to walk in, so it doesn't get crazy busy. It was perfect for us. Then, when he got older and didn't want to go to the beach with his mom, I'd come out here just to think. Or walk." I stopped to take off my shoes. "I miss the ocean. Walking along the beach."

Hand in hand, we did just that, quiet for a while as we strolled.

"In all our time together, Matt never came here with me," I mused as the wind ruffled my hair. "I never asked him to, not that he would've come if I had. But I never wanted him to come. It was my place *away*—away from my duties, from the mundane, from the grind."

"Maybe you would've preferred to keep it to your-self," he murmured, his tone and volume matching the vibe perfectly.

"You're not a person I want to get away from," I said, bumping into him softly. "When I need a break from my life, I go to your house."

"Our house," he amended, gently squeezing my hand.

"Listen, I was thinking about what went down with Matt the other day. Specifically about that divorce money. You've done so much to share your life with me, and I've had that money just sitting there, solely in my name. This is going to sound absurd, but I never even thought about it. It literally never crossed my mind. I've been dealing with the Ivy House funds and not thinking of Jessie Evans's funds. When we get back, we're going to use it to pay off your—our house or put it into retirement funds, or at least put your name on it with mine."

"No." He looked down at me. "Don't. Keep it as security. It's clear Matt was controlling you financially. I never want you to feel like you're in that position again. You need to have funds in this world that are solely yours."

I stopped and turned to him, running my hands up his arms before stopping on his chest. "You are unbelievably sweet, and your desire to make sure I have an escape route is…" My eyes misted. "It's really incredible. *You're* incredible. But I'm not the same person I was. If I need an escape route, I'll make one. I'm giving myself a paycheck through Ivy House, just in case something happens with the house, and we have the businesses and everything we're starting to work on. I have more than I ever did, both in terms of funds and control. Not to mention, I could just take a bar of gold out of the closet and be done with it. Or ransack the attic. Who would notice? No one has bothered with inventory."

He laughed, his eyes so blue, and ran his fingertips along my jaw. "True."

"That money is mine, less than I probably should've gotten, and I want to use it for what it was meant for—starting a new life. Starting *my* life. I've chosen to do that with you, and I want that money to back that choice."

He nodded slowly, his gaze lingering on my lips. "Fair enough. We'll pay off the house, then. Or look into using it as a down payment for a beach house for when we want to get away. Because, love…I don't think you are allowed to retire. Not in the way you're thinking."

I looked at the sky. "Right. Good point. That whole situation hasn't really sunk in. The living-forever thing. No compute."

"Especially since we're just trying to make it

through each skirmish."

We started walking again, and he took my hand.

"In other news," he said, his voice still subdued, "what are your thoughts about last night?"

I stopped him again, turning so I could look out at the ocean, and slipped my arms around his middle. I leaned against his body, and he wrapped his arms around me, resting his cheek against my head.

I'd always come here to run from my problems, to shed the emotional baggage for a short time. This place had been a haven. But now, with him, there was no emotional turbulence to table. No fear or dread of what I'd come home to—even though we were in a dangerous position. I was able to enjoy this place in a way I never could. It was just beautiful. Just peaceful. Tranquil.

"God, I love you, Austin. I love how serene you make everything. How you take care of me and look out for me. How you respect me, and how you're okay with my taking the reins at times. You're perfect for me." I hugged him a little tighter. "As for last night...I don't know."

He rubbed my back, chuckling. "Succinct answer."

"Those mages were shaken up."

"A powerful mage barged into their home and tried to kill someone at their party. As far as they were concerned, at any rate."

"Right, but…" I watched the waves for a moment. "Any powerful mage would have been able to waltz right in. Those wards would never have kept out a mage like Sebastian. If they were really serious, they'd have hidden some bear traps or something. Put in better locks, bought an alarm, I don't know." I pushed away a little, my mind still whirling. I hadn't entirely processed everything because it still wasn't making a lot of sense. "I'd thought attacks were more commonplace in the mage world. Arthur and his buddies said it themselves—if they got in the way of another mage, that mage would take them out. But none of them did anything. They just stared and then fell to pieces afterward. It took us half an hour to get Bert to stop screaming, for heaven's sake."

"It seems to me there must be levels. The people who would bother with Arthur and his lot are more on their level. Someone with a lot more power, like Sebastian, would have no use for Arthur's spells. They'd be way beneath his expertise. He mentioned that."

"He said a lot of things, and then tried to kill me."

"He didn't really try."

"Oh no, he definitely did. He didn't pull any punches with those spells he shot at me."

"He knew you could handle them."

"Maybe so, but that doesn't mean he didn't try to

kill me. Why didn't he tell me he was going to do that?" I sighed. "Besides the obvious."

Tristan had explained what Nessa had told him— that the whole situation had been engineered to boost my reputation. Though she hadn't mentioned why I'd been kept in the dark, Tristan surmised that they'd needed my reactions to be genuine. They clearly thought I was a bad actor, something Niamh had agreed with once we filled her in.

"I just don't like this whole thing," I finally admitted. "I don't like his sneaking around. It makes me nervous. What if he stays in character for too long and forgets our friendship?"

Austin squeezed me close. "He won't. And if he does, we at least know they have some sort of plan. They have an end game. Niamh, Tristan, and I are working on figuring out exactly what that end game is and how they might achieve it. It seems Nessa has been very good at eluding Tristan and Niamh, but now Niamh is starting to…*blossom*, is all I can call it. She's making connections and burrowing into the dark web better and better all the time. She calls it shaking off the dust. Tristan says she's becoming as good with the networks as she is getting information at the pubs. I have no doubt they'll close the distance, and soon we'll have a better idea of what's going on."

"It's just…why are we having to stalk allies?" I looked up at him worriedly. "Why don't they trust us enough to bring us in on these plans?"

He tucked a strand of hair behind my ear. "Tristan thinks Nessa is walking a dark, narrow path. He has a strange sixth sense where she is concerned. He doesn't think she's comfortable with that path, but likely feels she has no choice. She always presented herself as the ray of sunshine in our crew, right? Well, now she has to be the bringer of death or pain. Maybe she just doesn't want us to see it."

"She knows very well that most of my crew would be *desperate* to see it, and often want to take over the situation. No, it has to be something else." I chewed my lip. "I have a bad feeling about this, Austin. I think I need to step in. They are part of our crew, and therefore I am responsible for them. I won't just leave them out in the wilds on their own, regardless of if they think that is better for them. If Niamh and Tristan can track them down, then someone else surely can, too. It's not safe. They need to come back into the fold. We're better together. We've proven that many times over."

"I know, baby." He rubbed my back. "We're working on it, don't worry. In the meantime, we're giving them space to flex. We're giving them time to get their footing while we get ours. It'll all work out, I know it."

We started walking, but worry now pinched my gut. There was nothing I could do at the moment, though. I had to trust in my team to find them. Once they did, I'd make a decision then.

"I missed an opportunity for an ally, too," I said, sidestepping a nearly intact sand dollar. "There is no way those people are going to have anything to do with me with the threat of Elliot Graves hanging over their heads. No one in their extended circle will, either."

"That's probably for the best," Austin said. "None of them would add to our power. But you heard what Niamh said—your power and Elliot Graves's interest in you will be talked about. It'll lend credibility to the stories about your evading Momar. That'll interest mages with more power and more influence than Arthur and his friends, who will hopefully also want a change in the mage dynamic. This is a steppingstone. We have to believe that."

I nodded, trudging through the sand now, grumpy. "I know. I'm just really annoyed. Nessa was in the house and she didn't even say hi. Or leave me a note. Not to mention she never sends me messages through that phone. You don't just cut off friends, especially when you're the reason that friend is messing with mages in the first place."

"I think the phone has something to do with Tristan." He recounted what Tristan had apparently told him about tracking her.

"Ah. He never mentioned it."

"He's piecing everything together as we go." He swung our joined hands. "And if she tries to cut us off, we'll hopefully be one step ahead of her and save her from herself. It's all going to work out okay. You'll see."

"You need to tone it down with your optimism. It's making me grumpier."

He laughed, delighted. "Jess…" He stopped, reaching into the inside pocket of his trendy bomber jacket to grab his phone. He held it up, obviously taking a picture of me, and then slipped it into his back pocket. "Not to change the subject—"

"Please change the subject."

He smirked. "The mage situation is very important…"

"I thought you said you were changing the subject?"

His smile widened. "But I wanted to talk to you about tomorrow."

"Let's go back to talking about the mages."

He stooped to take off his shoes and then roll up his pants. He rolled up mine as well, and I let him, because whatever. It was in the middle of winter and cold (for Southern California), but you just kinda had to let non-beach people do what they thought was standard protocol. He probably thought dipping one's feet in the reaching surf was part of that protocol.

"How are you feeling about the party?" he asked, taking my hand again and veering toward the wet, hard-packed sand.

My heart had sped up the moment he broached the subject, but a new determination steeled me. The situation with Matt still made me uncomfortable, and the prospect of hearing constant slights from his mother for an afternoon made things worse, but I'd hit my threshold. I now saw Matt through a new lens that helped me make sense of my past—and also make peace with it. The last bits of the old me, the one who'd cared so much about pleasing him, had burned away.

This time when I went to a party with his people, I wanted to roll up as unapologetically me. Jessie, the socially awkward, weird-in-general girl from the "wrong" side of town. I wasn't one of them, but I knew their language, and this time, I wanted to talk back in a way they'd understand.

And then I wanted to close the door on the whole situation. It was time to move on.

"I feel like I have the ability to be on equal footing for once, and I want to see their expressions when I prove it."

He nodded at me as he stopped. A cresting wave

grabbed his focus for a moment before he turned back to me.

"You know that I love you," he told me, his expression turning serious. "You know that I consider us life partners. We're connected in a way non-magical people can't be. A way that is permanent, through not one but two bonds. Even if that weren't the case, you are my heart. You are my world. You are the reason I picked myself up and finally started to live again. For you, no obstacle is too tough. No challenge too great. I would die to protect you. I'd feel honored to do so."

I pressed my hand to the side of his face.

"I also want you to know this—I *will* take your magic. I will be your mate protector. The commander for the queen of the gargoyles. First, I need to organize the shifters and prove to them I am powerful enough to dominate on my own, but once that's settled, I'll join you with the Ivy House magic. I'll join you in your version of darkness, and we'll figure it out together."

I wrapped my arms around him, hugging him closely.

"He seeks to become the king of the shifters before he joins his queen," Ivy House said. *"He still seeks to earn you. You couldn't have chosen a better mate."*

I told him what she'd said.

"I won't ever deserve you," he murmured against

my lips. "You're much too good for me. Let's hope you never realize it."

I laughed.

He pulled back a little. More water washed up around our feet, reaching our ankles.

"In the magical world, you are my mate," he said. "That's known. But you were a Jane not so long ago. You have Jane friends and a Dick ex. It's important to me that they understand my claim, as well."

I furrowed my brow at him...and then he dropped down to one knee.

Butterflies exploded through my rib cage as he reached into his inside jacket pocket and pulled out a navy-blue, almost black box with an HW insignia.

Harry Winston.

Holy crap.

A wave washed up around us as he held the box up for me. It hinged open on either side to reveal a ring in its center. A round-cut diamond that had to be at least two carats was held in place by split prongs on four corners. Small round-cut diamonds lined the band, adding more carat weight and an insane amount of sparkle.

"Jacinta Ironheart, will you marry me?"

I gaped at him, suddenly shaking, tears springing to my eyes. Another wave washed up around him, and the salty air kissed his face. The morning sun highlighted his cobalt eyes.

"Yes," I said softly, then laughed, bending down to him. "Yes!"

He kissed me and stood, pulling me up with him. He took out the ring and dropped the box back into his pocket before reaching for my hand. It trembled as I stretched it forward. He slipped the ring over my finger, his eyes so soft.

"I love you," he said, and I kissed him again, wrapping my arms around him. "Now there will be no snide comments about my intentions toward you. There can be no doubt that I mean to stick around. Forever."

"Tell me you didn't get this just because Matt made those comments," I told him, wiping away a tear and holding my hand up to look at the ring in the sunlight.

"I'd already bought it. I bought it the moment I realized you didn't think being mates was the same as a Jane marriage. I didn't give it to you before now because there was never a perfect time. I wanted it to be special. I'm glad it worked out this way, though. I'm glad he made those comments. He thought he had wiggle room to turn me against you, but he'll see the way it is now."

"This *is* posturing," I told him, not able to look away from the sparkler on my finger. "A Harry Winston of this size? Give me a break. For him and his friends—his mother!—it's better posturing than any amount of alpha power you could pump out. I wish we were going to his club. I'd shove this in all of their faces."

He huffed out a laugh. "Next time. About the posturing, though… Not even remotely my intention, but tomorrow all his people will get to see that you've moved up in the world. I can't wait to rub it in their faces."

CHAPTER 26

AUSTIN

THE NEXT AFTERNOON, after an amazing Christmas Day in which their immediate family and crew all got together at the rental house and had a great time, Austin drove one of the Mercedes to the ex-in-laws' party in what Jess mentioned was a ritzy neighborhood in the Santa Monica Mountains. Some of the houses they passed were certainly extravagant, pushed back from the street and snuggled into the land. Jess had mentioned that those would sell for between five and twenty million. Multiple rooms, decadent pools, the works—they belonged to the filthy rich.

There were also plenty of moderately sized homes on average-looking streets, built in the early or mid-eighties and not updated. Their yards were tended and streets cleaned, but Austin couldn't see the point of paying two and a half million for what was essentially just an average house. That was the going price, apparently, and these people were forking out just for the prestige of the neighborhood.

"That really is a very beautiful ring, Jessie," Mimi said from the back seat, her little smile saying she was poking fun.

Aurora covered her smile with her fingers, incredibly expressive any time she was in the vicinity of Jess. This time she was sharing the joke, a joke Jess did not get.

Her parents wouldn't be coming to the ex's party, off the hook so that Jess could justify bringing Austin's family and a couple other additions. Jimmy was in a car with Mr. Tom—he was originally supposed to be in this one, but gave in when Mr. Tom caused a big fuss about his "inability to protect the young master when being relegated to an unimportant vehicle out of the way." Jimmy was proving to be just as easygoing as his mother, and just as willing to let Mr. Tom fuss over him.

Speaking of Jimmy, his smile had been bright yesterday when he saw Jess's new ring. If Austin had been at all concerned that the boy wouldn't want to see his mother remarry so soon after divorcing his dad, that fear would've been put to rest immediately. He'd given Austin "knuckles" and then pulled him into a one-armed hug before patting his back and hugging his mom. It was clear that he really wanted to see his mom happy, and it was just as clear he believed Austin would do that. The tears in her eyes made the Jane engagement that much more special.

Her parents, too, had been overjoyed. Her mom hugged him and smiled and then hugged him again, rocking him back and forth. Her dad gave a firm, gruff handshake and a nod before hugging his daughter, wishing her well. Good thing, because the shifters and gargoyles didn't really see what the big deal was. As far as they were concerned, she and Austin were already mated, so what was the point of a ring?

Hence the reason Mimi was poking fun now.

"He did a really great job picking it out," Jess said, putting her hand on Austin's shoulder, her eyes more dazzling than the ring could ever be.

Her gaze snagged on the diamond again, and an incredible surge of love welled up through the bonds. If Austin had known how something as simple as a ring and a proposal would have affected her this way, he would've done it a long time ago. He wished he could propose again, actually.

She rubbed his shoulder, watching the ring, and then put her hand on her thigh, still fixated on it. In a few seconds, she moved it again, watching it the whole time like a woman entranced. That was, until she beamed at Austin, so happy, so warm. So obviously devoted.

His proposal had spoken her language. It had said "forever" in a way she'd been brought up to understand. It was a symbol of his claim. A physical item to show others what a shifter did through posturing.

Emotion kept surging through her, the effect of accepting his claim. It made him feel like they were mating for the first time all over again.

"We're going to need to…cut the band at the bottom, maybe," he said, following the GPS directions. "I'm not sure what'll happen if you shift when you're wearing it."

"I won't be able to wear it most of the time," she said, giving it a little pout. "Today it'll be fine, though."

"I should hope so, since you brought the whole team." Mimi's teasing smile was a little bigger now. She did not understand the power of the ring. Different language.

The team would be stationed around the area, all under the influence of invisibility potions, to ensure Jess could safely show off his claim to all her ex-in-laws. He'd been all for it. He didn't want anything interrupting them today.

Besides, the team had lounged around and enjoyed the holiday all day yesterday.

MAGICAL MIDLIFE AWAKENING

He thought back to it again with a smirk, remembering the point at which Jess's dad had argued with Tristan about the right and wrong times to wear a cape. Tristan hadn't shown it on his face, but he'd been having the time of his life defending his stance that any affair where there was clam dip *should* have a cape-optional clause.

Meanwhile, Jess's mom had been in the kitchen, battling Mr. Tom about who was going to make the mashed potatoes. Jimmy had been at the island watching, eating the clam dip that only a couple of others were brave enough to try, and then gluttonous enough to hog. They'd had to make another store run for ingredients to make more.

The entire day had been amazing. They'd laughed and opened presents, had fancy drinks, and eaten too much food. Mimi and Aurora had totally relaxed, as though with their own family. Patty and Martha, Jess's mom, had chatted like they'd been friends all their lives, and the shifters and gargoyles had sat around and watched sports or helped with food prep. At one point, Indigo, after a few too many chocolate martinis, had wandered around touching everyone, seeing if they had anything that needed curing. When she'd gotten to Martha, she'd swayed, burped under her breath, and muttered something about a hip.

Martha, also on the too-much-alcohol train by that point, had ignored Indigo completely, not at all worried that a perfect stranger was leaning on the counter beside her, holding her hip.

Jess had gotten a phone call this morning asking what that lovely, mousy lady had put in Martha's drinks because her hip felt like new. And not "new" as in recently replaced, which it had been, but like she hadn't needed a replacement in the first place.

Austin was pretty sure Pete, Jess's dad, still thought they were a cult. Though he seemed to accept that they were a cult that did things properly, and it seemed to comfort him that Jess was only going to marry one of the members and not all of them.

Such an odd character, her dad. He could rationalize away the strangest things.

"I love you," Austin told Jess, swept up in the excitement of it all, soaking in those surges of emotion and throwing some toward her when he thought about how easily her blood family got along with her chosen family. All except her brother, who had missed his flight and hadn't been able to make it.

"I love you," she replied in a whisper, and this time her deep, heartfelt gaze lingered on him.

"You guys are gross," Aurora muttered, fighting a smile again.

"They can be much grosser," Mimi told her. "Don't challenge them. We want them to keep their clothes on."

Aurora furrowed her brow at Mimi, rolled her eyes, and looked away with a shaking head. Her smile shone through, though.

"Why is it you allow yourself to smile with Jess and no one else?" Austin couldn't help but ask as they wound closer to the house.

Aurora glanced at the review mirror, caught his gaze, and looked away again. She shrugged. "Because it's her culture. Because she can't understand my subtle movements, and it hinders conversation. Because she looks down on an expressionless face the way shifters look down on an expressive face—"

"I do no such thing." Jess twisted in her seat to scowl back at Aurora. "I don't look down on you ever, even when you're mean-mugging me." She turned back. "But I definitely can't understand your subtle move-ments. I'm not even convinced you're making any movements. I think you just think you are, but nothing is actually happening, and you are left wondering why no one answers you."

Aurora blurted out a laugh. "Maybe so." She looked out the window, then added, "Because she feels more like a sister than an aunt, and I've always wanted a sister. Mac is a dodo. He acts half his age."

"He actually acts his age, you mean," Mimi told her. "You act my age. You need to learn to live a little and stop worrying about the job so much."

"Dad never let me live a little," Aurora grumbled. "All I've been thinking about since I was five years old is gaining strength and learning all I could so that I could have a pack of my own someday."

Something tightened up inside Austin. "Or gaining strength so that if someone ever came after your dad again, like I did, you'd be able to protect your family."

Her eyes looked haunted in the mirror. She didn't comment, and his gut twisted. He'd apologized several times at this point, spoken to her about it one on one a couple times and asked if there was anything more he could do to try to rebuild that bridge. Every time she shrugged it off, telling him he was doing all the right things. She'd forgiven him.

He was having a hard time forgiving himself. He still looked back on that time with dread, though, with this horrible soul-crushing guilt, wanting a redo. Wanting to change it. He could only move forward, determined to always be there for her, always.

"I never had a sister, either." Jess turned in her seat again and reached back, putting her hand on Aurora's knee. She waited until Aurora looked at her. "I have a brother, too. He was older, but also a dingus most of the time."

Aurora smiled, but what Austin had said clearly affected her. She tapped Jess's hand, very clearly showing warmth and gratitude, before squeezing the band to point the diamond her way.

"It *is* a pretty ring."

Jess was beaming when she turned back. "Thank you. Austin has great taste."

When Aurora met his eyes in the rearview this time, her little smile and posturing said she thought their interactions over the ring were cute.

"At least you're living a little now, though," Jess said, and pointed at the house in question. "That one."

She watched it go by as they looked for a parking place amid the Lexuses, Mercedes, Teslas, and other luxury vehicles parked outside. Not supercars, though. Nothing that screamed *crazy* wealth. These people were prosperous, but there were no oil tycoons among them.

"My goodness," Mimi said, twisting a little to continue looking as they went down the street. "Brick facing in this part of the world? No, that doesn't work, especially with that color brown on the garage and...boards for decoration. That house is in drastic need of an update. At least peel off those boards and give it some paint. New garage doors. It would make the world of difference, even with the brick facing."

"I hope you mention every single word of that to Lottie," Jess murmured. To Aurora, she said, "It looked like you had a great time with Ulric and Jasper the other night."

Aurora laughed. "I'm a little ashamed to say it was the most fun I've had in my life. All I did was dance, too. Dance and joke and laugh. They are so much fun to be around. And so…" She gave Austin a puzzled look. "*So* sex positive. Like… Are all gargoyles that…"

"Loose? Free? Unencumbered?" Jess helped. "Most are. Garhettes, too. They have a very open culture. It's nice. I prefer it. They are respectful and easygoing and blasé, not at all worried about rejection."

"You got that right." Aurora shook her head with a grin, back to looking out the window.

Austin didn't comment. His brother would be freaking out if he knew this conversation was going on. He would not understand Aurora letting her hair down, even in such an innocent way. An alpha's kids usually had a very strict upbringing, Austin and Kingsley included. Shifters thought it was good training for a life as an alpha.

But Aurora wasn't Austin's kid—nieces didn't count—and even if they did, this wasn't a usual pack. The rules were different in the convocation. Austin didn't want to directly get involved, but he did think it was good for her. She obviously needed it, and she could be in no safer company to experience it.

He found a curb to park at. They were far enough away that the other cars in their party could park in front of them without raising suspicion. Austin watched as they did so. Those who needed to stay hidden would be taking the potions now.

"Jasper got shut down by this girl," Aurora said, "who was a real dick about it. He was like, 'Do you want to dance?' And she said, '*Ew*, are you serious? No.' And then he nodded thoughtfully, like that was some great philosophical question, and said, 'Me neither. Want to get a drink?'" Aurora started chuckling. "And she rejected him again, but more aggressively. I was getting pissed by then. I would've tagged in and knocked her down a peg, but he just nodded thoughtfully again and said, 'Me neither.'" She laughed harder. "He kept asking her more questions until she finally walked away. And when she did, she was half laughing because he was so chill about the whole thing. It was clear he didn't much care one way or another—he was having a good time. It was great."

"Never tell your dad if you get involved with a gargoyle," Mimi told her. "Or anyone else."

"Didn't need to be said," Aurora replied.

Jess nudged Austin before they got out of the car. "Did you hear that? Never tell her dad." Then she pointed back at Aurora. "But honestly, gargoyles are really awesome. You'd have a lot of fun. You should date one or two."

Austin stepped out of the car as doors opened and closed ahead of him. The potion was clearly kicking in, because only a few people from the group, those who'd be guests, were still visible. Patty was cheery and smiling, in contrast to Brochan, who would pose as Austin's brother and was intended to stress people out. Mr. Tom couldn't be talked out of "seeing to Master Jimmy's needs," so they would just have to deal with comments about his cape. Niamh was the last "visible" member of the group. Having failed to find any mages (or open bars) the previous night, she was excited about the prospect of messing with wealthy people. Matt's family had no idea what they were in for.

Jess stepped out of the Mercedes and braced her left hand on top of the door. She took a beat to watch the diamonds glitter before she cleared the way for Austin to shut the door. She didn't go far, though, reaching out to grab the edge of his jacket and step closer once he'd made it to the sidewalk.

"Will they at least have good food?" Aurora asked as she reached the sidewalk as well, wearing a snug maroon dress that ended just above her knees, showed only a tiny bit of her chest, and was adorned by a choker of pearls with five strands. Her hair was piled on top of her head with curls coming down everywhere, and a glittering diamond bracelet encircled her wrist. She looked prim and posh and sophisticated while still presenting as young and beautiful. It was the perfect ensemble for the situation. Not even Mimi could find fault.

As for Mimi, she wore black flared slacks, a long, bright red jacket with gold buttons, a glittering gold and diamond Chanel pin on her breast, and a white collared shirt beneath—a more flamboyant outfit than she'd usually wear. She clearly intended to stand out so people would come talk to her. Austin already felt sorry for those people.

"They get it catered, and it's usually pretty good, yes," said Jess, the belle of the ball. The whole house had weighed in on her outfit, but ultimately she and Austin had picked it out.

It was a champagne-colored satin dress with spaghetti straps and a cowl neckline. It was looser at the bust but then cinched in through the waist and flowed down her legs to her shins with a small slit up the right side, stopping just above the knee. The cut of the dress and fabric showed off the hard-earned muscle she'd gained this last year training and fighting, while emphasizing her feminine curves and showing off her natural grace. Her hair draped around her beautiful face with a soft curl. One of Austin's more extravagant gifts, a diamond and sapphire necklace, hugged her neck. She didn't wear a bracelet, not wanting to detract from her ring.

From his claim.

"I need to borrow that dress," Aurora said, looking her over.

Mr. Tom handed around revealing spells so those not invisible could see those who were.

"Your confidence that it would fit both of us is the best compliment you could give me." Jess laughed, smoothing the dress down her right hip. "They'll think it's loud. That a woman my age shouldn't be showing off her body like this."

All eyes turned her way. Patty pushed through people to step in close, frowning.

"You're joking," Patty demanded. "Tell me you're joking." Her pitch rose in volume. "Are you joking?"

"What does age have to do with wearing clothes?" Aurora asked, her upper lip showing a little snarl.

"I'm middle-aged and a mom," Jess said with an insecure shrug. "They'll think this dress is too showy, like I'm trying to act young. Older ladies should be covered up, in their opinion. We shouldn't be sexy, I guess."

Mimi didn't say a word, but her body language said she was enraged.

"Jessie, you look absolutely fabulous in that dress," Patty said, taking her hand. "*Fabulous*. It suits you perfectly. Those people really need to find some confidence and a hobby instead of trying to control one another. But we don't have time for those kinds of games, do we? No, we do not. We will wear whatever we want, whenever we want, and we will do it with style. And just look." She glanced between Austin and Jess, beaming. "You two are so handsome together! Suave and sexy and powerful and—"

"Are we plannin' on gettin' to this party anytime soon, like?" Niamh drawled from somewhere in the back.

"The Irishwoman has a point," Mr. Tom said, shooing everyone forward. "Though she is only making it because she isn't sucking on the end of a whiskey bottle."

"There are a lotta dirty jokes I could make after that comment," Niamh replied, "but yer face is joke enough."

"Lovely," Mr. Tom intoned. "Anyway, miss, the sentiment you expressed is exactly the sort of terrible conditioning we had to break you of when you first came to O'Briens, don't you remember? And look, you're more confident than ever. Let's take this party by storm, shall we?"

Nearer the house, the group spread out enough that Jimmy caught up with them. He walked on the neighbor's grass so he could be next to Jess.

"They're right, Mom," he said. "You look really pretty. And you look really happy. I know you never have very much fun at these things—not that I do, either—but this time you have all your people with you. You shouldn't worry what they have to say."

"Thanks, bud." She squeezed his upper arm.

"Also, can I have some of that invisibility potion? There's this—"

"No," she cut him off. "Absolutely not."

He let out an annoyed breath, tramping on some flowers.

"Careful there, Master Jimmy," Edgar said, suddenly behind them. "You are crushing some of the loveliest additions to this neighborhood."

"What are you doing after this, anyway?" Jess asked Jimmy as her son started weaving across the lawn more carefully. "You have another couple weeks before you have to go back, don't you?"

"Going home with you guys," he told her. "Dad's

going to be a nightmare after this. I'll see him for Easter."

Though Austin could feel her joy and also her frustration, probably because of how poorly her ex dealt with their son, she merely nodded. She didn't bash her ex, like Austin would've been tempted to do, or comment about Easter. She was still taking the high road, even after that disaster of a dinner. She was a remarkable woman.

The others fell away as they approached the door, Austin and Jess taking the lead. Jess fidgeted for a moment, shook it out, and then reached for the doorbell.

"It's going to go great," Austin assured her.

"It's not, but thanks for the vote of confidence."

CHAPTER 27

NIAMH

THE DOOR OPENED slowly to a young man in his twenties wearing a gray, chef-looking shirt with large black buttons, black slacks, and an apron around his waist. He was clearly a caterer.

"Come in, please." The young man offered a half-smile as he glanced at who was at the door. He did a double take when he reached Austin, his eyes widening slightly and his face going red. "Sir. Please."

He stared at his shoes and made himself smaller as Austin lifted his hand for Jessie to go first. She kept hold of him as she stepped through, and he followed her in, not sparing the boy a second glance.

"Go, go." Niamh motioned Patty in. The woman was practically bursting with energy. She did love a party with a bunch of strangers. Something was fundamentally wrong with her.

"I cannot believe you are going to embarrass the

miss by bringing a cooler," Mr. Tom told Niamh as they shuffled forward to the door. "Her mother never should've let you borrow it."

"I wouldn't have had to borrow it if ye hadn't taken mine out of the trunk before we left for the trip, ye donkey. Mine was at least cleaner than this one. And ye're talking about embarrassing Jessie? Cop on to yerself. Ye're wearing a cape, fer feck's sake."

"How dare you!" Mr. Tom replied in a frenzied whisper. "I'd expect something like that from the Dicks, but from you? I expect better."

"I haven't a notion as to why." They reached the door, and she passed through.

"Oh, ma'am…uhhm." The boy pointed at her cooler. "You don't need to bring that in. We are well stocked."

She paused and stared him. "Are ya now. Ye have *poitín,* do ya?"

"Wh-what?" he stammered.

"*Poitín.* The Irish equivalent of American backwoods moonshine. Highly illegal stuff. I met a lad last night who'd just come back from Donegal. Smuggled the stuff in. I traded him a flask of the basajaunak brew, which can curl yer arse hair, for a bottle of this stuff. It's lovely, actually. Flavored with blackberry. Much tastier than the basajaunak brew, but not nearly so potent. A nice sipping beverage, methinks. I'll give ya a taste if ye'd like? But no, ye are not well stocked. Try again."

She continued, clunking the cooler off the door-frame and then swinging it a little too much and hitting the back of Aurora's legs. Aurora half turned, everything about her posture giving a not-so-idle threat.

"Nice try, gorgeous," Niamh told her. "Ye're much too pretty to be taken seriously. Go flirt with married men and make all the wives jealous."

Her expression changed, the shift barely perceptible, and her eyes started to sparkle.

"I just might," she said with a little sass in her tone.

Their movement into the house, which looked like any old house to Niamh, with a front sitting room full of people staring at them and lowish ceilings, slowed and then stopped. Niamh edged out from behind Aurora as an older woman approached Jessie and Austin. Her gray-white hair was pulled up in a half-do of some sort with the ends curled under. Her flowered dress was god-awful, tied at the middle and hanging down past her knees, with a few strands of pearls around her neck.

She seemed to think quite a lot of herself, given the way she strutted up with her nose held high and a look of bored distaste on her face.

Niamh set down the cooler with a thump, pulled off

the lid, and took out a beer. She'd need a glass for that *poitín* because it had been put into a grape *schloer* bottle, and this wasn't the time for people to think she was minding her manners with a non-alcoholic drink. She had an image to project to these people.

She replaced the lid and sat down on the cooler, popping the beer as she did so. Broken Sue joined her by the wall, staring hostilely at everyone looking Niamh's way. He'd heard about the dinner between Jessie and her ex—they all had—and hadn't taken the news well. He was here to make his distaste known. Niamh couldn't wait to watch.

"Jacinta, hello." The woman looked at Austin Steele, who was looking very dapper this evening in a navy-blue blazer with faux-leather navy lapels, a crisp bow tie to match, and a pressed shirt underneath. He even had a little navy and white pocket square to accent the look— he bordered on being overdressed, but his messy hair and five o'clock shadow softened the look. He could do masculine in his sleep, but now he also came off as posh, rich, and stylish—perfect for this party of *eejits*.

"Lottie, hello." Jessie wrapped her arm around Austin's. Lottie's gaze zipped down to the new ring.

Niamh had to hand it to Austin Steele—she'd had no idea how much of a transformation a little piece of jewelry could have on Jessie. Normally, she didn't advertise her claim of Austin Steele—even though she'd most certainly defend it—but she was flashing that ring around like a billboard. Or a bullhorn. She hovered around Austin Steele like their mating was fresh. Like she couldn't believe her luck and wanted everyone in the entire world to know about it.

Basically, what Austin Steele always did with his posture and the intensity of his magic and power.

It probably should've occurred to all of them that Janes did mating differently. Now they had the proof. Good for Austin Steele to think of it right before it really counted.

Well…counted for Jessie. This party didn't mean *shite* for the rest of them.

"Lottie, this is my fiancé, Austin. Austin, this is Matt's mother and the host of this fabulous party. Her name is Charlotte, but she goes by Lottie."

"Austin, it's a pleasure to meet you." Lottie didn't smile as she held out her hand.

Austin Steele shook it, matching the expression. "Nice to meet you. Jessie has spoken of you."

Niamh felt a grin bud at the mild aggression in Austin Steele's tone. The undercurrent of disapproval.

Lottie's eyes narrowed just slightly, showing she'd caught his meaning. Jessie fidgeted.

"This party is going to go all kinds of wrong," Broken Sue said softly.

Yes, it would, and Niamh planned to help it get there.

"It's so unfortunate that your parents couldn't come." Lottie wasn't good at lying. "But I see their cooler made an appearance."

Jessie flinched, panic rising through the Ivy House bond momentarily before she calmed herself again.

"Yes, she's Irish," Jessie said with a small shrug. "She does as she pleases. Let me introduce Austin's family. This is his grandmother, Naomi…"

"Grandmother?" Lottie's surprise was a bit too dramatic. "Gracious, you look young enough to be his mother. You must've started young?"

"No," Naomi said without an ounce of warmness. "Good genetics can carry you a long way." She paused. "If you have them."

"Yes, and his niece, Aurora." Jessie stepped aside to showcase the rest of their group. "And his brother, back there. Brochan—"

"Sue," Broken Sue growled. "They call me Sue."

Lottie's eyebrows climbed, whatever humor she felt about his name struggling to break through the unease she felt about his intensity.

"Sue, fine," Jessie continued, undaunted. They'd gone off the rails now. Might as well accept it. "Our family friend Patty, just back there—"

"Hello, Lottie." Patty beamed. "Lovely home! I just adore your throwback to the eighties. Don't change a thing, no matter what anyone says. I do love the golden oldies, and what better way to express that than with your house, right? Fantastic!"

Patty for the win.

"Right," Jessie said, her face turning crimson and a smile threatening. "There's Jimmy, hiding in the back with our butler, Mr. Tom."

"Your butler?" Lottie gave Jessie a humorous though incredulous look. "Yes, Matt mentioned that when he arrived earlier. And your…butler tends to wear a cape everywhere he goes, correct?" She affected a baby-type voice. "Jimmy, come here, my little darling. Come say hello to Grandmama."

"Is she for real?" Broken Sue murmured.

Jimmy walked through everyone, prim and proper in a suit that was a little too small in the limbs. He wore that expression kids wore when they were meeting a family member they didn't jibe with.

"Hi, Grandma," Jimmy said. Lottie put her hands on his shoulders and exaggeratedly air-kissed each cheek. "Merry Christmas," he added.

"Yes. Did you have a nice day yesterday? We missed you! We'd thought you were going to spend Christmas with all of us." She pouted. "But I guess your mom's poor nerves come first. You're a good boy for making the sacrifice."

Niamh put out her hands, looking around with raised eyebrows. "It's as if she thinks Jessie buggered off or something."

"At least we don't have to worry about her talking behind our backs," Aurora said, turning to Niamh. "She's plenty happy to do it to our faces."

"I'm sure there'll be both," Broken Sue growled.

Apparently two could play that game.

"Run along into the family room—we have some presents for you to open." Lottie smiled up at Jimmy. "I think you're going to like them. You know how Grandmama always spoils you."

Compared to Mr. Tom, *Grandmama* didn't know what spoiling meant. That boy had gotten so much crap yesterday that Jessie had taken some of the gifts away, including a heavy gold and diamond necklace chain that some musician or other liked to show off. It had been obscene, though Niamh had to admit Jimmy's delight in each gift had been fun to watch. She'd imagined that was the only incentive that could have made Mr. Tom knowingly risk Jessie's annoyance.

"Is that everybody?" Lottie asked, her smile quickly dwindling. "With such a large party, I'd hate to miss anyone."

Aurora turned back again and rolled her eyes at Niamh.

"Please, welcome," Lottie said, stepping aside and lifting her hands. "Welcome to my home. The dining room has food and drinks...if you didn't bring your own, and there is plenty of room to mingle. If you need something, anything at all, like some ice for your cooler, just ask one of the service people in gray." She smiled condescendingly. "Thanks so much. Jessie, might I have a word?"

A wave of uncomfortable emotions surged through the Ivy House bond, but Jessie, thankfully, didn't show a reaction.

"Of course." She turned back to everyone, making sure they were all okay, before stepping away.

"What do we do now?" Aurora asked Mimi.

"You're hungry, aren't you?" Mimi replied. "Go eat. I'm going to get a drink and mingle, as the woman said. I want to see if the rest of them are as generous with their insults."

Niamh finished her beer, handed it off to the kid who'd answered the door, who was still waiting there, watching them with a disbelieving expression, and stood.

"Want me to get that?" Broken Sue bent to grab the

handle. "Do you really have…paw-chin? Is that what you called it?"

"Close enough. I do. Do ye want some? I only ask because they probably don't have enough bourbon or whiskey in this house to give ye the needed buzz. If ye're too sober, ye might lose yer patience and brain one of these idiots. I also have the basajaunak brew, but that might be a little too strong right out of the gate."

"This might be a stupid question, but are you never concerned about your liver?" he asked.

"That is a stupid question, yes, given I am magical and heal quickly, and also given my magical breed. I'm a creature who likes the *oul gargles.*" She tipped her head back and imitated pouring a drink into her mouth so he'd get the gist. "But if ye want to hope they have good bourbon in this mediocre house that cost too much, by all means…"

"Let's try the Irish moonshine."

"There ya go. *Schure*, ye might as well."

He led them into the dining room, where he set the cooler down by the wall and picked up two crystal glasses from the breakfast bar along the side. Austin met them there, still within hearing distance of Lottie and Jessie, who stood just beyond them, near the entrance to the kitchen.

"Gonna be a long day," Broken Sue murmured to

K.F. BREENE

Austin.

"Looks like it," Austin replied, barely moving his lips as he poured himself a generous helping of whiskey from the breakfast bar. Aurora grabbed a plate and headed to the other side, where a table holding various metal buffet warmers had been set up, all steaming, with a caterer checking the level of the contents. "This is about how it went the other night, though Lottie seems a little more obviously salty than her son. Quite the family."

"Quite the family," Broken Sue muttered, returning to Niamh and holding up the glasses to be filled.

"Lovely to see you again, Jacinta," Lottie said to Jessie, gesturing for a server to come over. "What would you like to drink? Or have you quit? I remember you used to indulge a little too heavily in years past. Matt tried and tried to get you to slow down, but maybe now you've seen the light?"

The last was said flippantly, accompanied with a little laugh, as though it was some sort of joke.

Aurora turned slowly from the line for food, looking at the pair of them. Broken Sue glanced at Austin for his take.

"It'll get worse," Austin murmured softly. "Let her get her bearings. She'll push back. After she does, we'll dominate this party."

"Matt didn't like my drinking at all, so a glass of wine after dinner was too heavy for his taste." Jessie paused when the server stopped behind them. She smiled. "Do you have sparkling wine?" He answered in the affirmative. "Great, I'll have that." She turned back to Lottie. "What can I do for you, Lottie?"

The other woman smiled without humor, spreading her hands a little. "Not a thing. I just wanted to check in and catch up. It's been an age! How are your parents? Are they okay? I really was sorry to hear they weren't coming this year. And here I was finally ready to break down and try those deviled eggs she always brings"— she reduced her voice to a murmur—"to a catered party."

Jessie's expression said she was not amused, but she kept her tone polite. Somehow.

"We had a big gathering yesterday. Family only," she said poignantly. "It was a late night for them. Since I was bringing more people to this party than originally planned, I figured letting them off the hook would be better for your numbers. I remembered that you gave *very* specific numbers to your caterers and didn't like any deviations, not even to allow me one special friend I never got to see because of Matt's jealousy and mistrust of me having friends at all." She laughed lightly, totally forced and not trying to hide that fact. "I didn't want to put you out."

Both Aurora's and Broken Sue's eyebrows lifted slowly. Austin grinned a little, and Niamh was in pure rapture. Imagine all this hostility without it tipping over into a brawl. Fascinating. Very good self-control.

"Oh yes. Diana, right?" Lottie nodded sagely. "I do remember her. Always meddling, from what I remember."

"You mean telling me I had a right to—"

"And I heard that you've moved away." Lottie gestured for the server to hurry up and hand Jessie her drink. "It's so...quaint...that you've settled into a rural sort of life. Big cities are hard to navigate. I remember you always had trouble. But now you can live a quiet life with your...new person and his...eclectic family. You were very quick to find someone new. But then, I suppose you've always been used to a certain lifestyle and needed to find someone to provide that for you..."

"Oh no, you've got that wrong, Lottie. Matt never took care of me. He paid for things so that I'd take care of him. But yes, I've found someone to handle all that. It feels good to be looked after for once. Not that you'd remember, right? How long has it been since your husband left?"

Aurora, who'd come away from the buffet with a full plate of food, paused with a mini hotdog halfway to her mouth, staring at Austin. Broken Sue wore a little smirk, lifting his glass to his lips.

Niamh could not believe they were still pretending to be civil. It was madness! They were outright fighting, throwing down with words, and still giving each other little smiles or chuckles. In the magical world, tension this intense always led to vicious spells or stab wounds.

"Besides, I clearly didn't find someone new as quickly as Matt did," Jessie said, a tiny bit of outrage working into her voice. "He moved on before the ink was even dry on our divorce. He's been engaged for months. I sure hope you gave him just as much derision as you're giving me."

"Is that what this is about?" Lottie's mouth puckered, like she'd won some sort of victory. "It's unseemly for a woman to move on so quickly; everyone knows that. It makes her seem desperate. But this makes more sense. You grabbed the first yokel you could because Matt had found someone else."

Jessie stared at her for a silent beat, and the emotions Niamh felt through the Ivy House bond were all over the place. Niamh couldn't pinpoint just one.

"I hadn't heard you'd gotten engaged, either," Lottie said, pushing her advantage. "That must've been recent." She tsked. "I hope it wasn't a Christmas proposal. That is so unoriginal. Almost tacky."

Jessie seemed to shrink before the other woman, as if the wind was going out of her sails.

Austin tensed and turned away, his emotions calm but his eyes tight. It couldn't be easy for him not to go to Jessie's aid. This must've been what it was like at the dinner the other night. These people used personal information to make vicious attacks, but their duplicity was hidden behind light tones and condescending smiles. Very effective. Niamh knew all about how that went down, having used the same tactic on enemies she wanted to incite.

But these people used it on *family*, and probably friends. They'd clearly used it on Jessie when she and that *bollock* were together. He'd give her a verbal battering, then the mom—whom he'd surely learned his tricks from—would follow up. It seemed Jessie hadn't been allowed to have any friends for backup or support. It had been just her, for all those years, dealing with this shite and not having the money to walk away, the know-how to fight back, or maybe even the realization that this was not normal. There were a lot of wealthy people in the world, but not many of them were this breed of arsehole. This family was...special.

"Come on, Jessie," Niamh whispered under her breath, trying to pump her full of the desire to fight. To battle. To blow things up.

Another wave of the same feelings came through the bond from someone else—Mr. Tom. He must've been within earshot somewhere. Then another, Edgar, probably having no idea what was going on but joining in anyway. You could always count on that vampire. Another addition, Ulric. Then Jasper, joining in for the sake of unity. Cyra's addition felt like fire itself—that was new—and Hollace's was a stiff breeze, igniting Cyra's feeling of flames. The bonds echoed with the crew's battle cry. With their need to rise up and fight back. To push Jessie to claim her destiny. Her freedom. Her self-worth. She wasn't alone anymore. She wasn't in this storm by herself. They were with her, in all things.

And finally Austin joined in, a steady drumbeat of power. Of strength. Of support.

Jessie's back straightened within the gale of the other woman's condescending smirk.

"I feel sorry for you," she finally said, surprising Niamh because it was clear she meant the words. It wasn't the war cry Niamh might've expected or hoped for. "If you truly think a woman moving on after a divorce is desperate, I feel sorry for you. If that double standard is the reason for your current loneliness, your bitterness, your…need to push these arbitrary rules on other people to drag them down to your level, then my heart goes out to you. Truly. But you are delusional if you can look at Austin and call him a yokel. You know as well as I do that there is no one in this house who is as handsome, successful, and, quite frankly, well dressed. He is also the most charming, considerate, and supportive man I have ever known. You can try to make me feel bad about a great many things in my life, but him and his—*my* family are not on that list." She paused for a moment, her bearing so incredibly casual. Nonchalant. "And he doesn't need the timing of a proposal to be original"—she lifted her hand, ring held out toward Lottie—"when he's slipping a two-carat Harry Winston on my finger."

She turned away like she'd just dropped a mic, strutting past two people who'd been blatantly listening in and staring to boot. Coming to a stop in front of Austin, she took his hand and gazed adoringly up into his eyes. He bent to her, a shifter and therefore not needing a piece of jewelry to show the world where his devotion lay. His posture screamed *mine* and his lips touched hers softly.

"What do you say we go see what Jimmy got for Christmas?" she said.

"Sure. Lead the way."

After they left, Aurora drifted in closer.

"Two things," she said, finishing off the last of her food and holding the empty plate. "First, where'd Mimi go?"

"Front room with Patty," Broken Sue said. "Next?"

Her brow quirked in a slight expression that meant *bollocks* to Niamh. These two were just too much work when they were together.

"Does that mean it's go time? Was that enough of Jessie pushing back?"

Niamh pointed at Lottie, who'd moved farther into the kitchen, and Niamh could see she was speaking to Jessie's ex. He looked a lot more haggard than he had in the pictures Niamh had seen. The man clearly wasn't aging well.

"Look at the state of that woman," Niamh murmured. "She's all flustered. I'd say that was Jessie pushing back. Green light. Let's rule this party."

"Right. Okay." Aurora looked around, and her gaze finally landed on Broken Sue. "Susan? Shall we mingle?"

"Sure," he replied, a smirk showing through his hostile expression.

"Do you know how? I'm not good at this sort of thing. Mac got the social genes. I got the…"

"Scary genes?" Niamh finished. "And what are ye on about, asking this one if he knows how to mingle? He's bloody useless at making friends. Everyone knows that. Make the best of it. Yis go and drift that way. Ye're both attractive and look the part. Hopefully that'll be enough."

"What are you going to do?" Aurora asked Niamh.

"Drift the other way and annoy people. I'll bring the cooler."

"And everyone knows you excel at that," Broken Sue said.

"What are ye, Captain Obvious?" Niamh refilled her glass, refilled Broken Sue's as well, and put the bottle away before picking up her cooler. "Or maybe I'll hang around here. I haven't decided yet. I need to feel things out."

Either way, it was time to make people uncomfortable and hopefully cause havoc.

CHAPTER 28
AURORA

"So..." AURORA PASSED Sue so she could get a drink, a white wine because it was easy, and then pointed toward the kitchen. "What do we do, do we just...go over there and stand around a little? Or..."

He glanced down at her. "You really are bad at this. Did you not talk to anyone in your pack?"

"I did, yes. Because I knew everyone in my pack, and if I didn't, they knew me. Did you not grow up as an alpha's kid?"

"No. I grew up as the adopted son of an older couple. I was shy and a late bloomer."

"Ah."

She nodded, no longer focusing on their surroundings. It wasn't prudent to ask more, given their respective positions within the pack hierarchy, but this was a family event, so she was just gonna kinda drift along and see what he'd say. She knew he'd shut her down if she overstepped.

"So you got picked on quite a lot, then," she surmised, taking a look around again. The setup of this house was a little odd. The kitchen was off to the left, and in it was another little, round table setup. Through a short hall of sorts to the right there was a family room out of the way, with a Christmas tree and people chatting.

They headed in that direction, meandering slowly.

"We should look friendly," she whispered as people glanced their way. This place was busy and pretty crowded. Gazes stuck to them, and some people outright stared, but no one stepped forward like they would've in her dad's pack.

"I am. I'm containing my aggression."

That probably wasn't going to be enough, but whatever. Judging by the body language of the people around them, they were making everyone uncomfortable just by walking around. Alpha energy for the win.

"I did get picked on, yes," Sue said as they arrived in the living room. Jessie was sitting beside Jimmy on the couch, looking over something in his hands. "Mercilessly."

Austin stood near her. Another woman Aurora didn't know sat on the other side of Jimmy, with tanned skin, straight black hair, and a big smile. Mr. Tom was off to the side, watching Jimmy and the room. He took his protection duties very seriously, it seemed. Jimmy was a cool guy who was easy to hang around with, though, like Jessie, so maybe Mr. Tom just enjoyed his company.

"It wasn't usual for a kid to get adopted into the pack," Sue said. "We grew up in a rural place. Seclud-ed."

"How'd you get adopted?" She half held her breath, knowing the question was an incredibly personal one to ask a beta.

"I got dropped off on the edge of town in a basket. Newly born with just the items from the hospital in the basket. I was left under a tree. The patrol brought me in, and my parents offered to raise me. They hadn't been able to have kids of their own."

She blew out a breath, not really knowing what to say and blurting out the first thing that came to mind. "Did your birth parents not want you?" She slapped a hand over her mouth. "I'm so sorry, that was incredibly rude. I didn't mean to say that. I—"

"It's okay. I asked the same question when I was told I was adopted."

"I don't mean to pry," she murmured.

"Yes, you do." He glanced down at her again with a small uptick at the corners of his lips, his version of a smile. He took a sip of his drink, then grimaced. "This stuff is intense. I tracked my birth parents down in my late teens. My birth dad had been an alpha. A gorilla, like me. He was up in his years and didn't relinquish the pack when he should have. He was challenged, given the choice to step down or fight to the death. He didn't step down, and he didn't win."

"And your mom couldn't stay in the pack and raise you?"

"She probably could have, but from what I learned, it sounds like she probably wanted a fresh start. She was my birth father's second mate. The first left when he started losing control of the pack but wouldn't make way. Seems she saw the writing on the wall. But my birth mom didn't. She was young. Too young to know better, maybe. Maybe too young to care."

"Maybe both."

"Maybe. She saw the opportunity to be an alpha's mate and took it. Or maybe my birth father had a lot of charm, I don't know. I didn't get any of his charm if he did."

"I don't know about that—some people find intense, menacing stares very charming indeed."

"Only Niamh, and she's not my type."

Aurora spat out a laugh and turned away so her uncle wouldn't see. Something about this dark, brooding beta made her feel lighter, somehow. Like he'd taken all the storm clouds for himself and she got whatever sunshine was left over.

"I got the feeling that she was very pretty but low on power," he said, watching as Auntie Jessie stood and slipped her arm around Uncle Auzzie. He pulled her in a little tighter, turning her way and bending toward her possessively, showing the whole room that she was his. His mate, his heart, his everything. "I guess she didn't see a future with a newborn and no mate. She thought it would be better to be without a baby."

"She wasn't there when you visited the pack?"

"No. She left before having the baby and never went back. I might've been able to track her down—I had her name—but I didn't bother. My parents were still alive at the time, and they'd cared for me all my life. Knowing my history was enough. Knowing my father was an alpha answered some questions. Questions that would later become very important as my power continued to grow. In my early twenties, with a newly established mate, I got to that precipice you felt before you came to this convocation. I needed a challenge. I needed *more.* I could've challenged for the pack I grew up in, but I knew it wouldn't be enough for me. Instead, I packed up and moved to the much larger pack of my birth father."

"Which had been taken over by another alpha."

"Taken over by a lackluster alpha who'd seen an opportunity and cashed in on it. He wasn't nearly as strong as me. Wasn't as strong as my birth father had been in his prime. The pack was languishing."

"You stepped in."

"Yes."

"But you didn't have any experience."

"No. But my birth father had been loved in his prime. He'd done well for the pack. The only issue they'd had with him was his refusal to step down when the time came. When she heard that I was taking up the mantle, his first mate returned, promising to help me where she could. The former beta acted as counsel, and so on. I cobbled together a good team, and they all helped me get up to speed. Once I got some experience, I found I had a knack for leadership. I got things back on track."

"And your birth father had no other children?"

"None. Just me. He might've succeeded if he'd had a child earlier, I don't know. From all the stories I'd heard of him, he'd been a true alpha. A good alpha."

"Part of being a good alpha is knowing when to step down."

"Yes, but if you have no one qualified to take your place except a stranger, an opportunistic, lackluster alpha…"

"Ah, the new leader was a stranger. You didn't mention that part. Gotcha. And your birth mother never came back even after you took over, huh?"

"Not that I know of. But like I said, I didn't keep looking for her. I wouldn't have known unless she came looking for me. I never asked for a picture, and she could've changed her name." He shrugged.

"I would have been burning with curiosity."

"I can imagine. You have no end of questions for me now."

She felt her face heat and didn't press further. Eventually the conversation would bump up against the battle that had taken all he cared about, and she didn't want to open those wounds. Instead, she watched Auntie Jessie chat with the woman on the couch as Jimmy and Mr. Tom tried to work out a puzzle box or something.

"Do you think she'd mind if I just call her Jessie?" Aurora asked, noticing people edging a little closer to her and Sue.

"I don't know."

"Jeez, man, stop with the long-winded answers, already."

Aurora could tell Uncle Auzzie had essentially tuned the conversation out. He was only hovering close to Jessie now because of their obvious and incredible love for each other. Aurora would never forget what it had been like when Jessie was on the brink of death. Her uncle had guarded his mate day and night, not leaving her side, openly crying in front of both packs. His desperation had far outweighed his training.

"I don't know if they are relationship goals," she mused, "or if I'm afraid of loving someone that much."

"She completes him."

Aurora blinked for a moment before slowly turning to look at Sue's face. Nothing in his demeanor gave his emotions away.

"Is that from the movie *Jerry Maguire*? Are you try-ing to be funny?"

"I never have to try. It happens naturally."

She could feel her smile bud, and when he looked down at her with glittering eyes, it grew.

"You're dumb," she said, turning away.

"I will say this much, since I'm older and wiser," he told her as a woman walked their way. She had hopeful determination on her face until Sue met her eyes, and then she turned, flustered, and quickly veered to a group of two couples.

"Quit scaring people away," Aurora told him out of the side of her mouth.

He grunted, taking the note.

"A love like theirs doesn't happen often," he commented, watching Jessie and Uncle Auzzie now—Aurora was just going to go with Jessie and watch her cues to see if it was welcomed or not. It felt more natural, because she was more like a friend than an aunt. "They traveled a hard road to find each other. But even lesser loves are worth it. It is better to know how love feels, how to give yourself to someone, how to form intimacy and create memories, than to travel through a cold life alone. It's a rush to feel truly vulnerable with someone. To fall to your knees admiring her smile." He paused for a moment, his sorrow leaking into his bearing. The air was thick around them. "I still remember the looks my mate would give me when I did something unexpected for her, like pick her some wildflowers, or take the kids to the park so she could have some alone time. She looked at me like I was her hero. I'll never forget that rush, and how it felt to be on my knees before her, looking up, feeling no regrets. I will never regret mating her, even though, on this side of things, I'd rather curl up and die than trudge through another day without my family."

Aurora stepped a little closer until their arms brushed each other, offering him her support. He leaned in a little, the touch firm now, suggesting he needed it. Great heavens, this man was hurting. He needed a bigger support system, more friends.

He needed help.

She knew he was too proud to ask, though. Or maybe he was still that shy, late bloomer, not good at making the first move.

"I had a lot of fun at Christmas yesterday," she said in a light tone. "It was a really good day."

He didn't respond, probably not trusting his voice to do so without giving anything away.

"We should do more gatherings. I'm sure Jessie would be game. Maybe some dinner parties. We could watch Uncle Auzzie try to teach Jessie to cook and eat whatever becomes of it."

She felt his movement and glanced up to see his small nod.

"And—" She cut off, noticing the woman from earlier turning.

With a plastered-on smile that amplified her nervousness, the woman took the few steps to join Aurora and Sue.

"Hello," she said, probably in her early thirties, with short blond hair, cheekbones to die for, and green contact lenses. Her mauve A-line dress was tasteful and conservative, and her chunky black boots were super cute and somehow worked. "I don't believe I've met you two." She pointed between them, including Aurora in the conversation just as much as Sue. "You're here with Jacinta's group, aren't you? Didn't I hear that…" She pointed at Aurora. "She's your daughter, right?"

"I'm his"—Aurora gestured toward Uncle Auzzie—"niece."

The woman blinked in confusion. "But aren't you"—she pointed at Sue—"his brother?" Then she pointed between Aurora and Sue again. She did love waving that finger around. "Doesn't that make you…"

"Ah." Aurora nodded, seeing that Sue intended to make her do all the work here. That wouldn't last much longer. "I see the confusion. They are both my uncles, actually. This one was adopted." She hooked her thumb at Sue. "But we're all family. My dad lives in Wyoming. I'm with these uncles for a work thing."

"Oh." The woman breathed out with a smile, bent, and gestured with her hand. Very expressive, this Jane. "I wondered because"—more pointing—"you two don't look the right ages. Well…unless you"—another point at Sue—"started *very* young."

"He would have needed to get started when he was about…fifteen, right, Sue?" Aurora prodded.

"Fourteen," he growled. "I'm thirty-nine for four more months."

"Possible, but improbable," Aurora said, noticing the woman's dazed, star-struck expression as she gazed up at Sue. She clearly wanted alone time and a phone number. Or maybe one of those quiet corners Jasper was so good at finding.

"Wait…did she call you…*Sue*?" the woman asked.

"I'll leave you to explain that one, Susan," Aurora said, stepping away.

He looked down at her, and his body screamed, *Don't you dare leave me with her!*

Aurora angled her head and twitched up her shoulder just a bit. *Good luck, sucka.*

She stepped away just as Uncle Auzzie and Jessie started toward her.

"Hey," she said, falling in with Jessie as they headed back toward the dining room. "What'd Jimmy get?"

"He always gets weird presents from this side of the family," Jessie said softly. "A puzzle box and an obscure comic book and some other things. The only good one was from his dad. Because Camila bought it."

"Was that the woman on the couch?"

"Yeah. She's had a couple hard days because of me. I feel—"

"It's not because of you," Uncle Auzzie cut in. "It's because of him. You are not in charge of how another adult behaves."

It sounded like he had said that before.

Jessie sighed as they reached the dining room,

where she checked in at the breakfast bar and asked for another glass of sparkling wine.

"I know," she said sullenly. "I just feel so awful for her. I think she's afraid to call and talk. He handles the bill. He can look and see who she's called."

"Yeah, but…" Aurora topped up her wine, spotting Niamh just outside the room with her cooler in hand, chatting with a man who was doing a terrible job hiding the fact that he was enraged. Niamh showed zero signs of a similar emotion. "What are the odds he'd look and spot your number, though?"

Jessie gave Aurora a look that said volumes.

"He checked my calls every month and quizzed me on several of them," she murmured as they headed toward the front of the house this time, slowly meandering. "If it was a call to a friend that was a half-hour or more, he interrogated me on what I was talking about."

"Hey, babe, I'm going to head back and save Brochan," Uncle Auzzie said, touching Jessie lightly on the arm. "You're good?"

"Yeah, I'm fine."

Uncle Auzzie headed off. As he went, Aurora noticed Jessie's ex heading back toward the kitchen area from somewhere deeper within the house. The guy saw her uncle heading his way and stopped dead. Fear lined every inch of his body. Uncle Auzzie had clearly made an impression. The ex quickly about-faced and headed back in the direction he'd come.

Not a minute later, three women about Jessie's age sidled toward them from the living room area, where Patty was still chatting up a storm and Mimi was standing by listening. Mimi was probably gathering the information Patty was sussing out and figuring out ways to blow up conversations with it. That or start trouble by gossiping about it. Mimi could be incredibly destructive when someone threatened her people. Her and Patty didn't always get along, but it seemed they could forget their differences when facing a mutual enemy.

"Dang it," Jessie muttered. "Spoke too soon."

She threw on a big smile for the newcomers, the women all kinda looking like different renditions of each other. Similar short or cap-sleeved dresses with reasonably high necklines, loose waists and skirts, simple necklaces with a few gems or diamonds, and a draping scarf and three-inch or less pump. They were conservative to the point of bland. Aurora would bet anything these were the people who'd convinced Jessie that a woman hitting middle age had to dress a certain way or be faced with ridicule.

"Jessie, hi!" The first, with perfectly straight,

bleached white teeth, threw out her hands in a faux display of excitement and friendship. They hugged, the woman rocking Jessie from side to side before stepping back so the next could do the same thing, and then the next.

"Hi, Pamela. Jody. Bess. How are you all?" Jessie said, her lack of enthusiasm evident.

"Just great! It's been so long," said the first of them, Pamela. She made a show of pouting. "I wondered if we'd ever see you again. You moved to the other side of the world."

"I don't know how you do it," another said, her hair fairly short and very blond. "Living in the sticks?" She gave Jessie an incredulous look. "All the bugs and critters." She issued a pronounced shiver.

"Not to mention everything shuts down early, right?" the third said. "What if you need to run out in the middle of the night for… I don't know, wine or something? You'd be stranded!"

"What would I do without delivery, am I right, girls?" Pamela leaned into the others, and they all started laughing uproariously. Jessie merely smiled at them, offering no comment.

"This is my niece, Aurora, by the way," Jessie said.

They looked Aurora up and down, the set of their shoulders and the tightness of their jaws saying they were intimidated.

"Well, look at you, girl!" Pamela leaned away and put a finger to her chin. She glanced at her friends and then leaned into Jessie. "To be young again, huh?"

"Yes," the second said, narrowing her eyes slightly at Aurora. "Though I'll never understand young women these days. They make a big stink about smiling. Don't they know they look positively wretched if they look miserable all the time? No offense!" She offered Aurora an insincere smile. "But you all don't care about marriage either, right? So I guess you don't care about getting a man."

Aurora added a heavy dose of power and hostility into her eyes and bearing. All three women's smiles faltered, and they quickly shifted their attention back to Jessie. How these women hadn't been killed by now was anyone's guess. They wouldn't last one day in a shifter pack.

"Too bad looks fade," Pamela said. "But look at you, Jacinta! You've lost weight."

"Yeah, I work out with Austin a lot. My fiancé." She showed them the ring.

"Oh my God!" Pamela turned and thrust Jessie's hand at the others. "I heard about this a moment ago. Is it really Harry Winston?" She narrowed her eyes at Jessie, dropping the hand. "He didn't just buy one of those boxes on eBay and slap another ring in it?"

They started laughing like it was a joke. Their bodies didn't lie, though. They were as jealous as people could be. Self-conscious, too, sucking in their stomachs or holding their arms in front of their bodies. Those things made them incredibly spiteful—and from there, it was a quick jump to destructive.

"Is he one of those Paul Bunyan types?" the second asked. "I mean, don't get me wrong, he's handsome, and he looks great for the party, but does he live in flannels and board shorts?"

"They live in the boonies." The third nudged her friend. "They don't wear board shorts—they wear holey sweats."

"He wears threadbare jeans a lot of the time, actually," Jessie countered, looking out at the other people, clearly bored. "White T-shirts." She looked back at the third. "And he looks hot in them. Well, you know, you've seen him. He'd look hot in board shorts or holey sweats, too."

Their "excitement" at seeing Jessie again was waning fast, and their scowls and snarls started to crack the façade of politeness.

"What'd you say he does?" Pamela quirked an eyebrow. "Venture capitalist?"

"Investor, but he also inherited a sizable trust."

"And you're…" Pamela was squinting and shaking her head slowly. "You take care of an old house?"

"Yes, basically. I manage a very large estate and the people who work there, like the cape-wearing butler. He came with the house. As such, I can use the funds for my own benefit. When needed."

"Like lipo?" The third lifted her eyebrows accusingly.

"I got a tuck done after I took on the house, sure," Jessie said breezily, explaining away what the magic had done. "But the rest was through working out. Again, you've seen my fiancé. How do you think he got that body? He's helped me get in shape."

"Well." The second showed disdain at Jessie's dress now. "You're sure showing it off in that dress. Are you sure you should be exposing so much of yourself with your son here? I mean…" She looked around and then lowered her voice. "He's probably embarrassed that his mother is dressing like the girls he's in college with."

"Or like your niece." Pamela indicated Aurora. She tilted her head to the side. "It's not a good look, Jessie. Your fiancé doesn't have any kids. He doesn't realize."

Jessie laughed softly. "You gals are really something. You know what? I'm glad he doesn't realize. And even if he did, he would be supportive of my feeling confident in my own skin and wearing this dress because I feel pretty in it. My son is not embarrassed, no. I'm happy that he is witnessing a woman in her midlife owning her body and kicking ass. I hope, when he's in middle age, he supports his partner like Austin supports me. And my niece? She can speak for herself."

Aurora waited for all three pairs of eyes to find hers again. She held them, letting loose more of her power, pumping out the wildness she struggled to keep at bay and slamming it into them. Their eyes widened, and Aurora leaned in a bit.

"Stop tearing other women down to feel better about yourselves. It doesn't help you, and it makes other women miserable. Build each other up. We should be sticking together and supporting each other. It makes us stronger. Enough strength and we'll be invincible."

"Well said." Jessie nodded at them. "Great to see you three, as always."

Aurora wouldn't wish their company on an enemy. She stepped away from them without another word, leaving them entirely speechless.

"Wow," she said as she followed Jessie toward the front room.

"That was nothing." Jessie stopped at the edge of a single step leading down to the adjoining room. She took a deep breath, her eyes on fire. "In the past I'd have frumpier clothes and a mate who belittled me. I'd try to stay on the outskirts of that group and not get noticed. I now realize I was easy pickings." She looked over her shoulder.

The three women stood with their heads together, speaking animatedly. Obviously pissed.

Jessie smiled in elation, looking away again. "That felt so good. I felt in control. Like I had some power for once!"

"You have more power than anyone in this house," Aurora replied, furrowing her brow.

Jessie shook her head, glancing back at Patty, who gestured wildly and then laughed. All the (very likely) stuffy, stuck-up people she was talking to laughed with her. She'd won them over. Not surprising.

Mimi stepped in and said something. One of the men, dressed in jeans and a blazer, lost his humor quickly. His eyes sparkled with anger, and the woman next to him looked embarrassed. Obviously, whatever Mimi said had hurt.

Aurora felt giddy at watching them operate. *Go, Mimi and Patty!* One was obviously setting the other up to take verbal jabs, which was apparently the Jane way.

"Magically, yes," Jessie said after a moment. "I was gifted that power. Socially?" She shook her head again. "I've never had any power socially. And while I was gifted the money to buy this dress and have nice things, it didn't fundamentally change me. O'Briens did. Austin did. Mr. Tom and Niamh, your dad and his pack, Sebastian and Elliot Graves—my new life has given me confidence. It's given me trust in myself and those around me. It's given me a sense of individual power and self-worth. I didn't let those ladies get to me. I held my ground. I came out on top for the first time ever, and it felt…freeing. Amazing! This whole trip has felt freeing. And I couldn't have done it without you all. Without your support."

Aurora was hugging her before she'd thought about it. It was easy to show affection to this woman. She felt grounded when she did it, rooted in the bond of family and friendship. They barely knew each other, and yet it felt like they'd known each other forever.

"You were meant to be in our family," Aurora told her as a balding guy in his early fifties sauntered closer. He had red cheeks and a red nose, with salt-and-pepper hair combed over his scalp in a sort of puff.

She hurried to finish what she wanted to say.

"You were meant to glue us all back together. I believe that. I've never much believed in fate, but you fit too perfectly for there to be any other explanation."

"Hello, Jessie," the man said, his smile a little…icky for some reason. Aurora couldn't put her finger on why, but something about this man threw her off. She didn't want him too close, a gut instinct. And if this were the magical world, she'd force him back or prepare to fight.

Given that it wasn't, she had no idea how to handle the situation.

CHAPTER 29

JESSIE

ANNOYANCE FLARED THROUGH me at the interruption by a man I'd always detested. A friend of the family who was high in the social hierarchy, had a great few dollars to his name, and was spoken of with an air of importance. Most of the men revered him, but the women detested him. It was an open secret that no woman wanted to get cornered by him. He got handsy when he drank, which was often, but no one would cast him out because of it.

I'd always been one of his favorite targets for butt pinching and breast groping. When I'd told Matt, asking that Ramous not be invited places (at the very least), I was shrugged off or told that I must've brought it on myself. I'd almost believed him. That had been easier than the truth, which was I had no one to protect me from being harassed, and if I wasn't careful, something worse might happen.

The thought made me want to run to Austin right then. He never would've allowed me to feel threatened. Ever. Hell, aside from his enemies, he wouldn't allow *anyone* to feel threatened, man or woman, pack or not. He'd set up O'Briens as a safe haven for just that reason. He was a true alpha, using his strength and power to protect those who couldn't protect themselves. He'd never asked for thanks. Never wanted fanfare. He kept people safe as a matter of course.

"Jacinta, my goodness." Ramous's watery gaze drifted down my body. "You look beautiful. Why didn't you call me when Matt left you?" He dropped his voice to a murmur. "I would've looked after you."

His tone dripped with innuendo. Aurora shivered, uncomfortable.

I hadn't been able to protect myself back in the day, but I could now.

"The very idea of that is repugnant, Ramous," I replied, wanting to look away but watching him to make sure he didn't get grabby.

"Please, call me *Uncle* Ramous." He leaned in a little closer, leering at my breasts. Clearly he hadn't listened to a thing I'd said. "Come to my beach house. You can sunbathe." He waggled his eyebrows suggestively. "Topless, if you want. Such a hot little body should be shown off."

"I'm going to tell you this one time," I ground out. "Your words and proximity are inappropriate and not appreciated. If you don't back off—actually, if you don't get lost, I'm going to knock you onto your ass. Decide."

I didn't use magic. Instead, I speared him with a hard gaze and bristled in the way a shifter might. I was ready for action, and I made sure he could see it.

Even still, it took him a moment to register what I was saying. My tone. My aggression. He was used to me backing down or scurrying away, making platitudes with an uncomfortable smile. He was used to me being prey.

Now he was on the other side of that dynamic, clearly an unusual place for him.

The sexual sparkle died in his eyes and anger took its place. His lips pulled away from his teeth in a silent snarl, and a crease formed between his brows.

"I gave you a nice offer, an offer most gold-digging whores would kill for, and this is the thanks I get?" he asked, a complete one-eighty from a moment before. "You better watch yourself. I will destroy you. I will put you out on the streets. You'd better reconsider your animosity, or there'll be hell to pay."

"So this is why no one will stand up to you," I said, suddenly understanding. "The husbands are afraid you'll make good on your promise and financially hurt them. Protecting their wives isn't worth being broke. You use your money and position to get a green light to act like a pervert. Since money is a god to these people, they just look the other way." I shook my head, uncontrollably angry. "Well, guess what? You can't do squat to me, and my fiancé won't look the other way. If you value those really expensive caps, you'll back the fuck off and forget you ever knew me."

His silent snarl continued as he stared at me. I held his gaze, daring him to press me. Several moments ticked by, and I realized the entire front room was as silent as the grave, everyone watching the situation. I'd probably raised my voice. Maybe I'd even yelled. I didn't know and I didn't care. I wanted this guy to reach out and try to touch me so that I could punch him.

I *so badly* wanted to punch him.

"No wonder he dumped you," Ramous finally spat. Literally. Spraying my face. "You're just like the rest of them. Money-grubbing sluts, always with a hand out. Get a little status and you think you rule the world. But you're still the same whore from—"

His body was ripped away before I'd even registered the familiar presence. Austin held Ramous's jacket in two fists as he spun and slammed him against the wall behind us. He leaned into the smaller man, his aggression throbbing, his control wobbly.

"What did you just say to my fiancée?" Austin growled.

"S-su-su… S-su…" Ramous's hands gently slapped at Austin's wrists, and his legs dangled. "S-su…"

It was unclear exactly what word he was trying to form.

"You do not disrespect women like that, do you hear me?" Austin said, pulling back and then slamming Ramous against the wall again. "You most certainly do not disrespect *my* woman like that."

Another slam before he yanked Ramous away and jammed him onto his feet. He spun him around like he was a doll, grabbed him by the shoulders, and thrust him my way.

"You say you're sorry," Austin commanded.

"Su-su." Ramous's jaw was slack, his hands up in front of his chest as if he were trying to ward away monsters.

"*Say you're sorry.*" Austin shook him.

"So-sorry," Ramous wailed. "Sorry. Sorry! *Sorry!*"

Austin flung him aside, letting go. Ramous staggered and then fell to his knees, pitching forward and bracing his hands against the ground.

"Sorry," he said again, shaking. "Sorry."

"He doesn't mean it. He's just scared," Aurora said, anger hot in her voice.

"Are you okay?" Austin clasped both of my shoulders, looking into my eyes.

"Yes, I'm fine. This time I'm fine, yes. He's been sexually harassing me for years, though. He's disgusting."

I turned to speak to the people in the front room. We'd just granted ourselves a disinvite from this party, I was sure of it. These people were the worst, but they were not physically violent. They'd call the cops if we didn't remove ourselves posthaste.

But I had three things I needed to do before I closed the door on this part of my life.

"That man"—I pointed down at him, to where he'd rolled up into a ball with Broken Sue standing over him aggressively—"has been touching and groping the women in these parties for years. Every one of you knows it. Austin is the only one who has ever stood up for any of us. The only one in...*years*. What is wrong with you people that you'd allow someone like this in here? There are no little girls at this party, but they're at other parties he attends. And yet you keep inviting this predator calling himself *Uncle* Ramous? Have you no shame? Have you no desire to do what is right and protect each other?"

Everyone looked at me, but silence met my words. Mimi stood off to the side, watching the scene, and

Patty nodded mid-conversation with whomever she was talking to.

"Do better," I told them. "You won't have Austin at those other parties to put *Uncle* Ramous in his place."

I turned and placed a hand on Austin's chest, sliding it up to cup his neck and pull him down to meet my lips.

"Thank you," I murmured. "Thank you for being there. In the past, I never had anyone to protect me. The contrast between then and now makes me appreciate you so much more."

His arms came around me. "I love you. Are you sure you're okay?"

He was clearly responding to my *blech* reactions through the bond. Maybe my anger.

"Yes. We'll be wrapping all this up shortly and heading home. First, though…"

Time for the second item on the to-do list.

Matt stood with two other guys, Ben and Lucas, his closest friends since college. His face was scrunched into a wary scowl, and his friends looked nervous about the way Austin had physically handled that situation.

"A word?" I said to Matt.

His eyes narrowed just a bit, and he crossed his arms over his chest. "You come into my mother's home and cause havoc with your Mafia boyfriend and expect to address me in private?" His huff of derision was ruined by his audible swallow. His friends' snickers rang false. "That was the sort of lowlife display I've always expected from you, Jacinta. I guess you've proven, once and for all, what you really are."

"And you've proven you're just as much of a coward today as you were the day we met, when a guy dumped soda on your jacket and I had to stand up to him for you. No surprise there, huh? What I was going to say is this—you and all your people are shallow, narcissistic nobodies with more money than sense. Your style is *gauche*, your suits fit poorly, and these parties are severely lacking in quality. What wine are you even pouring here? For a family that prides itself on wealth, you certainly look like a dying empire." I paused for a moment. This speech was intended to hit them where it hurt the most. "My dealings with you and your family are mostly finished. *Mostly* because auditors will be looking into the court-ordered funds you should be paying Jimmy. I'll also be providing him with funds so that he isn't dependent on you. Other than that, have a nice life. I hope you reap what you sow."

I didn't wait for him to respond, feeling a sense of relief as I walked away. He didn't shout after me. That wasn't his style. He'd try to find some other way to get back at me, and hopefully by then I'd be a phone call away.

I wouldn't be answering those calls.

Last order of business.

"Just what do you think—"

I ignored Lottie, veering by her to the family room where Camila was straightening up Jimmy's things. Given she wasn't socializing with any of the other guests or standing with Matt, I felt better about what I was about to do. Namely, reach back and try to help someone else out of this hellhole.

"Hey," I said, standing on the other side of the couch. She looked up, surprised.

"Oh, hi, Jessie." She gazed over my shoulder, obviously looking for Matt.

"Can I have a word?"

She straightened up slowly, suddenly fidgeting. "Uh…"

"Come on." I gestured, knowing she was like me, a little too easygoing for her own good at times. It would be hard for her to give me a flat no. "It'll only take a minute. I'm on my way out. I wanted to say goodbye."

"Oh…kay, but…" She looked around as she did what she was told. "Maybe just for a moment…"

She wasn't supposed to talk to me. That, or she knew talking to me would get her in trouble. More reason for me to force the meeting.

Broken Sue stood with Mr. Tom, Jimmy, and Aurora near the small kitchen table, clearly waiting for me.

"Where's Austin?" I asked.

"Using his presence and posturing to keep everyone contained in the front room," Broken Sue replied. "He wants to keep control and make sure everyone behaves."

"Everyone is afraid to move." Aurora smirked. "Your ex included. He and his boys are visibly shaking as the alpha stares them down."

"I just have one thing to do and we'll head out," I said.

"Need anything?" Broken Sue asked as I ushered Camila past him.

"Yeah. Watch our six. We need a second. Undisturbed."

"You heard her, Master Jimmy—let's get ready," Mr. Tom told my son. "Which of those presents do you want to take, and which of them do you want to stuff down the couch cushions and pretend you forgot?"

Broken Sue stepped forward to go with me, and Aurora stood her ground, presumably to guard the kitchen door.

"Oh…outside?" Camila said when we reached the back door.

"Yup." I gestured her through, and Broken Sue

pushed in behind us, his aura of intensity hurrying her into the backyard.

"Just…for a minute, okay?"

We took a seat on the cold patio furniture, metal chairs without cushions surrounding a dirty glass table. Though it was sunny most of the year here, and not cold by most of the country's standards, people didn't hang around outside during the winter without heating lamps and a firepit.

Broken Sue shut the door behind him and stepped to the side, leaning against the wall. My people spread out around the yard, perking up now that I'd come outside. I had a feeling they were bored out of their minds and would all be happy to leave.

"You didn't call me the other night," I started, knowing the clock was ticking. Her expression turned uncomfortable. "You worried he'd check the phone records and see my number listed."

Her uncomfortable expression turned guilty.

"Yeah." I nodded. "He did that to me, too. You were at that dinner. How he talks to you is the same as how he talked to me. It doesn't get better, Camila. And if you're cool with that, then great. I'm happy for you. But if you have *any* doubts, now is the time to fix your situation. Either push back or get out. Because once he knocks you up, things get a lot more complicated."

Tears filled her eyes.

"Oh God, you're already pregnant. I'm sorry, I didn't mean—"

"No!" She put out her hand. "No, it's not—"

The door swung open to reveal Matt, his face bland and composed and his body language screaming *furious*.

"Camila," he said in a disapproving tone. "You—"

Broken Sue flung out a hand, grabbing the middle of Matt's chest.

"This is a private conversation," he growled, leaning toward Matt with crazy eyes. "You're not wanted out here."

The color drained from Matt's suddenly long face, and his jaw went slack.

Broken Sue, with no visible effort, pushed Matt back into the house and closed the door behind him. He moved his big mass in front and crossed his arms over his chest, looking at me.

That meant *proceed.*

Matt trying to barge into the conversation meant *hurry up.*

"What were you going to say?" I prompted Camila.

"Oh, it's just…" She licked her lips as she glanced at Broken Sue. "Maybe I should go in—"

"Camila"—I laid my hand on the table—"talk to me.

I understand where you are. You know I do. You saw proof. You've seen how this family treats me. Is it different for you?"

She sagged a little, and a tear fell down her cheek. "That dinner the other night…" She shook her head. "It was like a cold splash of water. I'd been in denial, I think. It's just… He can be so charming. So, *so* charming. He always used to say the right things. To compliment me and seem to mean it. My whole family loves him. And he takes—or took, I guess, he doesn't do it much anymore—me out to these fancy dinners and everyone was all smiles to meet me…"

She leaned back in her chair.

"I don't know where it went wrong," she said, in almost a whisper. "I don't know how it got to this. Tripping over landmines. The things that used to make him happy now make him chastise me…" She shook her head. "But that dinner…" Another tear fell. "I just don't know how I ended up here. I thought it was so terrible the way he was treating you, and the things he was saying. But then I realized…"

The door bumped open. Broken Sue reached back and shoved it closed.

"And no," she said, her gaze unfocused now. "His family doesn't treat me well. I know it's hard to fit in when you're the second wife, but I still haven't found my way with them." She shook her head. "I don't know. He's been under a lot of stress lately. He tends to get frazzled."

And there were the excuses… The hope that it would get better again. That it would go back to the way it had been when he was that charming man who said all the right things and was liberal with compliments. The guy a woman couldn't help but fall in love with, not realizing that his entire personality was just a lure. It was a way to bring people in the door. Then the real guy took over.

"I'm going to tell you this, and then I'm going to go, because there is probably a passive-aggressive mob forming now. I blamed myself for him taking his anger out on you. Just earlier today I did that. Austin had to point out how irrational that was. That I am not responsible for the actions of a grown man. I also know how hard it is to distance yourself from feeling that way. To see things clearly when you're in the thick of it. It was only on this trip, coming back here with Austin, that I started to really process what my marriage was like. So I will say this to you… You are not alone. I am in your corner. If you need help in any way—*any* way— I can do that for you. I'll get you a burner phone so you can call me without his knowing. I'll get you a plane ticket so you can come to me if you need to. I can send you money if he cuts you off. If you need help, I am always available, okay? And we've got a lot of great guys around us. Guys who will treat you like a queen. You're young and vibrant—you deserve someone who is going to love and cherish you. Okay?"

More tears tracked down her face. "This sounds stupid, but I think maybe I was too eager to fall in love."

I reached out and rubbed her forearm where it rested on the table. "That doesn't sound stupid. Love is amazing. I hope for everyone to experience what I've found. And Matt makes it easy to fall for him. I should know—I did it, too. Just look after yourself, okay?"

A knock sounded at the door, and this time Aurora's voice came with it. Broken Sue stepped away and opened it, looking inside.

"Gotta go," she said with a smirk. "They called the cops on you, Jessie. Or maybe Uncle Auzzie."

"Crap," I said, pushing to standing. "They could take Austin in for assault."

I stopped beside Broken Sue at the doorway and dropped my voice to a whisper so Camila wouldn't hear. "Get our people to the front of the house. Wait until Camila is gone so she doesn't see you talking to invisible people."

After he nodded, I continued through, and Aurora stepped back as I passed her. A crowd had formed in the front room. Two policemen had already arrived, and they stood just inside the front door, facing Austin and Mimi, who were off to one side. Mr. Tom and Jimmy were nowhere to be seen, so I connected with Mr. Tom's bond to find them outside in the front somewhere, moving toward the car. Mr. Tom had taken my son and fled the scene. He was the best babysitter I'd ever had, and my son didn't even need one anymore.

And now it occurred to me that he'd been essentially babysitting me since I showed up on his doorstep. So there was that.

Patty stood next to one of the cops, a brick of a man with hard eyes and cut muscles. He didn't match the softer, rounder guy standing next to him.

"Isn't that a hoot, though?" Patty was saying. "I'll tell you what isn't a hoot—calling a woman a whore. That isn't a hoot at all. And sure as I am standing here, he called her a gold-digging whore. Well, let me tell you, if he'd called *me* that, I would've given him a fat lip. Don't underestimate me because of my size. I could do it…"

A spindly hand reached out and grabbed me as I made my way to them. I knew before I looked that it belonged to Lottie. She glared at me, her expression livid, and murmured in a low voice, "You have brought embarrassment to this family ever since my son brought you home two decades ago, but *this*…" She sucked in a breath, and her whole face puckered with anger. "You are a dis*grace*. This new group of people you hang around are a disgrace. Your outfit, your unabashed flaunting of your possessions, the way you've treated my son—a *disgrace*! I never want to see you in this house again as long as I live."

"The feeling is mutual, Lottie, I assure you." I yanked my arm out of her grip and pushed through the rest of the crowd until I stopped next to Austin. "Officers, what seems to be the problem?"

"Oh good, yes, here she is." Patty peeled to the side a little, staying close to the brick of an officer.

"I called them." Matt stepped forward like he owned the police force. "That man"—he pointed at Austin—"assaulted one of our guests, and the rest of you have overstayed your welcome. It's time for you to leave. These gentleman will escort you off the property and that man to jail."

"Well, let's hold on just a minute," said the brick of an officer, clearly the one in charge. "I'd like to get an account from the missus, if you don't mind."

"It isn't her I want charges filed against," Matt started, and then slunk down a little when the officer calmly looked his way.

The officer shifted his attention to me. "Can you tell

us what happened before Mr. Baker was pushed against the wall?"

Ramous stepped forward to stare at me from beside Matt, in front of the gathered people in the living room. He had a constipated but pleased expression, like he was in the right and now justice would be served on his behalf. It was an expression he'd probably worn a lot in his life, protected by the umbrella of being a rich businessman with great connections. Guys like that never seemed to be held accountable.

I didn't expect he would be now, either.

Starting with a little background on the nature of Ramous—something he tried to cut short, only to be silenced by the cop—I walked them through the infraction from beginning to end.

"Honestly, sir, we were about to leave," I finished. "We haven't had a very welcome reception here. I was just saying my goodbyes, and we were ready to head out the door."

The officer nodded, glanced briefly at the other cop, and swayed his weight a little with his hands on his belt. "I've heard all I need to hear. Miss, you can take your people. You're free to go. You too," he told Austin.

"*What?*" Ramous sputtered, his face screwed up in anger. "He's dangerous," he shouted. "He assaulted me!"

"Frankly," the officer told him, staring him down, "it's a wonder he didn't take it further. We'd better not hear about you sexually or verbally harassing women again, is that clear?"

"B-bu…" Ramous's fists balled.

"Miss, if you're leaving, best do it now." The officer stepped to the side, leaving the door clear. The other made room as well, watching.

"Yup." I threaded my fingers through Austin's and stepped forward immediately, more than ready to be done with all of it.

"Well, it was lovely to meet all of you," Patty told the room. "You'll be hearing from me."

"I doubt you'll like what you hear, though," Mimi said, following us.

"Oh no, definitely not, no." Patty shook her head. "I have no intention of keeping anyone's secrets. It was a very big mistake, telling them to me."

Niamh walked forward through the crowd, ramming people's legs with the cooler.

"Ma'am." The other officer stepped forward this time, his hand out to stop Niamh.

I paused on the porch, watching.

"We've heard that you have some illegal substances in that cooler." He pointed at it.

"Do I, me feck," she said, setting it down in front of

him. "Well, go on, then, have a wee peek."

"Open the cooler, please," he said, not budging.

She gave him a dramatic sigh before flipping the lid and exposing a flask and a couple of cans of Pabst.

"In case ye can't tell, I'm over twenty-one," she told them.

"What's in the flask?" the officer asked.

"Used to be a special drink made by a bunch of big-foots, but I drank all that." She unscrewed the cap and turned it over. Not even a drop leaked out.

The officer bent to the cooler and then straightened again and backed up. "Okay."

"Are ye sure now?" Niamh pressed. "Ye don't want a beer for the road?"

"Niamh, come on," I called. "Let's go."

She put the lid back on the cooler, and we were walking again. My mood felt light. Jubilant, even. I'd always hated going to that house. I'd hated being cornered by Ramous and getting snide comments from any number of people. I'd hated not living up to expectations and being ignored by Matt even though he'd ensured I had no one to talk to.

And now all of that was over. It was done. I never had to go back.

"I feel free," I said, half wanting to cry, half wanting to laugh. "I feel...like a weight has been lifted. Parts of this trip have been miserable, but they were important. Confronting a past I didn't know I needed to confront was necessary. And now I can look forward. Forever."

We stopped next to our car, and Austin pulled me into a tight hug. "I'm proud of you," he said. "I had no idea how bad things actually were. You were always so blasé about everything. But that's your personality, I guess. Easygoing…until you aren't. Bendable so that you don't break. Were you able to get through to Camila?"

"I don't know." I angled my face up for a kiss before I stepped back as Aurora and Mimi caught up with us. "We need to get her a burner phone—or Niamh does, because I have no idea how to do that—so she can call if she needs help. The choice will be hers, but I made it clear that she isn't alone. He won't be able to isolate her like he did me."

"Good." He crossed to the driver's side, glancing up as a cop car slowed along the street. It stopped even with our car, the more dominant cop driving. His partner was in the car behind him.

"I'm impressed by your control, alpha," the officer said, flashing a grin. "I would've ripped that guy's jugular clean out. But then, I don't associate with that brand of Dicks when I'm off duty. I look forward to seeing you guys again."

Austin bent a little to get a clear view. "If you're ever up in our neighborhood, stop in."

"Will do. Take'r easy." The officer pulled forward. His partner drove by, staring at us through the window, not at all amused.

"That guy was a shifter?" I whispered, watching the cars move slowly down the street as I sat down. "No way!"

"Just the one, yeah." Austin sat into the car. "I recognized his smell from the other night. Smart, having some guys on the police force."

"Is that why he let you go?"

"I don't know. In O'Briens they wouldn't haul someone in for what I did, but L.A. is a different situation."

"And it's an affluent neighborhood." We waited for Mimi and Aurora to get in and then pulled forward. Up ahead, Jimmy was being hovered over by Mr. Tom and, very similar to me, didn't seem to mind one bit. "I guess we got lucky," I continued.

"It's about time."

I dropped my hand to Austin's thigh as he drove.

"That party...was awful," Aurora said into the quiet car. "The worst. *How* did you stand those people for twenty years, Jessie? Are you some sort of saint?"

"She must be," Mimi said. "I had intended to stir up

a little drama, turn people against each other, but it turned out I didn't need to. The whole place is nothing but turmoil. They've already turned against each other. Then Patty got in there, and they spilled all their secrets. I just sat back and watched."

"When we get back to the rental," Austin said, "what do you say we make some dinner and relax for our last night, huh? Tomorrow we can head back early."

"Sounds like a plan." And it did. Maybe we'd even invite my parents over for dinner. I might be from humble roots, but my parents were genuine, caring people. I'd take that over Matt's family any day.

As we headed back, I watched my ring play against the light and enjoyed the sense of peace that flowed over me. I wore Austin's claim for all to see. I loved him, my new friends, my crew, and even Ivy House, as crazy as it had made everything. This trip had made me realize how much I loved my new life, weirdness and all. I wouldn't change anything.

Except for maybe those damn gnomes.

EPILOGUE

JESSIE

T HE STORAGE ROOM was empty except for one small pink note lying on a chair in the very middle. I stared at it for a long beat before casting magic through the space to make sure there weren't any booby traps. Not finding any, I cautiously approached the center of the room and picked up the note.

Jessie,

I have some new tricks! They come from a book I pinched from Ivy House. She didn't kill me, so I assumed it was okay to borrow. They could use a little refining, though (sorry about the burned areas). I see you've been finding some tricks of your own. That defensive spell was fantastic. A few little tweaks, and it'll be unstoppable.

Miss you guys. I'll do better about staying in contact—we're just busy kicking ass and tak-

ing...bodies to undisclosed locations to get rid of them.

That was Nessa's joke. She said to put it in.

Good job the other day. Thank you for trusting us. It couldn't have been easy to put on a dress like that and play at seriousness, but you did it incredibly well. Better than we anticipated.

As for the mages you were storing here, don't worry about those jokers. Nessa and I will record our dealings with them and send the transcripts to the resident monster. He seems to think he has the stomach for the big time—again, Nessa's words.

Tell Austin not to worry about how we snuck in. No other mage would be able to do it, regardless of their magical prowess. I knew Nessa and I would need to go our separate ways eventually, and I baked in a few magical tunnels that would get us past Austin's defenses. Even with fore-planning, though, originating from inside of the territory, we nearly got caught. So you guys are good.

I hope your visit went well!

And I sincerely hope you enjoy your presents.

Merry Christmas.

Best,
Sabby xoxo

I stared for a long moment and then read it again.

"What'd you find?" Austin asked, leaning into the room.

"An empty cell and a note. You?"

"A cell burned to high heaven, empty, no note. No holes dug through the walls or anything that would explain how they got out. The mages' dinner was eaten, so they were here to receive that, but they were gone before breakfast. The guards didn't see anyone coming or going. Cameras were put on a loop sometime last night and we can't get a time stamp. They were thorough."

I passed off the note to him and then looked around, not able to help a little smirk. "I'm not sure whether to be mad or impressed."

He breathed out slowly through his nose. "I guess at least it was them. Can you find these magical tunnels and...stop them or close them or...disable them?" He handed back the note.

"I...don't know. I can ask Ivy House. Maybe she'll lead me to a book? If that doesn't bring up a plan of action, though..." I looked at him seriously. "I can't compete with Sebastian, Austin. He isn't just powerful and incredibly experienced—he's a magical genius. A magical entrepreneur. A one-on-one fight I can handle. I have confidence there. But Elliot Graves doesn't do one-on-one battles. Not usually. He doesn't have to. And when it comes to sneaky mage magic, he's so far ahead of me…" I put my hands up. There really wasn't much else I could say.

"Maybe try—"

Austin paused as Tristan leaned into the room. "Anything?"

I held out the note.

"It's a good idea to ask Ivy House," Austin said as Tristan walked in and took it. "She must know the best spell books, at least?"

I nodded, hoping I could get her to cooperate.

"In the meantime…" He put his hands on his hips, staring out at nothing. "I have to figure out how to catch a magical mouse. I don't like people waltzing in here, helping themselves to whatever they want, and scurrying back out again. I don't care who they are."

"Agreed, sir," Tristan said. "I'm going to get with Niamh. We need a better setup. Nessa is running circles around us right now, but we have access to bigger and badder players. It's time we got serious about recruiting them. We need to take advantage of shadow worlds that we both have experience in. Though maybe we should come up with some parameters regarding the types of creatures we're willing to work with…"

Shivers covered my skin. This was starting to get

serious, dangerous in a way that might not just mean life and death. If there were worse things out there than straightforward magic, I wasn't sure I wanted to know about them. We'd only been home a day, and we were already back in full gear. I supposed it was for the best. Work today so we could live tomorrow. Literally. Get stagnant and we'd get killed.

"But what I really want to know is…" I took the note back and looked at it again. "What presents?"

We closed up shop. There was no point in sticking around, given there were no longer any mages to interrogate. I couldn't regret it too much. I hadn't been looking forward to prying information out of them.

As we headed home, Tristan and Broken Sue following in the car behind us, my mind continued down the same track as earlier.

"Seriously. What Christmas presents? Do you think they sent them to the rental we were in and we left before we got them? Or maybe they were stolen off the front porch? That's a huge problem in the city."

Once we got home, I had my answer.

A white box truck sat outside of Ivy House. Niamh was in her rocking chair in front of her house with what looked like a rock in hand, watching it until we got close. Tristan and Broken Sue were still behind us, and the rest of the team would be coming along shortly.

Austin parked at the curb out front, with Tristan pulling in behind him. We immediately moved in to check the truck.

"What is this?" I muttered to myself as I reached the sidewalk next to the box truck, sussing it out with magic. "All clear."

Austin peered into the cab. "Empty. And clean. No wear and tear."

On the back there was a little pink sign. *Merry Christmas.*

"Jessie, stand back," Tristan said, waiting until I backed up before he pulled the handle to unlatch the rear roll-up door.

A stack of wrapped boxes covered in bows and ribbons was stacked up halfway, filling the floor of the bed.

"What in the world?" Broken Sue asked as he came around the rear of the truck, peering in.

"Looks like we found the Christmas presents," Austin said, huffing out a laugh. "How many people did they buy for?"

Turned out, it was a great many. Anyone Nessa and Sebastian knew even reasonably well had gotten a gift, and those of us who were close to them had gotten a few, including high-end watches. Well...for me it was a pocket watch, and I was told to handle it carefully. That would be my thing going forward, obviously, a pocket watch sewn into a dress. Apparently, they thought my theme should be "weird and fussy."

Wrapping paper littered two large sitting rooms in Ivy House as everyone sat around grinning at their gifts. The presents had been as perfect and/or sentimental as the ones he'd given my team in the caves.

Ulric held up a card. "This was put in with mine, Jessie," he said, hopping up. A gold sign around his neck read, *Open for business.*

"What does the other side say?" I asked, pointing at it before I took the card.

He grinned before flipping it. *All sexed out.*

"It's for the bar," he said, laughing. "And look." He showed me his new watch. "The face is blue and pink to match my hair! So cool, right?" The band was a color-changing situation, too, a mix of blue and pink that changed as it caught the light.

"That's gotta be custom," I said, opening the envelope.

Ulric smiled brightly.

A couple of pieces of pink paper waited inside, along with a piece of parchment. I pulled one of the folded pages out and opened it up.

"Either they only have pink notepaper at their disposal or this is their new calling card," I said, peering down.

Jessie-

I'm still trying to figure out how to hide gargoyle wings. It's not as easy as it sounds. Other than investing in a lot of hoods to pretend like their wings are cloaks, you can try to make this magical serum and rub it on. It should be like an oil. Give it a try and see how it works. We can go from there.

Sabby xoxo

"Huh." I looked through the parchment, reading the instructions. It was probably a lot harder than it looked.

"What's that?" Ulric asked Tristan as he bent to clean up some of the wrapping paper.

Tristan held up his wrist, showing a beaded bracelet with two colors of metallic beads in a strange sort of design. "The beads represent Morse code. It's an inside joke."

"What does it say?" asked Jasper, who was also wearing a sign.

"I got two packages, each of them noting what the bracelets within say. One of them says 'daddy' and the other says 'owned.' I got one of the two bracelets. The other package is empty, meaning Nessa has kept that bracelet for herself."

The room ground to a halt, all eyes trained on Tristan.

"Which bracelet did you get?" Jasper asked, playing with his sign. Unlike Ulric's, both sides said, *Open for business.*

Tristan crinkled up a handful of paper. "*Owned.*"

A sly smile worked up both Jasper's and Ulric's faces.

"That sounds like a fun game," Jasper said.

"It will be, once I hold the other bracelet." Tristan grabbed more paper.

"Atta boy." Ulric slapped him on the back.

"Look at this." Cyra slowly put on a new pair of glasses, large and trendy, noticeable, and very clearly free of lenses. "Cool, right?"

I noticed her watch, white mother-of-pearl with small diamonds, a shiny white leather strap, and a simple, elegant design.

"Why does everyone get these really cool wrist-watches and I'm the weirdo with a pocket watch? What if I don't wear a dress—where is it going to go then?"

"In your...pocket?" Hollace asked, sitting beside Aurora on the other side of the room.

"Of my waistcoat? Oh God, what if he makes me wear waistcoats," I grumbled.

"Would anyone care for anything to drink?" Mr.

Tom asked, standing from his chair.

"What kind of watch did you get, Mr. Tom?" Dave asked, hulking at the side of the room, near the wall.

"We all know what kind you got," Jasper said to Dave with a grin.

It was true—Dave was the only one with a watch situation more absurd than mine. A large wall clock with a plastic frame and black numbers hung around his neck on a thick gold chain. It reminded me of Flava Flav the rapper back in the day.

Mr. Tom's wings rustled. "Master Jimmy's Spider-Man watch was repaired for me. I will be wearing that when the situation calls for it, and not before, so that I don't accidentally break it again."

I hadn't realized he'd broken it the first time. How sweet of Sebastian and Nessa to notice and fix it, and how sweet of Mr. Tom to prize my son's old watch as a memento.

"You still have that thing?" Jimmy asked with a grin, lounging on the couch with a pair of concert tickets he'd yelled about getting. Apparently Sebastian had asked Mr. Tom what Jimmy might like and come through with impossible-to-get, incredible seats.

"Of course I do," Mr. Tom replied. "What a stupid question."

Jimmy started chuckling. "So if I randomly send

you another of my watches, you'll wear that?"

"Of course I would. Another stupid question."

"How about your watch, Niamh?" Hollace asked, holding his up to the light and watching it glitter. "Mine is cool as hell."

She was sitting with a plain, waterproofed basket in her lap. It was filled with what Nessa and Sebastian had deemed "perfect throwing rocks." We'd all watched her go through them until she nodded, put on the lid, and held it in her lap. They must've gotten that right too.

She held up her wrist. Black band, white face, fairly simple.

"Wait..." Aurora, closest to her, squinted and leaned toward it. She started laughing. "It has two hour hands, one minute hand, and no second hand."

"Aye. And both hour hands work, but they go in opposite directions," Niamh said with a grin.

"Well, that's perfect," Jasper said, laughing as well.

"Sebastian was right about one thing," Austin said, holding up a set of keys intended for Kingsley. They went to some sort of collector's item car that Kingsley would apparently lose his crap over. The (pink) note that had come with it said:

Dear Austin,

I hope this note finds you well. We recently ran

into a mage partially responsible for the attack on Kingsley's pack. It seems he was at the battle, attempting to kill us all. Sadly, he got away.

Not any longer.

Please arrange transportation and pass this car on to Kingsley as restitution for the mage's terrible actions. The address where the car is located is below. Given my need to stay in the shadows, please transfer the car in your name. You can explain the situation in person, so the communication isn't overheard or intercepted. I thought he would be the perfect person to give it a new home.

One of your presents is to see Kingsley's face when his little brother gives him a car of this magnitude. You're welcome.

Best,

Sebastian and Nessa

Austin laughed. "I'm going to get a picture of Kingsley's reaction so I can show it to him someday."

"What was the one thing he was right about?" I asked, holding a little sleeve that would magically seal shut and stick to whatever surface I put it on. It would help me keep my engagement ring safe. If I had to shift at a moment's notice, I'd only need take a second to secure the ring. It would be wherever I'd put it when I got back, and it was equipped with a magical tracker if I was on the go.

It was perfect.

"Sebastian is very good at buying presents," Austin said, leaning into me.

He was exactly right.

A few days later, I woke up to a text message from Camila. *Thank you. I left. While it is sad, it is freeing. You helped me see my current reality, which wasn't the dream I'd been clinging on to. I know this is for the best. Please give me your address so that I can send the cash and credit card back to you. And thank Tom for me.*

I heaved a sigh. Matt would find another woman, I knew he would, but at least Camila was able to get out. At least now she had the ability to find someone who valued her for the wonderful woman she was.

I'd shut the door on the past. Now, I was looking toward the future while enjoying the present.

✧ ✧ ✧

SEBASTIAN

THE SCREEN CAME on, starting up slowly. The encrypted phone was old, the software outdated. It served its purpose, though. They only needed it to get messages from Jessie.

If only Tristan wasn't so incredibly good at tracking them. He had Nessa positively hopping with frustration. She hadn't had this kind of trouble before. It was a little disconcerting how quickly he and Niamh were picking everything up.

"We got one," Sebastian called to Nessa with a smile, waiting for the message from Jessie to come through. She wasn't one to receive presents without saying thank you.

He read the message too quickly at first, his heart hurting with how much he missed her. Then he read it again, slower this time, savoring each word.

"She's thanking us for the gifts, of course. She says they were perfect." He paused for a reply. When he didn't get one, he assumed Nessa was busy. She must have heard him in their tiny house. They were squatting in Arizona for the moment while they knocked out an important meeting.

He stood, muttering to himself as he went to find her.

"She wants to send us letters so she can write longer notes. That makes sense. We can set up a box or something, filtered through...some sort of system to hide the final destination." He smiled at the last line. "She needs help finding the perfect gift for us."

His heart squelched as he entered the short hallway, hearing Nessa in the living room.

"Your friendship has been the gift of a lifetime," he murmured, wishing he could say it to Jessie's face. He ran his thumb along the edge of the phone. "Your trust is more of a gift than I deserve…"

Closer now, he saw that Nessa was bending over the desk, tears running down her face, laughing so hard her face was red.

"What's…" He chuckled with her, caught up in the tide of laughter. "What's going on?"

She pointed at the two computer screens. Each screen showed four feeds from different surveillance cameras.

He leaned in closer as she banged on the desk. The images were frozen, and it took him a moment to recognize the gaudy décor.

"Arthur Godrick's house," he said, seeing Jessie standing in the entryway, dressed in the poufy gown they'd sent to her. "What's so funny?"

They'd watched the scene as it was happening, needing to get the timing just right. He hadn't paid attention to the details at the time, however. Apparently that was a good thing, given how much Nessa laughing.

"What is it?" he asked, still chuckling, pulling up a

chair to sit beside her.

"Lemme…start…it over." She tried to collect herself but gave in to another series of guffaws. "Okay, okay. Here we go."

They watched Jessie walk into the house, staring at the doorframe like she was trying to see the engineering. Austin had already entered, large and menacing and terrifying. The mage by the door, acting as a butler, looked like he was literally about to crap himself. He'd slunk as far as possible from the big alpha.

"This is the part where she starts to analyze the spell—" Nessa started.

"*It needs more punch,*" they heard from the distance, as the mics were in a different place than the surveillance cameras. They had been short on time and needed to make do. "*It's not grabby enough. Even with less power, I could devise something to slip past this.*"

"She is just spitting in their faces and has no idea how utterly rude it is." Nessa started chuckling again.

"Yeah…" Sebastian said slowly. "I never really taught her etiquette. I always welcomed her observations because it helped me formulate ideas. I can see how…I might've dropped the ball on that one."

"It's perfect," Nessa said. "The fact that she has no terminology and is explaining his shortcomings like she is talking to a toddler is absolutely perfect."

Sebastian grimaced. He wasn't sure about that. Trigger the wrong ego and things could get ugly fast.

Nessa's chuckles turned into laughs as Jessie kept going, nonchalantly saying, *"But it's fine. If they try to attack him, our people will kill you all."*

"She's talking like Elliot Graves," Nessa said. "Except she has zero swagger. She's just being truthful."

"It's terrifying because you can tell her people agree with her. It is entirely clear that it is not an act."

"Exactly." Nessa breathed out slowly. "Listen. She's detailing how easy it would be to get people in." She fast-forwarded a little.

Jessie's voice came through the tiny speaker. *"And locks don't matter for people who have soundproofing spells and can break a window without being noticed…"*

Sebastian didn't remember hearing any of this. Then again, at the time, he'd been focused on how his entry would go. Now that he was watching it…he didn't have words.

"I have a lot of magical spells for breaking and entering now. Anyway, no biggie. I was just getting the lay of the land."

The mage stared at her, and for good reason. That was a blatant threat in the mage world. Talking about breaking and entering with another mage was like running a finger across their jugular while making heavy eye contact. It held meaning.

She had no idea what she was saying.

"I think I might've missed some serious chunks in training," Sebastian said softly. "This is bad, Nessa."

"I think the opposite. Here, let me get to the funny part."

"I'm not so sure I'll think it is funny…"

Edgar popped his head into the visual and then looked around like his neck was a swivel. He walked in like some sort of ghoul, his hands held out in front of him, strangely swaying for no discernible reason.

"*Well, hello…*"

Nessa started laughing again, pointing at the screen. "He bleached his teeth. You know, and *I* know, that he was trying to look presentable, but instead he is basically saying, 'I'm a vampire, here are my fangs, I might kill you later.'" She laughed harder. "Can you imagine being that mage? Was he wearing a diaper? Because otherwise he probably needed new pants after that."

Sebastian couldn't help but chuckle a little. That vampire was so nuts.

"Wait, wait…" Nessa pointed at the screen again, and they watched Cyra be…well, Cyra. Zany and crazy in her own way.

"*This place is worse than the old Ivy House. Badly in need of a makeover.*"

"Another incredibly rude comment," Nessa said as though keeping track.

Tristan entered next, moving with the swagger and poise of a *GQ* model but ten times more graceful, as though he were gliding across the floor. The air around him darkened before the sheen in the doorway visibly melted away.

"Holy—" Sebastian leaned forward to get a better look. "I knew he could withstand spells, but melting them away is on a different level... Did you know he could do that?"

"No, I didn't," she said, watching closely while chewing her lip. "I've added it to the list of his traits. Which are incredibly perplexing, because I have a decent list, and he's not matching any of the beings I've looked up. He has attributes of several different magical creatures, but no overall profile fits. I can't figure him out."

"In more ways than one, huh?"

She fast-forwarded, ignoring that comment. There was something in her that was drawn in by that gargoyle, but she wouldn't admit it, not even to herself. Sebastian had tried to pry a little, but she wouldn't open up. He knew from experience that she wouldn't fill him in until she was ready. Whatever was going on was shoved down deep, where she didn't have to deal with it.

"What's next?" Sebastian asked to let her off the hook.

Broken Sue came through, another terrifying sight, followed by Mr. Tom with his box of disguises. It was entirely clear the host mage was beside himself with wariness. There was no mage group, not even Elliot Graves himself, who was this eccentric and this obviously dangerous all at the same time. Jessie was making a statement unlike any other mage Sebastian had ever heard of.

Unease pinched his gut again.

"*Missus Smith,*" Jessie said, holding out her hand.

Nessa started to chuckle again. In walked Dave, for all intents and purposes a bigfoot. His outfit was stolen from Phil and utterly ridiculous, the braids were insane, and his sheer size, topping even Tristan, was incredible. Terrifying. He was an actual urban legend walking in through the door. It was so over the top.

And then Edgar whispered, "*Did we break him already? Because usually it takes a little chatter to get to that point.*"

Nessa guffawed again, and Sebastian had to join in despite his misgivings. Jessie's team was so unbearably absurd. But they were also incredibly scary. And powerful. Still…so, *so* absurd.

They watched a little more, the laughter continuing to come because of that train wreck of a dinner. After, Sebastian sat in silence for a moment.

"What was the outcome?" he finally asked.

"Good. Arthur and his cronies are spreading the news about the dinner and her ensuing battle with Elliot Graves. Jessie now looks like she has no powerful mage allies. She's adrift. And Arthur or whoever said it right—she had an excuse for standing against Momar. Momar won't extend a hand to her because of her affiliation with the shifters, but the Guild might. Momar is growing more powerful than them, and they need a little might in their corner. She's inexperienced and malleable. She could be that might. They just need a little nudge to seek out the acquaintance."

"And we need to steer Jessie toward them." Sebastian's stomach churned. "I'm…reluctant. I don't want to steer her directly into harm's way."

"It's my turn to be tough guy, is it?" Nessa sagged a little. "You've said it yourself, repeatedly—we don't have a choice. You've made that clear. We're in it too far now. This is who we are. It's what we do. We survive."

Tears filled his eyes, and he stood. "I don't know if that's who I am anymore. They changed me."

She stared down at her hands. "Me too, but you've

assured me that we have no choice, right? This was the way forward that you *Saw*. I'm just seeing it through, like you asked, Sabby. I'm taking your lead and making it work, like I always have. I don't know what else you want from me."

Guilt ate at him. He put his hand on her shoulder. "I know. I'm sorry. It just hurts."

"I know," she whispered as a tear trailed down her cheek.

He left the room without further commentary. He knew she was right. His ability to see the future was only a sliver of what his sister's had been, but when he saw a vision, it always showed him what needed to happen. The problem was, how to get there wasn't defined. Not the way it had been with his sister's magic. They often fumbled their way to the finish line, and often people were lost along the way. Usually people they could replace.

Not this time.

This time, things were different. This time, he wasn't sure he had the stomach to follow through.

THE END.

About the Author

K.F. Breene is a Wall Street Journal, USA Today, Washington Post, Amazon Most Sold Charts and #1 Kindle Store bestselling author of paranormal romance, urban fantasy and fantasy novels. With millions of books sold, when she's not penning stories about magic and what goes bump in the night, she's sipping wine and planning shenanigans. She lives in Northern California with her husband, two children, and out of work treadmill.

Sign up for her newsletter to hear about the latest news and receive free bonus content.

www.kfbreene.com

Printed in Great Britain
by Amazon